| AUTHOR | CLASS | G |
|--------|-------|---|
| BRINK, A. | F | M |

**TITLE** States of emergency — H839

# STATES OF EMERGENCY

**ff**

# ANDRÉ BRINK

# States of
# Emergency

*faber and faber*
LONDON · BOSTON

First published in 1988
by Faber and Faber Limited
3 Queen Square London WC1N 3AU

Photoset by Wilmaset Birkenhead Wirral
Printed in Great Britain by
Mackays of Chatham Ltd Kent

*British Library Cataloguing in Publication Data*

Brink, André
States of emergency.
I. Title
823 [F]    PR936.3.B7

ISBN 0-571-15118-3

For
M
with love

The only safe place in the world is inside a story.

*Athol Fugard*

Despite the difficulties of my story, despite discomforts, doubts, despairs, despite impulses to be done with it, I unceasingly affirm love, within myself, as a value.

*Roland Barthes*

The year which ends at midnight tonight has been so full of violence and sadness that many will feel that the sooner it is forgotten the better. Yet 1985 was a watershed year and before its manifold horrors are thrust out of mind it would be as well to reflect on the significance of what has happened.

*Cape Times*

Notes towards a love story.

I never knew her. Not personally, that is. Yet she has infiltrated my life. The small report in this morning's newspaper (page four; I only noticed it on my second flip-through – there is so little of interest that can be printed in the present Emergency) should by rights have put an end to it. But on the contrary: I know now I shall not easily be rid of her again. (Nothing in her life became her like the leaving of it.)

It must have been about a year ago that the manuscript from the young woman in Northern Natal turned up in the mail. I receive many manuscripts, most of them unsolicited, most of them desperately boring. Occasionally one discovers in them a flicker of promise; how rare the sensation of that tingling in the spine with which, as Nabokov had it, real talent is acknowledged. Jane Ferguson's manuscript was one of those. Very short indeed, barely a hundred pages, at first sight a most conventional love story. Young woman, middle-aged man. In the end, when she is abandoned, she commits suicide in a way which, paraphrased, sounds hopelessly melodramatic: by immolating herself. (Quite early in the story she warns her lover: 'There are only three choices in love: freedom, or madness, or death. If you cannot be free and you dare not face death you must go mad. And do you know what happens to a woman who goes mad? Internal combustion. She burns. That's what happens. She burns.')

I am doing the writer an injustice with this crude summary. But that is precisely what I'm trying to convey: that the story as such was trite, even embarrassing, when reduced to a mere outline; but that in spite of this – almost as if the writer had deliberately chosen a framework as flimsy and sentimental as possible – it was one of the most delicate, and at the same time one of the most disturbing, texts I have ever been sent for scrutiny. I wrote back immediately to tell Jane Ferguson how deeply her manuscript had impressed me, offering to submit it to an agent I know in London. Prodded by curiosity I asked her to tell me more about herself.

'If you honestly think there is a chance of getting it published,' she wrote back, 'you may of course send it to your agent. But whatever you do, don't try to flatter me or give me false hopes. I don't think I could take that. I'd much rather have the truth. As for your questions about myself, there is nothing to tell. In terms of the calendar I suppose I'm still young, but I feel very old. I was in love, once. At the moment (for how long? nothing lasts, does it?) I live near the sea and spend my days walking along the beach, picking up shells, talking to myself, trying not to go mad. And that's all, really – '

I regretted my enquiry. Not just because I felt it had invaded her privacy but because the answer was so whimsical.

The manuscript was sent off to London. A few weeks later there was an enthusiastic reply – airmail, express – from the agency. One of the most moving stories they'd read for a long time. But, sadly, too short to be published on its own. Much too short. It would simply get lost in the annual torrent of new fiction. And then there was this feeling, shared by everybody who had read the manuscript – and they hoped I wouldn't take it amiss; how should they put it? – well, that South Africa was so much in the news these days, almost anything coming from that tragic country had the potential of attracting attention, provided it offered some insight into the political situation. Could I see what they were trying to say? Not just a simple love story. That was too easy, that avoided the issue. If it could be expanded, if it could be amplified by a political dimension to involve what was happening in the country right now (the actual phrase they used was 'at this point in time'), the book would really make people sit up. Did I think I might be able to prevail on the author – ?

I forwarded the manuscript together with a copy of the agent's letter to Jane Ferguson's Natal address, with a note to say how indignant I felt about their shortsightedness, but leaving it to her to decide how (and if) she should react to their recommendation. For two months there was no reply. I assumed that she had decided, hurt, not to pursue the matter. Perhaps I should have done more to encourage her, but I was trying to get into a novel of my own, *The Lives of Adamastor*, covering several centuries of

South African history. However, after a few months, after just over a hundred pages, I had to put it aside (temporarily, I still hope), for the simple reason that too much was happening around me – a whole country, it seemed, erupting in flames – to find the inner lucidity without which, even when one is in pain or rage, writing is impossible. It was only then that I decided to sound out Jane Ferguson again, pressing her in a short letter at least to allow me another attempt with her manuscript. In a sense, I suppose, I envied her for having managed to write that small gem of a love story in circumstances which had left me too numb to achieve anything myself. Perhaps, I told her, the agent might yet be persuaded, in spite of his own misgivings, to submit it to a few publishers; and who knows but someone might be found who would share my faith in the novella.

Without any covering letter the manuscript was returned to me and I dispatched it to the agent, accompanied by the strongest plea I felt I could make. An acknowledgement of receipt arrived in due course, assuring me of their willingness to do their best, regardless. (What a pity, though, that the author wouldn't consider their well-meant recommendations.)

After another delay (and another frustrated attempt to escape from the urgencies of the 'South African situation' to resume my own writing) the manuscript, rather thumbed and dog-eared by now, rearrived on my desk. Lengthy letter in a separate envelope. They really were so very sorry – no need to repeat how much they shared my own high regard of the story – but there seemed to be no point in continuing what had turned out to be a fruitless pursuit. Three publishers had turned it down, all of them responding in more or less similar terms. There simply is no market for such short novellas, at least not when written by young and unknown writers. So many sensitive young women sit down to compose exquisite accounts of unhappy love, and then turn out to be incapable of following it up with anything more substantial. Publishers, as I must be aware, are interested in long-term investments. In the circumstances they deemed it wise not to keep fanning the flames of futile hope. (But how about once again using all my powers of persuasion to try and twist the author's arm? It really would be a pity to see so much promise go unfulfilled.)

Glumly I returned the manuscript to the sensitive young woman in question, accompanied by as sympathetic a letter as I could devise, and urging her – rather against my own hope – not to give up. By return mail the manuscript was back, an impatient little note scribbled on the title page: *Why don't you just keep the damn thing? I have no further use for it. Do with it whatever you want, even burn it. At least it won't be on my conscience.*

Early yesterday morning, said the newspaper report, the body of a young woman, Jane Ferguson (23), was discovered on a footpath along the north coast of Natal, near Richard's Bay. An empty petrol container was found near by. It would appear that she had burned to death. Foul play was not suspected. She is survived by her father, Mr Charles Ferguson, a nature conservationist.

I wrote him a letter this morning to express my sympathy (rather formally, I'm afraid; it is awkward to approach a total stranger), and also to inform him of his daughter's manuscript still in my possession, in case he might wish to claim it. I hope he does. It has become a burden to my conscience, I should prefer to be rid of it. But perhaps, I must confess, there was another motive behind my writing: the wish that he might be prompted to tell me something more about the author Jane Ferguson. I don't want everything to end so abruptly, pointlessly. There may be more to my urge than the straightforward curiosity provoked, not only by the quality of her manuscript, but by the crude conclusion of her own life story: I need some reassurance that there is no link between her failed manuscript and her end. I mean, for heaven's sake, no one commits suicide over a manuscript turned down. Even in more melodramatic times than these such a thing would be preposterous.

It is not because Jane Ferguson as such concerns me that I have referred to her above, but only because her history – or that small part of it which has intersected my life – illuminates something of my own dilemma. For years now I have been

4

toying with the idea of writing a simple love story. Something like the perfect little novella she has written, uncluttered by any 'political dimension' of the kind demanded of her by the agents and publishers. I don't know what has restrained me all the time. A fear of escapism, of 'opting out', perhaps? As if a love story might imply some form of betrayal towards the great current of history sweeping past me: *this* torn and plundered country, *this* goddamned time? Does one not have a weightier 'obligation' – as a human being, as a citizen, as a writer – towards what is happening around one? (Barthes describes 'love' as 'a socially irresponsible word'.) It involves more than facile and often erroneous distinctions between the 'private' and the 'public', the old-fashioned *ars longa* and notions of 'commitment'. What is at stake is the whole concept of writing, of literature. The boundaries between 'text' and 'world', the 'responsibility' of the writer. How does one cope with a period like the one we have been living through during the past year or so, in the post-apocalyptic age *after* 1984? How can one even hope simply to report on it? Even as I sit down behind the typewriter (it is now the middle of 1986) my words are overtaken by events. The statistics are available for all to ponder, spread around the globe by the media (though, admittedly, it has subsided somewhat since it has become a crime to disseminate information not authorized by the State): almost two thousand killed, countless thousands wounded; a State of Emergency imposed throughout the country; the most peaceful forms of protest prohibited; well over ten thousand people, a third of them children, in detention; torture; strikes and boycotts; burning tyres and charred bodies; bombs and landmines; atrocities committed by the so-called 'security forces'; politicians holding forth, with apocalyptic arrogance, on 'a situation returning to normal', on 'law and order', on 'controlled reform'; Mandela still in prison and the ANC still banned; P.W. Botha* still in power, glaring at the world in myopic smugness, wagging a blunt admonishing finger on the TV screen. All of which

---

* At the time of writing, State President of the Republic of South Africa. But an explanatory footnote is necessary as future readers may not remember.

concerns me and violently involves me. Like millstones the placenames weigh upon my mind: Uitenhage, Queenstown, Mamelodi, Zwide, Tantyi, Langa, Alexandra, Crossroads, Soweto – the list is endless. I cannot, do not want to, avoid them. In these circumstances to write a story about two people who love – who try to love – who would like to love – each other: can it be done at all? Jane Ferguson did. (But does not the fate of her small novella demonstrate the futility of such an enterprise?)

It is not that I believe I 'owe' her something (or do I?). Yet what has happened to her has quickened – only much more disturbingly than before – my own unshaped ideas for a story. I have put aside *The Lives of Adamastor* once again (although I solemnly vow I shall return to it); I know that Jane Ferguson cannot be laid to rest in my mind until I have explored more fully the welter of thoughts she has stirred up. There is no story as such to which I am committed yet. The most I dare propose to myself is to explore the possibilities of undertaking such a story. It is, perhaps, no more than an attempt to test the extent of my own freedom – that freedom which may involve the choice to write a love story even (or especially?) when something else appears to be demanded of me (by whom, or what?). The freedom to follow a story wherever it may lead me. I do not know what will be happening ten pages from now – just as I have no idea of what may happen to me in a day or a month or another year.

Is it irrelevant to insert here a note about Wagner? I am reminded that, after his involvement in the uprisings of 1848 and 1849, and living in exile in Zurich with the Wesendoncks, working feverishly on his *Ring*, he fell in love with his host's wife Mathilde. This eventually prompted him to adandon the work he had been immersed in for years: literally leaving Siegfried dreaming in the wood in the middle of Act Two, and convinced that there were urgencies more pressing than those of politics, he began working on *Tristan and Isolde*. And only after finishing it in Venice could he return to the *Ring* and to Germany.

Every story can be traced back to a trigger character or episode, however insignificant at first sight, from which everything else develops. The reader may not recognize them as such in the final text (they may not even *appear* in the final text), but the writer knows that without these catalysts nothing else would have happened. In this case I have had for some time the mental image of two lovers in the night. (Who are they? I do not know yet, and it is too dark to see, anyway.) It is a windy evening; the street lamps, set far apart, seem to be inhaling light rather than emitting it. They are walking hand in hand. As they pass a stretch of bare brick wall covered with graffiti, I notice (among the many other, predictable, slogans: *Free Mandela – Botha is a terrorist – Troops out of the townships*) one which says:

*Life is a sexually transmitted disease*

For a moment they stop to read (the slanting light casts a pale glow over the wall, but their faces are still in the dark), just as a combi filled with students or some sports team back from a weekend excursion comes charging round a corner, heading straight towards them. The windows, even the sliding doors, are open: disembodied faces protrude from everywhere, shouting, jeering, wolf-whistling. Exposed in the glare of the headlights the couple try to back away. The combi follows, driving on to the pavement. Stricken by panic, they dodge round a corner and start running along an alley, but as they emerge at the far end the combi reappears, hooting with aggressive glee. Drunken jibes and maniacal laughter pursue them as they stumble along and resort to scaling garden walls or crawling through fences, taking short-cuts through backyards (sudden explosions of furious barking) to get away. But whenever they return to the streets, the combi is there again to resume the witch-hunt. Caught like two moths in the glare of the headlights, they feel stripped naked by the taunting voices.

Only after what seems to be hours, making a wide detour along back streets and dark vacant lots filled with rubble or overgrown with weeds, do they manage to shake off their pursuers and return, breathless, to the familiar space of the small white room in which she lives. Once inside, not yet daring to put on the light, he slides the bolt into its slot and secures the safety chain while she draws the curtains in front of the small window.

Standing close together, gasping for breath, still unable to speak, it is a long time before they can relax, trying to believe that they are safe here, that, surely, nothing can invade this little room.

A knock on my door, not half an hour after I'd finished the paragraph above, three days ago, in the evening. There is no reason to record it here, except that it does illustrate the circumstances within which I am trying to write. It was an unusual time of the evening for visitors, especially for Milton Thaya; even more so with the curfew imposed by the Emergency Regulations. Anything that moves in the township streets after nine is summarily shot. The Council police – the *amangundwane*, the 'rats' – are difficult customers in need of moving target practice, and not all that familiar with the firearms they handle with such abandon. But there is a State of Emergency, and questions are not encouraged.

From the outset it was obvious that Milton had something serious on his mind. It takes a lot to shake him out of his customary talkative good humour, but that evening he was clearly disturbed. Even so, he waited for me to serve coffee and then spent another half-hour on small talk – no matter how urgent his business may be, he regards it as impolite, if not quite unthinkable, to plunge directly into business – before he explained his mission. Mister Mtuze, he said, was dead; 'necklaced' the night before.

Milton's house is in B–Street, in Fingo Village; he has been renting it for years from his landlord, Mister Mtuze. He lives in it with his wife Thokozile, their two daughters and small son; but in the backyard there is a conglomerate of corrugated iron, wooden and even cardboard shacks abundantly inhabited by Mister Mtuze's other tenants. No problem to anybody, provided the rent is paid on time. In recent months, unfortunately, the situation has become rather tense, what with the South African police taking to patrolling the townships with Casspirs and machine-guns and arranging for their dirty work to be done by the *amangundwane*: the resultant vacuum in the day-to-day running of township affairs was soon filled by the people's own

8

network of 'street committees'. This created some complications for Mister Mtuze. I have not yet been able to get to the root of the problem as explained in confusing detail by Milton Thaya on previous visits, but as far as I could make out the trouble began with something going wrong between Mister Mtuze's only daughter Happiness and one of the young comrades on their committee. It would seem that Mister Mtuze tried to intervene in some way; and when he was told to mind his own business, he took it up with the *amangundwane*. Now, there is a state of undeclared war between the comrades and the *amangundwane*; and before long a rumour was circulating that Mister Mtuze had become an informer, an *impimpi*. The night before Milton so unexpectedly turned up on my doorstep matters had come to a head. Milton, it seems, had returned to his yard just in time to notice small groups of young comrades taking up position in the side streets. Knowing that Mister Mtuze was on his rounds collecting rent, it wasn't difficult to put two and two together. Without waiting a minute longer than was strictly necessary, Milton bundled his wife and children into his rickety green truck and drove off to spend the night with friends in Tantyi township, a few kilometres further from town. He returned the next morning to find his block ominously silent. Everybody in the yard seemed reticent, but it didn't take long to establish that the worst had indeed happened: Mister Mtuze had been taken away and 'necklaced' by the comrades in the night.

Milton went round to the dead man's house, but it was a futile visit. Only the mother still lived there and she was in a drunken stupor. (The daughter who had started it all, I learned, had left for New Brighton in Port Elizabeth more than a month ago.)

It is not easy to explain Milton's position. He is a teacher at Nyaluza High School in the township, but as a result of the schools boycott he hasn't been working for months now. In any case he has been moonlighting in a variety of ways for many years. In fact, ever since I first met Milton Thaya – which goes back a good ten or twelve years, when he approached me to help him with his correspondence course at the University of South Africa – he has always been involved in some 'project' or another. At one stage he was writing a novel; then he assembled a drama group; in the holidays he invariably went off to Cape

9

Town or Johannesburg, something to do with adult education, or self-help programmes, or outrageous get-rich-quick schemes. Once he started a brick-making concern, then a pottery, a weaving business, a school for basket-making – all of them well-intended attempts, always on a grand scale, at teaching skills to the unemployed. The fact that he tended to abandon his projects as readily as he embarked on new ones was not due to any lack of perseverance but only to his excess of energy, his impatience to leave nothing unexplored. ('Jeez, man, it doesn't matter if a man lives to thirty or to a hundred, as long as you done something worth while by the time your trumps come up.') As a result of these manifold activities he has come to occupy something of a unique position in township affairs. He has the confidence of the younger generation (with the establishment of the street committees it was Milton's advice the comrades sought); but as teacher and entrepreneur he also has the respect of the other side. Whenever negotiations between widely different groups are afoot – whether it concerns a consumer boycott of white business, or reopening schools, or bargaining for better conditions in the townships, or getting a crêche or a clinic or a soccer field going – one can be sure of finding Milton Thaya among the bargainers. Which he has managed, so far, without ever selling out anybody. (The only people he has no time for are the *amangundwane*: 'If one of those rats sets foot in my house, I tell you, I'll break his neck. Even if they come to shoot me afterwards. I don't mix with that kind of shit, man.')

In the event it was not surprising that Milton was the only person in the township available to identify Mister Mtuze's body in the police morgue. Which he had done that same afternoon.

'I never seen a thing like that in my life,' he told me that evening, looking ashen, and more corpulent than ever in the clothes which, as usual, were too small for him. 'Don't want to see it again neither, if I live to be ninety. You ever seen a log burning for some time and then doused with water? That's what Mister Mtuze looked like, I tell you. From the waist up it was just a kind of charred stump with a few branches sticking out. It was only by his feet I knew it was he; he used to have these crooked small toes.'

'And what is going to happen next?' I asked him.

'That's the problem, man. He must get buried. Soon, soon. The longer he stays where he is, the bigger trouble we got coming. Because the *amangundwane* are the hell in, they just looking for a reason to clean up the whole township. And the comrades are waiting for a big funeral to disrupt, because they believe they'll see there who are the friends of the dead *impimpi*. I tell you, we sitting on a bloody box of dynamite and the fuse is already burning. And all round the township the *boere* are ready, just waiting for an excuse to intervene. It's *mos* law and order.'

'But what can you do, Milton?'

'I got to organize the funeral. I'm the only one, man. Mister Mtuze's mother is no good. All she cares about is the funeral money, then she can get drunk for a week. So the first thing you can help me with is money for a coffin. I'll square it with the undertaker, and I know the chaps who dig the graves. The main thing is that it must happen now, now, before anybody can start organizing. I'll be talking to the street committee tomorrow to guarantee that I'll take charge of everything. We can bury him from my house, and only the tenants will be there, nobody else.'

'But he was nothing to you, Milton. Why don't you stay out of it?'

'Of course he was nothing to me. He was a bloody shit. And a shark too, with the rent he charged. But if he doesn't get buried the whole township will go up in flames. And it's my children I'm worrying about.'

'But suppose the street committee gives you permission to go ahead and the *amangundwane* come to your home for the funeral?'

'They won't.'

'How can you be sure? Suppose Mister Mtuze really was a friend of theirs – ?'

'I'll break their necks.'

'I thought you were trying to avoid trouble?'

'Don't you worry about me. Jeez, man, just lend me the money for the coffin. I'll pay you back. And perhaps a bit extra for the grave. I got a lot of expenses.'

'But where are you off to now? The curfew went an hour ago, you can't risk it in the streets. Why don't you sleep here tonight?'

'I got a place to sleep, no problem. And I don't want anybody to see my truck outside your house, the township people don't like us mixing with whites.'

'Not even with friends?'

'You don't know those young comrades. It's just black and white to them. And whitey can't be anybody's friend. It's an Emergency, man.'

Reluctantly, anxiously, I saw him off. Not knowing when – or if – I would see him again. Even in more peaceful times his comings and goings used to be unpredictable: but at least it was possible for me to visit him at home; now no longer. It's an Emergency, man.

It wasn't until early this afternoon that he returned. (No sign of the green truck: that, he explained, had to be left in town; he'd walked all the way from there – three kilometres – so as not to arouse suspicion.)

He'd managed to make arrangements for the coffin and the grave. The only problem was the post-mortem. The district surgeon had had a lot of bodies to attend to lately, there was a back-log. However, in the end Milton had persuaded the doctor to do the autopsy at seven this morning; the funeral was to be at ten. (Eleven, he'd told the comrades.)

At five past nine the doctor had finished. Milton drove straight to the undertakers who were standing by to collect the body. Just make sure you take an axe with you, he told them casually, because those arms sticking up like sticks won't ever get into a coffin.

From there he drove to the cathedral to steal a prayer book.

'But surely, Milton – '

'What else could I do? I only remembered at the last moment and we don't have that kind of thing in my house, man. It's an Emergency, isn't it?'

Next he went to an aunt of his wife's to enquire about what passage to read at a funeral. (No priest had been willing to lead the ceremony, all of them afraid – of both the *amangundwane* and the comrades.)

At ten to ten Milton arrived at the cemetery, where two gravediggers were already waiting; he handed them five rands and reviewed their instructions. At three minutes past ten the hearse drove up and the coffin was unceremoniously lowered into the grave. Milton took up position astride one corner of it and read the shortest psalm his wife's aunt had approved for the occasion; then the grave was filled up, the hearse drove off, and it was done. When the comrades arrived at his house just before eleven to find out when the proceedings were going to start, he could inform them with a clear conscience that it was all over. They were furious at first, but they may well have been secretly relieved too. The main thing was that, singlehanded, Milton had averted a possible bloodbath. (And the old lady, Mister Mtuze's mother, is now stumbling through the streets, singing and talking to herself, and clutching a new bottle of Ship Sherry.)

All of which happened while I was trying to sort out my thoughts about a love story untarnished by politics.

On page eighty-seven of his book on China, *A Quarter of Mankind* (Pelican, 1968), Dick Wilson refers to 'the astonishing affair of the novel *Returning Home* by Lin Shu-teh, a love story in a modern setting of social struggle, published in Shanghai in 1962. At first, it was well received, but in the spring of 1963 a conference of writers and artists was given an exposition of the new political line emphasizing the class struggle, and this novel fell victim to the new campaign. "Love," said one critic, "is of secondary importance . . . One should certainly not write about being intoxicated by love and absorbed in personal feelings and family quarrels; the effect of the novel would be the creation not of the new man but of the old." "The story of the love of individuals is meaningless," concluded another critic; "it has no ideological content". But the magazine *Literature* noted in the summer of 1963 that in spite of the disapproval, "young students are fighting to get this book and discuss it among themselves".'

If all the love stories in the world are mere variations on a few archetypal themes, it remains true that it is only in terms of its specifics that a story becomes persuasive. The local habitation;

the name. It is in the proper name that all the attributes and activities, all the biographical and psychological data converge to create the illusion of a person, a personality. What may appear to be a random choice to start with, gradually assumes the weight of inevitability, as the name functions like an electrical switch to turn on a whole current of associations within the text. So it would seem that, certainly at the outset, any name will do. Yet it is not quite so simple. Even names can condition readers, can 'tune in' a writer. What shall I call the young woman in my story? Isolde is too obvious, and besides, Wagner is not my favourite composer. Isola has a lighter tone to it and I could use the suggestion of an island in the name, but perhaps it is a trifle too pretentious. Clara has a clear and windblown quality, but isn't it too aloof? And perhaps a syllable too short, which is why I must also discard the lovely Lisa. Teresa? Too much of the crusty old saint in it and besides, it is too dark. Helena would have been perfect, were it not so burdened by mythology. Alison? In many ways this would convey just what I have in mind – it suggests Carroll without being wholly determined by its archetype – but that closed final syllable displeases me. And the grandmother she will acquire in the course of the story would never approve of such an English name. So it will be Melissa, even if the name may bring with it overtones from the *Alexandria Quartet*. But the reader would do well to abandon prejudice and at this stage to read into the name no more than the golden honey it alludes to.* It has a lightness and an airiness about it, but also the substance of three syllables, the last left open, inconclusive, tantalizing, a mystery, the beginning of a new alphabet in which anything is possible.

The important thing is that, at this stage, the name should still be open. All too soon it will be invaded and tarnished by meanings. Its limitless possibilities will be reduced to a circum-scribed set of codes. It may acquire connotations of blondeness, of tumbling tresses, of vulnerability and youth, perhaps a touch

---

* The original Melissa, I believe, was a Greek goddess who assumed once a year the form of a honey bee, in which shape she copulated with her consort and then killed him.

of recklessness and impatience, headstrong rebellion; the taste of the forbidden fruit, acrid, astringent, then a sudden sweetness; the name of a young woman eager to live fully, yet hesitant to take the plunge, caught in her own paradoxes: passionate and chaste, trusting and suspicious, carefree, wistful, mischievous, cynical, pensive and profane. All these attributes may, in time, be lured to the golden flypaper of that name. But for the time being, by all means, let us accept it as undetermined and intact, provisionally free, innocent. If only I could preserve it like that, protecting it the way one shelters a lit match against the wind for the briefest of moments before it flickers out, its existence accomplished and forgettable. In this instant, this last moment of freedom, it is equal only to itself: a name, a word, a triad of syllables, pure sound: Melissa.

She needs, of course, a male complement. The two of them must determine one another the way they determine their 'world' (as they are determined by it). In Jane Ferguson's novella, *A Sense of Occasion* (a title inspired, incidentally, by lines from Auden: 'For nothing can happen to birds that has not/ happened before: we though are beasts with a sense of/ real occasion, of beginnings and endings'), the setting is a hotel on the coast. The man runs the resort, the woman is a guest spending a few days on her own before she will go back to marry someone she has known from school. The hotel is built on a peninsula which sometimes, at springtide, is cut off from the mainland. Everything in the story is determined by this setting. Perhaps it was precisely this image of an island – a near-island – which caught my imagination from the start: outworn as it may be, the island remains one of our most persuasive symbols. Donne was undoubtedly right, but that does not prevent the urge which constantly sends us back to islands. Even the Garden of Eden, in its way, was an island surrounded by four rivers. It has become part of our collective cultural heritage.

Something of that insularity may well come in useful in my own novel. But I do not want blatantly to take over Jane Ferguson's setting; of course not. Anyway, there are many kinds of islands. Even a large office in a metropolis can convey this. Only I don't see Melissa as a secretary or a typist; nor can I visualize her man as a businessman. He may be an architect, I suppose, which would require her to be a draughtswoman, a final-year student doing her practical stint in his firm. But there is something too rigid in such a situation. A photographer and his assistant? An artist and his model? No, for Christ's sake, Melissa could never be a model.

And so, for various reasons, I have decided – provisionally – to try out the academic milieu I know from my own experience. She can be a student, all right. Postgraduate, she is no neophyte. And it would be useful if she could have finished her undergraduate studies at a different university (Cape Town?) before moving to this one. A constantly changing environment may well be part of her set-up. Never staying in any one place for too long. Her father may have been a magistrate, or a bank manager, a postmaster, something like that; transferred every few years, never allowed to put down roots, always subconsciously prepared for the next move.

My male lead, of course, must then be her professor. Not just because my story requires the stereotypes, but because I think the role of academic would suit him. History? Philosophy? Literary Theory. A sound structuralist: that is both fashionable and slightly, just slightly, *passé*. Middle-aged, fiftyish. Rather comfortably set in his opinions. With, above all, an implicit faith in the text as *Ding an sich*, an authority to be respected, because it is there, it will always be there, immutable, to return to and be tested. Not necessarily Leavis's 'one correct reading', but at least a predetermined, finite, circumscribed set of permitted readings. To thine own self be true. He would be circumspect, even suspicious, when it comes to post-structuralism, let alone deconstruction: too much emphasis on factors surrounding the text, on the fluid, the ephemeral, the elusive, the deceptive. The text, after all, is *there*: solid and reliable. Here it stands, it cannot do otherwise: God help it.

This is where she would challenge him. She is inspired by Derrida. (Not that she would ever become a disciple of anything, anyone; far beyond deconstruction she will go her lightfooted way through theory and philosophy as through the darkening trees of the wood into which she disappears at dusk when she takes her landlord's great Alsatian for his walk.)

It is settled then: Professor Philip Malan, MA, University of

16

Stellenbosch, DLitt, University of Louvain. Ms (she insists very strongly on this) Melissa Lotman, doctoral student and tutor in his department. Any university will do, but the Eastern Cape has the advantage of being the oldest historical 'trouble spot' in the country. Moreover, there is no Department of Literary Theory at any existing university in that region, which would emphasize from the outset that this is fiction. And, of course, I am familiar with the region. But that is neither here nor there.

That there exists an etymological connection between *life* and *love*, is obvious. But it is only via an excursion into German or a related language (*Leben – Liebe – Leib*) that the *body* is acknowledged as their connecting link. Donne: 'Our bodies why doe wee forebeare?/ We owe them thankes, because they thus,/ Did us, to us, at first convay.'

Beginnings fascinate me no end. That disquieting moment when the writer becomes witness to the translation of mere possibility into the signs of a new system, branding the paper. Suddenly, instead of unlimited potential, there are facts – a presence, a thereness – to be respected; or at the very least, traces to be acknowledged. Through words relationships are established which conjure up awesome horizons; suddenly one has to take responsibility for whatever tracks are followed to whatever horizon. No matter if it remains an eternally elusive horizon. The tracking process has begun and must be followed through. ('That first night we – ')

If there is truth in the old quip that marriage is the most important reason for divorce, it also follows that nothing determines an ending so fatally as a beginning. I have begun to write: surrounding my words lie the horizons of their end. (Graves: 'Take your delight in momentariness,/ Walk between dark and dark – a shining space/ With the grave's narrowness, though not its peace!') Perhaps our most profound consciousness is this sense of an ending. Perhaps our most basic drives are those directed towards countering, or negating, or rebelling against it. Art, love, work, religion, language, sex. Even if each of them ends up by confirming what it has set out to deny.

In Jane Ferguson's opening situation the girl is walking along the beach, away from the isolated hotel, across the dunes; the weather is gloomy, a strong wind blows, she walks bent forward, straining against it, barefoot in the wet sand. When she stops at the far end of a bay's deep curve it is just in time to see her footprints being washed out by the tide until there is nothing left of them, leaving her a person without traces, all the signs of her individual existence obliterated. She is beset by a primitive dread, but it is mixed with ecstasy: as if, unexpectedly, it has become possible to start anew, and innocent. In the distance, following exactly the route she herself has taken, she sees the figure of a man approaching. Her first reaction is panic, the natural impulse, I should imagine, of a woman who sees a stranger coming towards her in a desolate place. She wants to turn and run, make a detour back to the hotel, to other people. But she is restrained by something stronger than her fear: the tide has turned – the foam washing across her footsteps was but a last petulant display of energy – and over the shimmering smoothness of sand she watches him treading his own row of footprints exactly where hers were, as if to reopen the way back, making her possible again.

For the story I am contemplating various beginnings would be possible. For example:

1. After a meeting on campus one evening (addressed by a famous speaker from elsewhere, Beyers Naudé or Allan Boesak or Molly Blackburn or Bishop Tutu) the professor retires to the Arts Building and goes up to his study to finish a pile of unmarked essays or chase a reference for an article he is working on. The main reason, I suspect, is that he has been disturbed by the speech and now needs some time on his own, reluctant to go home and face his family straight away. Some time later Melissa appears in his doorway, framed in darkness.* Has she seen him

---

* This scene is, of course, a reinvention of the first meeting between Van Heerden and Nicolette in my early novel, *The Ambassador*. No doubt other

18

go upstairs? Have they arranged it before the meeting or is it coincidence? At this stage I prefer to leave the options open. What matters is the setting, and the atmosphere. The university has been going through a period of political turmoil recently; the Black Students' Movement, after a long time of patient negotiations, has become more aggressive in its strategies, which in turn has antagonized some of the whites, and it may well be that this evening's meeting has set a match to an already smouldering situation. The Security Police was present in force; it is conceivable that the meeting was disrupted by violence before the end. Outside the building, on the dark campus, there may be a chorus of angry voices, the sounds of fighting, possibly even the reports of teargas canisters exploding; snatches of *Nkosi sikelel' iAfrika* being sung, defiantly, interrupted by shouts of *Amandla!* and *Ngawethu!* Inside, surrounded by books and furniture and tidy stacks of paper, the two of them. After an initial embarrassment he remembers, grateful and amused, a bottle of sherry a visitor had recently given him and which he has forgotten to take home. There are no glasses, though, only a single brown coffee mug. 'If you don't mind sharing – ?' he says, grinning. 'Why not?' she smiles. 'If it is poison we can share a spectacular death. That will give the university something to talk about.' In a disarming, somewhat old-fashioned donnish way he offers her the mug, and in mock solemnity she drinks before passing it to him. It turns out not to be poison after all – good enough, in fact, to be a love potion. In any case it is a beginning worth exploring.

2. Another possibility, more dramatic – a sense of real occasion? – would demand a death in Melissa's family. Her younger brother, perhaps, who has died 'on the border' when his army vehicle detonated a landmine.

---

parallels with my previous novels will be explored in the course of these notes. Part of the satisfaction of making them lies precisely in the exploration of alternatives, not only within the emergent text but also in terms of the larger framework of one's work as a whole; and, in fact, of the 'subtle immensity of writings' mentioned by Barthes, which surrounds every newly written text.

On her return from Johannesburg or Kimberley or wherever the funeral took place (the family was not allowed to see the body: 'Burnt beyond recognition', some officer told them, 'when the Buffel he was in exploded'), she is met at the airport in Port Elizabeth by her professor. (What is he doing there? Perhaps they happened to travel on the same plane: he may be returning from a conference. Perhaps, his family being away – in which case it would have to happen during the school holidays – he decided to take a break, and telephoned her at her parents' home to tell her he would meet her. Otherwise she would naturally have been worried about getting back: it is a drive of 120 kilometres from P.E. to their university town. But these are details one can work out later. What matters is that they are at the airport together.) On an impulse (or has he planned it beforehand?), on the way back he turns off the main road to one of the small coastal villages where he has a beach cottage. (It may also be a friend's; or he may have rented it.) It is a small blue shack, set far away from any other human habitation, among the dunes, tucked into a tangle of milkwood and euphorbia. There she can have the peace and quiet – 'silence' will be the word she uses – she needs to face the world again. At first she is scared, suspicious of his intentions (God knows, after what has happened she is in no mood to have to fend off the advances of an amorous middle-aged male): perhaps it is the natural impulse of a woman left alone with a stranger in a desolate place. (Though of course he is not a total stranger: they know each other quite well, after all, as professor and student, head of department and tutorial assistant.) But her grief – and her relief at being sequestered from the world for a while – is greater than her fear. And during the three days she spends with him (they even share the same bed and she huddles in his arms at night, but chastely) she gradually comes to trust him. He looks after her like a father, cleaning the house, making food, allowing her many hours on her own each day. As in Jane Ferguson's story, nothing 'happens' between them initially, not in the customary narrative sense of the word. Yet, in a more profound sense, *everything* happens. Their brief retreat from a violent and urgent world fosters one important discovery: that they can be good for one another; that, possibly, they need each other.

3.   There is a third beginning which has been haunting me for years, ever since it was suggested by something that happened during 1968, which I spent in Paris. It involves a middle-aged man walking through the deserted streets at night and finding a girl abandoned in a wretched condition by whatever companions she may have had. Drunken? Out of her mind with *dagga* or some stronger dope? The victim of a gang rape? Whatever it may be, he is old-fashioned enough, gentlemanly enough, to pick her up and take her home. (For a beginning like this he should ideally be divorced, or a widower; but perhaps his family has simply gone on holiday for a week or so.) Coax her as he may, she cannot – or does not want to – divulge her name or address. Because of the state she is in, he has to clean her up, bathe her, put her to bed. She is mumbling and sobbing; the moment he leaves her alone, she starts screaming in terror or rage. There is nothing he can do but get into bed with her and hold her in his arms. Gradually she begins to relax, grimacing at him in confusion and mistaken love, caressing him, her eyes mischievous through tousled blonde hair. (This really has the makings of a Mills & Boon.) He tries to subdue her, even gets angry at her, slaps her; that sets her screaming again, abusing him in the filthiest language he has heard in his life. At long last she goes limp in his arms, a crooked little childish smile on her lovely depraved young face. This is the moment of transition towards a darkness he has not acknowledged in himself before. His soothing attentions turn, imperceptibly, into caresses. In vague bemusement she seems to acquiesce. Fired by her shop-soiled innocence, his prudence and concern overwhelmed by the urgency of his own arousal, he forces himself on her. (Forces? It is met by no resistance; even in her dazed condition she seems capable of lust.) The following day, when she wakes up – it is almost noon; she is languid and exhausted, with a wan and perplexed smile – he is overcome by remorse at the thought of what he has done. If only he could ask, and receive, her forgiveness: but how to broach it? She appears to have no recollection of the previous night at all. Her only sentiment towards him is one of almost slavish gratitude. For the time being she stays with him; in complete chastity he nurses her back to health. Only much later will sex enter into it again; and

by then it is impossible to disillusion her about his shame. 'What made you care about *me*?' she asks him once, in awe, in love. 'You're the first man I have ever known who hasn't abused me. Jesus, d'you know, I was ten years old when a cousin of my dad's started "playing" with me – he was supposed to baby-sit with me when I was ill. I didn't even understand what was really going on. He just said it was "our secret". I was scared as hell. I wanted to tell my mom, but I knew she wouldn't believe me, she always blamed me for everything. Then I thought I'd write a note to my dad – surely *he* would understand, and help me – but I wasn't even sure what I was protesting against or what words to use. And here you are looking after me and caring for me and loving me. Jesus, I can't *understand* it.'

Throughout the course of their love there will be the growing apprehension inside him: one day she is bound to find out; one day she'll know that the man she has been regarding as her saviour has just been another of her exploiters. And then he will be the one responsible for her inevitable final collapse.

Except that, when finally he is driven by despair and self-loathing to confess it all to her, she may well respond with irony and compassion: 'But, my love, I've known it since that first night. I just never wanted to tell you, in case it spoilt everything.'

Oh, Melissa.



It should be clear by now what kind of episode I'm looking for: an emergency of an intensity which must strike them both as extraordinary. What else would drive them so fatally together? There must be something about her which involves him so deeply that he cannot let go again. Something sufficiently different from other escapades in his past to mark the course and texture of his life: for, surely, if he is no compulsive womanizer he is no blameless bougeois either; in the twenty years or so of his marriage he must have had his share of brief liaisons, mostly away from home, at congresses or conferences, but possibly even within the university. (Never, categorically never, with a student. He has too deep a sense of propriety for that. Over the years he has been father confessor to many a young woman – something in him appears to inspire confidence – but not once has he taken advantage of them.) Perhaps he has even come to regard himself as 'safe'. He 'knows' the world, doesn't he? He even 'knows' – he would be convinced, like any chauvinist unaware of his own chauvinism – women.

Furthermore, he is really quite happy with his wife. Theirs is known as a 'good' marriage, an example to others.

So why should it be so different this time?

Is it implicit in the situation? (In which case there must be at least some suggestion of danger, of a menace; an unusual circumstance which threatens to intervene in all that is predictable and turn it into anarchy.) Or is it something about *her*, this girl, this Melissa? It cannot be simply a matter of her youth. Here, too, a hint of the unusual must be evoked, to make of it the kind of experience in which, suddenly and violently, one is confronted with *the other*. Which illuminates both the freedom and the boundaries of the self. Here ends the 'I'; here begins the 'you'.

Dear reader: by now you should have seen it for yourself. Nothing exposes one to danger quite so much as a beginning. Which is why I have been writing twenty-two pages without arriving at a beginning yet. I keep on postponing, prevaricating. Quite frankly, I am scared.


For South Africa, the year 1985 began on 21 March in the black township of Langa, outside Uitenhage in the Eastern Cape – not on 1 January as conventionally indicated on calendars. What had happened between 1 January and that day in March can now be seen as mere attempts of history at finding a starting point, a testing of paradigms, a playing with limitless options. It was still possible, if only just (in spite of the wave of violence which had submerged the country since the previous September in reaction against an infamous new constitutional dispensation) for history to find a different course. What complicates the issue is the fact that this clear-cut beginning in itself was merely the result of an event of many years before, the massacre at Sharpeville exactly a quarter of a century earlier. As if life itself is moving in circles, or in spirals, continually passing the same beginnings.

On the date in question, as everybody knows, for it is history now, police in two armoured vehicles cut off a march by an unarmed crowd on their way to a funeral and eventually killed some twenty men, women and children (most of them shot in the back), wounding scores of others. A triumph, once again, for Law and Order; and at least one of the police officers in charge of the massacre was promoted soon afterwards.

Through one of the cruder juxtapositions of history another disaster took place within days of the Uitenhage outrage, when a school bus in Westdene, Johannesburg, drove into a lake, leaving forty-two children dead. It was revealing to note the different ways in which the press reported the two events. For weeks on end English and Afrikaans newspapers ran 'human interest' stories on Westdene: interviews with all the parents and kin, biographies of all the dead, moving comments on funerals and memorial services. Photographs: a mother collapsing with grief, a school tie and a pair of shoes on a coffin, houses marked with white crosses. Every drop of sentiment squeezed out of the occasion for consumption by the masses. A fund was established for the bereaved families, supported by the Government and amounting to hundreds of thousands within days, although no-one was really sure what the money was meant for. There was no fund for the bereaved of Uitenhage. Press coverage was, of course, massive, but almost without exception these reports discussed the massacre within the context of politics. No 'human interest' here, no attempt to report the feelings of a woman whose child of two or three years old had been shot dead on its mother's back, or the reactions of a man who had seen the body of his wife kicked about by police trying to establish whether she was dead, or the reaction of a survivor with a bullet in his spine, paralyzed for life. No biographies, interviews, commentaries to establish that what had happened belonged not only to the political statistics of the country but concerned ordinary men, women, children. For these victims were black; this incident had occurred far away, in limbo, beyond the periphery of white suburbs and consciousness. The poor children of Westdene, on the other hand, were white, cut off tragically in the prime of their youth, the elected of Lord Jesus, the purest pearls of His eternal crown. Furthermore, think of it: all those beautiful white children would have married in due course, to produce children of their own. One can calculate for oneself what a loss was sustained by the white race of Southern Africa, established here by the will of God Almighty. The others had sprouted from the soil by themselves, like weeds in a well-planned mealie land.


In these turbulent times – late March, early April; during the Easter vacation – the professor is to attend a literary theory congress in Cape Town. He has been invited to read the final paper. Prior to the congress he spends a week in Cape Town, with a senior colleague, as delegates of a Senate committee to explore inter-university programmes in the Humanities (he serves on many committees; he has ambitions to be elected Dean later in the year). Originally his wife was to have accompanied him, but something of a domestic crisis developed. A sick child? But that may have been no more than a pretext; the roots lay deeper, untouched by the clichés of their superficial conversation: 'I'm not begrudging you your congresses, Philip,' she told him. 'But when last did we have a holiday, just the two of us? There was a time when we used to do most things together.' 'Please don't exaggerate,' he would have replied. 'We can discuss it later. Can't you see I'm busy? I've got to finish this paper.' 'You're always busy, you always have excuses.' Nothing more was said, but it was enough to disturb him. One does not always recognize an emergency when it comes. Only when it is too late – No, this is ridiculous, there is no reason to overreact. Once the congress is over they can sit down and sort it all out, calmly, like adults.

His lecture, on the final afternoon, is well attended. He is regarded as an authority: many of his colleagues have been waiting for him to do this neat academic hatchet job on the recent proliferation of lunatic-fringe heresies in literary theory. It is time to return to the text, the text *über alles*. The very hegemony of the word is at stake. 'The rise of the textocentric approach and its refinement in critical debate with the so-called "new paradigm".' He is a balanced, restrained, urbane speaker, not dogmatic or categorical in his approach, open-minded, yet passionately convinced of his cause. The discourse is followed by prolonged debate in which, like an experienced batsman, he flicks one question after another to the boundary. Applause. Then a brief intermission before the closing reception in the Otto Beit Union. He has been planning (secretly, like a truant schoolboy) to skip the reception and slip away into town. A Capab production of *The Valkyrie*. Marita Napier as Brünnhilde. (He adores Wagner. The profound pleasure and reassurance of a structure shaped by interlocking symbols.) But a colleague from the north corners him to discuss his paper, and while they are talking several other delegates join them. Regretful, but also flattered by their interest, the professor relinquishes his evening at the opera.

The reception is in full swing by the time he and his colleagues, having reached consensus, arrive at the Union. And almost immediately, in a small opening in the crowd, he sees Melissa. During the three days of the congress he had noticed her from time to time in the audience, or in the throng surrounding the tea-tables. Once he had given her a conspiratorial little wave over the heads of the people separating them, pleased and touched by her loyalty to their subject. But this is the first time they have a chance to talk.

'Not too bored, I hope?'

'You were brilliant, prof.' A flicker at the corner of her mouth, which he remembers from her Honours seminars. 'But I don't agree with a word of it, of course.'

They have often argued in the past, but she has never been quite so outspoken before.

'Have you joined the heretics then?'

'Perhaps I just belong to a generation less inclined to faith.'

'What has faith got to do with it?'

'Everything. What is a conviction about the authority of a text if not a confession of faith in an author? A good old-fashioned naturalistic God, present everywhere but nowhere visible?'

'Wait a minute, Melissa. If you start with de Saussure – '

'You see? Already you are looking for an author again. Poor old de Saussure has had so many things ascribed to him without our knowing what he really said. You know very well his lectures were written down and probably distorted by his students. For all we know they may have created a deliberate fiction. Perhaps de Saussure never even existed.'

Her cheeks are glowing. Too much wine, so early in the evening? How little he really knows about her.

Other guests intervene in their conversation before he can reply; he is dragged away, she is dragged away. But he feels irritated. Something has been left incomplete. He has been challenged, he must respond. But whenever he tries to find her again in the crowd they are kept apart. Now and then he catches glimpses of her, usually in earnest conversation with younger guests; once he hears the clear cascade of her laughter and sees her for a moment, her head thrown back, a tumbling mass of blonde hair, a flash of light sparkling on the wine glass in her hand. When at last he does track her down again – now grimly determined not to be waylaid again – he finds her talking to a young man with tousled black hair, his face almost overgrown with beard. There is something so easy and intimate in their manner that the professor feels an instant grudge, prey to a possessiveness he himself cannot explain. (Where does she know him from, this hirsute young male animal with his faded jeans, the chain around his neck, the hint of a foreign accent? Did she spend last night in his bed?)

'Excuse me,' he says brusquely, taking her by the arm. 'There is something I still have to discuss with Ms Lotman.'

The stranger shrugs and turns away to someone else.

'What's the matter, prof?' she asks, startled by his vehemence.

'We'll keep on getting interrupted here,' he says recklessly. 'Can't I kidnap you and take you somewhere else?'

A brief, intense examination with her eyes before she says, with a generosity he has had no reason to expect: 'Why not? Where are you taking me?'

'Dinner, perhaps. I can't stand all this small talk and drinking.'

On their way through the city in his small rented car he asks: 'Do you know Cape Town?'

'I studied here, remember. And I still spend most of my holidays here. Especially in winter.'

'Why on earth in winter? It is so miserably wet and cold.'

'Perhaps you only learn the meaning of love once you've

learned to love Cape Town in winter. It's really the most beautiful time of the year, didn't you know? The rain. The wet misty mornings. To lie awake in bed at night and listen to the gutters dripping. To wrap yourself in someone's jersey or overcoat or blanket and wander through the streets, or spend long nights drinking wine in front of the fire, or talking nonsense, or making love on the rug, or just dropping off to sleep. The only time in my life I almost consented to get married was here in the Cape. High up against the mountain, in Kloof Nek, an old-fashioned house so ugly one could hug it. Fortunately I realized just in time that if I really said yes it would only be for the sake of staying here forever, not because I cared for the man. And somehow it never works out for me anyway, staying in one place for too long.'

'Now come on,' he says with almost paternal concern. 'A responsible person like yourself.'

'Responsible?!' He is surprised by the scorn in her short laugh. 'I envy you your certainties, prof. But I don't think I'd like to swop.'

'How old are you, Melissa?'

'Twenty-three.' A shrug of her smooth shoulders, their late-summer tan offset by her white dress. 'But don't let that fool you. Sometimes I feel positively ancient. One of these days I'll be all grey and haggard.'

'Leave age to me,' he says lightly.

'My generation is supposed to prefer older men.'

'Who was that hairy young ape who annexed you at the party?' he asks, more tartly than he meant to.

'Julio?' She seems flattered by his curiosity. 'Just somebody from the congress. I rather enjoy arguing with him. We're at it all the time.'

Now he'll probably never find out, he thinks. And why should it be so important to know – not only about that man, but about everything that concerns her?

There is no parking place in front of his hotel and they have to leave the car right down on the beach and walk back to the entrance in the gusty night wind. The palm fronds in the garden rustle like the sea.

'Is this where you've been staying for the congress?' she asks.

'Yes.' Somehow her question makes him feel guilty, caught

out. 'I thought we could have dinner here, it's as good a restaurant as any. Rather than driving all over the place trying to find something else.'

She gives no answer. The wind sweeps her loose white dress up against her body. She is dangling her small handbag from the crook of her little finger. Her windblown hair makes it impossible for him to see her face.

'There was something you still wanted to discuss with me, you said,' she reminds him with a straight face after they have ordered.

'Was there?'

'That was your reason for kidnapping me.'

'Oh. It isn't important. You were the one who still had to explain why you dismissed my talk.'

'Dismissed with acclamation,' she corrects him slyly.

Their conversation returns to the academic, to his confidence in the text and her suspicions about it; throughout the starters and the main course the discussion continues eagerly, without any strain. But he becomes more and more aware of shutting himself off from her arguments as he concentrates on the movement of her mouth while she speaks, or the caressing motions of her hair on her cheeks, the gestures of her hands which cause a gentle tinkling of thin golden bracelets, the curve of her shoulders. Without warning he wonders: Suppose he asked her if she – ? But he must put it out of his mind. If she were to refuse, how can he face her again? She's his assistant. He should be concentrating on what she is saying. Soon, distressingly soon, dinner will be over, their coffee drunk (will she order Irish?), and then he will have to take her back to wherever she is lodged. A hotel? Friends? That bloody troglodyte?

It is just after the waiter has brought back the menu for dessert that there is a sudden change in the evening's course, a small deviation which, in retrospect, will prove decisive. Instead of coming to take their order, the waiter leans over to announce as casually as possible (though it is obvious that he is very tense):

'Sorry to disturb you, sir, but would you mind going outside for a few minutes? There's been a telephone call about a bomb scare in the restaurant and the police would like to – '

All around them chairs are pushed back from the tables as

people prepare to leave. There is no panic, everything is happening with almost excessive decorum; many of the guests carry their drinks with them. Perhaps they have already become used to such interruptions. (It is only Melissa's tight grip on Philip's arm which makes him realize how nervous *she* is.) Outside on the terrace, in the first premonition of autumn in the air, small groups of guests continue their conversations as if nothing at all has happened. From the parking lot below a phalanx of police comes swarming up the broad stairs, several of them with dogs on leashes. Without interrupting their conversations the diners on the terrace adapt their postures so that they can keep an eye on what is going on inside without making it too obvious. Not that one can see much through the forest of palms and potted shrubs in front of the plate-glass windows – except for a slow, deliberate wave of uniforms unfurling through the restaurant from one end to the other. Five minutes later the police return through the front door and lead their dogs into the night. There is a rumble of vehicles starting up and driving off. Soon afterwards the sound of waves breaking on the beach below can once more be heard.

'It is all clear, ladies and gentlemen, thank you,' announces the head waiter from the front door. And with the same casual movement as before the crowd drifts back into the restaurant.

'Shall we go back for a dessert?' asks the professor as they reach the door.

'I don't think I feel like it any more,' she says, subdued, glancing up at him. He realizes that she is trembling. In the uncertain light he tries to see the colour of her eyes, but it is impossible. Blue? Green? Grey? Even brown? It can be anything.

'Do you mind – ?' she says.

There is a sudden small flicker of panic inside him. She cannot leave now! Something has happened, somewhere in this tentative night a shift has occurred: he can no longer let her go. A great invisible fist of danger has momentarily clutched them in its grip – it is only now, after it has passed, that he is struck by the fear she has been feeling – and something has irrevocably changed.

'Won't you stay with me tonight?' he asks, not daring to look at her. 'Please don't go.'

30

She does not answer. Behind her, very far away indeed, he can hear the uneasy sighing of the sea.

'Will you stay?'

'Suppose the bomb is still somewhere?'

'My God, yes. I'd better take you back.'

In a strange calm, her eyes fixed on his, she says: 'No, I'll stay.'

'But – '

'I'll take the chance.'

Walking ahead of her down the interminable passage and up the gleaming wooden staircase to his room, he feels his stomach contracting in fear. Are they not walking more deeply into danger with every step? Suppose she was right and the bomb is not lodged in the restaurant but somewhere in the deeper recesses of the hotel – a linen closet, a toilet, a broom cupboard? Yet here he is, and she with him, following him to God knows what doom.

Key in the lock. The door pushed open. Light on. 'Here we are.' He stands aside to let her pass. 'Come into my parlour.' His throat feels dry.

'Nice room.'

'Just an ordinary hotel room.' (What will the debris look like?)

She picks up a much-thumbed book from the long dressing table and begins to flip through the pages. (Relieved to have something irrelevant to concentrate her mind?) Donington: *Wagner's 'Ring' and its symbols*.

'Found it on the Parade on Saturday,' he says too eagerly. 'Been chasing it for years. First edition. I was actually planning to go to *The Valkyrie* tonight.'

'Now I have made you miss your date with Brünnhilde?'

'I'd rather spend time with a woman than with a symbol.' (Is violent death preferable to an evening of make-believe?)

She continues to leaf through the book as if it really is of great importance to look at every page. 'I can do without Wagner,' she says. 'Personally I prefer Chopin. Or Bob Dylan. Wagner is too heavy, all that violence and fate and *Sturm und Drang*.'

Finished with the book, she puts it back on the dressing table (not quite as squarely as it was, he notices). Then remains standing as if waiting for something. For the bomb to go off? The night is fraught with danger.

31

He lifts a hand to touch her, to reassure her, but lets it drop again.

She turns round to face him, a strained smile tugging at her mouth.

'Well?'

'I'll wait on the balcony,' he says deliberately. 'In case you feel like – '

Was it really out of tact that he has left her alone inside? he wonders on the balcony. (Far below the sea is tossing restlessly, murmuring, spending itself on the sand.) Or is it to escape? Or the better to see the explosion when it comes? But he should be inside with her; no, rather, they should be racing out into the night, to his car, and through the streets, back to where she will be safe. (Will she really be safer somewhere else?)

'I must go down to the sea again,' he mumbles in a transparent attempt to restore order to his mind, stilling the panic. He has found, in other situations of stress or distress, that it helps to think of a poem and start analysing the lines. It shuts out the world very effectively. '– And a star to steer me by – ' (An illustration from his paper this afternoon. How long ago? Before the Bomb.) Now, ladies and gentlemen, why would Masefield –

'What's happened to you?' she calls through the open french doors. He hurries back to her. 'If you'd stayed away a moment longer, I would have run away,' she says. She is standing with her back pressed to the heavy dark curtains, waiting for him, undressed, but with her white clothes and underclothes bundled against her, a scared beautiful white moth that has lost its way in the night.

When he takes her by the arms he discovers that she is still trembling. Perhaps the bomb has nothing to do with it, he thinks, startled. What if she is still a virgin – ?

'Don't be afraid,' he tries to reassure her, himself unnerved, leading her to the bed and pulling back the bedclothes.

'Please put off the light.'

In the instant before he leans over to find the switch beside the bed, as she drops her clothes to the floor, he tries to impress on his mind that first view – the mere glimpse – he is allowed of her body, how smooth she is.

Hurriedly stripping off his own clothes he moves in beside her, groping for her in the dark.

'Take off your watch,' she says quietly. 'It scratches.'

He finds the request unsettling. Whenever he wakes up at night it is his habit first of all to check the time; there is a reassurance to be drawn from the small illuminated disc in the dark. An indispensable calculation: so many hours since last night, so many hours before he has to get up: here, in between, is he. Almost as if relinquishing something he draws the metal links across his palm and puts the watch on the table beside the bed.

'Suppose the bomb does go off in the night,' she whispers in his ear. 'Doesn't it scare you to think we may be dead by the time the sun comes up? This may be our last night.'

'Thank God I found you just in time,' he answers, trying to sound flippant. 'Imagine dying without having spent a night together.'

'We'll be part of the country's statistics,' she says, entering into his mood. 'We'll have our niche in history.'

'Living dangerously. Isn't that a maxim of your generation?'

'Isn't it for you too?'

'Perhaps it hasn't yet been necessary to consider it.'

'Prof.' Unexpectedly, she pushes herself up on an elbow; in the dim glow from outside he can see the outline of her body, a breast, a shoulder. 'Why did you really kidnap me from the party?'

'Don't call me "prof".'

'I can't suddenly start calling you by another name.'

'Philip.'

'No, Prof is my name for you. And you still owe me an answer.'

'I'm not sure I have one ready. Perhaps I was just jealous of the other people talking to you. Here we can be alone. Listen to the sea: we can pretend we are marooned on an island.'

'Do you believe in islands then?'

'I believe in the two of us here, tonight.' In a slow, gentle caress he starts tracing the outlines of her body.

'A night doesn't last very long.'

'Long enough.' ('*Ewig wär uns die Nacht –* ')

33

'For what?'

'For many things. Being together. Whatever you want to call it. We are here now.'

'And tomorrow?'

'We needn't think about it now.' He smiles. 'You *have* made me take off my watch.'

'Perhaps you're right.' A small sigh of contentment.

'Anyway, tomorrow morning we can sleep late, the congress is over.'

'I'm afraid I have to get up early,' he says, apologetic. 'I must be at the airport by half-past seven.'

'Damn. Why didn't you warn me before?'

He is piqued by the reproach in her voice. 'I can still take you home if that is what you really want. At least your honour will be saved.'

'You're talking too much, prof,' she says with a ripple of laughter, pushing him back against the pillows and putting her finger to his mouth. Off his guard, he abandons himself to the unexpected energy with which she starts fondling him, amazed by the curious mixture of shyness and expertise in the necromancies of love she performs on him, his eyes peering into the semi-darkness as he tries to familiarize himself with her silhouette against the pale glow of the window. After a while he pulls her down beside him to involve himself more actively – she, nervous and passionate, at times almost in a rage, possessed – until he hears her breath coming in deeper gasps and she begins to utter the moans of her imminent orgasm, her hands pressed against the sides of his head as she tries to force him more urgently into what writers of love stories would call the ozone of her overwhelming femininity; while far outside the sea turns and sighs like some vast dark animal in the night, its wet waves breaking on the sand.

This is the moment I shall choose – perversely – to intervene in their story. With diabolic design I cause the telephone beside the bed to ring, so that she instantly tenses up in shock, caught already in the first spasms of her coming, while he is struck dumb as his mind tries furiously to run down the possibilities. It must be two or three o'clock in the morning. None of his colleagues or acquaintances knows where he is staying. His wife? Unlikely. He had spoken to her shortly before the afternoon session; in a few hours he will be home. Unless something drastic has happened. But damn it, he has arranged for a student to sleep in the house during his absence, and he knows the young man is mature and competent enough to handle most crises. It can only be a wrong number.

Through her fingers pressed against his ears he hears her whisper: 'Shouldn't you answer?'

'No. It must be a mistake. The night porter must have rung the wrong room. It cannot possibly be for me.'

'But suppose – '

He gets to his knees, loses his balance, half-falling over her, smothering the telephone with a pillow, knocking over the lamp on the bedside table in the process. She starts giggling, with a hint of hysteria. He is furious. After a few more rings the telephone falls silent.*

Still a bit shaky, Melissa gets up and goes to the dressing table where she rummages through her handbag in the dark. He hears the scraping of a match, briefly sees her body illuminated by the small fierce flame. Then she utters a sharp: 'Shit!' and starts laughing nervously.

'What's happened?'

'Lit the wrong end of the cigarette.'

She stubs it out and takes a new one from the packet; then comes back to the bed, pulling up the sheet to cover her breasts, and sits smoking in a tense silence.

'Do you think it could have been – ?' she asks after a while. Her voice still sounds unsteady.

'It cannot possibly be anyone we know.'

'Unless someone saw us leaving together.'

'Who was that young – ' Without finishing the question he

---

* How will he ever find out that it was I who rang? What would he have said if he had indeed picked up the telephone? What would *I* have said?

Would I have said: 'For God's sake, man, think of what you're doing, consider the consequences, think of the whole train of events set in motion by a beginning . . .'?

Or would I have said: 'By all means go ahead, Philip. No matter what pain and exposure and terror and chaos may spring from it: go ahead, it *is* worth it, it is the only thing really worth while'?

gets up to pull the telephone plug from its socket in the wall. More from a need of movement than from thirst he goes to the bathroom and returns with a glass of water.

'I'd like some too.' Her voice sounds more easy now. 'From your glass. If it is poison we can still share a spectacular death – even if the bomb fails to go off.'

He moves in beside her again. While she goes on smoking, he starts stroking her shoulder, the bend of her arm, gently tugging at the sheet to peel it from her. And after she has finished her cigarette and stubbed it out she turns back to him. The numbness ebbs away. At last they can resume; in the open french doors the curtains are swaying in the late night breeze. ('Now are we consecrated by the night'.)

The first daylight is already filtering into the room when at last, exhausted and replete, they come to rest, she sheltered in his arm, the sheet pulled up to her shoulders, her hair a dark patch on the pillow. He has no wish to sleep. In the gathering light he lies gazing at her in wonder, this beautiful strange face next to his, remote in sleep, partly hidden by her hair. This is what it really means, he thinks, 'to sleep with someone'. Not just the writhing and celebration of bodies, but this: this lying together in silence afterwards, this abandonment to sleep in someone else's arms. How vulnerable one is in sleep. Anything may happen, anything may be done to one, even one's life may be taken: yet you close your eyes, trusting me enough to fall asleep beside me, your whole life delivered to me. And who am I to dare concern myself with you? What right have I, what choices are available to me? A single night have we shared, a few hours of darkness: a shelter, a station where we stopped before resuming our separate journeys. Or will it turn out to be more? – A beginning, a point of departure, from which to set sail on an undetermined, indeterminate voyage across uncharted seas where God knows what terrors may await us, and God knows what ecstasies.

Without adding sound to it, his mouth forms the name he has hardly uttered yet: *Melissa*. Whatever that may mean. *Melissa*.

He keeps all thoughts at bay. (Except: The bomb has not exploded after all. We have strangely survived.) Too soon they must rise and go away from here.

She is silent when, on his way to the airport, he makes a detour to the address in Rosebank she has given him.

'Any regrets?' he asks, without considering what he says, instantly wishing he can undo it.

'Why on earth should you ask that?' Her eyes are still dark with sleep.

He makes an effort to laugh it off: 'Didn't your mother warn you not to sleep with strange men?'

A flickering of her mouth. 'It's easier with strange men.'

He stops at the street number she has indicated (will he ever find it again on his own?). An unattractive pink house in a style of the twenties or thereabouts, 'added to' over the years, now clearly in need of new paint and repair.

'Whose house is it?'

She shrugs. Her long white dress appears surreal against the dark green grass sparkling with dew; pigeons are cooing in the tall pines. 'Just people I know.'

'You sure they'll wake up if you knock?'

'I have a key.'

'Will you be able to sleep again?'

'I can sleep any time, any place. Don't you know? Even in your lectures.'

She starts walking towards the glassed-in front porch.

'Melissa!'

'Hm?' Glancing back, her face obscured by her swinging hair.

'Will I ever see you again?'

'Sure. Next week. I'm starting the new term with a dawn patrol.'

'That's not what I meant. Will you – '

She comes back to the car, leans through the window, touches his cheek with her lips, then runs off to the ugly pink house, past the front door, round to the back.

He has to go. Return the rented car. Check in his suitcase. Catch the plane. Back. Back – to what? Work, wife, children, everything. 'Life'. One always has to go back. Always. So why this paralysing resentment, as if he really doesn't know how?

The road to the airport is lined with army trucks.

At least this is a beginning. Tentative; a trial run; no more. But a beginning of sorts.

*

'I had to come past here on my way to Cape Town, so I thought
why not look you up,' says the stranger on my doorstep (I greet
him with diffidence; I frown on visitors who turn up unan-
nounced). 'One cannot trust the telephone these days, and the
mail even less.'

Even when he says his name – Charles Ferguson – I do not
recognize it straight away. He must have noticed, for he hastens
to explain: 'You wrote me a note about Jane's manuscript.'

The kind of man who may be seventy but looks fifty, grey,
crew-cut, a leathery skin cured by sun and wind, clean white
shirt fraying at the collar and the cuffs, jeans, Jesus sandals.

'Of course.' It is unnerving suddenly to be confronted with a
total stranger with whom one is supposed to commiserate. 'I'm
terribly sorry – about what happened. The report in the newspaper was such a shock. I suppose you came for the manuscript?'

'No. There's nothing I can do with it. You're the only one.
Who showed any interest, I mean. Can you spare me a few
minutes?'

'By all means,' I say, feeling guilty. And after offering him a
drink (he asks for orange juice), I once again assure him of my
annoyance about the publishers' shortsightedness.

'That's neither here nor there now,' he replies. 'Look, I don't
what to waste your time. I've brought you something.' He tugs
at the clasp of the kind of khaki satchel children drag to school; it
is dilapidated and stained, as is the dog-eared scribbler he takes
from it. 'It's a diary she used to keep.' Noticing, no doubt, my
guarded look, he smiles to reassure me: 'No, please don't think
this is another of those requests writers are always pestered
with. You needn't do anything at all with it. Don't even read it,
unless you really want to.'

'But – '

'In one of your letters you asked her to tell you more about
herself. She showed me the letter. We were very close, Jane and
I. Ever since she was a child. You see, her mother – well, let's
just say she left us when Jane was still quite small. So we had to
sort things out on our own. Living in the veld, most of the time.
She practically grew up among the Zulus. Spoke Zulu before she
learnt any other language. In fact, the first day she went to

38

school, when the teacher asked her who her father was, she said: "*Baas* Charles".' An impish grin, which makes him look younger still. Even the insides of the wrinkles on his face are brown. 'The only time she let her defences down to any stranger was with this man. I guessed how serious it was because it was the first time she ever tried to keep anything from me. Only afterwards did she show me the diary; even then she was reluctant to talk about it. It was I who encouraged her to turn it into a story – she'd been writing stories since she was a kid – I thought it might help her come to terms with it. Kind of therapy. But I'm sure you know more about these things than I do.'

'But the diary must mean more to you than to anybody else.'

'I may come back for it one day. But at the moment – I may just as well be frank with you – well, you see, I don't want the Security Police to get hold of it. Which is why I prefer not to keep the manuscript with me either. They were bad enough before, but ever since she died they've been a bloody nuisance.' He stops abruptly, as if he hasn't foreseen where the conversation was heading.

'Security Police?' I ask, bemused. 'I never knew she was – '

'I can assure you Jane was as apolitical as I am, if that is what worries you. She was like a little veld animal. It all happened because of this man.'

'Who was he?'

'Didn't you know?' He looks at me in disbelief, then nods. 'But of course you wouldn't. Chris de Villiers.'

'Good God,' I gasp. 'Was *she* the girl – ?'

And this was the woman the publishers urged to add a political dimension to a love story.

Chris de Villiers.


Places. Her room. The forsaken garden. The wood. The night streets. The geography of love.

She lives, I imagine, in a room in the backyard of an old ramshackle house, one of three or four stables or other outbuildings from a century ago and restored cheaply to serve as student digs; each with a minuscule cubicle with shower, washbasin and toilet, and a small kitchen. He is reluctant to visit her there: it seems to him too blatant and definite a move, too defiant. In a small town like this, on a campus like this, where everybody knows (or tries to find out) everything about everybody else.

But what else can he do? A few hurried minutes in his office from time to time, if he can devise a pretext to call her in; or in the one she shares with another assistant – and then he must take the precaution of carrying books or notes or forms with him to maintain a pretence of official business. In these circumstances it is no wonder that he should find her reticent, evasive, always fearing an unexpected intrusion.

At home: the postponed discussion with his wife has remained unbroached. If they had talked it over before the congress, it may well have been resolved quite easily. Now it has become much more complicated. What is required of him above all is to keep all the components of his life meticulously separated. His family. His work. And now – Melissa. Exposed to each other, these parts can invade and injure and even destroy one another. Only by keeping them apart – himself the sole link – can survival, and sanity, be ensured. But that demands a separate space for Melissa.

And so at last he ventures to her room, picking his way – guiltily, like a would-be burglar – through the backyard where piles of rubble among unkempt shrubs and weeds form a veritable obstacle course. Someone must have pruned the climbing roses on the hedge; the entrance is blocked by thorny branches through which he has to battle. Behind a tall fence of wire mesh her landlord's large Alsatian rages furiously until a sleepy Melissa emerges from her door to restrain him with a pat on the head.

'Did I wake you up?' he asks.

'It was high time. I feel as if I've been sleeping for a hundred years. So you've risked it at last?'

There is something formal in the way she sits on the narrow bed in the corner with her cup of tea, while he perches on an uneasy chair from which she has cleared clothes and books. There is no flow in their conversation. He enquires about the progress of her research, the tutorials and lectures she has been giving, the – what else is there to ask about? It is only when she gets up to put away her teacup that, suddenly, in the way she tosses back her long blonde hair, he is reminded of the night in Cape Town (the first evening in his study – the night in the cottage by the sea – the night he brought her home from the streets where she had been abandoned). A flood of memories return, so vivid and violent that he is forced to admit: No, it hasn't been imagination; it really happened; it was she, I, we.

She remains standing at the table, rummaging through books and papers, brightly coloured socks, wine bottles, empty tissue boxes, fruit in paper bags, retrieving at last a packet of cigarettes. Jumping up to take the matches from her, his hand brushes against her wrist and for a moment he clutches it.

'Do you remember?' he asks. 'How you lit the wrong end of the cigarette that night?'

'I got such a fright when the phone rang. Did you ever find out who – ?'

'No. I'm sure it must have been the wrong number.'

'I still get the shivers when I think of it.'

'So you do remember.'

'Did you think I would forget?'

Her eyes should be blue, he thinks. Or green. Or grey. But they aren't. They have a colour still unnamed, they change from one moment to the next, sometimes agate, smoked glass, sudden darknesses in which one could get lost.

'I was hoping you wouldn't. I was afraid you might think – '

'What?' She doesn't afford him any easy way out.

'That it was just a one-night stand.'

She turns away, as if to go to the window. 'I have nothing against one-night stands, prof. If you know there's no tomorrow and no further scheming to worry about, then it's OK. Provided both want it. And as long as it isn't just the result of an argument or a struggle, or because the man feels he's expected to perform.'

'Are you talking' – he decides to risk it; he must know – 'from experience?'

'Last year one of my Cape Town professors came up here on a visit,' she says; he cannot make out whether it is meant as an answer to his question. 'In our undergrad days we worshipped the man. Most of the girls, I think, were secretly in love with him. So I was terribly flattered when he wrote to tell me he was coming and to invite me to dinner at his hotel.'

There is again a hint of nervousness in the way she stubs out her cigarette in a saucer; then she carries their cups to her tiny kitchen.

'Well?' he asks when she comes back.

'Well what?'

'Your visiting professor?'

'*Ag*, it's nothing really.'

'Please tell me, Melissa.'

'It isn't important. I don't know why I even brought it up.' She goes to a long mirror against the shadowy far wall (the two small windows do not let in much light) and starts brushing her hair. 'We had dinner. Then he invited me to his room for coffee and port. I accepted, of course. Why shouldn't I? It was a cold night, it was raining outside, I enjoyed his company. Only, as soon as the coffee was brought he locked the door and suddenly things got heavy.'

'Did he – ?'

'It was awful. He was so drunk, so crude. When he discovered it didn't work out that way, he asked me if I knew the Tarot and took out a pack and started telling my fortune: and each card had something to say about a new lover who was going to change the whole course of my life, things like that. I couldn't help it, I started giggling, it was so obvious. I swear he carried his cards with him the way some men make sure they always have a Durex in their pockets. And when he saw it was no good, he lay down on the bed, turned sideways so I could see his profile, not that he has much of a profile, and started telling me about his romantic, sensual nature and his poetic soul. Adding, in passing, that he had a lot of influence at this university and with committees that dish out scholarships for studies overseas, and that there was no limit to what he might still do for me – '

'But in the end he did let you go?'

She shrugs. 'Sometimes one tries to resist, one fights like a *meerkat* with a snake, but oh Jesus, it's such a schlepp. So sometimes you just learn to switch off and for God's sake let them do what they want to if it's really so important to them. It's

42

the quickest way to get it over and be rid of them.' The small cynical laugh he has already come to know. 'At least, when he did allow me to leave, he told me I was a beautiful and precious person.'

'Melissa.'

She looks at him.

'That early morning in Cape Town when you told me it was easier to sleep with someone you don't know – what did you really mean?'

With an absentminded air she starts rearranging some of the books on her table. After a while she looks up at him through strands of hair: 'Was that what I said?'

'You know it was.'

'Do you think it's better for a woman to put up a struggle and fight for her "honour" even if it goes on for hours, even if it goes on for a whole night? Does "honour" enter into it at all? Honour is a word. What does it mean? You tell me.'

Quietly he asks (is he deliberately trying to provoke her?): 'Is that why you said yes to me that evening?'

She turns on him so fiercely that he starts. 'Don't ever say that to me again!'

For a moment they stand opposite each other in terrifying exposure, more naked than in that remote impossible night. Then she says, very calmly: 'I said yes because I wanted to. Do you understand that? Even though I knew it would be difficult. It's always difficult with someone you like. Because you have no idea of what may happen. Because there's nothing you can take for granted. Because, suddenly, it's just the two of you. You're on your own. There is no other loneliness quite like it.'

He moves towards her to take her in his arms.

Once again it becomes necessary for me to intervene. The dog starts barking outside; in a panic, Melissa ducks away from the front window. The visitor is known to both of them, but their experiences of him are different. To her, Lucas Wilson is an ex-lover. To the professor he is an up-and-coming member of Faculty (Department of Political Studies? Psychology?). I see him as thirtyish: someone once referred to as 'an angry not-so-young man'. Highly talented, limitless ambition. A brilliant PhD, I can imagine, with a thesis that caused quite a stir in

Liberal circles when it was presented a year or two ago. Active in a variety of political organizations, an acerbic polemicist who loves writing letters to newspapers. Something along these lines: once again, the details can be filled in later, depending on the kind of role he may be required to play if I do decide to pursue the story.

Philip, with his back to the window, cannot see the visitor arriving, only hears the barking outside, the squeaking of the iron gate on its hinges, as he watches Melissa cower.

'What's the matter?'

'I think it's – oh God, yes, it *is* Lucas. Don't move. Please. Don't make a sound.'

'But – '

'Shhh!'

She seems ready to burst into tears from fear. He stares at her in amazement as she stands contracted into a small bundle, hands clutching her stomach as if racked by cramps.

A knock. A pause. Another knock. A voice calling: 'Melissa! Melissa!' A long pause. Another knock.

'Is he never going to leave?'

'Melissa!'

At last the sound of the gate turning on its squeaky hinges again. A car starts up in the backyard. It takes at least another minute before she dares to move.

'Melissa.' He holds her tightly in his arms, feeling her tremble like a hare saved from the hounds. 'Now you must tell me.'

A strangled laugh. 'I'm overreacting. I'm sorry, prof. Just hold me. You must think I'm out of my mind.'

'Nothing will happen to you while I'm with you. I promise.'

She keeps standing pressed against him; slowly the trembling eases.

'Do you hear me?' he asks gently. 'Do you believe me?'

'I want to, prof. I really want to.'

'This relationship you had with Lucas – was it serious?' he asks. He knows very little about it; it hasn't concerned him before.

She nods, goes to the table to light another cigarette, then stabs it out again. 'I must stop smoking. I don't want to depend on bloody cigarettes or anything else. That's why I broke with

44

Lucas. Yes, we were together last year. Not for very long, a matter of five, six months. Even so, it was the longest I've ever been with anybody. He asked me to move in with him. I had misgivings, being independent has always meant a lot to me, but he kept on nagging, so in the end I did. And it wasn't too bad in the beginning. Except that he was terribly possessive. Every evening he'd go out with his friends to drink and play chess, while I had to stay in the flat. And when he came back, long after midnight, he would wake me up to make love. He could never take anything easy. He just had to prove all the time how strong and virile he was. You'd never believe it, listening to him in company: in public he was just about the greatest champion of women's lib you've ever seen. Anyway, it couldn't go on like that. A few times I tried to move out, but he would always come to fetch me back. He'd even beat me up when he was in one of his rages. One night he threw me down the stairs. I ran outside to get away from him. He locked the door on me. It was winter, I was almost naked, I went on pleading with him for hours to let me back into the house, but he refused. In the end I crept into the garage and got into his car. Thank God he hadn't locked it. And the next morning I moved into this room. The place wasn't even finished yet, the builders were still painting and hammering and cleaning up, but I couldn't wait. I rounded up a few friends to help me carry my stuff over from his flat while he was at lectures. Not that I have many friends here, he never allowed me to have any of my own, and he could be incredibly rude whenever I had a visitor. Anyway, for a few weeks he left me in peace. Then he tried to persuade me to come back. He still comes round almost every night to make sure there's no one here with me. I usually don't even open the door for him. Once or twice he actually tried to kick it down, but then Jack threw him out.'

'Jack?'

'My landlord. A down-to-earth soul who won't hurt a fly. He runs a small shop downtown, mainly for black customers. You know the kind of shop? Iron pots, bags of samp and beans and mealie meal, bales of chinz, things like that. Jack's a bit of a plodder, I suppose, but the kind of big strong hulk that makes one feel safe. And he certainly gave Lucas a fright.'

'But do you really believe Lucas will harm you? I've always found him – well, rather civilized.'

'I know him better than you do.'

She stops him with a finger on his lips when he tries to speak again; for a long time he holds her in silence, until at last she seems calm again.

'Is it better now?'

She nods. 'I'm sorry I was so hysterical.'

'Forget about him now.' He moves a hand across her breasts but she takes it in hers.

'Not now. I'm still too shaky.'

'I'll come back. As soon as I can get away without anyone knowing.'

'Can't you stay?'

'No, it's getting late.'

'Yes, I suppose so.' A small sigh. 'Oh well.' If there is something on her mind she keeps it to herself.

'I'll be back. I promise.'

'Yes. Then we must go out somewhere. Away from here. Where we won't be cornered again.'


At this stage I am not yet sure to what extent Lucas Wilson should become a 'presence' in the story. Should he be allowed a 'voice' of his own in the narrative? From what private emergency does he operate? Ambition? Sexual frustration? Fear? Possibilities to be explored: a youth prone to illness (a weak chest?) – a Willy Loman father, a driving mother (or the other way round?) – the need to compensate, to achieve, to 'show them', in order to suppress his own secret sense of inadequacy – a desperate yearning for recognition, for love – the early discovery of sex as a means to dominate, etc. A hint of the mephistophelian? According to the Larousse *World Mythology*, Loki was a maker of mischief, frail in appearance, almost effeminate, always active; witty, congenitally disloyal, with a passion to expose the most sacred things to ridicule, a betrayer of his friends, a seducer of their wives, a gambler by nature, recognized everywhere by his evil laugh.

46

*

What is at issue in a love story? In languages like Spanish and Portuguese the word for 'to love' – *querer* (besides *amar* of course) – is related to the concept 'to want' (cf. in English 'acquire', 'require'). Which would tally with our ordinary, superficial experience of love as a personal form of imperialism. But should one not, in addition, acknowledge in it some relation to words like 'quest' or 'request'? Love as ceaseless interrogation, as a search without end – not necessarily moving towards a Promised Land where sooner or later the pilgrim arrives, but a voyage which, in search of sense, demonstrates only the sense of search (i.e. the very fact that it is a *process*, an experience of being in motion, without any clearly defined point of departure or arrival).

The notion of 'sense' is in itself problematic. 'Sense' in the sense of 'meaning', something given, like clothes packed into a suitcase and taken with one on one's journey, ready to be unpacked, intact, upon arrival, seems reassuring enough. But so much of this sense depends upon mere hunch, or on what can be conveyed to us by a notoriously untrustworthy physical apparatus. The English language does not even differentiate between 'sense' (meaning), 'sense' (feeling, intimation, awareness – 'a sense of occasion') and 'sense' (the organ through which we apprehend sense).

The situation is both illuminated and complicated by the discovery that there are languages (like Dutch or Afrikaans) in which the words for 'sense' and 'sentence' are identical: *sin* or *zin*.* Perhaps our traditional confidence in syntactical wholes rounded off with full stops is misplaced: who knows but that language, far from resembling a train consisting of a row of coaches, may not really be an unbroken flow, like a river, in which for pure convenience we artificially isolate moments in order to grasp at meanings drifting past like bits of flotsam and jetsam on the tide? To regard a sentence (or a narrative, of which the sentence is but an image) as a product, rather than as a continuous, forever unfinished process, may be as dangerous an

---

* I am tempted also to speculate that the Dutch *zin* (sentence; meaning) may be etymologically relevant to the notion of original sin (in English) and the expulsion from Paradise as a result of eating the fruit of the Tree of Knowledge.

illusion as to conceive of life itself as a satisfying syntactic encapsulation of sense.

To tell a story is to drift on language. To be is to be in motion. The very root of *I am* is inextricably linked to *amo*, I love. Which takes us back to where we started from.


Apropos of the reference to sin and the Garden of Eden above, it is amusing to think that, just like the forest and the enclosure surrounding the mystical castle of love in the *Roman de la Rose*, the circle of fire in which Brünnhilde is secured by Wotan in the woods, and the tangled thorns protecting the Sleeping Beauty (all of them but variations of Paradise) may be, quite simply, like the ring of the Nibelungs, metaphors of the vulva. It requires a knight brandishing his blade to break the taboo; Eden is guarded by an angel with a flaming sword; and the fire which finally gives access to the Castle of the Rose in the Garden of Earthly Delight is caused by a candle – '*qui ne fu pas de cire vierge*' – lit by Venus.


The forsaken garden. From the memory of a fantastic and decaying old farmhouse I saw near Franschhoek many years ago (before restoration became the vogue) I fashion this rustic hotel in the mountains and transplant it to the Eastern Cape, a few kilometres out of town. Make it an old mansion built by ambitious British settlers a century ago and converted by some baroque imagination, fired no doubt by ostrich palaces from the turn of the century, into an hotel; much favoured by tourists until more modern accommodation close to town – and perhaps a deviation in a main road – made it obsolete. That was the beginning of a long decline. The sprawling lawns are still mown from time to time, but without much enthusiasm; in autumn the grass is strewn with fallen leaves. Oaks. Plane trees. Poplars. The outbuilding, originally labourers' quarters, then a ballroom, at one stage even a disco, is falling apart, its windows broken, doors torn out, the thatched roof plundered by vandals and the wind. I even write a swimming pool into it, half-empty and slimy green, a breeding place for frogs and mosquitoes. On the lawn beyond the trees and overgrown terraces a number of garden chairs and tables have survived, most of them with legs or other vital parts missing; one or two have been half-heartedly repaired with wire. As I imagine it, new owners recently acquired the place, doing their best – with much good will but little capital – to make it habitable again, but they are battling against the odds. The kind of establishment one might imagine somewhere in the heart of Africa, where ages ago colonial masters in white flannels played cricket or croquet on the lawns before withdrawing for sundowners under the trees or thatched shelters where blacks in ill-fitting white livery waved plumes and palm fronds to keep the flies from bwanas and memsahibs. A park garden of the imagination, a state of mind rather than topographical reality.

The first time we went there (I am trying to imagine how Philip would recall it) I came to your room in the morning, a translucent autumn morning. The preparations and schemes and strategies it took to arrange a few hours' absence! Carrying a pile of books to serve as alibi, I was on my way down the stairs in the Arts Building when Lucas Wilson (who else?) came up from below, his mop of red hair partly obscuring his bespectacled eyes.

'Oh prof, I was just on my way up to you, there's something rather important I'd like to discuss. It's about the next Senate Lecture.'

'Can it wait until tomorrow?' I tried not to sound too abrupt. He serves on several committees with me and in the last year or so, especially as chairman of the Lecturers' Association, he has become spokesman of a group of radical young academics wielding increasing lobbying power; they might swing a decision on the deanship later in the year. But that was not what weighed on my mind as I looked at him. It was you, Melissa. From what I now knew about him and you I felt the urge, hard to control, to snap at him, if not actually to throw him down the stairs. But it was precisely because of you that I had to keep my cool and maintain an air of complaisance.

'Whenever it suits you, prof.'

'About ten tomorrow morning?'

'Right.' He turned round and walked back down the stairs with me. For a moment I thought he might accompany me all the way, but on the ground floor he waved cheerily – 'See you tomorrow then' – and went off in the direction of the library while I stopped at the mailbox to collect our post (a single airmail letter from the Cape for you).

The street running past your landlord's house was lined with armoured vehicles. Casspirs, Hippos, even a few Buffels. Young men in riot gear chatting without a care in the world; some were drinking Coke, others eating chips from greasy paper bags; preparing, it seemed, for a 'show of force' in the black townships. (Another funeral? At which more people would be killed, leading to the next funeral, where yet more would be killed, causing a further funeral – ). It looked as if the whole street was under siege. As I turned down the narrow side street towards your backyard I had the uneasy feeling of being watched by scores of eyes, staring right into the quick of our secret.

Your hair was wet and tousled, newly washed, and you were still in your dark-red dressing-gown. From the small transistor on the chest of drawers (two burnt-out sticks of incense drooping over small mounds of ash as delicate as the dust from butterfly wings) came Morning Concert: Janet Baker singing 'Non temer, amato bene'. How perfectly I can recall it all. I took you in my arms, all damp and fragrant (watch out – perfume persists!), and you said: 'The bloody hair-drier has conked out.' But is wasn't the drier, it was a power failure, so you couldn't even make us tea. You were in a foul mood. 'What are we going to do?'

'I'll take you out for tea.'

'Don't be ridiculous. There's nowhere we can go. We'll be seen, it isn't safe.'

'How about Fortnum and Mason?' I proposed. 'Or the Brasserie Lipp. Unless you prefer the Negresco in Nice. The Algonquin isn't bad either, of course.'

'You're impossible, prof.' You began to laugh. 'I'll get dressed.'

We were already on our way out of town – I felt so carefree and irresponsible that it wouldn't have taken much to make me go all the way to Cape Town or Tristan da Cunha – when I remembered the letter I'd brought you from the university. Eagerly, avidly (those quicksilver moods of yours) you tore it open and started reading, a secret smile on what I could see of your face through the golden mass of your hair.

'Good news?' I asked lightly.

A mocking sigh. 'Poor man. Why didn't he say it three years ago? I was head over heels in love with him then, but he couldn't care less.'

'Another skeleton in your cupboard?'

'Why does it always seem to work out this way?' you asked, ignoring my question. 'Whenever I fall in love with someone he's already occupied. By the time he gets interested in me, I'm no longer available.'

'Where does this one fit in?'

'Just somewhere in my depraved past.' Meticulously you folded the letter and put it back in its envelope.

'Have you ever seriously considered getting married and settling down?'

'God, no. What I've seen of marriage has been a total turn-off. I mean, look at my parents. And babies give me the creeps. Awful, sour-smelling little things.'

'You must have had *one* good love in your life!'

You stared thoughtfully ahead, then said with unexpected gaiety: 'Yes, I have, you're right. Back in Cape Town. Early one morning. It was winter. Raining. Normally I love the rain, but that time I was terribly depressed. I'd just had a very bad time with – no matter. I tell you, I felt suicidal. In fact, I was thinking about taking the cable car up the mountain and then jumping off a cliff. I mean, *really*. And then, right out of the rain, came this strange man. No raincoat, no umbrella, he was dripping wet. Fell in beside me. I didn't even look up. He started talking. I don't have the faintest recollection of what he said, but he just went on talking. He was funny, amusing, warm, sincere, irrepressible, wonderful. We walked for blocks and blocks through the city and then through the gardens, and he just talked and talked. And then he began to sing. He didn't have a particularly good voice, as I remember, but it was pleasant. In the rain it was beautiful. He sang – not very loudly, not attracting attention or being embarrassing – but it was as if his whole heart was in it.'

'And then he took you home with him?'

You stared at me with the kind of indulgence (it seemed to me) one feels for a child who cannot understand. 'It wasn't necessary. When we came out of the gardens, at the museum end, into Queen Victoria Street, he just said "Ciao!" And off he went, running through the rain, leaving me behind with a feeling of fulfilment and almost reckless joy. I never ever saw him again. But I tell you, that was the most perfect love I've ever had.'

The road wound uphill. From the top there was a wide view of the town nestled cosily among hills, the opposite range disfigured by the sprawling black townships, row upon row of shacks and shanties from where a large column of black smoke came drifting towards the town. Did that explain the military vehicles of an hour ago? To our left a scraggly wood, or what remained of it. Years before, when I had first come to the town, it was a dense forest covering whole ranges of hills: the remains of early plantations (pines, bluegums), luxuriant stretches of Port Jackson willow, and in the deeper folds of the hills thickets of indigenous forest. Over the years it had been plundered – by inhabitants of the black townships in search of firewood; by municipal workers in vain attempts to establish some kind of order – while in dry seasons veld fires had devastated large areas. But it had survived, somehow.

'You must go there with me one day,' you said eagerly, 'I often go for a walk in the woods.'

'It isn't much of a wood.'

'Once you're inside it's beautiful. Do you know, one evening when I stayed rather later than usual, until long after dark, the whole place was glittering with fireflies. It was magical.'

'But isn't it dangerous all on your own?'

'I had Rex with me.'

'Who's Rex?' I asked (the jealous lover).

You couldn't help chuckling. 'My landlord's Alsatian, stupid. Wonderful dog. If he were human I think I'd marry him.'

'We can drive there now.'

'No, I'm thirsty. You promised to take me out to tea, remember?'

Only then did I think of the derelict old hotel and its abandoned garden in the mountains. I wasn't even sure that it still existed; I hadn't been there for years.

We drew up beside the main building. There was only one other car in the shaded parking lot, a battered old blue Valiant with one mudguard half torn off, and the driver's door gangrenous with rust. Not very reassuring. Warily we walked past the old farmstead, hand in hand, to explore the gardens first, passing under autumn-coloured oaks and plane trees, past a great wave of purple bougainvillaea. A golden leaf came zigzagging from above and landed on your hair still dark with damp.

'Now you can wish,' I said.

'It's no use.'

'Why not?'

'Wishes never work out the way you want them to.'

'But suppose you *could* have a wish?'

'Then I'd wish for us to stay here forever, and never go back again.'

Far below us, on the main road, cars came sweeping past, almost soundless. Near by, birds were calling in the trees and bushes. On the grass were starlings, hopping about in search of seeds or insects.

Beyond the lawns, where the earth began to slope upwards to the mountain, we could make out a small rectangle which must have been fenced in once; now the rusty broken wires lay strewn across the grass ('like the hair of a drowned Ophelia', I thought in literary whimsy). A deserted graveyard, we discovered as we went nearer, with a few grey headstones still around, mottled with lichen, some of them broken or toppled. Only with much effort could one still decipher the odd inscription:

OUR BEL

J   HN WILMOT

RIP

A single complete date: 7 September 1873. British Settlers?

'At Arniston on the South Coast,' I told her, 'I once came upon a tombstone on which somebody's whole life history had been engraved. A man called Sylvester, if I remember correctly. Then, after lines and lines of boastful biography, it ended abruptly with a single sentence: "But what will it matter, by and by?" '

53

You weren't really listening, I noticed.

'Something wrong?'

You looked up from the fallen headstone where you were kneeling. 'I don't know what to say, I feel quite stunned. D'you know I dreamed about this place last night? And I swear I've never been to this graveyard before. I'm sure it was the very same grave.'

'What did you dream?'

'If this really was the place in my dream then we were making love right here on the grave. And then a skeleton appeared and tapped you on the shoulder, and asked whether you didn't think it was a bit too much in the open, people might see us. So he invited us into his coffin where we wouldn't be disturbed. And when we looked up there were eyes all around us. It was dark, we couldn't make out whether they were people or animals or whatever, it was just the eyes, hundreds of them glaring at us like headlights.'

'Did we accept his offer?'

'I don't think so, I can't remember. I suppose we felt too intimidated.'

In a curious way your words stirred up half-submerged memories in myself. 'I also thought the place seemed vaguely familiar,' I told you (remember?). 'Not a dream, but something that happened long ago.' And I told you what I could recall of that holiday, in my first year at university, with distant relatives of my mother's on a farm near Stellenbosch – how it had come about, I couldn't remember; and it was the only time we ever went there – a farm disturbingly similar to this one, only not quite so neglected. There had been peacocks in the garden, I could still remember them screaming in the night, and how unreal they seemed by day, strutting among the shrubs: creatures as fabulous to me as unicorns, unheard of in my youth. And then the late afternoon when my great-aunt, or whoever she'd been, had come to me from the massive ivy-covered stone house and awkwardly took my hands in hers to break the news: 'Now, Philip, there's something I must tell you. I know it's rather sudden, but try to take it like a man. Your mother is no longer with us. We think it must have been a heart attack.' Years afterwards the great-aunt had written to me again, urging me to visit them on the farm, but I'd never gone. Did I somehow dread the prospect of returning to find the place different from my memories of it, the peacocks a figment of my imagination, my mother's death itself a fantasy? Only after the death of the great-aunt did I learn that she had meant to make me her heir and leave that mythical estate to me, on the sole condition that I visited her before she died. Now I had forfeited it all; yet the memory of what might have been had remained with me as an unrealized parallel to my 'real' life, forever.

'If only I'd taken the trouble,' I told you, 'it would have been mine now. We could have gone there and lived there happily ever after.'

You stared at me, a curious expression in your shaded eyes. 'Do you realize this is the first time you've ever told me anything about yourself?' you said. 'You're the most secretive person I've ever known. Perhaps nobody will ever really know you.'

'My life has been unremarkable.' But that was not what I wanted to say. Not at all. How could I convey to you the sudden panic inside me? I wanted, desperately, to throw open the remotest recesses of my life and let you in, but there was this fear that you might find it merely boring. There had been that one occasion, years ago, in Paris – But how could I explain it to you? The terror that lies in exposing oneself totally, unreservedly, the readiness to risk everything. *Can* one do it more than once in a lifetime? Can one survive it more than once? The few times, through the years, I had had brief liaisons with women, now seemed to me, in the fierce illumination of your words, to have been no more than urgent attempts to suppress the unbearable awareness of my own solitude, the feeling of being 'stuck' in myself. Really to get involved, to mean it seriously, to commit myself and place everything at risk, had never occurred to me. Not after that one month of heaven and hell I'd known in Paris with Claire. But now, in a single casual remark you had torn away all my defences. *Perhaps nobody will ever really know you.* Don't you realize, I felt my insides crying at you in the silence, don't you realize I *want* to open myself up to you, to deliver myself to you; I want nothing of my life to remain secret to you; I want to share everything, even the most insignificant part of it, with you. I'll tell you all, I'll give you all: just never, never, let me hear those words again.

'When you talk about your past,' I said, trying to scrape lichen from a headstone to reveal a lost inscription, 'about your childhood, your studies, your lovers, anything: somehow it makes sense. I see you as the result of it all. It all adds up to you. But if I grope into myself there is nothing I can grasp, it's just a hollow, an absence. Why did I tell you about that distant aunt's estate, just now? I don't think it was because it mattered to me as such, or even because this place reminds me of it. Perhaps it is because in losing it I really let everything else slip out of my grasp as well.'

'You're being too hard on yourself, prof.'

'I'm not. I'm not even sure of what I'm really trying to tell you. Perhaps just this: if I suddenly have to think back and come up with the clearest, the most meaningful memory from my past, the kind of thing which makes one feel that you belong *here* and nowhere else, in this goddamned land, do you know what I come up with? It's an image from my childhood. The farm where I grew up. It is late afternoon, the sun is setting. We're bringing in the cattle to be milked, I and the black boys on the farm, the ones I grew up with – we would swim together, and play together, make clay oxen together, steal fruit together, play ghosts together, get hidings together – and then we tie up the cows in the shed and start milking them. The sound of the milk in the pail. The foam on top. A warm jet spurting straight from the teat into your mouth. The smell of cow and dung and grass. The prickling of hay in your nose. The blood-red sky darkening outside. A flock of wild geese flying past. Those terribly forlorn cries. That feeling, above all, of the world opening up on all sides in the dusk, pure, limitless space.' For a moment I found it almost impossible to go on, the impression was so vivid. 'It's the kind of memory which lures me back, which makes me think that, somehow, it was all worth while – the endless fights with my father who wanted me to become a farmer and who could never forgive me for going to university and giving up my "heritage" – but then I realize: I *cannot* go back. *That world does not exist any more.* That space, which shaped me and defined me and turned me into what I am, has closed up behind me and there is no going back. I've lost touch with part of myself,

perhaps the most vital part. And everything that came afterwards – the studies abroad, my academic life, my involvement
in literature, my marriage – now seems to me like an endless
series of hopeless efforts to compensate for something I have
lost: something I never even realized I had at the time it was
mine. Can you understand that?'

You leaned over and kissed me.

'Or do you think I'm just a doting middle-aged man
succumbing to romantic delusions?'

'What makes you think *my* life makes sense?'

'We must be doomed,' I said, and laughed, I didn't know why:
there was just, suddenly, such a feeling of relief in me. 'If I'm a
nut there is no need for you to crack up too.'

'What we need above all is some tea,' you said, and took my
hand.

I picture them as they return to the main building, that
outrageous Gormenghast. In the hotel lobby (a disconcerting
assortment of furniture: a few impressive pieces, old and heavy
and solidly beautiful, but mainly second-hand junk, outmoded
and rickety chairs and tables; one wonderful old rosewood
grandfather clock with its insides missing) they have to wait for a
long time after Philip has pressed the service bell on the counter.
But when at last reaction comes it happens on a surprising scale.
A stout elderly man, bald, in baggy khaki shorts; a run-down
woman of uncertain age, her hair in pink and green curlers; a
younger man in a foul temper, with sideburns, and one hand in
plaster; and two youngish girls (one severely plain, looking like a
housekeeper, in green overalls; the other wearing an amazing
*décolleté* evening gown in black velvet, which seems to suggest
that she hasn't been to bed at all since last night or, alternatively,
that she has been nowhere but in bed, an impression heightened
by the unmistakable *odor di femina* she smilingly, languorously,
invitingly, exudes) – all of them erupting from an inside door,
with three or four more female servants, black, also in green
overalls, hovering in the background.

'What can we do for you?' several of them chant, more or less
in chorus. The woman in the evening gown approaches to lean
on the counter, which causes the *risqué* dress to slip from one

shoulder, almost wholly exposing a bosom lurking in the shadows like a pale pawpaw ready to be plucked.

'Have you come a long way?' enquires the portly gentleman, beads of sweat glistening eagerly on his purple face.

'Our tariffs are very competitive,' assures the siren.

'We're just working on a new menu,' sighs the mother figure.

'Got any baggage?' asks the aggressive young man in an accusing tone of voice.

In this confusion it takes the two guests a little while to get their message across: no, they have not come a long way, they are from town, and they do not wish to stay over (but they may well decide to give the new menu a try on some future occasion), all they really want is tea.

'Tea?'

'Tea?'

'Tea?'

'Tea?'

'Tea?'

Which covers five tones of the sol-fa.

'If it's possible. We shouldn't like to – '

'Everything is possible in this place,' assures the old man, beaming, as he tries (in vain) to tuck the front of his shirt into his shorts, over the blubbery mass of his stomach. Followed by a roar of instructions over his shoulder: 'Sophie! Dinah! Where the bloody hell are you? Christ, mister' – back to Philip – 'these blacks are useless. We're up to our necks trying to cope with the rush of visitors, but they just take their time over everything.' Another great roar over his shoulder, down the passage: 'What's happened to the waiters again? Simon! Johnson!' Followed by a string of other names, not all of them proper nouns.

In the mean time various other personages have started pulling out chairs from different coffee tables – ranging from ball-and-claw to 'Swedish' and cast-iron – inviting the visitors to be seated.

'Can we have it in the garden?'

Consternation all round, urgent whisperings – only the girl in the evening dress remains unmoved, gazing ahead with a beatific smile suffused with sensual memories – resulting in a chorus of emphatic assurances: In the garden, of course, obviously, where else, Johnson, good God, where the fuck are you when one needs you, two teas for the master and madam, outside on the lawn, and move your arse.

At last they are released by the throng of eager hosts and allowed to return to the garden. After an unusually long half-hour a black man in a dirty white jacket and dark trousers approaches from the gothic mansion, carrying a tray ('Just leave it on the grass, thank you, the table is broken'); goes off, unmistakably satisfied ('Keep the change'): and then they are left alone again under the warbling birds and lightly falling leaves drifting on a wind that comes from very far away (Rilke: 'The leaves are falling, falling, as from far – '), from inhospitable, unimaginable vastnesses of air and openness.

'Is the tea OK?' he asks, offering her the cup he's just poured.

She smiles, sun on her face. 'After all this trouble – ' She tastes it. 'Good. You know, prof, I was brought up to believe that there are only two criteria I would have to meet in this world: to make tea, and to look pretty. Nothing else really mattered, since my parents decided, from the time I was a baby, that I would be good for nothing else. Because I was a girl, you see.'

'I love your tea and I think you're beautiful.'

'My parents won't agree with you. Even if they did it would make no difference. To them, our family's hopes for the future have always been tied up with my two brothers. No matter that Louis was always at loggerheads with them: he was their son, anything could be forgiven him. Together, Louis and Tinus were the two white males who would ensure the survival of the race on the dark continent.'

'Now there is only one left.'

'Yes.' She turns her head to look at him. 'Do you think it's unnatural that I haven't been able to cry once since Louis died? There was a time, you know, when we were quite close. In a sense he was my only ally in the family. When he was called up for military service he considered refusing and going to jail. But eight years in the can is a long time when you're twenty-one.' A brief flash of anger. 'What I shall never forgive them for is that eighteen months in the army turned him into a believer. He used to be so free, so unruly, so eager, so sure of himself and of the way he would change the future of the country single-handed. But during his months of training I gradually saw him change. It was one of the most unnerving experiences of my life. I tried to draw him out, to discuss things with him the way we used to. At first he was hesitant, then he became sullen and withdrawn; by the time he was sent to Namibia he was openly hostile to me. The fact that I'd joined ECC* made him mad. The last time I saw him – ' She stops, finishes her tea, looks down at her feet. (Her legs are drawn up; she has taken off her shoes; her toenails are painted dark red, small perfect drops of blood.) 'Died a hero's death, they said. They'll probably award him a posthumous Honoris crux yet.' She looks up, straight at him. 'What is heroic about getting blown up by a landmine, prof?'

'How did it happen?' (During those distant few days they spent at his seaside cottage after she'd returned from the funeral, she didn't talk about it at all – although it was there, between them, all the time, a heavy unspoken presence in her silence.)

'I don't know. They didn't even allow us to see him before the funeral. One of his friends told me he'd been charred like a log, the arms sticking up like two branches. I wonder how they got him in the coffin?'

'Don't torture yourself,' he says quietly.

'Of course, we don't know for sure what happened. For all we know it wasn't even a landmine. It may have happened deep in Angola, in a battle with the Cubans or whatever. Or he may have been shot by one of his own colleagues. They never tell the truth, do they? Sometimes at night I wake up in a sweat, thinking it wasn't even Louis we buried but someone else's body. There's no way of telling. And perhaps that is why I cannot grieve. But at least my parents are content. His death has given them a new status among their friends. God knows how I'll get through the next holidays at home. He'll be the only topic of conversation. Now that he's dead and can't talk back I know he'll be a saint to them.'

'Must you go? Why don't you break away from them?'

'I've tried. But I don't think I have the guts. There's nothing I desire so much as to be on my own, to be free. At the same time

---

* End Conscription Campaign.

the idea of being free scares me out of my wits. Does that make sense to you, prof?'

'Surely they must realize that you're no longer a child?'

Her small bitter laugh. 'You should see how mother prepares my room when I go home. It looks like a Sunday school concert, all pink bows and frills and ribbons and gentle Jesus meek and mild. Dolls all over the place, in the sweetest little frocks. Enough to make you puke. She stubbornly believes that I'm still four years old.'

'It needn't be like that,' he insists. 'While I'm with you, you can be whatever you wish to be.'

'For how long?'

'How can you ask a thing like that?'

She stares past him, to where the invisible wind comes from. 'You'll soon grow tired of me.'

Without thinking he blurts out: 'I love you, Melissa.'

She shakes her head slowly, not bothering to reply.

'Don't you believe me?'

'It's not a matter of believing. It's just the way it happens. Only the impossible, the dangerous, seems to attract me. Which is why whenever I get involved with someone I know it cannot work out.' He is struck by the calm, detached way in which she says it, with no hint of melodrama or adolescent self-pity, as if she were discussing a literary text.

'How can it work out if you're so negative about it?'

'I'm not being negative. Not even cynical. It's just something I *know*.' She is silent for a while. There is only the wind ruffling the hair on her shoulders; and the birds. Overhead, in a sudden burst of eerie sound, a couple of hadidas come past. She pours herself another cup from the stainless-steel teapot. 'During my first year at UCT there was this man – I think it was the first time I really was in love; he's living in Canada now, emigrated a year or two ago, he's a photographer, Ron, we still write to each other from time to time, but it's long been over between us. I was ready to do anything for him, try anything, sacrifice everything. But I suppose I was too inexperienced, too shy perhaps; anyway, he kept on making demands, expecting all kinds of things from me. Dragged me into bed all the time, and of course I wanted him to be happy, but still there were times I didn't feel like sex, sometimes I just wanted him to hold me, to lie in his arms and talk. Then he would fly into a rage, he had a hell of a temper, and he would make a scene and rush out. He always came back in a day or two, to show me nude pictures of other girls he'd been with in the mean time.' A defensive shrug. 'Perhaps I deserved it, I was so uptight, I had so many hang-ups. I always let him down. Couldn't live up to his expectations. But I did love him, prof! The ones who came after him – ' She pauses, closing up quietly. 'One gets more cautious as one grows older.'

'You're twenty-three!'

'Don't patronize me,' she says sharply, then smiles. 'I've lived a lot since then. Maybe, after Ron finally left me, I deliberately tried to get rid of my inhibitions. It worked, I suppose, "technically", I mean. But in other ways – ' A pause; she sighs, clasping her feet in her hands. 'One loses out too. Too much perhaps. You lose touch with yourself. You must, otherwise you won't survive. But you pay for it, all right. I've never realized it so deeply as these last few weeks, since that first night with you. I mean, so much has happened between then and now, between Ron and you. Disillusionment especially. Through being used, manipulated, hurt, raped, possessed, scared, scarred. Oh, it makes one tough too. But at a price. Sometimes I'm not sure whether they used me or I them. Not that it makes much difference.'*

'You mustn't always be haunted by the past,' he says. 'There's a future to think about.'

'My vision of hell is to think of myself as forty, all used up and with my boobs and bottom sagging, desperately trying to seduce first-year men to persuade myself I can still make a catch.'

---

* There is a certain danger in the projection of Melissa's character at this stage. If she shares with female characters from some of my other novels a certain 'history of calamities', what is important to me is not the way in which she resembles them but the way in which she is different. To make sure the reader is alerted to this the dialogue above may be extended. If Philip responds, in a natural rush of protective feelings, by putting an arm around her, she will look him in the eye, cool, almost amused, to remind him: 'This is not a table of woe, prof. If you think I'm telling it to you because I need your sympathy you don't understand at all what I'm trying to say. Look, I'm not a victim: I'm a survivor.'

He bursts out laughing. 'When you're forty I'll be seventy, remember. That's worse.'

'Anyway, there isn't much point in talking about the future, is there?' she says. 'If we were black it would be different. At the moment we're living on borrowed time. Even while we're sitting here – I'm not talking about the possibility that people may find out about us, that there may be a scandal, or anything like that. But the mere fact that we're here, that we're white, and all around us the country's burning, the troops are massing – it may explode at any moment, and what will be left of *us* then? There's no security in our love. Nothing. Every moment we are together may be the last, and that changes everything. It changes *us*. Nothing is normal.'

'We'll survive,' he says almost angrily.

'Is it me you're trying to convince, or yourself?'

'Melissa, you've got to believe me.'

'Can you really be optimistic about the future?'

'I still have hope. Not much, admittedly. But I cannot bring myself to despair.'

At this point I can see him hesitate. Should he – shouldn't he? But there really is no choice, he must take the plunge. So must I. Even if I'm not yet quite sure about the form his 'confession' should take.* Most likely, a neatly structured summary, informed by hindsight, of the years he studied in Europe. The sixties. ('I suppose I belong to the last generation that still genuinely believed in hope.') What may look like a lost world now, he will insist, was very real then. Even in the excesses surrounding them – the flower children, the anti-Vietnam protests – there was a kind of furious innocence. It really did seem as if a better world could still come about. And perhaps, he will suggest – disarmingly if disingenuously – that something of that attitude must have persisted in him.

Will she interrupt here? A comment like: 'But wasn't your

---

*I must remember to insert, a little later in the text, a note on this phenomenon: the passion of lovers to trade recollections ('Show me yours and I'll show you mine'), even at moments when they appear to be concerned only with being together here, now. The past not as an escape from the urgency of the present but as a manifestation and confirmation of it.

childhood your true image of innocence? Those things you talked about: the cows being milked, the sunset, the wild geese, the feeling of space. And the peacocks in that other garden.'

Of course those were his images of paradise, he will have to admit. But that lay at the root of his problem which, summarized, was his early conviction of having grown up in a perfect world. Everything was preordained, every person knew his proper place. On the farm: the whites were the masters, the blacks their trusty servants. It had the reassurance of biblical sanction. And it lasted right through his university days and while he was a teacher, saving money to go to Europe. But then, from there, ten thousand kilometres away, suddenly it was all so different. It was only at that great distance that he discovered what was really happening over here. What he'd taken for paradise was, in fact, hell. It had seemed like paradise only because he was white, and privileged. Now all the customs and habits and traditions and structures which had bolstered his life turned out to be evil, the very opposite of what he'd always taken them to be. It was as if, in one stroke, the validity of all his memories was cancelled. He had nothing left but shame. And when he came back at last – that was even worse – he discovered there was nothing he could do to change an iota about it. So he retreated into academic life. But there must be times when he fears that one day this, too, will be turned inside out, just like his youth. And then there really will be nothing left at all to bolster him.

'What *happened* in Europe, prof?'

He hesitates. 'Nothing specific. I mean, there wasn't one dramatic episode that changed it all. It just happened slowly, naturally, inevitably.'

'A woman?' she asks, her eyes too wise for comfort.

'You're jumping to conclusions.'

'Are you sure?'

'It was not so simple, Melissa.'

'But there was a woman.' This time it is a statement, not a question.

He shrugs, avoiding those knowing, probing, challenging eyes.

'And one day,' she says in a voice suddenly strained, 'when

I'm older, and mature enough, and when you trust me enough, you will tell me about it. Is that it?'

'All right. There was a woman,' he says painfully, as if the words are wrung from him; it is so many years since he has dared to talk about what matters most to himself. 'Her name was Claire. We met in Paris, in '68. I'd gone there for a weekend, to old friends of mine, and then got caught up in the student revolts and stayed for almost two months. It was like living without a skin, without eyelids, all the nerve-ends exposed. In the end – well, it just didn't work out.'

She looks at him serenely, as if she knows exactly what has been left unsaid; but she makes no attempt to prod him further. For the moment she seems almost content.

In writing this, now, I know it is an area of my character's life I shall have to come to grips with. Philip's debt to Melissa is mine to my reader. That is the danger intrinsic to the story-telling act: having committed oneself to it, there is no turning back. Which is why I still insist that this is only a preliminary exploration, a testing of possibilities. I have not yet undertaken anything.

But to keep Melissa satisfied (I know by now she will not easily allow him to avoid his own secrets and truths and shames and agonies) an interruption of some kind is necessary to alter the course of their conversation. Anything will do. In this case I contrive a yellow police van approaching from the main road below, driving through the front gate and up to the main building. Almost detached, Philip and Melissa watch from the lawn. Two constables get out, doors are slammed, they go in through the front door. Something like a chill ripples through the autumn morning, almost imperceptible, like the merest breath of wind upon an expanse of water. A few minutes later the two constables come out again, get into their vehicle, and drive off. In the front door all the characters we have met earlier are huddling together in a knot, looking after the cloud of dust as it subsides and settles on bougainvillaea and dark green shrubs. There is a sound of loudly arguing voices, but at this distance nothing can be distinguished. After a while the young man breaks away from the bunch and stalks off through the trees, past the outbuildings; his father (?) calls after him but when he stops it is only to raise his plastered fist like a half-hearted Africa salute before he marches on. It is like a sudden eruption in a chicken run; but after a few minutes of furious cackling and squawking the ruffled feathers begin to settle and peace returns. One becomes conscious once more of the birds in the trees.

However, the hotel crowd has barely withdrawn when the enraged young man re-emerges from behind the nearest outbuilding, this time dragging a green garden hose after him, on his way to the slimy pool. As he comes past them he half-stops.

'Trouble again,' he mumbles without looking at them, tugging at the hose. 'It's just bloody trouble, trouble all the time.'

'What was the fuss about?' asks the professor.

'Bloody police haven't got enough work to keep them busy, that's what. A summons.' He nearly chokes. 'Brought me a summons.' He gesticulates with his plastered hand. 'Now they call it assault. Just because I taught a fucking waiter who's the boss. One can't even hit one's own kaffirs these days, then it's trouble. Next time, I swear, I'll take my gun, then there won't be so much explaining to do afterwards.'

He moves on again, tugging at the hose to make it reach the pool, but it falls short.

'Oh *fuck*!' he shouts and stalks off, leaving the hose just as it is, bleeding its water on the half-dried grass.

Every now and then, it seems, a shiver or a shudder moves through the world around them, momentarily interfering with their silence before it passes on, leaving them in peace again, exposed to one another. He has rolled over on his stomach and is playfully caressing her feet, kissing her toes, flicking the tip of his tongue in between them. On the small web between two toes of her right foot he discovers a tiny white scar, almost invisible, a mere little ridge to the tongue.

'Where did you get this?' he asks.

She laughs. 'How can it possibly matter to you?'

'Everything about you matters to me.' He says it with mock seriousness; but he knows it is true.

'I must have been about five or six,' she says. 'Tinus got a cricket set for his birthday. All the boys in the neighbourhood came round to play. Even Louis was allowed to bat, although he could barely walk. Only I was shooed off, I was a girl. So I just

66

grabbed the bat and refused to let go. Tinus began to yell all kinds of dire threats at me but I stood my ground. I must have been an insufferable little brat. But I was damned if I'd give in. So he hurled the wicket at me and it caught me right here between the toes, pinning me to the ground. I howled blue murder and they all ran off, leaving me behind. When mother came out to see what was going on, she fainted. And there I was, like a stuck pig. Until at last one of the servants, I think, came to set me free.'

He continues to stroke the little nick: not the way one would try to ease the pain from a wound, it occurs to him, but more like Aladdin rubbing his magic lamp: as if in that small motion of his finger he would like to conjure up everything she has ever been, the baby and the little girl, the child growing up, the adolescent, the young woman, all her pain, all her joy, all her secret wishes, everything she may yet become, oh God, Melissa, I love you.

High above her head a bird is calling in sweet shrill tones in the dark leaves of an oak. From far away an answer comes back: the same three small spikes of sound in the light breeze. They have stopped talking. Now it is only the birds, defining the immensity of space with their various trills and warblings. He strains to listen – as if, with only a bit more effort, he will be able to understand them. But a vital key is missing. Incomprehensible, the bird-calls pass overhead, leaving them isolated in space, remote from it all.

She presses her head against him. 'Let us go back,' she whispers. 'I want to make love.'

And they run back to the car, and speed along the highway through the deep green valley under the mountains, over the rise from which the town and the townships beyond become visible (in their ears, almost subliminally, a dull, distant crack-crack, crack-crack-crack which may be gunfire), and tumble head-over-heels into the small room from where they first set out.

For the first time I felt at home in the room, and accepted by it; the rough white walls, the crevices in the ceiling, the few bright prints and posters, the red French shopping bag behind the door (now locked, the safety chain securely in its slot). The front

67

window was almost overgrown outside by a profusion of shrubs and foliage, so that the very light seemed green, lending your room a submarine aspect, as if we were inside in a bathysphere, sinking slowly through deep, unknown and dangerous waters. You stretched to reach the high white curtains and undo the yellow ribbons which held them open; and immediately the day outside was shut out, a mere brush of light on your extended arm, your shoulders, your stretched back, the smooth curve of your bottom; before you returned to the narrow bed in the corner where I was already waiting ('Take off your watch'): this time with all the frankness and assurance of love, as if, at last, you *wanted* me to see all of you, to share and explore and probe and know and imprint on my memory the miracle of your presence.

I am having problems with Philip's past. If he was in Paris in 1968 – and I need him there – he would already have been well into his thirties. The only solution would be for him to become a teacher after completing his studies, and even to get married. Perhaps they can be saving for a trip to Europe. After five or six years of marriage his wife dies. Car accident. In her third month of pregnancy, to add to the trauma. He is suddenly cut loose, at odds with himself and the world. Then he goes to Europe, to Holland, for his doctorate. Which would get us to 1968 without further problems. And it would add to the weight of loss and sadness he feels in himself.

A few remarks (not so much statements as questions) on the historical impulse in love.* Why this compulsive interpellation by my characters of their past, the constant exchange of memories? If it were no more than a convenient narrative device it would render diminishing returns: in each episode the two elements of a setting in which the lovers meet (geography), and

---

* Cf. footnote on page 63.

a conversation in which they discover – or invent – to each other their respective pasts (history).

In part, of course, it is the inevitable result of their condition. The settings of their fleeting, secretive encounters represent a retreat from the world which exists both in space (out there) and in time (the present); the nature of their love precludes, at least at this stage, a future. Which means that the movement inward can only be manifested in terms of a delving into the past.

At the same time *their* discovery, rediscovery or invention of the past coincides with *my* exploration, as author, of their historical dimension. *Their* love is *my* narrative. (Barthes: 'At the origin of narrative: desire.') In both cases there is a breaking into language: the language of history, the language of story. As the simplicity of the statement *I love you* is (tragically) complicated into questions (who is this I? who is this you?) the weight of history increases. It is not a matter of encapsulating lived experience in a word, but of finding the word which will liberate experience. An entering into history, an assumption of responsibility, an extension – not an evasion – of time and space. It derives from the need to explain, to find reasons; the quest for meaning or the illusion of meaning; the creation of a mythology. There is a dimension in which each individual (character) also 'represents' humanity (a narrative insight developed with remarkable dexterity by Jurij Lotman). Through the excursions/ incursions into collective or private history one deliberately runs the risk of whatever these exposures may entail, as the instant is penetrated by time (a defloration of which the sexual act itself may be but a metaphor). At each moment, when we are in love, we cannot but live fully the presentness of all our past selves, all our past certainties and vacillations, attempts, failures, delusions, sufferings, victories. It is no good simply to exist on the surface of love: that is infatuation. We must know where we come from and where our earth comes from. The archaeology of love.


The massacre at Uitenhage had introduced a new element into the violence which had become endemic in South Africa since

September of the previous year: attacks by blacks on the homes of black policemen, members of community councils, and others regarded as sell-outs to the apartheid system, became prevalent. Not 'black-on-black violence' as it was so gleefully represented in the apartheid press, but an expression of rage by victims and opponents of racism against everyone perceived to be a collaborator of the system. The first such episode occurred within two days of the Langa outrage, when a mob set on Mr Kinikini, an affluent undertaker who had been running a thriving business during the turmoil. Kinikini was killed together with two of his sons, a nephew, and a friend. Afterwards the bodies were doused with petrol and set alight on a pile of burning tyres – the beginning of an epidemic of 'necklace murders' in the townships. (The following day children were seen playing with part of one of the charred bodies.) A community frustrated by its inability to strike directly at the oppressor, was turning against itself. At the same time police and army forces became more unrestrained in their provocative and/or repressive actions in black townships. The only political expression still open to blacks was provided by funerals, and the month of April saw the beginning of a seemingly endless series of mass funerals all over the country. On the thirteenth of that month, twenty-eight victims of recent violence (nineteen of them shot by the police in the Langa massacre) were buried from Kwanobuhle Stadium. Between 70,000 and 100,000 people attended; led by Bishop Desmond Tutu and Dr Allan Boesak, it was the largest funeral in the history of the Eastern Cape. On that occasion police kept a low profile, although they were out in force to protect the white suburbs and industrial areas of Uitenhage. (During the weekend seven more people were killed.) Other funerals throughout the country were not allowed to proceed so peacefully. It became a favourite tactic of the security forces to disrupt services and processions by firing tear-gas at the crowds; when younger elements responded in anger by throwing stones, the police would open fire with R1 rifles, shotguns and rubber bullets. In this way, almost every funeral led to new deaths and follow-up funerals. In many areas the only response the security forces could think up was a 'show of force', with hundreds of police and army vehicles parading through the townships, for hours on end, sealing them off from the outside world while a large task-force conducted house-searches (often accompanied by renewed violence, intimidation, and killings) to arrest 'suspects'.

In many cases the official version of such incidents had very little to do with what eyewitnesses reported under oath. (When a Motherwell woman, Violet Fulani, was killed by police in her house and her nine-year-old daughter shot in the eye, the official report claimed that they had been shot outdoors 'in a riot situation'.)

On 30 April the Minister of Police reported in parliament that more than ten thousand people had been detained in the country since the first outbreak of violence.



It will become necessary, I think, at some stage to introduce Milton Thaya into the lives of Philip and Melissa.* Or, more accurately, into Philip's, as it seems likely that Melissa may already know him. How? Perhaps through her landlord Jack, whose dingy little backstreet shop may well be supplied with fresh produce from the Port Elizabeth market once or twice weekly by Milton in his rickety green truck. This truck, I should have mentioned when I first introduced Milton to the reader,† is Milton's pride in life. Kept going more by goodwill than by the laws of mechanics, this vehicle has crisscrossed the face of South Africa over many years; little of its body and few of its parts are still original; most of it appears homemade – among his amazing range of interests Milton also counts a fondness of mechanical engineering, though even he would concede that in this case it is a matter more of enthusiasm than of skill.

Milton, I am sure, is the kind of person Melissa would have taken to immediately. Before the Emergency she would have paid regular visits to him and his family in Fingo Village; and in

---

* I shall of course have to change his name if he functions in the story; but for the time being he may just as well remain Milton Thaya.
† Cf. page 8 etc.

spite of Jack's uneasy reprimands (one can imagine his feelings about the 'impropriety' of a black man visiting a young white woman in her room) Milton would undoubtedly have spent long afternoons of boisterous conversation and coffee drinking in her place, discussing his latest schemes or enlisting her financial or moral support for this and that. The Emergency would have introduced a darker note into their now less frequent conversations, although I cannot see it dampening the man's exuberant spirits.

On this particular occasion I imagine Milton discussing with her some of his worries about the disruptive effects of the schools' boycotts in the townships. 'Look, man, I can understand these kids rejecting the bloody inferior stuff they getting. You remember Big Boss Verwoerd telling the country way back in the fifties that blacks got to be prepared from childhood to accept they'll never be equal to whites? "Why teach a black child maths if he can never put it to any use later?" Something like that. So there's sense in what they doing. But this new slogan – you know, *First liberation then education* – I mean, that's just plain stupid. Playing right into the government's hands. So we trying to set up some kind of scheme for an alternative education. Make sure they learn the basics. Reading, writing, maths, a bit of history – the real stuff, not the "Whites Only" variety – know what I mean? And I thought perhaps you could give a hand.'

It is agreed she will take a class of first-graders. That is the easy part, and her enthusiasm inspires Milton to proceed to his next problem. Money. Not the ten or twenty rands he's 'borrowed' in the past, but big money. His truck has broken down and it may cost a thousand or more to have it repaired. At the moment, with little scope for any of his other large-scale schemes, his livelihood depends on the cartage and conveying he can undertake with his truck. But it goes beyond personal considerations (he comes closer to her, lowering his voice): there are youngsters in Fingo Village and Tantyi and Makana's Kop who are being sought by the SB; most nights there are raids. It is often necessary to get them out to safety at short notice. Same goes for people in other towns. Which is where his green truck comes in. For months now, he tells her, he's been smuggling people to and fro between various townships in the Eastern Cape, concealed inside bales of wool or woven materials, behind crates of pottery, under mounds of fruit or vegetables or whatever. Now if he has to wait for parts to be plundered from vehicles elsewhere and fitted in his own backyard like before, some of his clients may get picked up. And you know what that means, don't you? So it's a matter of urgency.

But Melissa does not have that kind of money and so, quite naturally, there must be a meeting in Philip's study at the university. Late one afternoon, after the secretary has left, when all the offices on their floor are dark and empty, and before the cleaners come in.

'Milton is a good friend, Philip. I can assure you if he says he needs the money it really is for a very good cause.'

'But dangerous.'

'Of course it's dangerous. But how can we carry on with our lives pretending nothing's happening over there?' She motions through the window, in the direction of the invisible sprawling townships on the hills beyond the town. 'People are being detained, and tortured, and killed, Philip. While we – '

'No, it isn't fair on the man,' says Milton, rising from the chair into which he has eased himself immediately after being introduced. 'I was just taking a chance. But I don't want to endanger other people's lives. It's bad enough as it is. I mean, suppose they find out about the money and they accuse you of helping me to – how d'you call it? – "defeat the ends of justice"? I mean, jeez, it's serious. No, Melissa, leave it to me. I'll find a way.'

'Philip.' She looks at him very quietly.

'Don't go, Milton.' He takes a deep breath, turns away from the window. 'How much is it you need?'

'I thought about twelve hundred – make it thirteen. But look, I promise you – '

'Can I give you a cheque?'

'If you don't mind, cash will be better. I mean, I don't want to have to explain to the bank and so on. Perhaps I can drop in tomorrow afternoon? But only if you quite sure – '

'Of course I'll help you.'

'Thank you, Philip.' She kisses him. 'I knew you would.'

'Hey, look, it's not charity,' says Milton. 'I don't just want to

73

take your money, man. I'll give you this – ' He puts a hand into the back pocket of his jeans and takes out a knotted handkerchief which he undoes meticulously to reveal a small box covered in stained, moth-eaten black velvet. Inside, when he opens it – both of them leaning over to see – is a gold coin, shiny enough but rather the worse for wear.

'A real Kruger pound,' Milton informs them with great pride. 'Take it out, look for yourself. See the date? 1898. Now that must be worth something, don't you think?'

'Where did you find this?' asks Melissa.

'Long story. Belonged to my grandmother. That's what my father told me. She was working on a farm in Graaff-Reinet, see. Hell of a long time ago, turn of the century, must have been. Beautiful woman she was, that was what everybody always told me. In fact, even the white farmer couldn't resist her. So – ' A shrug of his large shoulders, the daylight glaring on his glasses. 'But of course he couldn't face the scandal when she was with child. Tried all kinds of things to make her lose it, but we're a tough lot, I tell you. Even gave her a thrashing with a sjambok, thinking I suppose that would bring off the child. But no go. So he chased her away. Gave her this pound and told her to get the hell off his farm. She walked all the way to Port Elizabeth. That's – what? – almost two hundred miles. No matter how bad things got for her, she held on to this. Later my father got it, now it's mine. So!' A great burst of laughter. 'There you got my whole history in your one hand. Isn't that something?'

Almost roughly Philip thrusts the coin back into the little box and holds it out to Milton. 'I can't take it, Milton. I don't want it. For God's sake, you keep it.'

'No, it's yours. And one day when you marry this one' – he winks at Melissa – 'you can set it in a brooch or make a pendant out of it or something. I don't want it no more.'

'Milton – '

'It's to show I trust you, dammit. So you keep it.'

After he has left – after she, too, has left – Philip remains behind at the window. Absently he weighs the dirty little box in the palm of his hand. He'd rather not have it. But both Milton and Melissa were adamant. ('At least, then, keep it till one day I can pay you back, OK?') At last, he thrusts it into his pocket, guiltily aware of the bulge the way a schoolboy is conscious of an untimely erection.

He should have preferred to undo the whole afternoon. But it has happened. It is there, with him, its memory burning in his mind. As if, through a simple transaction, something immeasurable has shifted in his life, in his relationship with Melissa. It has become part of them now, introduced into their deepest shared consciousness. It is not just a worn coin from another age, but an uneasy reminder of history itself, of everything happening out there, on those hillsides, in those burning smoking streets, invisible from inside this ordered comfortable room, but no less there for all that, a small fierce stab in the mind.

Gadamer paraphrased: The literary text as paradigm of human communication – a dialectical game involving, among other things, distance and nearness, aloofness and involvement, alienation and appropriation, understanding and interpretation. Changing the world through play implies the playful transformation of the self. And this transformation of the 'I' demands a moment of alienation, a 'losing' of the I in the text in order to find it: in this way appropriation also becomes divestiture. Not by exchanging one mask for another, as that would maintain the experience on one level: extending the I demands a change of level as well.

Adapting this to my own view of literature one might say that, just as the text detaches itself from the world in order finally to be restored, in a changed form, to the world, the reader, through the process of reading, is also first withdrawn from the world, transformed, and then restored. In this resides the element of risk which lends the adventure of literature its sense of 'value': it is *worth while* running this risk.

*Chris de Villiers.* The first mention of the name in Jane Ferguson's diary occurs in the entry dated Sunday 6 January. *At least I know* this *now*. *For the past days he has been Clive de Vos. That is what he wrote in the hotel register. In his own handwriting. A stranger arriving from nowhere at this remote resort in the mountains. All I knew about him was his name. Now everything has changed, now I know him. Better, I think, than I have ever known another person. But now his name has changed. Suddenly he is 'Chris de Villiers'. And 'Clive de Vos' has literally become a series of meaningless syllables. In the beginning name and person matched each other exactly, the way a drawing on tracing paper can be placed exactly on the lines of the original. The name 'Clive de Vos' was the man I came to know. Now the new name reaches out past him, to something, someone, I do not (yet) know; something which cannot be he, as my knowledge of him – as an individual, a person, a man, a lover – is enclosed in a different name.*

*The two names are so similar, the initials, C de V. C de V. Yet they are light years apart. But that is what disturbs me so: surely he is still the same, the man he was, is. Why should another name be of any consequence? Suppose I suddenly became June Farrell, or Joan Fisher, would that make any difference to who I am? Or is it conceivable that truth can be relative to the name one calls it by?*

*Perhaps it would have been easier to talk it through with him. But I am alone tonight. He insisted. 'You know how much I want to be with you,' he said. 'But this is a choice you've got to make on your own. I shall accept whatever you decide. Even if it is to hand me over to the police. It is not only your life which is in my hands: mine is in yours too. Take your time. Think about it. About all that's happened. About everything that may yet happen.'*

*What has happened: could it possibly have happened in another place, in other circumstances (named by other names)? Or does a place, a specific defined space, really determine one's possibilities, the risks one is prepared to take?*

In another entry, a few days earlier, Jane Ferguson had given this description of the place:

*A forsaken garden. Going to seed. The lawns are still mown from time to time, but only halfheartedly, it seems. The main outbuilding, originally labourers' quarters or stables or something, later converted into a ballroom, at one stage even a disco, is falling to pieces, windows broken, doors torn out, the thatched roof plundered by vandals. There is even a swimming pool, half empty and green with slime, a breeding place for frogs and mosquitoes. On the lawn behind a row of trees and terraces overgrown with flowers and weeds a number of garden chairs and tables have survived, most of them with parts missing. One or two have been unsuccessfully repaired with wire. It's only a few months ago that Uncle Jock bought the place and set about the job of making it habitable again, but he has more good will than capital and it's an uphill battle. When he first phoned Dad to ask if I could come over for a few weeks to give them a hand, he made it sound rather different, like the kind of establishment one might have expected somewhere in Africa ages ago, with colonial masters in white flannels playing cricket or croquet on the lawns before withdrawing for sundowners under the trees or thatched shelters where mute blacks in ill-fitting white livery would be waving plumes or palm fronds to keep the flies from bwanas and memsahibs. Now transferred to the Drakensberg Mountains.*

*Beyond the lawns I found a small rectangular space which must have been fenced in once – but now the rusty broken wires just lie strewn about on the grass. A deserted cemetery with a few mottled headstones still around, most of them broken or toppled.*

This is the setting for the occupants of the place as she describes them: Uncle Jock, an old university friend of her father's, always involved in one 'scheme' or another, the holiday farm being the latest; his mousey wife, Auntie Maud, her innate viciousness blunted into mere nagging by years of forced resignation to his male whims; the eager but plain young householder, Wendy, who turned up penniless one day, on a hitchhiking tour from London through Africa, and offered to help out for a few months in exchange for free board and lodging; and the 'problem case', Sylvia. As far as one can make out, Sylvia arrived on the farm as an appendage to the young man Uncle Jock had appointed as his manager; but then there had been difficulties with the police following an assault on a black waiter, as a result of which the manager was now in custody (nobody being prepared to fork out the bail money), leaving Sylvia behind as a more or less available partner for whoever wanted her. The young man's arrest had left Uncle Jock and Auntie Maud no choice but to leave their home in Durban to take over the management personally until such time as a new manager could be found; and very soon, Uncle Jock being infinitely more of a hindrance than a help, the place had begun to subside into a state even worse than before.

*Poor Auntie Maud*, writes Jane, *isn't much good at anything either, spending most of her time complaining about how badly life (meaning Uncle Jock) has treated her. 'There used to be a time, dearie, when we had our own fabulous estate near the Cape, peacocks and everything, place would have been worth millions today, but of course Jock just let it go for next to nothing, so one thing led to another, and look at us now.'*

Jane had been reluctant to give up a beach-bumming holiday on the coast in response to Uncle Jock's distress signal, but she couldn't say no to her father, so in the end she had grudgingly consented to come and help out during the rush expected in December and January. However, no rush materialized, and one can imagine her frustration; though at least she was now free to spend most of her time wandering about in the mountains (pointedly ignoring Auntie Maud's dire warnings about what might happen to a white girl on her own) or exploring the surroundings on horseback.

The first hint of a change in the dreary daily routine appears in an entry dated 4 January:

*We actually have a guest! Panic stations all over the place of course. I was out riding when I saw the car coming up the dust road. A battered old blue Valiant with one mudguard torn off and the driver's door all rusty. As I came into the lobby, after handing Beauty over to Simon at the stable, I found the whole bunch of them crowded round the stranger. Uncle Jock, Auntie Maud, Wendy, and – honest to God – even Sylvia, who'd been out for most of the night (picked up after dark in a black car white with dust). She probably crashed straight into bed when she came home, for there she was, still in her black velvet, her eyes drooping on her cheeks like two cocktail onions, smudged with eye-shadow, one tit practically hanging out down to her navel. All of them talking at the same time, offering accommodation and pretending the place was a going concern. Uncle Jock had the audacity to say he'd have to check the register first for vacancies, but he had to drop his pose when it turned out no one even knew where the book was. It took ages before Dinah or someone found it in the pantry and brought it round for the poor visitor – all flustered and annoyed – to sign, the whole lot of them watching over his shoulder as if it was a marriage register. Clive de Vos. Johannesburg address. (Odd. The car registration said ND, but perhaps he'd hired it in Durban.) Then he asked whether he could have tea on the lawn, which caused an even greater commotion. Everybody wanted to be* involved. I'd have preferred to stay out of it, but it was clear that nothing at all would get done, so in the end it was I who carried out the tray to where he was sitting on the grass among the broken chairs.

As I squatted to put it down he suddenly chuckled and said: 'I'm glad to see you're free.'

'What do you mean?'

'Well, you brought two cups. So I presume you're going to join me. Aren't you?'

I was flustered, mumbling something like: 'Oh, I'm sorry. There were so many people in the kitchen trying to help – '

He laughed, a clear uncluttered kind of laugh. 'Tell me,' he said, 'is this really an hotel? Or is it an institution?'

'No, it just looks like that. We're not properly organized yet. Uncle Jock wanted to have everything ready before the builders' holidays began in December, but it didn't work out.'

'I was just looking for a place to get away from everything for a couple of days.'

'You'll certainly be away from it here. You're the only guest.'

We drank our tea. We talked. We took a walk. I showed him round as well as I could, through the shrubs in the large decaying gardens, up to the old cemetery. He seemed fascinated by the graves. While he was moving from one to another trying to decipher half-obliterated inscriptions I kneeled beside a grave and began to weed the unkempt little plot. A rather futile attempt, but at least it gave me something to do. In a sandy spot I started digging with my hands, heaven knows why. I became conscious of Clive standing behind me, watching, which made me persevere as if it really was important to get the digging done. Only an inch or so into the sand my nails scraped on something. Too smooth for a stone. Like an archaeologist making a breathtaking discovery I smoothed away the earth and took out what looked like the rim of a red plastic mug, which I dusted meticulously before I held it out to him.

'The remains of the Grail?' he asked, laughing. 'Or the lost ring of the Nibelungs? Or perhaps this was the end of the rainbow. For all you know it was once filled with gold.'

'It's empty now.'

'Perhaps you should dig deeper.'

'Too macabre.' Feeling inexplicably guilty, as if I'd robbed the dead, I reached out for the poor little mug again. 'Let's put it back. What's buried should stay buried.'

He squatted down beside me to cover it up with sand the way it had been. But he said: 'I'm sure they wouldn't have missed it.'

'Someone once stole a vase of flowers from my mother's grave,' I said. And immediately wondered why on earth I should have mentioned it.

'When did she die?'

I didn't feel like talking about it, but now I had to; and it turned out to be strangely comforting.

'She went away when I was quite small,' I told him. 'I grew up with Dad. When I was seventeen, we heard that she was dead. Suicide. At first neither of us wanted to go to the funeral, which was in Johannesburg. I mean, we'd managed perfectly on our own, without her, for so long. But in the end we went.'

'Must have been traumatic.'

'Not really. That was the strange thing about it. I felt – Dad too – completely detached. The shock came afterwards. When the little note was found she'd left behind as a kind of will. Not much in it. She wanted to be cremated and all her belongings to be burnt. And her urn inscribed only with a question mark. Imagine! Only Dad refused to have her cremated, he couldn't stand the idea of her being consumed by fire. It was the only serious quarrel we've ever had. I told him his own feelings had nothing to do with it: if she'd wanted it that way he ought to respect her last wish. But he refused, and so she was buried and in due course the stone was put up, with the question mark chiselled into it. That was all she'd left behind, all she had become, to herself and to us. That question mark.' I got up; I felt I had already spoken too much. 'We put flowers on the grave,' I said. 'But then the vase got stolen and it was never replaced. Now there's only the question mark. I've always felt she was done an injustice. I wish I could think of a way to make up for it one day. But how?'

He said nothing, just stared at me in a way I found unnerving.

'Let's go,' I said. 'Graves make me feel creepy.'

'In this land one never gets away from graves.'

'You a preacher?' I deliberately tried to be flippant, anxious to change the tone of our conversation.

'Certainly not!'

'Then you must be in politics.'

'Don't be ridiculous!' Why did he seem so upset? He must have noticed that I was puzzled, for he sounded contrite when he said: 'I'm sorry. I suppose I'm a bit overworked. Well,' almost breezily, 'I think

I'm going for a walk.'

'It's nearly time for lunch.'

'Please apologize for me, will you? I really don't think I can face that whole reception committee right now.'

I looked after him as he sauntered off with a curiously deliberate air of casualness. I could see that, underneath, he really was very tense. He walked past the cemetery, up towards the mountain, and disappeared among the trees of the pine plantation. Something about him had touched me. Even though I'd just met him. His guardedness, a cautiousness? Not so much that as a sense of – well, call it desolation. No. Too strong a word. But there was in him the kind of intense loneliness I'd known in only one other person before and that was Dad.

He stayed away all afternoon. After I'd given Auntie Maud a hand in the kitchen I went out to the stables to see to the horses. By that time the sun was setting. There was the usual rumpus at the low bungalow Uncle Jock had turned into his private 'office'. Apparently the building had been in ruins upon their arrival but he'd hurriedly restored it to get away from Auntie Maud's whining. Even did the rewiring himself and nearly got electrocuted in the process. But converting the place into a private hideaway created other, unforeseen problems. During the years in which the place had been unoccupied a flock of guinea-fowl had begun to roost in it and even after the new door and window had been bricked in and the roof rethatched they kept on coming back. Every sunrise and sunset there was no end to the noise they made as they trotted round and round the little building trying to get in; some would even fly up on the window-sills to peck furiously at the panes.

I was still standing there watching their fluttering frustration when our guest spoke behind me: 'More visitors?'

I told him about the crisis Uncle Jock's refuge had created for the guinea-fowl and his endless efforts to scare them off, to the point of firing buckshot at them.

Whereupon he asked: 'But why? It's very selfish of him. They were here first, weren't they? Surely he's the one who must learn to live with them, not the other way round.'

(Exactly the way Dad would have argued, I thought!)

'You try and tell that to Uncle Jock.'

'I will.'

And at table that evening he did. Everybody was there (except for Sylvia who, once again in the black velvet she insisted on wearing even

81

*in midsummer – this time complemented with a red hibiscus behind one ear – had been spirited away in a Jag at dusk), all nervous and excited after Auntie Maud and her full staff had spent the whole afternoon in the kitchen preparing a memorable dinner.*

*Uncle Jock, I could see, was furious about Clive de Vos' temerity; at the same time he didn't want to offend his first guest. Heaven knows how the argument might have developed if it hadn't been interrupted in such a dramatic way. Carried away by his own eloquence, and at the same time choking in the too-tight collar and tie Auntie Maud had forced him to wear, he jumped to his feet to carry on the argument standing up ('My God, this is my property, I bought it, do you know what it cost me, and now you're trying to tell me I must go down on my knees to a lot of bloody guinea-fowl – !'), when he suddenly stopped in his tracks in front of the open window, unable to say another word. All he could do was gasp for breath as he pointed outside in a series of short stabbing gestures. We all jumped up to see what was going on. It was the bungalow going up in flames. Starting as an ominous red glow, it changed into a raging blaze as we watched. Leaping flames, billowing smoke, casting an eerie flickering light over the whole backyard.*

*A terrifying sight, yet incredibly beautiful too. All my life, this fascination. Camp fires in the veld with Dad when I was small. I could stay awake all night just gazing into the flames. Perhaps the single most vivid memory of my childhood: Dad drawing or writing with fire in the night. He'd select a burning stick from the camp fire and form letters or patterns with it, his movements so swift and sure it was breathtaking. He never allowed me to try. Said I'd wet my pants in the night if I did. It was a game for grown-ups only. Once, while he was pottering about in the tent, I couldn't resist the temptation. The feeling of power, of being in command of something awesome. Then a glowing ember broke away from the stick and landed right between my toes. I started hopping about on one leg clutching my foot and hollering like hell. 'Daddy, Daddy, it bit me, it bit me!' It took him a long time to make me stand still so that he could dislodge the coal and apply some spittle. To this day there's this little scar between my big toe and the second one. It made me a bit more careful, I suppose, adding fear and the memory of pain to my fascination, but it didn't rid me of the spell. Nothing can. And this fire, that night on the farm, was one of the most spectacular I'd ever seen.*

*Our guest was the first to come to his senses and start organizing and ordering us about. Auntie Maud got on the telephone. Uncle Jock,* instead of giving a hand with dousing the fire, trotted laboriously down the hill to the Zulu village in the valley to round up help. The rest of us were milling about in the yard between the water tap and the burning building. The heat was so fierce it singed our hair. All of us, including neighbours who turned up in response to Auntie Maud's telephone calls, were black with soot and smoke. From time to time the flames seemed to subside, but the moment one stood back to catch one's breath or survey the scene they would flare up again. At some stage Sylvia and her beau also arrived, promptly to be commandeered, in spite of their protests, to join in the fight, he in his tuxedo, she in her velvet, the hibiscus already fading.

It was hours before we heard the siren of the fire brigade approaching, by which time the outbuilding was just a ruin anyway. My arms felt torn out of their sockets from carrying so many buckets of water. But right through my exhaustion I suddenly discovered that Clive wasn't with us. My first thought was: My God, he must have got caught inside the bungalow. Shouting at the others, without waiting for the firemen, I rushed headlong into the still smouldering rubble, tearing myself away from the hands that tried to pull me back.

I suppose I would have been burnt pretty badly if they hadn't overpowered me and dragged me from the ruins. All the time I kept on struggling to get loose, and I only gave up when it got through to me that it was Clive himself who was shaking me and talking to me:

'It's all right, Jane, it's all right. Don't go on like this. Nothing has happened to me.'

'I thought you'd burned to death!'

'One of the black children got hurt in the fire, so I took him down to the village to treat him.'

His voice sounded flat with tiredness, but he was so calm that I was ashamed about my own hysterics.

In the meantime the firemen had put out the last flames and to make their long trip worth while they also doused the roof of the main building, drenching in the process most of the furniture. An unholy mess, when at last we all dragged ourselves indoors again. Clive carried me back to my room and put me down on the bed and then he cleaned and treated my burns and bruises. (Where did he so readily find ointment and bandages?)

'Now close your eyes and try to sleep.'

It is with embarrassment that I now remember mumbling in reply: 'Please don't go. Stay with me. I'm frightened.'

*'You need rest more than anything else.'*

*He went out. The door was closed. But I couldn't sleep.*

*Every time, through all the burning images in my mind, my thoughts go back to the man who plucked me from the smouldering bungalow. Ridiculous. I hardly know him. A total stranger. And yet.*

*This is why I couldn't stay in bed. I had to get up and do something. So here I'm sitting now, at my table under the bad light (forty watt, Uncle Jock refuses to buy a stronger bulb), trying to write it down and compose my thoughts. I know I'll be ashamed of myself tomorrow. But for the time being I*

At this point the night's entry comes to an abrupt end. There is nothing more before the one of Sunday 6 January which I have already quoted in part. From the latter it would seem that while she was still working on her notes during that night of Friday or Saturday she was interrupted by a knock on her door. It was the stranger. Clive de Vos.

'I saw your light still burning.'*

'So you couldn't sleep either?'

'I was worried about you.'

'I'm all right. Really.'

'Shall I go then?'

'No!' she cried, reckless. 'I'll go and make us some tea. Or coffee, whichever you prefer.'

Through the lugubrious old house – creaking boards, a pattering in the attic, outside the crowing of cocks and the first excited clicking of the guinea-fowl – they went to the kitchen. Where they started talking, she seated on the table, he leaning against the window sill. A great flood of conversation sweeping them along until the black women came in through the open door to start the day's work. And even then they couldn't stop. There was too much to be said, two whole lives with which to catch up.

Only when the others in the house began to stir and move through passages, opening taps and flushing toilets and ringing for tea, did he take her back to her room. Where she fell asleep in blissful exhaustion, dreamless; and it was almost time for lunch

---

* From this point on I have to invent most of the dialogue and some of the particulars, as Jane's account becomes more and more laconic, even cryptic.

before she woke up – to discover, with a shock, that he was gone. But he'd only gone for a walk, and before they had finished their meal he was back.

In a short paragraph Jane Ferguson notes that they returned to the burnt-down bungalow in the afternoon and discovered among the rubble the charred remains of a bird. A guinea-fowl? Had this been the culprit that had caused the fire by roosting among Uncle Jock's precarious wires? 'Poetic justice,' commented Clive de Vos wryly. Afterwards Jane went down to the Zulu village with him. He wanted to check on the child who'd been injured the night before. She stood watching as he tended the boy, amazed at the dexterity with which he removed bandages, cleansed and sterilized wounds, checked the temperature with a hand on the small forehead.

'One would almost think you were a doctor,' she remarked on their way back.

To which he reacted with surprising sharpness: 'Nonsense!' Her startled expression must have alarmed him, for he composed himself to explain more gently: 'My room mate at varsity studied medicine. Suppose I picked up a few tricks from him.' Adding, after a pause: 'Why are you staring at me like that? Don't you believe me?'

'You're so strange, Clive. I don't think I've ever met anyone like you. I wonder whether anybody can really know you?'

'Don't say things like that. I *want* you to know me, Jane.'

(What did she tell him in return? The diary doesn't say. One has to reconstruct, from what Charles Ferguson later told me, a life dominated by a single male figure, that of her father; an almost wild childhood in the veld, along the coast, in nature reserves, sometimes in the mountains; the years at university where she went very much against her own wishes, only to please her father, and there, to her surprise and his joy, turned out to be a brilliant student.)

Coming home in the late afternoon, the sun already sinking, she suddenly stopped, and clasped his arm. 'Look!' Among the charred remains of the bungalow the guinea-fowl were scratching and pecking and bobbing busily, clearly content with having reclaimed their territory.

'So perhaps it was worth while after all,' he joked.

The evening meal was not a success. Sylvia was in a foul temper, presumably because there was no prospect of going out that night, which she tried to cover up with snide insinuations about Jane and Clive; and Uncle Jock made it plain that he did not approve of what was happening either.

To the open dismay of the whole company they withdrew to her room after dinner, where they resumed their endless, unbridled talking. The window was wide open to the peaceful sounds of crickets and insects. No fire that night.

Did they ever go to sleep? They must have, for Jane gives an account of a dream she had. *We were in the little cemetery, making love on a grave. And then a skeleton came up and tapped Clive on the shoulder, and asked whether we didn't think it was a bit too much in the open, people might see us. So he invited us into his coffin where we wouldn't be disturbed.*

*I told him about the dream this morning. We were up in the mountains. I wanted to show him 'my' waterfall. The weight of his body on mine. So many birds in the trees. I thought the dream would amuse him, but he seemed curiously depressed. Once or twice on the way back I asked him whether anything was wrong, but he just shook his head. Perhaps he was feeling guilty about us, I thought. Perhaps he's married. 'You can tell me, Clive,' I said. 'I'm not expecting anything or asking anything of you, I'm happy just to be with you.' No, he said, very emphatically, he wasn't married; had no intention of ever getting married. 'I don't lead the kind of life I can expect a woman to put up with.'*

*On our way down from the waterfall we saw a yellow police van driving away from the farmhouse. A cloud of dust hovered above the road for minutes afterwards, there was no wind. Clive stood staring at it as if petrified. His face was terribly pale.*

*'What's the matter, Clive?'*

*'Nothing. Nothing.'*

*'Are you ill?'*

*'I told you it was nothing.' He grabbed me by the arms so forcefully that I cried out, but he didn't even seem to notice. All he kept on saying was: 'Jane, Jane, Jane – '*

*'Please tell me what is wrong.'*

*'Jane, I want you to promise me one thing. Do you hear? Whatever happens, promise me you will remember that I loved you.'*

'Of course I shall. But why are you saying such things?'

'Just remember it. Please. That's all I ask of you.'

He turned round to look at the mountains as if he wanted to go back to where we'd come from. But after a moment, with a small sigh, he went down the slope with me. It was like dragging a truant boy to school. When I asked Uncle Jock about the police he said they'd come about the fire. Possibility of arson. (But who on earth would do a thing like that? And what about the dead bird we'd found? He shrugged it off. Feeling guilty about his wiring, I suppose. Didn't want people to find out, which might cause a lot of trouble.)

Clive remained withdrawn all afternoon but I didn't want to prod him again. I knew he would make up his own mind about when to speak and what to say. But when at last he did it was unlike anything I'd expected.

'There's something I must tell you, my love.'

'What is it, Clive? I've been waiting all day for you to talk.'

'I'm not Clive de Vos.'

I could only stare at him.

'I am Chris de Villiers.'

Bewildered, obtuse, I said something like: 'But in the hotel register you wrote – '

'The Security Police are looking for me. I'm in hiding. I'm on my way out of the country.'

There are no further particulars in the diary. Perhaps even at that stage she was concerned that the Special Branch might somehow get hold of the book. Unless her silence was due to the same reticence which marked her references to their love.

Of course, by the time her father brought me the diary for safe keeping the name Chris de Villiers was no longer a mystery to anybody. All that fuss in the newspapers. But Charles Ferguson's view of the matter was, inevitably, more personal than the sensational 'exposures' of the press.

'Look, all I can tell you is what I heard from Jane afterwards, when she came to unburden her heart to me. By that time it was all over, of course. He was a doctor, as you already know, as everybody knows. One of those who really take their Hippocratic oath seriously. Which isn't always an easy thing to do in this country. I'm not sure how and why it all started, but one got used to seeing his name in the papers in connection with complaints against the police about assault or torture. I remember an occasion a few years ago when the young son of a trade union leader was assaulted so badly that he nearly died. The father had gone into hiding a few weeks earlier, and they wanted information about his whereabouts from the child. He was only thirteen or fourteen. After the assault Chris was called in and he managed to pull the kid through. But then they came back: in the light of "new information" or whatever they called it they demanded to interrogate the boy again. Chris refused to hand him over. Said it could kill the child. So they arrested him too. Defeating the ends of justice. But some of the hospital staff who'd been present contacted Chris's lawyer and late that same night an urgent interdict was granted forbidding the police to assault either Chris or the child. Not that it was much use. When the boy was set free the next morning he was already in a coma and a day or so later he died. At which stage they let Chris go as well.

'He immediately laid a complaint about the death of the child. Got the top lawyers in the country. But of course it was impossible to pin down the police. Honour among thieves. From then on Chris got even more involved with the black unions, and campaigns against the government, and the UDF and so on; by then, of course, he already was a marked man. Especially after he said quite openly that he subscribed to the ideals of the ANC. Who had driven them underground? he would say. Who had made it impossible for them to function as a political organization? Who had first started the violence? Who were the real terrorists? Anyway, now we know where it all got him.'

He pushed his fingers through his brush of short grey hair and crossed his legs. I couldn't help noticing his tanned feet in the open sandals he was wearing: the feet of a young man.

'But what made him go underground?' I asked.

'As far as I know there was a case coming up against some of the top officers in the SB. Chris was going to give medical evidence. According to Jane he'd somehow got hold of documents smuggled from John Vorster Square. But it seems to me that even without any specific reason they would have closed in on him sooner or later: he'd become an embarrassment to them, he knew too much.

'One night a friend of his came round to warn him that there

88

was a raid going on in Soweto and that several people he'd been working with had been detained. "A routine enquiry", the minister called it afterwards. Words don't seem to mean what they used to. Anyway, Chris got the message and thought it would be wise to go underground. The trade union leadership decided it would be better for him to leave the country for a while until things had quietened down again. He was worth more to them abroad than in detention. And you know how things have deteriorated these last few months: a man can't blow his nose without being accused of high treason. So Chris left Johannesburg, changing cars several times on the way to Durban, where he was lent the battered old Valiant with which he turned up at the holiday farm. The whole cloak-and-dagger bit. From there he planned to go to Swaziland, then on to Mozambique. You will appreciate how much those few days in the mountains meant to both of them.'

*Perhaps it would have been easier to talk it through with him. But I am alone tonight. He insisted. 'You know how much I want to be with you,' he said. 'But this is a choice you've got to make on your own. I shall accept whatever you decide. Even if it is to hand me over to the police. It is not only your life which is in my hands: mine is in yours too. Take your time. Think about it. About all that's happened. About everything that may yet happen.'*


Here is a note I made recently while on holiday in Mauritius:

Every work I write, I write for the sake of – in the name of – by virtue of – that which cannot be written, that which must be forever unwritable.

The profound disturbance of the unwritable by the written: like submarine currents of which you are only half aware while swimming in the sea. With, at most, sometimes, while diving off the coral reef, a brief glimpse of a previously unimaginable world suddenly coming into focus in front of your eyes, before your goggles become waterlogged and your snorkel gets clogged – for it is a dangerous exercise.

Likewise: the body I love, I love in the name of – by virtue of – the woman who can never be circumscribed in a body. Not to escape from the body or the mortal, but on the contrary as an affirmation of all that is mortal, in order to get to know it, to explore it, to learn to live with it, to acquiesce in my own death.


On 4 May Andries Raditsela, Transvaal vice-president of the Federation of South African Trade Unions, was stopped by police in an armoured vehicle and taken into custody. Eyewitnesses confirmed that he was assaulted at the time of his arrest. He was detained in terms of Section 50 of the Internal Security Act. Two days later, on 6 May, he was set free again, but by that time he was already in a serious condition and a few hours later he died in Baragwanath hospital. His funeral was attended by between 25,000 and 30,000 people, marching through Tsakane township outside Boksburg in a procession two kilometres long. Some newspapers subsequently reported that only 'hundreds' had attended the funeral and that 'the expected thousands of mourners were not there'. On TV news ten seconds was devoted to the event. Two days later there was another funeral in Tsakane, and one in Duduza soon afterwards. These received no coverage at all in the white press.

On 14 May police undertook to 'keep a low profile' at the funeral of yet another victim of violence in Grahamstown. But as the procession of peaceful mourners left Joza Stadium, police opened fire, killing a girl of sixteen and a boy of seventeen. At the funeral of the girl on the twenty-sixth an angry mob swarmed towards the home of a town councillor, and to deter them the police once again shot into the crowd, this time killing a young man of twenty-six.

Towards the end of the month South African commandos were sent deep into Angola to the oil-rich province of Cabinda to sabotage refineries and other installations. (One can imagine the spectacular eruption of fire in the tropical night.) Two soldiers were captured. At a news conference one of them admitted that the mission had been aimed at mining American oil depots to cripple the Angolan economy. The event did not deter the Reagan administration in the US from pursuing its policy of 'constructive engagement' with the Pretoria regime.

*

Secondary characters can be problematic; yet sooner or later, even in a love story which aims to focus on two lovers within the exclusive territory of their relationship, they become indispensable. Now I have already sketched in Lucas Wilson, incorporating a few lines which may be developed in due course. But at this stage the story urgently requires another personality, that of Philip's wife. It would have made things much easier to keep her in the background as a convenient stereotype: the woman who 'doesn't understand her husband', one whose apathy renders her husband's actions acceptable to the reader, not only in terms of the story, but also morally.

But I do not want to take the easy way. Much of Philip's personal agony should derive from the fact that the woman who has been, for so many years, his ally and his confidante, should now become a potential adversary, a role which both of them will find profoundly disturbing. Even more so as I conceive of no natural animosity between her and Melissa. On the contrary, there should be a hint that, in other, more 'natural' circumstances, they might have become friends. This will be the element which introduces danger into the relationship. Philip has not remained loyal to his wife over the years because it was expected of him, because it was a matter of convention, but because he has *chosen* to be loyal. (The occasional brief affair was no more than an incidental piece of driftwood on that broad current.) And Melissa represents a challenge to that loyalty, as she challenges most of what he has come to take for granted in his situation.

What I need is not just a character, but an episode, a context within which her narrative validity will be demonstrated. The kind of episode which should, among other things, illuminate that banal yet decisive question: How does a woman first discover that her husband has a mistress? Surely not the time-honoured long blonde hair on his shoulder or the note in his breast pocket. It is only after she has already found out, or already suspects, that she goes in search of such confirmation, plagued by an awareness of humiliation no one realizes more disturbingly than she herself. Scent? Undoubtedly. How unbelievably acute the sense of smell in a suspicious person. But it goes beyond smell, it is much more subtle. A woman like Philip's wife, Greta, is bound to make the fatal discovery precisely in those areas of action where he himself would least expect it: in the small, new signs of attentiveness to her needs and feelings; offers to run errands for her in town; a proposal to take the family to the seaside for a weekend, where he will play cricket with the boys (if they have sons) or spoil the girls (if they have daughters) with little gifts and fond embraces. (Then again, without reason or warning, he would wander off on his own, walking for hours along the beach in fog or drizzle.) She would find his attentions painful, discovering in them his need to convince himself of what a good husband and father he really is. (In order to sanction those other evasions and interludes? – the appointments, meetings, official duties which keep him from home for longer than before.) Even when he touches her, which he does frequently, fondly, she will find in it something repulsive (while at the same time submitting to it with an exaggerated sense of relief), suspecting that his thoughts are elsewhere, that it is someone else's heart he is carrying on his sleeve.

And then the self-reproach, the guilty soul-searchings: It must be my own fault, something in myself which has driven him to other comforts, which has caused 'this' to happen. If only I can be given another chance I shall make up for it. Whereupon she will proceed to smother him with fond attentions, driving him to despair through the newly kindled discovery of his own guilt. He must keep his different worlds apart, otherwise everything will fall to pieces. It is the condition for his survival.

This is the stage they must inevitably arrive at, a crisis all the more unsettling because it has never gone quite so far before. They have been together for, say, fifteen years. Perhaps he was already not so young when he first met her.* Let us imagine her registering as a first-year student in his department. In which case he would have had to wait patiently and discreetly for her to finish her degree, possibly even her teacher's diploma afterwards.

Only a week or so ago somebody told me the story of his own great love. (He'd heard that I was working on a novel: amazing

---

* Cf. page 68.

how such news can inspire people, even strangers, to confide their private lives to one: 'By all means use it in your book if you want to – ') Fifteen years ago, when he'd been in his early thirties, he had met this young girl on the beach; love at first sight; but when he asked her how old she was she answered: 'Fifteen'. So he gave her a coin and playfully instructed her to telephone him the day she turned eighteen. Which, against all odds, she did. And they have been together ever since. So something similar may well have happened to Philip and Greta.

Only, she is no longer twenty-something, but nearly forty. In fact, why not choose this as the year she will turn forty? Which will bring with it the inevitable stock-taking brought about by this first reminder of middle age: What I have, you have given me; what I am, you have made me. What now? I have never had a 'life of my own': for as far back as I can remember you have taken responsibility for me. You have really been the only man in my life. The two others I had known before you – all right, three, if we include that brief, unhappy business with Geoffrey – were not important. And then we got married. You were already settled in your work, I had to adapt to it (which I did, with such abandon); even your home had been furnished to your own taste and it took years before I dared to change anything in it; and then the children were born, you didn't want to postpone a family as you were already getting on (except that for me you were young, you still are). One day, I used to promise myself, one day as soon as the children are more manageable, I shall catch up. Not that I bore them any grudge. I loved them, fulfilled myself in them. Were they not the very proof of our love, our faith in belonging together? I wanted to bring them up to do you proud. Only, this didn't leave me much time for anything else, you see. Even to that I resigned myself without resentment. Sooner or later they would be off my hands and then I would resume my own career (I'd barely started when we got married, remember). It's a way of keeping oneself going. Always continuing to believe in that magical 'one day'. Then, all of a sudden, you open your eyes and discover that you are forty: and you know that distant 'one day' is *now*, and all that has happened in the mean time is that life has passed you by, you're no longer young, you're afraid of facing anything on your own. And this becomes the most horrible of all one's fears: to be left alone.

Her fortieth birthday on 16 June will require a special celebration. 'Shall we invite the usual crowd?' he may propose. 'We all get along so well, your parties are always such a success.'

'Not this year,' she says. 'There's something obscene about the idea. The sixteenth is Soweto Day, remember?'

'It is also your birthday.'

'All right,' she relents at last, adding more quietly: 'If that is what you want.'

For a moment he gives her a probing look, then nods. 'Good idea. I'll get out the invitations today.'

(She thinks: Why didn't you suggest taking me away for my birthday? It needn't be anything exotic – not Rio or Mauritius or Paris, not even the Cape or Durban; Port Elizabeth will do, or even our beach cottage, just the two of us, we can easily leave the children at home for a few days. We never had a proper honeymoon, remember? You had to come back to your work immediately, so we promised each other: One day – We can walk along the beach and lie in the dunes, and at night you can hold me in your arms and whisper in my ear that I needn't be afraid, you'll never leave me.)

He makes a list of the twelve or fourteen people to invite, leaving it to his secretary to make the telephone calls.

Melissa? Something of a problem there. For one reason or another – nothing important – she hasn't been to their parties before (except last year, when she came with Lucas Wilson). Now he is hesitant: at the same time, defiantly, he *wants* her to come.

'Apart from anything else it'll be just too obvious if you stay away,' he tries to convince her. 'People will start asking questions.'

She shakes her head. (She is brushing her hair, looking at him in the mirror.) 'No way, prof. Don't be naïve.'

'No one will know. Only the two of us.'

'No. Just forget about it. If I go I'll never be able to face your wife again.' She turns round to him. 'Don't make things difficult for me, please. When you and I are together, we can forget about anything else. When those curtains are drawn, the world no longer exists. But the moment we go through that door, among

94

other people, it is different. Then it can so easily become nasty and sordid. Just another little affair.'

'Does it matter what people call it?'

'Yes.'

Grudgingly – even though he knows that, obviously, she is right – he gives up.

But that is not the end of it. The very next day Lucas turns up at her place. For weeks there has been no sign of him; he seemed at last to have accepted that the past was indeed the past; she has begun to relax. Lately she has stopped taking precautions, leaving the door open during the day when she is working at home. And that afternoon, as she looks up from her table, very suddenly, he is standing inside the room. Immediately: the contraction of her heart, the feeling of numbness as the blood drains from her face.

'You're not scared of me, are you? I'm not exactly a stranger, you know.'

'You are.'

'Melissa, only a few months ago – '

'Please don't start with that again. You know damn well there is nothing between us any more.'

For a moment she fears that he may close the door behind him and turn the key – how many times in the past has he done that! – but then he casually comes past her and stops at the opposite side of her table, hands in his pockets, his pale eyes flickering across her books and notes and letters. There is nothing, she knows, he does not absorb and file away in his mind for later use: from whom she has received letters, what notes she has been making, which books she's reading. When they still lived together he regularly read her mail, sometimes even tearing open sealed envelopes to make sure there was nothing secret going on in her life.

'Actually I just brought you an article I've done for the *New Statesman*,' he says, maintaining his casual attitude. 'Thought you might be interested.'

For a moment there is a hint of pleading in his voice; briefly she relents.

'You can leave it here.' She points, still on the defence.

'I wouldn't mind a cup of tea.'

'No, Lucas.'

'Why so uptight?'

'You know very well if I offer you tea you won't be leaving soon. And I'm not going through all that again. Please, Lucas, why can't you take it like a grown-up?'

Without any warning he changes the subject. 'So the Malans are having a party again.'

'Are they?' She tries to keep her cool, sensing trouble.

'Surely you've been invited?'

'I don't think it's any of your business, Lucas.'

'Last year we went together.'

'That was last year.'

A sudden, unnerving change of mood: 'Jesus, Melissa, I love you. Don't you understand? Perhaps I was a selfish bastard, I handled you the wrong way. But I've changed. Just give me a chance to prove it. For God's sake, I'll do anything to get you back.'

Is it the Mills & Boon style of his pleading which riles her, or the undertones – unperceived by himself, most likely – that converted the final promise into a threat? Whatever the reason, more frightened of herself perhaps than of him, her only response is to avoid his eyes and shake her head.

He is silent for a long time.

When at last she dares look up again there is something terrible in his stare: rage, yes; but also the blank incomprehension of a pain so intense that it hits her in the pit of her stomach.

His voice reduced to a whisper he enunciates each word separately, like a row of small angry candles that must be lit one by one: 'I want you to go to the Malans' party with me.'

She starts rummaging among her books in search of a peppermint in a small jar. In a tumbler next to it is the bunch of white daisies Philip brought yesterday.

'So there's someone else in your life.'

'What is it to you?'

'I know you have a lover, Melissa. And I know it's Philip Malan. You can't fool me. Just remember, I warned you before: I won't allow you – '

'You won't allow me! I have my own life, Lucas. I can make my own decisions.'

'I never thought you'd carry on with a married man.'

She takes a deep breath. 'You won't provoke me,' she says, very calm. 'You're just taking a chance. I can call your bluff.'

'I saw him coming from your back yard yesterday.'

'He – he brought me some essays. I happen to be his assistant, in case you've forgotten.'

'If you don't go with me I'll know for sure that you're afraid people will notice something. That'll prove me right.'

'And if I go?'

He pushes his hands through his red hair. (A second-hand merkin, she thinks viciously.) 'Then I'll soon find out how well the two of you can play-act.' He stares steadily at her through his thick lenses, his colourless eyes like coals of fire, burning into her. At last, with a sudden smirk, he goes back to the door. 'So it's a date,' he says. 'See you tomorrow night.' And goes out.

In a belated futile rush of emotion she runs to the door, grabs it with both hands and flings it shut, then turns back to the table to lean on it, shivering, waiting for the nausea to subside.* Only minutes after she's heard his car drive off (why didn't she hear it when he came?), she goes to her tiny bathroom to rinse her face in cold water; then fastens the safety chain on the door, shuts out the daylight from her windows and sits down with her books again. But her eyes cannot focus, her thoughts are scattered, and in the end all she can do is remain where she is, unmoving, staring into space.

She attempts to warn Philip the next day, but she hasn't reckoned with his full programme of lectures and meetings; and even the urgent little note she leaves in his post box remains uncollected.

So one can imagine the barely concealed flicker of shock in his eyes when, that night, he opens the front door of his elegant old Victorian home to them.

'Hi, prof,' she says before either of the men can speak. 'Lucas insisted on bringing me with him.'

'Of course,' says the professor, studiously civilized. 'Glad to see you. Come in.'

---

* Too melodramatic? But I need this emotional display. Lucas is the one person she cannot handle at all. (*Why* not?)

Behind him Greta appears, her shortish dark-blonde hair immaculately done; looking thirty. Good figure, Lucas may observe, tall and well groomed, the kind of person who can cope with any situation without being overbearing (which he doesn't approve of in women).

What else would he observe in the course of the evening? On the surface, nothing. Everybody is cordial, the atmosphere easy, the wine mature; most of them know each other, have been to many parties together, are prepared to make allowances for the sake of harmony. (Even Lucas's few attempts at stirring up arguments go unchallenged, except for the odd good-humoured put-down.) Without any sign of strain the conversation flows and eddies around university matters, personal observations, politics, food; and the meal progresses without either delay or undue haste.

Tonight after they have gone (Greta may think on her way to the kitchen with a tray of empty aperitif glasses), when we are in bed, he will say: 'Thank you, my love. It was a first-class dinner.' And what he will really be trying to say will be: 'I love you.' Only, we no longer use those words. One develops different codes, a private shorthand, one's personal cryptography. Words no longer mean what they meant before. And why should this touch her so deeply, suddenly, that she has to grip the sides of the kitchen sink to control her tears? But other women are following on her heels to help clear up and stack away the dishes; she must put on her smile again and be prepared to play the game of good manners to the end, not be a spoil-sport.

There is a brief disturbance just before the vichyssoise is served, when the family dog, a smelly shaggy creature of dubious descent and even more dubious age, inexplicably escapes from the shed where he has been locked up for the evening (one of the children must have crept in in search of a hammer or a screw-driver or something and left the door open), and starts cavorting among the guests, farting and slobbering and shedding tufts of hair.

'For heaven's sake, Philip, do something. I'm trying to dish up.'

'But I'm pouring the wine. And you're the only one he ever listens to.'

Resentful, humiliated, Greta drags the dog to the kitchen where he baulks, refusing to budge. Her angry tugs at his collar are met with enthusiastic lickings of her hands.

'Damn you!' she exclaims in helpless rage, discovering too late that there is someone standing behind her. The blonde girl from Philip's department, the one who came with Lucas Wilson. Melissa.

'Can I help?'

The girl kneels down beside the dog, presses her head against his shaggy body as she starts talking to him, running her fingers through his knotted pelt.

'Nothing will move him once he's set his mind to it,' says Greta. 'And you shouldn't fondle him like that, he's filthy.'

'He's beautiful.'

'I think so too. But most of our guests find him a bit much.'

'Don't worry, I adore dogs.'

'So do I.' Greta stands watching them with a feeling almost of complicity, fascinated by the way the girl handles the crusty old animal as she laughingly tries to stop him licking her face. When she gets up again the dog follows her to the back door.

'Where do you want him to go?'

'There's a shed just round the corner. But you really shouldn't – you're all covered with hair.'

'Come on,' says the girl. Open-mouthed, drooling, waving his tail, the dog follows her, a sinister old wolf now docile and subdued.

Her good mood restored, Greta starts ladling out the soup. The meal begins with a round of predictable but sincere compliments; the hostess relaxes. It may yet turn out to be a good evening.

In the interval between main course and dessert the smokers among the guests light cigarettes; some go to the bathroom. And when the bathroom downstairs is occupied they know the place well enough – good, solid friends all of them – to find their way upstairs (what a splendid collection of paintings the Malans have) to the *en suite* bathroom at the end of the passage. Throughout the house the conversation expands, flowing freely past small islands of people. Some of the men, awaiting their turn, go out on the upstairs balcony to enjoy the balmy late-autumn air and look out over the peaceful town reassuringly demarcated in rows of lights. It is only when one of the guests happens to look in another direction, towards the black townships on the opposite row of hills, that they discover an ominous red glow against the sky like an untimely sunset.

'My God, what's that?'

It must be buildings – a school? – on fire. What started as a glow soon changes into a raging blaze: leaping flames, billowing smoke, casting an eerie light over the whole hillside.

Somebody runs inside to spread the news among the guests who have just begun to drift back to the dining room for the dessert. (It is becoming a habit, Philip may think with wry amusement, for my meals to be interrupted between main course and dessert.) In their eagerness to see the spectacle everybody rushes upstairs, leaving Greta behind at the table. Composed, with a resigned little smile, her glass in one hand, she sets about tidying the table, shifting forks and spoons into position, folding up napkins, gathering ash-trays to empty in the kitchen bin. Annoyance at the disturbance – she sets store by routine – is tempered by relief at having a few quiet moments to herself. Not that the evening has depressed her; on the contrary. Her self-assurance has been restored. Philip has been so helpful, so genuinely complimentary, that she has begun to master the shadow creeping up on her during the last few weeks. Perhaps she really should broach the subject of a holiday for the two of them. Almost light-hearted, she returns from the kitchen, once again checks the table, refills her glass, and follows the others upstairs.

Fascinated, the guests watch the flames which are by now illuminating the whole town. In the distance, the sirens of the fire brigade (ambulances?). The deeper rumbling of military vehicles. Bursts of rattling sounds which may be gunfire. Eruptions and ululations of human voices. The sharp shrill screams of children. And behind it all, a barely recognizable murmur, an almost imperceptible motion, as the whole town uncoils and comes to life in the dark. Without actually seeing anything, one becomes aware of people emerging from their darkened doors or clustering in windows, even crowding on rooftops the better to see what is happening.

Once or twice fantastic explosions reverberate through the night. (Cars? Classrooms?) But in reality it doesn't last long. Twenty minutes, half an hour. The noise begins to ebb away. A few more clattering salvos. Another round of sirens. Then the flames begin to sag, smothered in smoke, until nothing but a dull red glow remains.

'Soweto Day indeed,' says one of the guests.

'I was at a party a few nights ago,' says Melissa. 'All postgraduates. Someone brought out a newspaper to check on the movies. There was something on the front page about the sixteenth. It turned out that no one in that kitchen – and there must have been thirty or so jammed together – knew what it meant. No one *cared*. I remember one guy kept on talking about his great ideal in life: to possess a red Ferrari. Another, who'd already had too much to drink, kept on declaiming the truth he'd just discovered: "Language is useless. Shunting is the only valid form of communication." '

'Shunting?' asks one of the older guests.

'Fucking.'

There is a sudden uneasy silence as they stare at the dying red glow in the distance.

One of the guests clears his throat. 'Well, guys.'

'You really think of everything, Philip,' someone else remarks. 'Even a free show thrown in.'

Bantering, laughing, a few in more serious conversation, they begin to move back downstairs, suddenly stung by feelings of guilt about having left their hostess in the lurch. But Greta accepts their profuse apologies with her customary little smile, pressing her back against the wall in the passage to let them pass before she switches off the light and goes to close the balcony door.

There are only two figures left in the dark outside. She can see their silhouettes against the reddish afterglow. Philip, and a woman. She cannot immediately identify the latter; then recognizes the shiny hair. Melissa Lotman. They are not touching; in fact, they're standing a yard apart. No hint of any intimate exchange. A very ordinary scene: two people in the dark, talking; it is mere coincidence that they should be male and female. And they are, obviously, already preparing to come inside again. Only as they turn towards the door, Philip briefly – so briefly it may be by accident – touches the girl's shoulder. She moves forward ahead of him, turns back her head to look at him. There is the suggestion of a smile in the light coming from inside. Nothing more. Except for something, heaven knows what, it is quite indefinable, something like confidence, trust, something which suggests a more intimate knowledge, in the movement of that blonde head, turning to look back and up at him, as if she feels secure with him, as if in the easiness of the gesture her eyes convey a question – 'Tomorrow?' – to which the merest nod of his head appears to respond: 'Yes. Of course.'

Then it is so. Then it is she.

The next morning he finds a small bunch of fearless daffodils in a vase on his desk, with a note:

> *I have decided it will be better if we do not see each other again. Please try not to make it more difficult for me than it is.*
> *Love,*
> M.

Donington (a passage which Philip may well sometimes look up in one of the opera programmes he keeps so neatly filed in his study): 'The strength of our desire and longing gives woman her power, and she may use it to destroy us or create us or both.' It is relevant to Lucas too. Wouldn't it be possible to interpret the very 'Mills & Boon style of his pleading' (cf. page 96) as the clumsy articulation of something really felt very deeply? What if he *is* desperately in love with Melissa – a desperation his intellectual pride (itself a mechanism of defence) dare not articulate? Perhaps even Loki's vicious revenge on Balder should be read as a sign of love gone wrong.

Lately I have been reading *Alternative Shakespeares*, edited by John Drakakis, which illuminates in an exciting way the thesis paraphrased on the back cover, that 'there is no unified subject "Shakespeare", but a series of alternative "Shakespeares" each of which is defined oppositionally, and each of which it must be the business of criticism to contest in the face of opposed perspectives'. This, I believe, captures something of my reservations about writing a love story. After all, the genre creates its own set of expectations: namely of a certain consistency, a beginning, a middle, and an end, a centripetal structure. It is concerned with *this* love relationship, not with anything beyond its boundaries. The least one can expect is that all the components should be 'integrated'.

But the more I allow these notes to develop, the more I discover that the story I should like to write does not allow me to focus only on itself. For to what extent *can* any love relationship truly be regarded as exclusive, insular, unique? Granted, 'to love' implies, at first sight: *I love you, here, now*. But this 'I', this 'you', this 'love': do they not already include all my own previous experience of love, and yours, and of all others who have been involved in it? An entire history and literary tradition converge in us. Every new love repeats Romeo and Juliet, Heloïse and Abelard, Siegfried and Brünnhilde, Tristan and Isolde, Samson and Delilah, Adam and Eve, Isis and Osiris, *ad infinitum*. At every moment meanings tumble into *this* love from outside, while at the same time, from inside, it keeps spilling over its own boundaries. Its sign is the *hymen*, to take an example from Derrida. Summarized, the relevant passage from *Dissemination* boils down to this: the word *hymen* does not refer only to the virginal membrane – that precarious divide between a woman's interior and her exterior, between desire and fulfilment, between past and present – but also to marriage, to coitus. At the same time, according to some etymologists, it is related to *hyphos* (a weaving) and to *hymnos* (a hymn, an intricately woven bridal song or elegy). The word that signifies separation, division, boundary, also signifies the transgression of the boundary, the celebration of unity.

Similarly, this time with reference to Derrida's *Of Grammatology*, the very boundary (hymen) between this text on paper and whatever lies beyond already signifies its transgression. Which means that when he states: 'There is nothing outside the text' (his most widely misused pronouncement?), it should also be read together with a line from Barthes in *S/Z*: 'For as nothing exists outside the text, there is never a *whole* of the text'. Love, and the text I should like to write about love, cannot be separated. They are one hymen, one weaving (*text* and *textile*, too, are derived from the same root), each the supplement and surrogate of the other.

Is that why I am still hesitant to commit myself to a love story? What I have done so far is no more than fore-word, pre-text: isolated moments, episodes, character sketches, intuitions, trial runs, to find out whether it may, eventually, 'work'. (Knowing at the same time that, as with love, *unless* one is prepared, from the outset, to risk everything, there is no chance of making it 'work' at all.)

Perhaps the making of notes has become compulsive in itself. I have no choice but to continue. Not just because I've stepp'd in blood so far, but because all around me, if I were to stop, there would be only that other inextricable weaving of a land in flames.

Seismographic tremors of the news about the raid on Cabinda were still reverberating through the news media of the world when South African forces undertook a terrorist raid on the neighbouring state of Botswana to destroy alleged 'ANC bases' (mostly private homes) and eliminate 'ANC terrorists' (including women and children). The burden of language becomes increasingly unmanageable.

Inside the country the first half of the year culminated in the murder of four black community leaders: three from Cradock (including the impressive champion of peaceful protest, the teacher Matthew Goniwe, whose long detention without trial or charge had caused the worst schools' boycotts and civic unrest in decades), and one from Oudtshoorn (the school principal Sicelo Mhlauli). Their charred bodies were found beside the wreck of the car they had been travelling in from Port Elizabeth, some days after their alleged 'disappearance'. It is significant that only hours before leaving on that fateful journey Mr Goniwe had told several of his supporters that he had received threats of an attempt on his life, as a result of which he assured them that he would only stop his car if it was flagged down by police in uniform.

At their funeral, a few weeks later, the flags of the ANC and the Soviet Union were defiantly displayed by the vast crowd of mourners. This was the first time it had happened so openly. And the government, whose only response to violence so far had been a recourse to even greater excesses of violence, reacted the very next day by declaring a State of Emergency in thirty-six districts, banning meetings by seventy-four organizations, embarking on a new wave of detentions, and sending the army and the police into the black townships with what amounted to a licence to kill and destroy at random.


It was by way of a challenge more to myself than to my characters that I inserted on page 102 the paragraph about the note which accompanies Melissa's bunch of daffodils. But having written it (I needed at the time the ironical juxtaposition with Greta's discovery) I will have no peace of mind until the complication has been sorted out. What I propose is an episode written from Melissa's perspective. This will offer a glimpse into the turmoil in her mind and the ways in which she tries to contain herself before I bring Philip on the scene; the black children may be a significant factor; and there may even be an opportunity to prepare the reader for Melissa's grandmother who, in one way or another, may yet enter the story. If only I had the leisure to elaborate, to develop possibilities as they announce themselves. But now there are these many demands on my time. (I have just had another visit from Milton Thaya; perhaps I shall find an excuse for telling more about it later: his insider's view of the gloom which pervades the township like a pall of tear-gas smoke, the mounting rage among the young who, left more and more leaderless as the police arrest everybody wielding some authority, are driven to a spree of violence no one and nothing can check.) In the hour or two – sometimes no more than a few minutes – I have each day to retreat into a tentatively shaping story, it often seems like an act of betrayal to shut out the outside world as surely, as precariously, as Melissa tries to exclude the unrelenting daylight when she reaches out to undo the ribbons on her off-white calico curtains.

I imagine her a day or two after the party episode in her room with a group of black children. Four or five of them (sometimes there are more; the word spreads), ranging from nine to twelve or so, a few much older. She has fed them all (they have probably been going without food for a day); they have yelled and chortled and cavorted under her shower; she has patched up the scars and wounds and sores and bruises caused by family feuds, stones, falls, fights, police quirts, dogs or whatever; and now they are at work on their lessons. She's been doing this as part of Milton Thaya's project, usually once a week; but with the schools boycotts (and the black consumer boycott which curtails the supply of food in the townships) they drift back more often, some weeks daily. It began with a few kids sent to her by Milton; then her landlord's char Rosie asked whether her child could also attend – a bright, mischievous, large-eyed girl called Ntombazana – and soon their friends began to come along too, some of them for the lessons, most of them for the food, all of them for the fun. There are afternoons when the whole room seems to be teeming with them. On other days, after a raid or a tear-gas attack in the township, there are fewer; invariably there is news of someone detained, or beaten up, or missing – off to Lesotho, to relatives in other places, gone to earth, or simply 'disappeared'. From the way they tell it, it sounds like one great adventure, a comedy series. She is startled by their wisdom, the agelessness of ten-year-olds in charge of a whole family in the absence (or during the drunken comas) of parents or older siblings. The girls love her hair: brushing it, stroking it, plaiting it, just feeling it. The boys sometimes slyly touch her breasts, which annoys her; yet the guileless exuberance of their laughter when she rebukes them is disarming. ('Perhaps they *are* taking advantage of me,' she will say to Philip if he gently reprimands her, 'but so what? If I'm a soft touch or a sucker, it's all right by me. I do get bloody mad at them when they take up all my time playing the fool or watching TV or running riot – you should hear Jack when they're gone – but can you imagine what they have to go back to? So why shouldn't they enjoy themselves for a change?')

They are sitting and standing around her table, one or two on her bed, or kneeling on the floor with their backsides stuck in the air like bird-dogs', their pencils scratching in the silence (never a very long silence); her thoughts will be elsewhere (the night on the balcony, the fire in the dark, Philip; perhaps with Louis, the way he'd used to be before the army; or, with a touch of amusement, with her gran, from whom she has just received the customary stern fortnightly letter bristling with texts from the Bible: what would that fierce little old lady say if she were to see her grandchild here today, surrounded by these children, the descendants of the very heathens God himself had sent the Boers to save and subjugate and, if necessary, eradicate?). She will be longing to be out of this small room, perhaps in 'her' wood above the town, out of sight of the world. And yet, in a sense, it would also be a relief being here, overrun by their demands and needs: she does not *want* to think too much. Not now. Not after what has happened, she has done.

Then the knock, and it will be Philip. The children tensing in suspense, ready to make a run for it.

'Prof!' She cannot conceal her joy. But immediately represses it. 'Why did you come? I *asked* you not to.'

'That is why. I had to find out. I just can't believe you.'

She lowers her head, her eyes closed for a moment. 'I asked you not to make it difficult for me.'

'May I come in?'

Only then does he notice the children. He will find their presence disturbing: all those inquisitive eyes watching, the ears eager to catch whatever is to be said.

'Shall I come round later?'

But she draws security from their presence. 'No, come in. Coffee? Tea?'

'Melissa, I – really – '

They are already scurrying about, collecting their books and the paper and plastic bags in which they have stuffed the excess fruit and bread she dished out. 'Don't go,' she tries to stop them. 'It's my prof, he's a friend.'

'Is he your boyfriend?' asks one beautiful, bold, bright-eyed girl staring cheekily at him.

She will blush at this. 'No, Ntombazana!' she says sharply. 'I told you I have no boyfriends.'

'But I don't believe you.' The girl giggles, shoving her books into an OK bag. 'Bye-bye, Melissa.' The others repeat it in chorus as they traipse out. (One or two say impishly: '*Sala kakuhle.*') Melissa goes with them to make sure that Rex will not molest them.

She comes in again. She closes the door but remains standing with her back against it.

'What happened, Melissa?'

'You shouldn't have come.'

'But I love you.'

What will she reply? Not: 'It is because I love you that I – ' Though that may well be what she thinks.

'Two nights ago, at the party – '

'I don't want to hear about two nights ago!' she cries angrily. And that gives it all away. It is as simple as that.

'Lucas came back here with you?' he asks slowly.

She comes quickly past him and starts tidying up where the children have left their mugs and plates and peels and scraps of paper. 'Does it matter?'

'You know it does.'

'I couldn't stop him.' A sudden pleading, urgent look in her eyes. 'Please believe me.'

'Of course I believe you.' He struggles to control his voice. 'You – invited him in?'

'Do you really want to know it all?' she asks with a weary, blunt tone in her voice. But without waiting, she says: 'He insisted. I knew if I tried to stop him he'd make a scene and I couldn't face it. I thought, perhaps if I offered him something to drink he might – '

'He stayed?'

'He was still here by four o'clock. By then I was so tired I just fell down on the bed. He was going on and on, accusing me of "carrying on" with you, of being a slut, of being cold and nasty to him – oh God, I've been through it so many times already. In the end I told him he could go on drinking and talking as much as he liked, I was going to sleep. That made him mad.'

'So he didn't leave.'

She stacks everything on the table. Shrugs. Turns away. Picks at the ribbons on the curtains, and lets go again. At the approach of winter the shrubs outside have lost their leaves; the light inside is no longer green but colourless, bleak, disinterested.

'Did he hurt you?'

'He always has to prove how strong and manly he is.' She comes back and lights a cigarette, blows out smoke.

He moves towards her to put his arms around her but she discourages him with a small shake of her head.

To his surprise there is the hint of a smile – a rather wan one, admittedly – on her face when she looks up after a while. 'The weird thing is that in spite of everything I felt *sorry* for him,' she says. 'Can you understand that? Sometimes I think I must be mad. But I can't help it. Let's face it, I did give him a hard time, I never really cared about him, I always let him down. I remember thinking, as he was panting and raging away – God, has it ever occurred to you how ridiculous the postures of sex are? – I was thinking that, perhaps, in a way, I owe him this bit of consolation for the misery I've made of his life.'

'After what he's done to *you*?!'

'I'm not sure.' She seems amazingly composed now. 'In a sense he never really touched me. I just let it happen, let it pass. Not just the other night, but always. The way the shadow of a cloud passes through a landscape. It leaves no mark, no imprint, nothing.'

'*I* know how much he's hurt you.'

She comes to him. This time she allows him to put an arm round her; but her body remains unyielding, tight, collected. 'I don't know how to explain it,' she says. 'Perhaps I shouldn't even try. Just listen. And if you don't understand, then don't ask questions. For I have no answers.' Her eyes demand a solemn promise; he gives it; she goes on: 'In Cape Town I went out with a student in my class. Herman. We got along quite well. Which was something of a suprise, I suppose, for usually I only fell for men much older than me. There was no question of being in love with him. But he was, well, not bad. Trouble was, he was madly, obsessively, ridiculously in love with *me*. Always tried to drag me to bed. But I refused. I think I felt vulnerable. No, that doesn't sound right. What bothered me was that I got the impression he believed if only he could get me to bed I would be "his", he could stake a claim to me, he would "possess" me. And if I allowed him to have his way he *might* have possessed me. Do you understand? But then things changed. I met somebody else; we clicked; I slept with him. When Herman found out I thought he'd kill me. Kicked up such a row I could only stare at him in disgust. I felt nothing for him, not even anger. I couldn't care less about him any more. I suppose I no longer saw him as a threat – except "threat" isn't the right word either. Anyway, *then* I could go to bed with him.' She looks at him. She leans her head on his shoulder. 'You see why I wrote you that note, prof? It's no use. I'm bad news. I cannot complicate your life with mine.'

'I'm not discouraged so easily.'

She seems almost let down by his answer. As if threatened by his embrace she shakes off his arm and goes to the bed in the corner where she sits down, her back against the rough whitewashed wall, hugging her knees. Looking straight at him – but with the safe distance between them! – as if to check his reactions very carefully, she says: 'My best friend at UCT was a girl who'd also been to school with me. Irene. We'd known each other since we were fourteen or fifteen. Neighbours. Her father was a dominee. Which probably accounted for her wildness. Everybody regarded her as a "problem child". Rebellious as hell. But brilliant. And beautiful. At university we'd sometimes get together for a "spree". Especially on weekends. It was usually her idea, but I never needed much coaxing. She'd come over and just say: "Hell, *jong*, I need some fun tonight. Shall we go out and check the male talent?" Right, and then we'd go pub-crawling till the wee hours. Just for kicks, really. It was a game more than anything else. Like playing chicken, you know. More often than not we finally staggered back tired and drunk and laughing our heads off. I mean, she wasn't a nympho or anything. God, no. But of course' – she is watching him very intently now, nervously – 'there were times when it turned sour, when it got bad, when there was no way out. That would sober us up for a while, sometimes for months. But sooner or later she'd come back, with that same look in her eyes, and say:

"Well, how about it?" '

This time she breaks off very suddenly. Her eyes are still on him, but there is a darker look in them now.

'Why am I telling you all these things?' she asks. 'You must be disgusted with me.'

'I love you,' he would like to say. But he doesn't: that is not adequate, not now. He goes to her and kneels beside the bed, clutching her ankles. 'Did you really think you could scare me off? Why are you trying to warn me, to persuade me you're a witch or something?'

'I'm a nut case.'

'Makes two of us.'

She cannot help smiling. 'You're such a model of self-assurance, your life is so organized. How can you stand someone like me?'

'It's just because you don't know about all the confusion and fear and self-loathing and God knows what else in *me*.'

And he begins to tell her –

Each character in a story, in my experience, ultimately wells up from a single sharp image, a flash of memory, a sensual impression. Innumerable other things may eventually combine with it, of course. But that initial vital shock must be there. In Melissa's case: the girl running in the wood with her long hair flying, caught in the sunset, with the great dog; and the death-cries of hadidas above. An image so vivid – a red-hot coal to the touch – I have not yet attempted to translate it into an 'episode'. In Philip's case the character derives from a memory. And it is this recollection he now finally shares with her.

Claire. In the turbulence of Paris, 1968.

The city seemed relaxed when he arrived in late April, unfurling itself in the balmy days of early spring. It went to his head so much he couldn't bring himself to sleep, not wanting to miss anything, day or night. Those late nights he wandered through deserted streets past cafés with chairs up-ended on small round tables inside; isolated lovers or small knots of people in bistros that stayed open late; groups of boisterous youngsters drinking beer or playing pinball machines; kissing couples on green benches on the pavements; a *clochard* sleeping on a metro grille like a bundle of rags abandoned in disgust; bits of papers scurrying in the late-night breeze; traffic lights monotonously changing colour; a solitary young girl slumped on a bench, yawning hopelessly; a group of revellers clustered round their cars saying their good-byes, their voices ringing too loudly in the dark emptiness among the buildings. How rapidly it all changed. In the early days of May, the first clashes between police and students. The ever-increasing demonstrations, walls covered in slogans, streets ringing with chanting voices ('CRS – SS!' *'Libérez nos camarades!'* 'Gestapo! Gestapo! Gestapo!'). Poor old white-haired Aragon trying to placate the massed students at a sit-in in front of the Sorbonne (*'Cinquante ans de trahison ne s'expliquent pas en dix minutes!'*). Cohn-Bendit. And suddenly it was a global issue: Vietnam entered into it, and Prague, and Warsaw, in a cumulative rage directed against anything that smacked of imperialism, of a 'system', as an entire generation exploded in revolt against obsolete forms, clamouring for the new world they so passionately believed in and which, in those heady spring days, suddenly, brilliantly, seemed to loom as a reality. (This was the massive movement De Gaulle subsequently dismissed so contemptuously as a collection of 'groupuscules'; he paid the price, of course.)

And then the night of Saturday the tenth.

He'd had a meal with his friends, in the rue du Dragon. They went home after it was over; he wandered off on his own. Coming back, it must have been close to midnight, he found the Boulevard St Germain flooded with people and blockaded by the police, so he took a short cut along the rue Monsieur le Prince. But where it opened into the Boulevard St Michel it was chaos. The evening's big peaceful demo from the Place Denfert-Rochereau had ended there, blocked by a phalanx of police. Spontaneously – it seemed – the decision was taken to dig in and occupy the Latin Quarter. By the time he arrived there barricades were going up in all the streets. Unbelievable organization: hundreds of students (some of them couldn't have been older than fourteen or fifteen) lining up to dig up cobblestones and pass them on to the barricades; or stripping building sites, uprooting traffic signs and felling trees. An air of serious industry – yet the atmosphere was exuberant, it seemed like one great carnival. He couldn't get through to his friends' apartment and had to make a tortuous detour, across several barricades, along the rue d'Ulm, down the rue de l'Estrapade, past a massive wall of police cordoning off the rue St Jacques directly opposite a barricade in which a car was tightly ensconced. Here and there red or black flags began to sprout. All the time police reinforcements were approaching from the direction of the Seine, massing behind the front lines of the CRS. Outbreaks of song, the 'Marseillaise', the 'Internationale'. Some of the students had transistor radios on which one could follow the progress of the talks going on between Cohn-Bendit and the rector of the Sorbonne. Towards one o'clock there was a surreal interruption: a door on the opposite side of the rue St Jacques opened and out came a lame man in a wheel chair, into the no man's land between the forces of law and order and the barricades. He moved swiftly to the middle of the street where he stopped to salute, first the police, then the student crowd, before he proceeded to the other side where another door opened to receive him. At that moment came the news: the negotiations had broken down. Now it was war. It began a little way down in the rue Le Goff with a spectacular volley of flares fired to illuminate the swarming scene, followed by salvo upon salvo of tear-gas and heaven knows what else. Within minutes everything was shrouded in dirty yellow clouds of gas that caused even the police momentarily to fall back. Then they regrouped, the solid wall of helmets and *matraques* and shields parting only to let through the black water-cannons. An awning in front of a green-grocer's in the rue St Jacques took fire; soon red flames came leaping through the yellowish fog. Cars in the rue Gay-Lussac behind them exploded, hit by police fire-bombs. This inspired the crowds on the barricades to set fire to other vehicles. The whole neighbourhood seemed to rock and shudder under the explosions. From the radios – blaring on forlornly in the din – came urgent calls for doctors, ambulances, medicine, helpers, as wounded or hysterical people were dragged into the buildings on either side of the streets where the fight was raging. Standard police tactics: select a victim, spray gas into his face until he falls down, then attack him with matraques before dragging him off to the long line of *paniers de salade* waiting ominously behind the troops. Even ambulances were turned away. Red Cross teams coming in to save victims were themselves attacked ferociously by the police. Daylight, when at last it came, revealed a devastation difficult to believe, with streets dug up and reduced to rubble, blackened carcasses of burnt-out cars obstructing the way, sobbing girls wandering among the torn-down debris of barricades, people with head wounds lying sprawled along the sidewalks to be kicked or dragged off by squads of police. In all the doorways stood bunches of bleary-eyed, gawking people, women in curlers and flapping night gowns, men in striped pyjamas, watching as rows of young prisoners, hands on their heads, came shuffling past, under police guard, to be thrown into the vans. Down the rue Gay-Lussac came a solitary policeman, long after the others had withdrawn, shouting hoarsely, beside himself, lashing out with his baton at whatever came in his way – automobile wrecks, piles of rubble, corrugated iron shutters, railings, grey walls; disappearing at last round the corner of the rue Le Goff.

(Later in the day, the parade of the bourgeoisie arriving in their cars or by taxi from the suburbs to come and see for themselves the destruction they had heard about: rotund little men in Sunday suits, dressed-up madames with gloves, soft fat etiolated children picking their way in polished shoes among the rubble, the felled once-beautiful chestnut trees, the charred wrecks, the shattered shop windows, the twisted remains of traffic signs.)

It was in the midst of all this, that night, that he met Claire, her eyes streaming from tear-gas, and brought her home to recover; before they went out again, lured by the terror in the streets, into what seemed like the apocalypse, caught in the fascination of violence in which there lurked, even while they furiously tried to deny it, Yeats's terrible beauty. And only after it had subsided, in the light of the new day, did they trudge back through the devastated streets to the building where he lived, and up to his room on the sixth floor, at the far end of the small courtyard with the single tall chestnut tree (the riot of birds in that early morning).

It lasted for more than a month. Together they lived through it all: the great strikes paralysing the city, the mounds of rubbish piling up along the streets, the fetid smell of decay, the non-stop oratory in the Odéon (*'L'imagination prend le pouvoir'*), the sit-ins, the demos, the occupation of the factories, the people on bicycles after the petrol stations had closed down, the crowds overflowing inside the Sorbonne (the statue of Richelieu carrying a red drape on the arm) – like those massive paintings of the popular tribunals in the first Revolution – the measles of graffiti and posters (*'Plus je fais la révolution, plus j'ai envie de faire l'amour'*).

'Six weeks, in all, without any restraint, without having to think about tomorrow or anything else, six weeks of boundless, ecstatic lovemaking and laughter and talk and roaming about and believing in the new world dawning around us. And then it was over. I had to go back, take up my life again. Be responsible and mature and sensible again.'

'I don't see why,' Melissa says, disturbed. 'If you loved her so much, if she loved you, why couldn't you have stayed together?'

'It just wasn't possible, Melissa. Everything was against us.'

'No! Not if you were really in love.'

'Claire came from Martinique.'

'So?'

'Don't you understand? In South African terms she was "coloured". We could never come back here together.'

'And you couldn't stay there?'

It is a long time before he dares to look up at her. 'That is where I failed her. Don't you understand? When I had to make the choice I was a coward. Through her eyes, through loving her, I made the first real discovery of what was happening in this place, of what "my people" were responsible for. That was what brought the change in me: it wasn't an abstract, theoretical process of political growth, but the shock of reality.' He presses his head against her knees. 'And in spite of all that – when the moment of choice came – I left her. Not because there was any great cause I wanted to get involved in. Not because of any romantic sense of "destiny" or whatever. But simply because I didn't have the guts to stay with the woman I loved more than anything else in my life.'

'And then you came back?'

He nods. 'I think I'd made up my mind never again to get so involved. I couldn't face it, I would lose whatever wholeness I had left. Then I met Greta. I fell in love. In a way the years we have been together has strengthened it. All right, so much of it may become a habit. But one acquires something at the same time, a kind of inner peace, trust, a readiness to forgive, compassion perhaps. Only, you see, it's like living on a high plateau. There are no dangerous cliffs you can fall down. But the problem is: once you exclude hell, you also exclude heaven.'

'There have been other women in your life.'

'Of course. But never seriously. In a way it was a game. To allow a bit of adventure back into my life from time to time. Without taking any risks. Until I met you.'

She looks at him, making no attempt either to avoid him or to encourage him.

'You are the first person I've met since Claire who has made me *want* to take risks again. To put everything at stake. Even if it is unbearable. To love *is* unbearable. You understand that?'

'Yes.'

'May I come back?'

She barely nods. There are tears in her eyes. They do not touch.

(An interim episode: I visualize him in his study at home – high-ceilinged, two walls lined with bookshelves, an old-fashioned roll-top desk, a spare table stacked with books and files, everything in immaculate order; a collection of sharpened pencils and ball-point pens, blue and red, lined up with military precision on the desk – late at night, under the angle-poise lamp, leafing through a pile of old theatre and opera programmes. Two full cycles of the *Ring*; Glyndebourne, Bayreuth. A season of the Berlin Philharmonic in Amsterdam. Segovia at the Pleyel in Paris, the only concert he and Claire went to together.

Greta brings him a cup of cocoa. 'Will you be late?' she asks. 'A while,' he says. 'I'm going to East London tomorrow,' she says, looking back from the door. 'Shopping with Elaine. She asked me this morning, I forgot to tell you. We probably won't be back before dark.' 'Good,' he says, both surprised and pleased: she hasn't indulged herself like this in years. 'I'm sure you'll enjoy the outing.')

In the morning there's a committee meeting that cannot be cancelled at such short notice (Lucas Wilson is involved too; one cannot afford to antagonize him even further, not with the deanship coming up soon and the powerful lobby Lucas commands). Which leaves them only with the afternoon; yet even that seems like a gift from the gods. Normally they have, at most, an hour or two.

He will pick her up at two. Perhaps they can drive to the sea. Or go for a walk in 'her' wood. A whole glorious endless afternoon.

But as he comes downstairs from the bedroom, a few minutes to two – freshly bathed, shaved, in casual shirt and trousers – the doorbell rings.

Here I can work in Milton Thaya's most recent visit, every detail of it just as it happened. I was at work when he turned up two days ago. As always, he chose the largest easy chair, the only one which can accommodate him without too much overflow; two buttons on his generous stomach missing, the lenses of his gold-rimmed glasses opaque with fingermarks and dust.

'Well! So! What's news?' Not waiting for an answer, he went on, his stomach trembling with repressed laughter: 'Why's it so quiet in this place today?'

'One needs peace and quiet to get some work done.'

'Jeez, no, that would give me the creeps. People got to be together, that's the fun of it, man. I mean, hell, suppose the SB were to come in here and drag you away, no one will even know about it.'

I knew what he meant. Before the Emergency I'd been to his shanty in the township. Eleven or twelve people crammed together in two small rooms, visitors coming and going all the time, each of them greeted with a handshake and a blow between the shoulder blades and a great burst of shouting and laughter. And it was in that cramped little place that he'd studied for his degree (no electricity; only paraffin lamps at night; a small black Dover stove in the kitchen), in between teaching and his innumerable other 'projects', weathering with unfailing generosity all the blows fate seemed to reserve so specially for him: his father died (tuberculosis), one of his sisters was assaulted, his brickyard was robbed several times, every now and then he was done out of all his money by strangers whose transparent sob-stories he couldn't resist. The Emergency has curtailed our contact. But here he was back, as buoyant as ever.

After the second cup of coffee he explained the reason for his visit. His *buti* – who might be anybody from a real brother to a superficial acquaintance: to Milton the whole of humanity is family – had picked up problems with the SB. Vuyani. Still a youngster, eighteen, nineteen: it was only last year he'd gone to the bush to become a man (I remember; I had to fork out a substantial amount for the goats they required). After that he'd joined COSAS. Became quite a kingpin, as far as I could make out, what with the dizzying turnover in the leadership as a result of SB raids and detentions. No matter that in recent weeks he'd actually been a peacemaker ('Look, we all know black education is shit, but what'll become of us with no education at all?'). During a mass meeting early in May he led his group from the soccer field, refusing to join the boycott. But once the SB get it into their rigid little minds that a person is an agitator nothing can ever get it out again. 'So now', said Milton, 'they've decided he was the gang-leader when they burnt down that school two nights ago. They spent this whole morning at my place asking about him. I told them it was nonsense, Vuyani left for Cradock in the afternoon before the school was attacked, but no go, man. They looking for him and if they get him, I tell you, we going to have another death in detention.'

'I'm sure you're exaggerating, Milton.'

'They took him in for a few weeks last December. You should have seen him when he was released. And now they looking for culprits. I wish I could take you up to Tantyi township right now and show you. Army cordon right round the place, and the police moving from house to house, taking in all the kids. And it's just: "Where's Vuyani? Where's Vuyani?" all the time.'

'You sure he's in Cradock?'

'I phoned my people there early this morning and they said he's OK.'

'What can *I* do, Milton?'

'I don't know. But you white. I'm black. I can't do nothing. You just got to help me.'

How many times has he given me that line? Only, usually it concerns a (non-refundable) loan, a camera, a typewriter, a testimonial, the use of my car. This time it clearly was more serious.

There was no way out of it; I had to leave Milton behind and pay a call to SB headquarters, following Milton's instructions. An unmarked door on the top floor of the OK shopping centre. Actually there are two doors, Milton warned me. One leads to a toilet. ('So no matter which one you take, you land in the shit.') No bell. You simply have to knock, and then wait, hoping someone will open. It is only when the door is opened and you see the steel grille inside that you realize this is a different world, another kind of space altogether, which has nothing in common with that outside where children are running about, and newspaper vendors call out, and women come past pushing supermarket trolleys, and students chat on the corner, and arm- or legless beggars stretch out their hand expecting charity.

'I'm sorry,' said the colonel in the safari suit, helpful, remote, 'but you really are on a wild-goose chase. Where did you get that information?'

'I have friends in the townships.'

'Well, it isn't my job to give you advice, but the townships aren't all that safe these days.'

'I believe Vuyani has been trying to make it a safer place.'

'Then he doesn't have anything to fear, does he?'

'I've been told that he is being blamed for burning down the school.'

'Why don't you just leave that to us? We'll track down the criminals, I give you my word for it.'

'I have no doubt about that, colonel. But what I'm trying to tell you – '

'If that really is all you wanted to discuss – ' He got up. 'We'll bear in mind what you have told us. In the mean time I'm sure you can use your time much more constructively.'

His hidden warning did not escape me.

What next? A call to Molly Blackburn (who was still alive at the time). A letter to the minister.

'I'm not very optimistic, Milton,' I told him at last. 'All we can do now is wait.'

'I'll make sure the message gets through to Vuyani.'

'But it's dangerous, Milton. For you too.'

'So? That's life, man.'

By that time the afternoon is almost over; and when Philip reaches Melissa's room there is no sign of her. It is hardly surprising. It is past five: how could he have expected her to wait patiently from two o'clock? But he must find her!

The campus is deserted. Not a soul in the Arts Building. Her office locked up, the whole floor in darkness.

For a while he drives aimlessly up and down the streets. The sun is sinking. Another hour or so and Greta will be back. This whole day, bursting with glorious promise like an overripe exotic fruit, down the drain.

There is one last possibility (why hasn't he thought of it before?), which sends him out of town, off the main road, uphill against the low mountain slope which leads to the straggling woods above. He leaves his car beside the road, watching in the rear-view mirror the dust subside, gleaming golden in the late sunlight. Which way now? This is Melissa's wood, and he's a stranger here. Low dark drifting thunderclouds make it seem later than it is.

Tentatively he walks towards the nearest copse. The warm smell of eucalyptus. But here, he knows, he will get lost. (He should have brought bread crumbs, or pebbles, he thinks, like Hansel and Gretel.) Is it voices he hears coming from the road? Hurriedly he returns through the trees and sees a rickety donkey cart approach from the thickets along the slopes above. Two thin mangy little donkeys are straining against the weight pushing from behind. They are harnessed with thongs and wire; one has bleeding sores where the wire has cut into his neck. The cart is piled high with firewood, two or three small boys perched on top like meerkats (four or five others skipping along beside and behind it). There is also, Philip sees as they approach, the body of a gaunt old man stretched out on the branches. His clothes in tatters. Tufts of grizzly beard. And, most upsetting, an ugly red smear of blood on the side of the head. He shows no sign of life.

'What happened?' said Philip, stepping from among the trees at the side of the narrow road.

To his surprise the inert body jerks to life again as the old man sits up, glowering, his face breaking into furrows of rage as he shouts: '*Hamba!* Go away! Go away!' Fumbling among the branches he pulls out an axe which he brandishes in his stick-like arms like a sword: 'Go away, *mlungu! Hamba suka!*' And suddenly the attitudes of the boys also change. Some stop in their tracks, ready to scatter into the wood; but others, the older ones, grab sticks from the cart, and one stoops to pick up a stone.

'Wait, wait!' calls Philip, startled by their animosity. 'I only wanted to help.' Cautiously he begins to back in among the trees again.

For a while they seem ready to attack. Then the old man groans feebly, struggling to remain upright – a hieratic posture, like a praying mantis – before he presses a gnarled, skeletal hand against the bleeding wound on his head, and collapses on the load of wood. This seems to decide them. With wild cries and furious lashings the *kwedini* get the wretched little donkeys going again and they continue their wobbly trot downhill.

At the back of the cart, draped over a protruding branch, hangs the long thin form of a snake, its head a pulpy red mass coated with dust and twigs.

More upset than he would like to acknowledge (what on earth has happened? Why were they so hostile? Is the old *mkulu* dying?), he looks around him, uncertain about how to proceed.

The sun reappears through a patch of thunder clouds, suddenly lighting up the whole wooded hillside as if it has been set on fire. But it is late, late. And he has yet to find her.

Moving on blindly, pressed on by an inexplicable urgency as if his very life depends on finding her, he stops only to pick up a stout straight branch and proceeds to strip off the side twigs and the bark (that snake – ). Remembering – suddenly, but why? – a small flute he once cut from a red reed among the rushes in the *vlei* near the sheep kraal on their farm when he was small. Thinking – and smiling at his own foolishness – that if only this stick could be another flute he might blow on it and call her to him with the magic of its sound.

A massive cloud obscures the sinking sun again. Soon, soon it will be dark. Another memory: those endless afternoons in his boyhood when – alone, or with a few black boys to help him – he had to bring home the sheep; and that one day when three or four had strayed and his father sent him back in the gathering dusk to find them. 'If you dare come home without them I'm going to give you the hiding of your life.' His mother tried to intervene: 'But Hans, you can't do that, there's a storm coming. He's only a child.' His father in that implacable voice: 'He's a boy. For some reason God saw fit to give me three daughters and only one son. How can I bring him up to be a sissy?' It proved impossible to track down those recalcitrant sheep, it was already too dark. Scared to go home and face his father he spent the night outside. The sounds: a night-jar; the jackals crying like lost souls in hell. And then the storm broke. He nearly died from fear and he was delirious when they found him the next morning. After that, in disgust, his father gave up trying to 'make a man' of him; he was left to his shame. And his mother was the only one who understood and cared, who shielded him, and kept her faith in him and his studies. (Then came those holidays on the dream-farm where the peacocks pierced the night with their dire shrieks.) Even after his father died there was no respite. The problem was: he wasn't dead when they buried him. For years and years that stern face, that voice dark with scorn and disappointment, has continued to haunt him. How many years does it take for a father to die within a man? How long to make one's peace with the dead and with oneself? Has that brooding, grieving old man finally been laid to rest, or will he always be revived in quests like this? (Will the old black man be dead by the time the cart reaches the township tonight?)

Moving through a clearing in a patch of Port Jackson willow he hears a rustling among the fallen twigs and leaves littering the path. A snake? On edge, remembering that limp shape swaying, green, behind the cart, he brings down his stick where he has heard the rustling. Silence. Cautiously, he clears away the undergrowth, stepping back when he sees a minute angry head, a flickering tongue. But it isn't a snake, only a lizard, its smooth small body split open by the blow. Ashamed, revolted, he kneels down to watch the tiny creature writhing in its long final agony until, after a last shudder, it lies still before his feet. Involuntarily he puts out a guilty hand to touch it, but draws it back quickly when he discovers a drop of blood on his finger. The fierce little dragon face stares blindly up at him.

God, he thinks wryly, embarrassed, through what other ridiculous dangers must I still battle my way before I find her?

Once more the sun emerges, poised now on the rim of the hills. Another moment and it will be gone. The light is an unearthly blue. The clouds turn red. The entire woodland is briefly, dazzlingly, illuminated by the dying light, each tree a tongue of flame leaping up towards the sky, individual branches blazing like swords. Odin's fire.

A stinging, itchy feeling in his finger. Instinctively he puts it in his mouth, remembering too late: the blood; and pulls a face.

High above the hills a flock of hadidas come winging towards him, and past. Three – four – six – eight – nine of them. Their blood-curdling cries. Except, suddenly, it sounds to him as if they're screaming: 'There! There! There!' And as he follows them in their flight he sees her at the edge of the next stretch of wood – dark pines soughing in a mere intimation of wind – as she runs along, fleet-footed, lightly, her hair streaming after her like liquid gold. She stops, bends over, picks up a stick or stone – it is too far to see – and hurls it away from her; barking in frenzied glee the big dog chases ahead to catch it and bring it back. Only a moment, then she disappears among the trees and is gone, as if she hasn't been there at all.

In the distance he hears, almost subliminally, a droning of bees.

'Melissa!' he shouts. 'Melissaaaa!'

There is no answer. Only, very far away now, the sound of the hadidas as they veer over the wood, their hideous grey necks and long curved beaks stretched out: an ancient sound, older than human memory.

There are other bird sounds too. Clear bell-like calls, and cooings, chortlings, twitterings, as if the whole wood is briefly transmuted into sound. He is caught in the magic of it, that uncanny light of the setting sun still lasting, persisting. And again it is as if he can understand them, as if they point the way to her.

A bush-dove nearby: 'It is my little girl! It is my little girl!'

'Melissa! Melissa! Melissa!'

At last he finds her. In a clearing in the enchanted forest, surrounded by the flaming trees, on a large flat surface of rock near the edge of an escarpment where the mountain breaks down, she has lain down, quite motionless, her golden hair gleaming like an ancient helmet.

He runs towards her, through the circle of flames – dying away now in a final shudder of light; and then it is dusk, and the sky begins to bleed – calling again: 'Melissa!'

Near by, the Alsatian pricks up his ears, ready to charge; then recognizes Philip and relaxes.

She sits up, smiling, as if she has been expecting him.

'Melissa, I've been looking for you all over.'

'And now that you've found me?'

He sits down beside her. 'Are you angry with me?'

'Why should I be?'

'It was Milton Thaya. He turned up just as I was leaving. A crisis.'

'That means he's come to trust you.'

'But why *today*!' He strikes his stick against the rock; the tip is shattered. The dog jumps up eagerly to catch a piece that whirrs away. 'I was really counting on it.'

'You know there's nothing we can count on. We're not "entitled" to anything, we have no "right" to anything. All we have is the little bit of time we can steal from a day, now and then. That's the whole extent of our freedom.'

'How can you accept it?'

'What difference does it make?'

Fatalism? Cynicism? Nonchalance? No, it isn't that. Isn't it, rather, the attitude of someone existing beyond disillusionment, knowing – believing? accepting? – that nothing, no one, can be trusted ultimately; that the deliverance of the self to others (parents, friends, lovers) must inevitably lead to denial and suffering? (Or is this very suspicion confirmation of how little he truly knows about her?)

'Did you wait all afternoon?'

'When it seemed you weren't coming any more I decided to come out here with Rex. I needed silence.'

'Your room is quiet enough.'

'I'm not talking about an absence of sound.'

Bird-sounds – now peaceful, drowsy, tentative – in the darkening trees around them.

'Listen to them,' she whispers. 'It's sounds like those that make silence possible. They define silence. That's what I'm trying to say.'

'Sometimes I cannot believe that you are so young.'

'I warned you. I'm ancient, really.'

He smiles, holding her. 'You're a stream of water I'd like to dive into.'

'Old-fashioned romantic twaddle.' She kisses him fondly. 'Beware. You'll only break your own reflection.'

'I love you, Melissa. Even though I don't know who you are. There's so little I know when I am with you.'

'There is no mystery. I'm just me.' Dusk is settling on them now; he can hardly make out her face. Almost like a chant (is she reciting something?) she says: 'What you don't know, I'll know for you. If I have your love I'm you.' She looks up. 'That's why I was in need of silence, you see. Without silence one cannot love. Without love you can never be free.'

'Is that what you're looking for?'

She looks past him, into space. 'There *are* only three choices in love, aren't there? Freedom, or madness, or death.'

He gazes at her but she says no more. Something tremendous has happened, he thinks. But what it is still lies beyond the reach of his words. Later, perhaps. Some day. At the moment there is only silence. And the knowledge that nothing can ever, really, be the same again.

The dog is getting impatient to go back. In the deepening darkness they follow him through the silent wood; the birds are asleep now. Only space is left, surrounding them on all sides, endless.

He leads her back to where he has left his car. She turns down a back window to let in fresh air for the dog. (When he gets home he must remember to brush off the hairs, wash off the spittle. Before Greta comes back.)

Youth; age. It's not the age difference as such which weighs on him, he'll think when he is alone again. Almost thirty years separating them: but it's not that. What matters is the simple knowledge that however long the road ahead may be, it must be shorter than what lies behind. There is an end he is aware of. The intimations of immortality are behind him now.

What I should like to introduce here is an episode which happened when my youngest son was three or four years old. His first discovery of death, and my attempt to allay his fears, using a box of matches. In the novel it may function as a personal recollection of Philip's:

It wasn't Grandpa's funeral that brought it home – even though Ma often reminded me of how inconsolably I had sobbed, it isn't part of my own memories – nor the many forms of dying one grows up with on a farm: slaughtering chickens or sheep, finding a dead animal in the veld, my dog bitten by a snake, a black child drowning in the irrigation dam (the straight narrow backs of the other children waiting on the edge; grown-ups gathered in a silent crowd, staring dumbly at the trembling of the wind on the surface, the wails of the women as Pa waded out with the small body). No: it was a leaf. A yellow loquat leaf falling on my head, in the backyard. Ma was gathering eggs, I remember. I asked her why the leaf had fallen from its tree. She said: 'I suppose its time has come.'

'How d'you mean, Ma: its "time"?'

'There's a time for every plant and animal and person. Nothing lasts forever, you know.'

'And you and Pa and me?'

'Same with us. Hand me the basket.'

'And then?'

'Then nothing. Then you're buried and that's that.' (Of course she added a bit about the Lord and going to heaven and children turning into angels or stars, but to me it was beside the point.)

'Then you just lie there?'

'Yes. But you don't know about it, you're *mos* dead. So you needn't worry. Now make sure you close the gate properly, you know Pa gets angry if the hens come out.'

'When will *my* time come, Ma?'

She laughed. 'It's a long way off still.'

'But how long?'

I nagged and nagged until, patient and meticulous as always, she brought a new box of matches from the pantry and came to sit with me on the kitchen floor. She emptied the box on the shiny red tiles and started counting – I remember every minute detail – up to eighty. (The rest she carefully set aside; in those days there were more matches to a box than at present.) Then she put those eighty matches side by side on the floor, in a long straight line. She showed me where I was – third, or fourth, or fifth, or whatever – and explained: 'See? This is where you are now. One for each year. Now look at all the years that are still left – more than you can count. So there's nothing to be scared about.'

I struggled to free myself from her suffocating embrace and returned to the matches, gently moving my finger along the entire length of the line until it reached the final one, the eightieth. And I said: 'But what happens here, Ma? When there's no more left? One day I'll be here.'

'But it's such a long time still.'

'I'll get there. And what then?'

It was, I'm sure, the most terrifying moment of my life. And long after she'd gone back to her work – absent-minded and perturbed, no doubt, otherwise the rest could not have happened – I put all the matches back into their box and went out to the shed where I'd always hidden when I felt the need to be on my own. And there I started striking them, one after the other, all eighty of them, transfixed by the small flicker of each flame against my fingers, and the slow decline of the brave little flare, until it died away. Only after I'd burnt them all up did I go inside for supper.

It was when Pa got up after the meal to fetch the Bible from the sideboard – a chore he always insisted on doing himself – that he stopped in front of the window and exclaimed: 'My God, what's that?'

We all jumped up to see. The shed was on fire. A deep red glow, rapidly changing, as we watched, into a raging blaze. Leaping flames, billowing smoke, casting an eerie light over the whole backyard.

Et cetera.


*'Fire. Violence. Blood. Death. Sometimes I think to be scared of death is a form of self-indulgence.'*

There is no date above this entry in Jane Ferguson's diary. It appears on a separate page at the back, simply headed: *C*. The only sustained piece of dialogue she has recorded:

'*If you move about in the townships the way I do death becomes part of the context, part of one's given, real, world. I'm not only talking about actual violence – assault, rape, police raids, torture, reprisals – but about the daily doses of suffering which are the symptoms of the system. Losing your job because you talked back to the white foreman. Landing in jail because your wife from a distant homeland spent the night with you in your hostel. Seeing your child die because the queue at the clinic was too long. Snarled at or patronized in the post office by a dumb white girl half your age. There are more kinds of death than just dying, Jane.*' Looking at me, almost pleading. '*I wish we could forget about all this, my love, if only for these few days. But I can't. It's not a coat one can take off, not even a skin one can shed. It started as an act of choice, now it's part of my guts.*'

'*How did you first get involved?*' I asked him.

'*It's a long story. I'd just started working for the District Surgeon in Joh'burg. I was called to John Vorster Square one day to examine a detainee. Young chap, eighteen or nineteen. Seems he'd seen police shooting a man in Orlando to death – just like that, for no apparent reason. The man didn't even live there, he'd just arrived to look for lodgings. Anyway, the youngster ran away but in the end he was caught in someone's backyard where he'd tried to hide. They wanted to make sure he wouldn't talk about what he'd seen. Tried to persuade him to make a statement that the dead man had been a terrorist and that he'd fired at the police. He refused. By the time I was called he was in a pretty bad shape. It was my first personal experience of this kind of thing and I can't tell you how shaken I was. Like a kick in the stomach. It's one thing to read about it in the papers, but it's different when you suddenly find yourself face to face with it. But that wasn't the worst: the greatest shock still had to come. It was when I reported the matter to my boss. He just shrugged. "What else do you expect?" he said. "You can't put on gloves when you're dealing with terrorists. The sooner you patch up your bleeding heart, the better your chances for survival in this business." I objected. He lost his cool. In the end he threatened me. Don't rock the boat, he said, we're all in it. So I went over his head and laid a complaint. You can't imagine the shit that caused. The pressure put on me to withdraw the action. That really brought me to the boil. In the end*

I lost the case, "lack of evidence". Lost my job too, of course. From that moment my whole life changed. Black people just turned up on my doorstep. All kinds of personal problems. Some came specially to tell me they wanted to be friends with me. Took me to their houses. I spent more nights in the townships than at home. A whole new world opened up to receive me. Alice through the looking glass. I tell you, on this side of the wall people haven't the faintest idea of what goes on "over there". But it's exhausting, believe me. Every waking moment you're exposed to suffering: just the endless pain that goes with being black in a place like this. And there's so little one can do. Save a life here, patch up a broken leg, comfort a widow, work in the unions, join a march, lead a deputation, land in jail – then start all over again.'

'How do you survive, Chris? Do you ever have a moment's rest?'

His sudden crooked smile. 'Don't worry. I assure you, if I had the choice, I'd do the same thing again. Because it's worth every exhausting instant. A party in a township – a quiet talk with a man you didn't know from Adam the day before and who all of a sudden is hugging you like a close friend – a meeting – an impromptu game of soccer – the laughter, the jokes, the generosity, the friendship, the shared tears and anger and defeat and sometimes success – I tell you, I won't exchange it for anything. A guy may have only a crust of bread in his house but he'll share it with you. If you need a place to sleep, someone will offer you his bed and sleep on the floor himself. There's a togetherness, a kind of infectious faith in the future which goes beyond anything I've ever known on the "white" side.' A silence. He shook his head. 'But it's changing. It's changing fast. You should see them. Ordinary decent people caught between their own black policemen and the angry youngsters who reject them for having consented through their silence to be turned into victims. And those kids, the new generation. They're not scared of anything, not even of death. They have nothing to lose. They're beyond language. Violence is the only articulation they've been left with.'

'I know so little about it, actually,' I confessed. 'I mean, really know. One reads the papers, of course, but it seems so remote. When I listen to you I begin to feel guilty about everything I've always liked about my own life.'

'It's not you, Jane. It's all of us. Damned to privilege, sentenced to comfort, imprisoned in our own whiteness. Not caring, or even knowing, about what's happening to "them". Jesus, my love, how did *we ever get into this mess of "us" and "them"? For God's sake, we're all in it together. We're all "us". It's like being deprived of one's own shadow: we of them, they of us. You know what really happens when one loses one's shadow? – it means the sun has set, the light has gone out. We're all groping in the dark. Will we ever find each other again?' A pause. A sigh. 'Apartheid.' And again: 'Apartheid. The great either/or. Never the whole. Apartheid. Love gone wrong.'*

'No prof, one must go further than Saussure. In his paradigmatic category each word in the sentence "displaces" all the other possibilities that *might* have operated there. But we tend to forget that this displacement is never absolute. It's not just either/or. All the others still resound in the one which actually materializes, like vibrating strings. The totality of language vibrates in every word; in every word language itself is at stake. Like – what do they call it? – "white noise". And even more than language, the sayable. Because it includes what Wittgenstein called the "unsayable". In every word silence reverberates. It is a terribly dangerous game in which nothing is ever unambiguous or final or "stated".'

There are two clearly defined movements in the story told by Jane Ferguson in her novella *A Sense of Occasion*. In the week during which the relationship between the two main characters develops in their hotel by the sea two phases can be distinguished, both placed under pressure. After this week which the initially nameless young woman spends on the coast (it is only during the second half of the story that she and the man are given names, Ilse, Stephen) she must return to her inland town to get married: she practically grew up with the man she is to wed, the two families have been friends for years, ever since their primary-school days it has been tacitly assumed that they are 'meant' for one another. But the effect of the pressure on the first half of the week is different from that on the second. When they first meet (remember the episode on the beach, the misty twilight, the tide receding and washing out her footprints, the stranger approaching across the virgin sand, her initial panic, the instinct to flee, changing into a curious acceptance of the inevitable as she stands waiting for him)* there is an almost immediate discovery of mutual attraction. For the first time in her life – the situation as such is familiar enough in fiction – she faces something utterly unpredictable. Accustomed always to be regarded (even admired) by everyone as a person with 'common sense', 'reliable', with 'a cool head', she now becomes aware of forces inside herself which threaten to engulf her. It goes beyond rebellion against the idea of getting married after this brief escape, even beyond the fear of a totally predictable future: these can but lend a peculiar urgency to the discovery of the need to live a lifetime in a single week. Whatever may happen afterwards, however monotonous or horrible the rest may be, this week she can – must – break out, do whatever she wants to, taste everything, try everything, risk everything. This week is hers. She must live it to the hilt, challenge her own possibilities to the utmost. The immemorial, romantic dream of total escape, the island, the encapsulated paradise, that frozen eternal moment in which man and woman and fruit and serpent are caught, motionless and achingly beautiful, in some early Renaissance painting. To each other they are without history, weightless, even nameless. He knows nothing about her, nor she of him. All that is relevant is this given moment. Except for the point, the still point,/ There would be no dance, and there is only the dance.

Where, when, how does the shift occur? Reading the manuscript I found much of the magic of the story precisely in the almost imperceptible nature of the transition: the mere fact that they come to know one another, that their knowledge expands, the loving and breathless accumulation of detail, the exchange of dreams, excessive wishes, memories, possibilities, acquire a weight which slowly wells up from inside until the drop must fall.

The moment arrives when he is forced to confess: he is married.

---

* Page 18.

What difference can it make? They are already conditioned to accept that there can be no sequel to their story: their genesis, like the Biblical one, will forever be contained within these seven days, no more. She will get married; he already is. Such facts belong to another dimension altogether. And yet it is not so simple. Not the fact of his being married can influence their lives, but the fact that it becomes *known* to them, and that this knowledge informs their island existence. It gives a name to what exists between them. Suddenly it is a 'relationship', it is an 'affair'. Through the intrusion of language this experience can now be compared to others. It can be defined, circumscribed. A tone of desperation enters into it: What is going to become of us? How can we return to our separate lives pretending this hasn't happened? In the beginning no questions obtruded; now calculations and decisions are imposed on them. They are surrounded, invaded by meaning. What started as a process of creation now turns out to contain the germ of its own destruction. Decay sets in.

(A small episode in the novella in which Ilse subtly – with carefully controlled obliqueness – illuminates the shift involves her recollection of her first orgasm:

*One of my most intimate memories. I was still in primary school. We lived in a house on a steep incline. Approaching from the hillside above our house on my bicycle I had to calculate very swiftly and carefully the exact moment to veer left into our narrow driveway without either losing my balance or hitting one of the gate posts. On that particular day I suddenly became aware of 'something' happening to me. I had no idea at all of what it was, there was no name I could give it, I only knew there was something strange going on, a kind of madness welling up inside me. I thought it was some kind of attack coming on, although I'd never experienced it before. The bike was going faster and faster and I could do nothing to control it. My eyes were wide open, but I wasn't conscious of seeing anything. I couldn't even call for help. And then, just as inexplicably, it subsided, it was over. By that time I was right at the bottom of the hill. Shaky, still panting, I got off, and slowly started pushing the bike back up the hill. When I got home I shut myself up in my room, just lying there on my bed, staring at the blank ceiling. Feeling – what? I don't know. Suffused with a nameless excitement, a kind of afterglow, a kind of guilt. There was no one I dared discuss it with. Only years later, when I learned the word for it, I realized what had happened, and then it caused an extraordinary feeling of being doubly displaced. I was transported back to the day it had happened (which nevertheless remained unattainable in time and space, since I wasn't really 'there'); and at the same time propelled forward from that day to the subsequent discovery of the word. And these two impulses seemed continually just to elude each other: the experience was too early; the word too late. I was neither wholly 'here' nor ever adequately 'there'. A kind of suspended existence, somewhere in between (but between what and what?). And it occurred to me that one is almost never where one is. Zeno's arrow. Part of you is always somewhere else. You so seldom catch up with yourself. Language keeps you at a distance. And perhaps the only truly memorable moments in life are those rare, precious instants when you truly are where you are – knowing you are there – containing within yourself the whole of yourself and of your knowledge of yourself.)*

Futurity breaks into their present; pastness gnaws at it. ('What are you thinking about?' 'Nothing.' 'You're thinking of him.' 'You're thinking of her.') You cannot say you love me and then let me go. But it was you yourself who said: Let's plunge into this one week as if nothing else has ever existed, will ever exist again. Hold me. Don't let me go. Promise you won't abandon me.

Because in itself this moment is so fleeting it needs to grope for reassurance in notions of immortality. Time *infected* with immortality. Eating the forbidden fruit is to enter time, to enter history, to submit to meaning.

'Look, I don't want you to think I have any doubts about the quality of the story,' Charles Ferguson told me the day he brought me the diary. 'But for heaven's sake don't try to read too much into it. I mean, it's a *story*, nothing more. Jane was always writing things. Even as a little girl she used to bring me her poems and stuff. Wonderful imagination the child had. And the dreams she had at night and could recall, in detail, in the morning! All I'm trying to say is don't look for too much autobiography in *A Sense of Occasion*. After all there's a world of difference between Jane and the girl in the book.'

'And yet,' I said, 'I hope you won't mind my saying so, but in the end she did exactly what Ilse had done in the story, didn't she?'

'But that was the wrong way round. Life imitating art.'

'All right, I promise you I'll keep my perspective. After all, I'm a writer myself.'

'Instead of searching for clues,' he said, as if still not quite satisfied with my attitude, 'I think you should simply accept that her meeting with de Villiers – and the shocking outcome of it, of course – drove her back to writing. You should read it the way one interprets a dream. And I'm sure you realize what a dicey business *that* can be.'

The bodies of two lovers fitting each other perfectly, every contour and inlet of the one matched by its complement in the other. Like the two halves of the original *symbolon*: the stone the ancient Greeks used to split so that each of two friends or relatives could keep one: and when they were parted and one of them wished to send a private message to the other, it would be accompanied by his half of the symbolon to guarantee the authenticity of the message. *Symbolon*: symbol: the bringing together of two halves, one close at hand, the other from afar, the abstract and the concrete, the matching of opposites.

There is another connotation of the word which may be illuminating. *Symbolon*: *symbalon*: cymbal: two discs brought together in order to produce a sound (that clanging sound which indicates that one hath not love).

Body and body: I love you.*

In one of his writings Barthes says something to the effect that it is the incompleteness of life which makes writing possible.

This is how I imagine Greta coming back from East London in the early evening: collected, sensible, unsentimental. The shopping outing with her friend has gone well. It was good to get away, to put physical distance between oneself and one's

---

* This warrants further examination, later.

worries, to discuss the situation with an impartial friend. Her mind is made up. She has gained a new insight into her own past: fifteen years of giving up all claims to a life of her own in order to provide a 'happy home' for her husband, to bring up the children, to live vicariously. She has discharged whatever 'duty' may have been expected of her, by whomever. It is not too late to make a new start. Elaine has helped her see that: forty-two, Elaine was divorced a year ago and is now running a successful fashion boutique in town.

Oh, there are pangs in the memories of the years she's been with Philip. The first time he came into the lecture theatre and she looked at him from that eager crowd of first-year students and just knew, calmly and for certain: this is he. The first meal he cooked for her, after he'd patiently waited three years for her to graduate. The wedding, where the minister they'd booked for the service had been called away for an emergency at the last moment so that an old emeritus dominee trembling with Parkinson's disease had to stand in for him; the grey woollen socks he wore with his too-short black pants. And it was only after he'd already monotonously intoned the first paragraph of the funeral ceremony that one of the elders, in a loud whisper, pointed out the mistake, and he switched to the marriage service. The birth of their first child when he'd spent the whole night beside her bed holding her hand and doing his best to hide his tears from her. But there was no point in dwelling on the past, Elaine had made her realize. She could retain the memories and still survive as a person in her own right. In fact, the surest way of damaging the memories would be to sit back and allow Philip to keep on taking her for granted, carrying on with that little blonde bitch and expecting *her* to keep his home in running order.

There need be no humiliating, violent scene, Elaine had impressed upon her. A responsible discussion between two mature people. This is the choice I give you, Philip: it's between her and me. Simple as that. If you choose her, you move out immediately and take the consequences. If it's me, you fire her and make sure she leaves town at the earliest opportunity. At the same time you must realize that if you do choose me it is a different me you'll have to contend with in future. You will have to accept that I have my own needs, my own expectations of life, and that I am no longer just a housekeeper and a nanny. I still love you. But that doesn't mean I'm a masochist. It isn't going to be easy for either of us but I'm willing to give it a go. Provided you consent to be totally honest with me. Otherwise it is an insult and a humiliation which inevitably degrades your own love. So: this is it.*

Assured and competent she steers the small white Mazda down the last incline; the street lights below them are already burning. Beside her, Elaine is smoking in silence.

As she enters the town there is a suggestion of inchoate, massive movement swarming ahead, just out of sight. Only when she comes closer does she recognize it as a crowd of black people coming up from the township on the left and damming beside the street; a low menacing murmur of sound. Further ahead, the flickering bluish and red lights of what may be police vehicles, ambulances, the fire brigade. The wail of a siren. Unexpectedly a few youngsters detach themselves from the

---

* An alternative sequence of thoughts: 'It is not too late to make a new start. It would be wrong to overestimate what is happening to Philip (that is, if my suspicions were true; they may yet turn out to be unfounded). It's "that time of life" for him, that's all. Like a summer cold. Unpleasant and untimely, but nothing desperate.

'Those early romantic memories: the first day he entered the lecture theatre – the years of waiting – the first meal we had together – the first night – the wedding – the birth of our eldest child. All right, so a shift has occurred between then and now; but those moments are still valid, stored somewhere. I know that. Two nights ago, when you were carving the joint at the party, do you know what was really on my mind? Not the thinning of your hair and the first baldness appearing on your crown; not the deep lines habit and middle age have carved beside your mouth. But the youthfulness of your embrace; the memories of the many times I have lain in your arms, snuggling in a safety and a feeling of peace I have known nowhere else in my life.

'I know I'm guilty too, Philip. Just as much as you, I have allowed habit to take over. I have allowed the children to take precedence over the two of us. I have not done enough to keep the sense of adventure alive. But my eyes have been opened in time, and this brief outing with Elaine has helped me to see straight once more. I know I can convince you of my love. Just give me the chance. It will be worth our while again, the way it was when *I* was twenty-three.'

crowd, only yards away, leaping right in front of the car, half-bricks in their raised hands. 'For God's sake, step on it, Greta!' screams Elaine. 'They're going to kill us!' Involuntarily she ducks, and swerves, then charges ahead. The sound of a kierie or a stone thudding against the side of the car. Then they are through. Police vehicles close up the road behind her and there are voices asking whether she's all right. She just keeps on stammering: 'Yes, yes, yes, it's OK.' All she can think of is to get home. Her husband will be waiting for her.

They turn off into the narrow dirt road that winds uphill towards the hotel in the mountains; behind them every yard of their progress is betrayed by a lengthening cloud of dust. Once again the feeling of security as soon as they stop under the trees, now bare in the first chill of winter; the whitish grass of the lawn is littered with brittle leaves. Here they can withdraw from the world, a brief suspension of the everyday.

He would have preferred to spend the morning in her room – they have so little time; it takes a quarter of an hour to get here – but her landlord Jack was working on a friend's broken-down car in the backyard (what with the boycotts he is spending less and less time in his shop), and there was no other way to escape from the racket he made, tinkering and starting and restarting the engine and revving like mad.

As always, they find the lobby deserted and have to press the service bell on the counter for a considerable time before there is any response; then, again as always, people suddenly come tumbling head-over-heels through the inner door, like the entire cast of a farce who have missed their cues. Only the portly old gentleman is missing today; but him they discover on the terrace above the main building, tending the pool. Rather to their surprise they find it topped up, crystal clear, an icy blue. The old man is meticulously skimming fallen leaves from the surface.

'Well?' he asks, obviously proud of himself. 'Getting on, aren't we?'

'Pity it's winter now,' says Philip. 'But after the holidays, I'm sure – '

'It'll be ready and waiting for you. And down there too.' He points towards the main building, then strides off with an air of proud ownership.

They remain behind at the pool staring at the pointlessly clean, irrelevant water. Both of them are conscious of the phrase he used: *After the holidays*. This terrifying emptiness ahead: winter, July. Four weeks to be spent with her family on the farm of her terrible grandmother. But it is not just the emptiness, not just the time. That is a mere surface, leaves on a face of water. Underneath lurks the real dread: the awareness of how vulnerable their love is, how easy to be invaded or denied. It involves so much more than a fear of discovery, of exposure – his wife, friends, colleagues, others, 'them' – for with that in itself one can (must) learn to cope. It is, rather, the consciousness, usually stowed in a back corner of the mind but at moments like this an acute and unavoidable pang, of an emergency within themselves, and between themselves. Something whose entire worth lies in its exclusiveness to them, and which can at any moment be taken from them to be degraded, tarnished, distorted, even turned against them. To love, surely, is to know how dangerous it is to live.

She presses herself against him as if the chill is too much for her. 'How will we ever get through this month?' He presses his face into the wilderness of her hair. (Whence the line that breaks into my thoughts: 'Woman is wilderness enough to wander in – '? Durrell.)

'We'll manage,' he says, doing his best to sound cheerful. 'You know, when I was small, I used to keep a shoe-box in which, three or four weeks before my birthday was due, I'd store a number of pebbles, one for each day ahead, and every evening I'd throw one away; some days, when I grew too impatient, I'd throw away two at a time, but of course that didn't help. Still, sooner or later the waiting would come to an end. It's bound to happen to us too.'

'Four weeks, prof.'

'Twenty-eight days. It's not so much, if you think of it.'

'A lot can happen in twenty-eight days. You may come back and find you don't love me any more.'

He tries to smother her mouth with a kiss, but she breaks

away and walks towards a higher terrace from where one can overlook the valley below, and the distant line of the main road.

'I took my kids home to the township yesterday,' she says suddenly, not looking at him. 'They'd stayed later than usual, and I didn't want them to get into trouble. So I borrowed Jack's car. When I came back I was followed all the way from the township. I couldn't make out who it was; they kept their lights on bright all the way. When I told Jack he thought it might have been the SB. Why do you think they'd do a thing like that?'

He feels his stomach contract. 'They may've been watching Milton Thaya. I'll never forgive him if he lands you in trouble.'

'What kind of trouble? For heaven's sake, my love, we're just helping some kids learn to read and write. That's not breaking any law.'

'Anything can be subversive to them.'

'If they think I can be intimidated so easily they've got a surprise coming.'

'But if something were to happen to you – ? Melissa, they can destroy us.'

Her serene eyes studying him. 'There are things more important than you or me, prof. Our love can't be worth much if it's threatened so easily.'

'But suppose – '

'While those kids are with me, at least their parents – and ironically, even the police! – know they're safe, dammit.' A pause. 'Sometimes I wonder what it must be like to be black in a time like this, and to have children. Suppose I was expecting your child – what would I do, how would I react, knowing this is the world it's going to grow up in?'

He feels a great invisible hand clutching him, crushing him: not the thought of her being pregnant, but the renewed discovery of how precarious their existence together really is.

'I had a strange dream last night,' she interrupts his thoughts. 'It was very upsetting. I actually dreamt we *had* a child, you and I. But you weren't there. We were looking for you everywhere. A little girl. And then, for some reason, I was forced to give her up. She had to be left behind, there was a war on, something like that, I can't remember clearly. She was about two years old, and the whole dream was one long confused leave-taking. I

139

remember pressing her small naked body to me, clinging more and more tightly to her – I was suddenly reminded of it when you were holding me just now – and she couldn't understand what was going on. Somewhere there was a dog in it too, he had to be put down. But why? It's all so confusing.'

From the far side of the tatty lawn a waiter approaches with their tea. He is wearing a spruce new white jacket, but it is too tight for him. For a while he stands looking in all directions, completely at a loss, until they signal to him to leave the tray on the grass.

'And what about December?' she asks suddenly. 'This time it's only four weeks. But in December – what will become of us?'

'It's no use worrying about that now,' he says soothingly. 'Let's just take each day as it comes.'

'I suppose you're right.' She withdraws into that remote calm where nothing can touch her. 'Anyway by December you will have left me long ago.'

'You know very well I won't. Not ever.'

'Everybody grows tired of me.' A sudden shift in her mood. 'For God's sake don't feel sorry for me. I'll survive. Whatever else I may be, I'm *not* a poor little helpless waif!'*

'I never thought you were. Not even that first night I found you in the street and brought you home.'

She smiles, almost with compassion, as if she is the one who is thirty years older; and takes his hand to lead him to the abandoned tray. 'All I want you to realize, prof, is that I'm not "expecting" anything of you, OK? I'm content with what we have and I'm trying my best not to ask questions about what comes after. Even if the pebbles in the box grow fewer and fewer every day because somebody may be throwing away two at a time.'

They sit down on the dry grass beside the tray; she pours for them. On the terraces opposite a gardener in tattered blue overalls is halfheartedly trying to scrape away leaves with a broken rake. In silence, almost ceremoniously, they drink their tea.

---

* Cf. footnote on page 62.

'The first time we came here,' she says, lying back on the dry grass, propped up on her elbows, gazing into space, 'a leaf fell on my head, remember? You said I should have a wish. You know what I'd wish today if I could? To be different from what I am – for you. Not so used, second-hand, shop-soiled. Know what I mean?'

'No, I don't,' he says. 'Surely you don't want to be a virgin again?'

'I wasn't thinking of that.'

'Nothing can corrupt the innocence I love in you.'

'Innocence?! How many times must I tell you that you're an incorrigible romantic?'

Before he can protest there is a flurry of sound in the ramshackle outbuilding opposite the lawns, the one with the doors and windows torn out, the plundered thatch. The gardener has gone inside, presumably in search of other tools, or a wheelbarrow, causing an unexpected rumpus: flutterings and chirpings, a few ear-splitting shrieks, and out comes a flock of guinea-fowl that must have been nesting inside. One bird, in totally surreal fashion, comes flying through a hole in the roof. Excited and indignant, they flee through the trees, past the broken cemetery, into the mountain.

'It was terrible having to give up that child,' she says, returning without warning to her dream. 'I never thought I had any motherly instincts, but when I woke up I was sobbing.'

'You must have been beautiful as a little girl,' he says.

'I was an insufferable little brat.' For a minute she is silent. 'Still, I'm not sure I always deserved what I got. You know, the first day I went to school, Mother just dropped me at the school gate and drove on, leaving me to cope on my own. And after the first six months or so even that was too much trouble, so I was packed off on the bus. But nobody had told me about bus tickets and things, so on that first day I exchanged mine for a box of silkworms. And when the conductor asked for my ticket on the way home and discovered I didn't have one, he promptly stopped the bus and ordered me out. I didn't have the slightest idea of where I was. Just stood there beside the street, bawling my heart out, still clutching my box of silkworms. But I suppose the other kids spoke to the conductor, or perhaps he'd just

141

meant to give me a good scare anyway, so the bus stopped again and I was called back. And when I got home and told my folks about what had happened all I got was a hiding from Mother. And the silkworms landed in the dustbin.'

Every time, he thinks, a new segment of landscape opens up in her: every time there is something more of her private wilderness she entrusts to him.

The bare trees are shuddering in the light wind.

'Let's go back,' she says. 'Perhaps Jack will have finished with the car by now. It's too cold and exposed up here today.'

She carries the tray back to the hotel; he waits beside the car. Behind him the gardener is still moving about energetically, but there are so many teeth missing from the rake that it hardly makes any impact on the leaves of the lawn.

In front of her small window, too, the branches are now bare; unchecked, the cool white light spills on to the threadbare carpet, until she unties the ribbons from the curtains (a little girl undoing her plaits) to turn the interior of her room into a safe and shadowy place again.

There is a certain visual intensity I should like to convey in this scene. The gentle dusk blurring all shapes – muted pain – yes, but only to begin with, as a general context for more acute perception; the way one might recognize, in a dull grey matrix of pain, the sudden scream of an exposed nerve. And so, because it is chilly and she is trembling lightly, I shall have her turn on the old-fashioned little convex heater; stooping over it for a while to make sure it is working; and from the bed one will be able to watch the reddish glow licking like a tongue of fire the contours of her breasts, the outline of her stomach, the hair hanging down over her face, the roundness of her shoulders.

(V.S. Naipaul: 'If only the world outside could be shut out, and men could be made to forget what they knew.')

'Come to me,' he says.

This time –

I should prefer to draw the customary veil of silence over the rest of the scene and leave it to the reader's imagination. Any description of the act of love runs the risk of degenerating into either a naming of parts, a purple rain of adjectives, or a pretence of metaphysical agonies and ecstasies. Language baulks at shouldering the burden of meaning involved in an experience it prefers to reduce to titillation, or to cliché. Semiotics appears, with exquisite irony, to retreat before this essential act of communication in which, precisely, everything 'stands for' something else while yet affirming its own value as pure form: the merest trembling of the skin, the tautening of a nipple, the flickering of an eyelid, the shudder of a sigh, the gorging of a penis, the secretion of fluid, the contraction of vaginal muscles: medium transformed into message, an act of elementary and dangerous transgression.

Therefore I shall refrain from the explicit. Yet I cannot be altogether silent; pause or asterisk would not only be an evasion but a denial of significance in a moment of illumination as momentous as the meeting in the wood, whose sequel and complement it is. So:

This time she cannot let him go again; she clings to him with a passion which confounds him, a hunger which has to be sated against all the empty unpredictable days ahead ('Are you not burned by the fire in my blood?'): fighting him, with the angry thrashing of her body against his, to draw from him, not seed, but reassurance and hope and faith with which to counter a surge of fear she has never felt so urgently: a fear of the future which has already begun to invade the present, a fear of the ultimate, of death. In the violence of her orgasm she bursts into uncontrollable sobs. Not in the way she often cries at the moment of climax, but in a total abandonment from which, after a long time, she only half-emerges, gasping and trembling. He feels left behind, stunned by those unknown silent regions she has traversed in her coming.

'What's happened?' he whispers in her ear, amazed, in awe, exhausted.

She stares at him with vacant eyes. 'I don't know. I think I died.'

They remain locked together in silence, oblivious of time. Absently, without being conscious of it, she lies toying with his wedding ring. They cannot speak. They have given up words; it will take time to catch up. No one can tell how long it is before the implacable ticking of the small alarm clock beside the bed imposes itself on them again.

He sighs, and sits up. 'I must go.'

'It's too late.'

'No,' he says, uncomprehending, putting on his watch, 'it's still all right.'

She shakes her head. 'I mean: whether you go or stay, whatever you do now, it is already too late. Something has happened. We can never go back.'

He gets up, and puts on his clothes, and braces himself against the blinding light awaiting him outside.

There are, as always, *Casspirs* in the street.

A note on Philip's perception of innocence in Melissa: I fully agree with him, of course; and I suspect that even Melissa would have to concede the rather precious point he made: 'Nothing can corrupt the innocence I love in you.'

De Sade's Justine regarded herself as innocent for as long as she retained her hymen, no matter to what excesses of debauchery and humiliation she was submitted. All imaginable (and several normally unimaginable) forms of penetration were permissible save only the vaginal. Which may seem like a purely technical conception of innocence. And yet Justine was right in a very profound sense, namely be defining innocence as a *state of mind*, of which the hymen was a mere semiotic function. In Melissa's case no penetration was relevant as long as what she called her 'silence' remained impenetrable. If I read her correctly, she was never really 'present' (in Jane Ferguson's sense of the word*) on any of the occasions where, at first sight, she became the victim of her abusers and exploiters. By distancing herself from whatever was happening to her body she was never really involved.

Even on that first night when Philip picked her up (if for argument's sake we accept that as the starting point of their story), she was left untouched both by what had occurred before he found her and by the way in which he himself took advantage

---

* Cf. the passage from her novella quoted on pp. 133–4.

of her. Which explains why, afterwards, she could continue as if nothing had happened: in her deepest experience nothing *had* happened.

Am I right in suspecting that the first time she fully inhabited her body in making love to him was that early winter's day tentatively described above, when she began to sob so uncontrollably as she came? Because that would be the moment she consciously and decisively, and unconditionally, offered herself to love – which also meant exposing herself to the possibility of being hurt, betrayed, wounded to the quick. Putting her innocence at stake.

If that is so then this would be the territory where the signs of the inevitable shift in their relationship will most readily be noticed: that uncertain landscape where 'guilt' is equated with 'knowledge' (cf. in German: *Schuld*, guilt – *Schule*, school).*

Here is the end of Jane Ferguson's diary entry dated 6 January:

*For how many hours have I now been sitting here, writing, hoping that by committing it to paper I can bring myself to understand what happened, is happening? The more I write the more I realize that it is hopeless to recapitulate: what happened did not 'take place' (in the most literal sense of staking out a territorial claim) somewhere out there, yesterday or the day before. It is happening right here, now as I write it down, trying to come to grips with the shift from 'Clive de Vos' to 'Chris de Villiers'.*

*But I can't go on like this. A little while ago, to ease the cramp in my hand, I went outside for a walk in the garden, round the dark main building where the only lights are his and mine. And I know he's waiting and waiting for me. He must be under the impression that I'm still trying to make up my mind about his political involvement; about whether to inform the police or not. But that's irrelevant! My only problem has been the displacement caused by his change of name. And*

---

* 'School' in the sense of a place of learning; but also in the sense of a grouping, a multitude ('a shoal of fishes'): it refers to that moment when one has to come to terms with the knowledge of others, of outsiders, of the masses.

*surely it is pure selfishness on my part to split hairs about the only thing I 'have' of him, his name. I must get past the self. Mine. His. Past language. Back into the basic simplicity of living, loving, accepting. A love as simple as the honest sweat of toil. Perhaps it is illusion. Paradise no longer exists. The acrid tang of that fruit is on our tongues, tasting of words.*

*I do not want to postpone it any longer. I'm going to him. Now. God knows how little time we may have left.*

The diary is not resumed before Thursday the tenth, by which time there clearly was so much to catch up with that many of her notes are extremely cursory. Much later, with hindsight, she would formulate it like this:

*What's in a name? Everything. When he was Clive de Vos we were naked in Paradise. Then he became Chris de Villiers and everything changed. Because then, whatever we did we did knowingly, in full consciousness, taking upon ourselves the whole burden of our separate histories in this violent country.*

But on that Thursday, still heavy with grief – it soon becomes evident that the visitor had left that morning – there was very little interpretation in her notes, as if she were concerned only with jotting things down in order not to forget, to remind herself, perhaps simply to do something mechanical to concentrate the mind.

*From Sunday night (early Monday morning really) till today: three days. Enough to last a lifetime? Went back to him in the first grey light of day. To tell him: Here I am, I'm not asking anything of you, I love you. Do you want me?*

*Woke up in his arms. Almost 10. Knock on the door. Jackson with the coffee, only one cup of course. Shuffling sounds in the passage. All of them eagerly trying to catch a glimpse? Not a word at breakfast. An atmosphere you could cut with a knife.*

*Then: Auntie Maud trying to lure me to the kitchen. Which I pointedly ignored. Went out with Chris\* instead. All those eyes in one's back, like daggers. Down the slope to the Zulu village again to visit the child hurt in the fire. This time I could understand the care and professional skill with which he examined the small body. The boy was*

---

\* Here she first wrote 'Clive', then scored it out.

much better, thank God. Chris had the people's confidence by now, they all wanted to chat. I had to translate. The old woman Demazane invited us to her hut for sour milk. Thought Chris might be hesitant but he was eager. Which made me happy, as Demazane is the most wonderful storyteller. Wizened little thing, not a tooth in her mouth, two wrinkled skins for breasts, nipples like tortoise heads. They're all scared of her. But once she starts telling stories the whole past of the Zulu nation seems to unfold like an old map. What will happen if she dies? She's a living archive. One should really tape it for future reference. (No, says C. It won't be the same. It's not just the stories, it's the way she infuses them with life, embodies them. Without her it would be archaeological material, no more.)

She told us the story of Ntombinde, daughter of Usikulumi, the girl who married the Sun.*

C. enthralled. Old Demazane would have gone on all day if I'd let her. But I was possessive of C. Laughing, his arm around me, he at last consented to go. ('Promise: once we're married you must bring me back to this wonderful old woman.' All day long we spoke like this. As if the future had already been decided.)

The whole suspicious crowd awaiting us at the hotel. Couldn't face them. Packed a picnic basket in the kitchen (Auntie Maud: 'But I've been slaving away all morning to cook lunch for the man!') and went up the mountain with C. Back to 'my' waterfall. The pool I christened Ilulange, after the old woman's story. On the way up a mountain eagle tumbling from above. Its forlorn cry. Then another. Then four or five more. Nine in all. The first time I'd ever seen so many together. Something ominous about it? I know how the Zulus interpret it. But with C. so close I shook off the slight apprehension. We went higher, to Ilulange. A blazing hot day. Took off our clothes to swim. I stood under the waterfall – barely a cascade, only a very fine spray ('like a veil, and you're the loveliest bride that ever was') – eating a mango. He rubbed the sticky sweet juice into my breasts. Made love on the grass. Lay there talking endlessly. The whole future seemed so close, so disarmingly possible. Told each other stories.

Fell asleep on the grass, then woke up, and started talking again from

___

* I am not familiar with the story. But I have written to Charles Ferguson; perhaps he can fill me in.

*where we'd left off, and slept again. Until it turned cool and we had to go back, the sun already setting.*

*Once again that atmosphere at table, but we pretended not to notice and slipped away again after dinner. Wandered through the night. Forgot about time. Unaware even of tiredness. At last fell asleep in his bed.*

*'Such shameless behaviour under my roof. Jane, if you were my child – !' That was Uncle Jock, next morning. Purple-faced. Auntie Maud nodding assent in the background. Lost my own cool too, I'm afraid: 'Well, what's my sentence for the crime I committed?' 'You've bloody well sentenced yourself,' he stormed. 'One day this thing will be a flaming sword between you and your husband in your marriage bed. If you ever get a husband after this! You're not a decent woman any more. You're just – you're just – ', looking for the worst insult he could find, apoplectic with rage, 'you're just what you are!' Such* opaque *rage! That was casting me into outer darkness all right. Sent me to my room as if I were a naughty child. I bet he wished I'd sleep for a hundred years. But I wasn't going to be disposed of so easily.*

*I did go up, but only briefly, to wash my face. Flushed with anger. And then Sylvia, of all people, cornered me. 'Jesus, how can you be so cheap?' 'Who are you to talk?! Your husband or boyfriend or whatever in jail, and you go gallivanting with other men every night.' 'At least I know who I'm going out with. This man is a total stranger. For all you know he's an escaped convict or something.'*

*Et cetera, et cetera. I felt polluted, dragged through mud and shit. I thought: God, all we've got is these few days, you have no right to mess it up like this. It's ours, you stay out of it!*

*To get away from her I ran out of my room again, right past Uncle Jock who just stared in disbelief seeing his orders ignored like that. C. waiting for me outside. Didn't want to tell him about it all, but I was so upset I just had to. It took a long time before I calmed down again. Patiently, lovingly, he just held me in his arms. In a way I found that even more disturbing, for it made me remember a dream from the night before. About our child. Little girl. Only, he wasn't there, we were looking for him all over. And then I had to give her up, there was a war on or something. She was about two, I think, and the whole dream was one muddled leave-taking. I could remember pressing her small body to me and how she couldn't understand what was going on.*

*Gradually the tension left me. Started talking again. No longer the wild romantic dreams about the future. But memories, facts, our two realities. I wanted to know everything about him. Couldn't stop listening.*

What a pity she does not give more information. But presumably, by the time she wrote it, Jane already realized the risk attached to it.

*Was the day overcast? Honestly can't remember. But I know he once said: 'Don't worry, tonight the Sun will be back.' (Referring, of course, to Ntombinde's story which the old woman had told us.)*

*'As long as you don't leave me.'*

*'I'm with you now.'*

*'But soon – ' I clasped his arm. 'Why can't you take me away with you? If you must leave the country, I'll go with you.' It suddenly seemed so easy, so obvious.*

*But he said: 'Going away means having to come back again later. I can't do that to you. But don't worry, one day we'll be together. And there will be peace in the land again. I'm sure of that.'*

*Coming back to the hotel, a curious sensation: like seeing a film one's already seen. The yellow police van driving away from the front door. C. stopped short. (This time, at least, I understood.)*

*Once again, as it turned out, it had nothing to do with him. Two of the staff taken away for questioning, Uncle Jock snapped when I asked him about it. In connection with the fire. After all, the culprits had to be found, not so? The police had to start somewhere. And these blacks are all in cahoots. Even if Jackson and Freddie turn out to be innocent they're bound to give the police some useful information. You can trust the cops, they have ways of getting to the truth all right.*

*Then C. intervened. 'Did you tell them about the guinea-fowl?' he asked.*

*'Of course I told them!' said Uncle Jock.*

*'No, you didn't,' said Auntie Maud. 'You were scared they'd find out about your bad wiring.'*

*C. was pale with rage. Said he was going in to town straight away to tell them everything. And if the police wouldn't budge, he'd arrange for the two waiters to get a lawyer.*

*'You stay out of it,' said Uncle Jock. 'None of your business. The cops know their job.'*

*'That's what I'm afraid of,' said C. And went out to his battered old blue Valiant. I followed him blindly. Tried to plead with him. I could*

*understand his anger, of course. But he had to think of his own safety.*
*Suppose – I couldn't even think of what might happen.*

*He held me. Kissed me. Smiled palely. 'Jane, why are you going on*
*like this? You know I must do what I have to do. Otherwise, what's the*
*use?'*

*So I let him go. Ashamed. But fear burning inside me worse than fire.*


It will not be strictly necessary, of course, to include the July
vacation in my story. It represents an emptiness of time and
space between them. Withdrawal, the more surely to return. But
it may be an opportunity to fill in something about Melissa. Her
'context'. The family holiday on her grandmother's farm in the
Northern Transvaal. How she will experience it; how, afterwards, she will relate it to Philip:

An arid region, no rain in five years. The earth blood-red
and exposed, like a carcass skinned and left to bleed. Cattle
slaughtered. Emblematic skeletons among rocks and the last
surviving thorn trees, bleached horns still brandished against an
empty sky. The intricate patterns of parched mud on sunken
surfaces around windmills that haven't given water in years.
Ouma – shrivelled, tough, angry, tight bun behind the head,
mouth sunken (the dentures worn only for meals and for
reading the Scriptures at night), always sheathed in black or
navy blue, mesh stockings fastened with peach-stones below the
knees (revealed at night when the feet are ritually washed before
supper), buckled shoes. With her small angry claws, contorted
with rheumatism and discoloured by liver blotches, she rules the
farm like an absolute monarch of old. You won't believe your
own eyes, prof. Even big strong men among the workers, men
who could pick her up in one hand, start trembling when she
addresses them. And she seems to take an evil pleasure in
humiliating them, forcing them to crawl in the dust at her feet,
wounding them in their masculine pride in the presence of their
wives and children. You should see their eyes sometimes. Like
the eyes of an ox flogged for taking the wrong turning in front of
the plough: that wild rage, a white madness; yet one knows he'll
just stand there and submit to whatever is done to him. Except

that these are people, not oxen. And some of them have begun to make this momentous discovery. I became aware of strange cars arriving on the farm after dark. When I spoke to the kitchen servants about it they refused to talk – they're not used to having conversations with whites – but once a young girl let it slip out: 'They city people, Missus. They talk strange things.' So even on that distant frontier something is stirring. But they still fear the old woman. She's the one who hands out mealie meal, who heals the sick, who offers employment, who sends people packing from the farm at the slightest provocation. Their very lives depend on her.

There's something terrifying in it, prof. The ferocious way in which this shrivelled, dried-up little *biltong* of a creature clings to her archaic power, reigning like a queen. Only, what is there to reign over? Red dust and flint, whirlwinds dancing across the bare plains, white husks. A kingdom of nothingness, growing more barren every day. When one goes for a walk in the veld – something drives one outside every day, there's nothing else to do – one is exposed to a naked fear as scorching as the sun. No metaphysics here. *Mayibuye iAfrika.*

But she persists, by God, and how. Looking at her one begins to understand those female ancestors who crossed the Drakensberg Mountains barefoot when the menfolk thought of submitting to British rule in Natal. It's her type that survived the concentration camps in the Boer War (she herself was born in the camp at Norvalspont), and clung to the hard earth like aloes through poverty and depression and world wars. She can look God himself in the face and challenge him: 'Behold me, Lord: not even You can eradicate me – white, and woman – from this soil.' She actually has the unnerving habit of addressing the Lord as if he's some obstreperous male at her side while she feeds the chickens or kindles the black stove or sweeps the yard or drives the *bakkie* in to town: 'Lord, I asked you to give us rain, so what are you waiting for? Can't you see the cattle are dying?' Or: 'Lord, didn't I tell you last night we needed someone to fix the pump?' I've heard Father say – when she couldn't hear, of course – that he was relieved he wasn't the Lord, he wouldn't be able to take such constant bickering.

When one arrives on the farm, even invited family like us who wouldn't dare to turn down an invitation, she stands waiting at the front door (there's no verandah; the moment you go through that door you're right outside in the sun), arms folded on her bony chest. Eyes beady and black and savage like a hawk's. A stark figure in that dusty white yard – the whole farm looking like an over-exposed photograph – tough and forbidding, unmoving: you have to go to her to greet her and receive a dry kiss. 'How long are you staying?' As if it's a burden to be borne with much resentment. And that is exactly how it is, for she makes it abundantly clear that the moment strangers set foot on the farm (and on that Godforsaken farm *everybody* is a stranger) things start going wrong: the cows stop giving milk, the goats start dying, the hens stop laying, the labourers get unruly, the last barbels in the stagnant stinking puddles refuse to bite, even the clouds stay away. Here everything has a cosmic dimension. And the horizon is ablaze with the coming Apocalypse.

There are innumerable rooms in the sprawling old farmhouse, but most are locked; in front of the windows, even of the few reluctantly set aside for occupation, the wooden shutters remain closed to keep out the dust. At five in the morning you're awakened by one of the four or five black women working in the house and in the yard (what do they *do*? what does Ouma do?), with a cup of coffee and a carefully rationed plate of rusks. Now you'd better hurry, because there's family prayers before sunrise. The earth hard and white with frost outside. And then it's up to you to find a way of getting through another endless day. (I go for walks, several times every day, and whenever I return, grey with dust, I'm greeted with the same reproach: 'Melissa, it isn't proper to wander about like this. A white girl on her own. These kaffirs can't be trusted.') At night, before supper, one of the kitchen servants carries in a dented zinc bath with lukewarm water for us all to wash in: face, hands, feet, in that order, from the oldest to the youngest. (And invariably I'm the youngest; the water bears a grey lather by the time my turn comes.)

After supper it's time for Scripture reading again, Ouma grimly working her way through Revelations, right through to chapter twenty-two, and then back to one, in order to remind us of the End which is nigh.

*And I saw the dead, small and great, stand before God; and the books were opened: and another book was opened, which is the book of life: and the dead were judged out of those things which were written in the books, according to their works.*

*And death and hell were cast into the lake of fire. This is the second death.*

*And whosoever was not found written in the book of life was cast into the lake of fire.*

That Patmos must have been a damned desolate island.

Then follows the anachronism of TV, to which Ouma is religiously addicted. The daily quota of depressing news. Arson, murder, stonings, bullets, the interminably repeated vicious circle of violence.

Ouma: 'Bad times we're living in. Ja, these are the last days. And no sign of rain either.'

One night I dared to comment: 'Perhaps the two go together, Ouma. Perhaps we're being punished for our sins.'

Almost a rupture in the family.

'What I fail to understand,' Philip says when I tell him about it, 'is how can you keep on going back for more. Why didn't you break away long ago? My God, you're twenty-three. Nothing forces you to spend all your holidays with them.'

(We're in my room behind the drawn curtains; a cheerless August wind tugging at the sash-windows; the deep red glow of the heater.)

'Perhaps I need them, even their irritations. D'you think there's a streak of perversity in me? I've never been able to get on with them, yet I cannot survive without them. I already told you: my sole function in life, as far as Mother is concerned, is to make her feel proud; mostly I've let her down, and she's made damn sure that I'm not left in any doubt about that. As for Father, you know, if I think back, there's only one image of him I can remember from my childhood. I must have been very small. He came home from work. I'd heard his car outside and went running to the front door to meet him. He came in with a colleague. Didn't notice me, walked right past me to put away his briefcase in his study. It was his friend who picked me up and swung me into the air and kissed me.'

'You forgave him for that?'

'It's not a question of forgiveness. Perhaps the knowledge that, no matter what I did, I could never please them, never be to them what they wanted me to be, made me need them even more. But nowadays it's different. A year or so ago it struck me for the first time that they were getting old, even though they're not much older than you. There's a kind of vulnerability that comes with age, I suppose. When I go home it's no longer my mother who organizes everything. She's leaving more and more to me, she can't cope any more. Even if she never stops criticizing, I get the strange impression that she's leaning on me, needing me. And Father too, in his own way. Nowadays I'm the one who has to pour his scotch and tell him which wine to open. They're more exposed now to the approach of death, I think. The defences are coming down. How can I not feel sorry for them?' I look at him. 'I don't blame you if you don't understand, prof. I know it must sound terribly mixed-up.'

'Perhaps I do understand,' he concedes, lying back against a large pillow. 'I also used to hate my father, I told you. Perhaps "hate" is the wrong word. I just cut myself off from him totally. Especially after that night out, when I couldn't find the lost sheep. We lived in the same house like two strangers from different countries, not even sharing the same language. There was only Ma to keep us going. And then he had a stroke. One of my sisters took him in, he didn't need me. I visited him only a few times. He couldn't speak. There was nothing I could say to *him*. But the last time – ' He hesitates. 'I just saw him slipping away. A shadow against the bedclothes. A narrow bundle of bones. And suddenly I felt hopelessly sorry for him: not because he was dying, but because of everything we'd missed. Suddenly I understood something about the terrible disappointment I'd been to him all his life. An only son who'd failed him in all his dreams. No matter if they were unreasonable. They were his dreams. His vision of making a "man" of me may have seemed crude from outside, but to him it was entirely reasonable, it was the only logical expectation his own upbringing had allowed him. And when I'd let him down it was he who was diminished by it; he was the one who'd made a mess of his life. This was what I wanted to ask his forgiveness for. But there he was, slipping away, and he didn't even hear

154

me when I spoke. I couldn't make my peace with him. Or with myself, for that matter. In that last hour I knew the only thing that mattered was that he was my father. For the first time I understood something of what that means. A father. A son. But it was too late.'*

His confession has moved me; leaving the towel on the floor by the heater I go to him, snuggling up against him for warmth. Yes, I think, perhaps we share more than we have thought. There may yet be hope for us.

'I can understand your feelings about your parents,' he says. 'But what about your grandmother? Surely there cannot be anything in her which attracts you? Not from what you've told me.'

'Sometimes I think I hate her,' I admit. 'She can be so destructive. But there's something in her, something she's always tried to keep away from us and which I found out quite by accident – '

My pathetic old Oupa, dead now, and what a relief it must have been for him. Ouma used to treat him like one of her good-for-nothing labourers. Whenever he opened his mouth in company she would find a reason to berate him, or a pretext to send him out to fetch and carry. In front of others she would take bitter pleasure in accusing him of being a weakling and an alcoholic – the latter because he couldn't do without his glass of invalid port at sundown every day. Which he had to take in the shed as she refused to allow 'drunken orgies' under her pious roof. None of us could ever understand why he ever married

---

* This scene, even more than some of the others, will require drastic revision if it is to be incorporated in a novel. The tit-for-tat confessions are too glib. In addition I should like to work in references to her brothers: the elder one who has always been the parents' favourite; the younger who died, leaving in Melissa a lacuna she has not yet dared to explore consciously. What is important is the filling in of the characters; but other means must be found by which to convey it. And even if the setting – her room – is retained and the point of view – hers – remains the same I should like to find a way of conveying, in addition, *his* perception of her as he rediscovers all the small, precious aspects of her life a month's absence has rendered unfamiliar. (Her motions as she dries her hair with the red towel in front of the heater, hands raised, her high breasts trembling in the red glow.)

someone like her. Perhaps it was his henpecked misery which drew the two of us together. Behind her back, of course, for she would never have approved. And in a moment of weakness – I'd found him in the shed where he was crying because she'd discovered and thrown away his meticulously hidden bottle of port – he finally confided in me. How she'd been the wildest and most beautiful girl in the vicinity, surrounded by suitors; and how madly he himself had been in love with her, but without ever daring to say a word to her about it. (Such a banal little sob-story, really, but because I had such a soft spot for Oupa I couldn't help being moved by it.) Then she discovered she was pregnant, and the man responsible for it refused to face up to it. So she turned to Oupa and asked him to save her reputation by marrying her. If he turned her down, she solemnly warned him, she would pour paraffin over her and set herself alight. Can you imagine? He didn't even think twice. He'd do anything to make the miracle come true and be by her side for ever. (If he so much as breathed a word about the truth, she warned him, she would promptly carry out the paraffin threat.)

And this more or less summarizes their story. Unhappily ever after. Oupa wasn't used to pouring out his heart to anyone. But he told me enough to make me realize that in all their years of being together the marriage had never been consummated. By the time he died they'd been married for forty years.

'There's something terrifying in a person like that,' I confide to Philip. 'And no matter how mad she sometimes makes me I cannot help feeling sympathy for her. Even a sneaking kind of admiration. Because it wasn't only Oupa who'd been suffering all those years. She'd had her share too. She'd had the guts to do the kind of thing I wouldn't ever dare to. Perhaps deep inside every person there is this urge to plunge into something romantic and reckless and wild, even if it's only once in your life. And even if you have to go to hell for it afterwards. She was prepared to take the jump. She's been burning for the rest of her life. But I – '

'You needed guts just to survive the holidays,' he says.

'There certainly were days I felt I'd never make it. But I suppose what fascinated me was the desperation with which she clings to what remains of her life. Seeing her whole familiar

156

world changing in front of her eyes. One night, shortly before we left, the old shed behind the house – Oupa's hiding place – burnt down. A dilapidated old ruin, really. But it still came as a shock. I mean, the possibility that it might have been arson. It happened on a Saturday night, you see, just after she'd had an argument with a couple of labourers about leaving the gates open or something. She'd slapped one of the men in the face. Gave them until sunrise the next day to get off the farm. So there certainly was enough provocation. Not that it made much impression on Ouma. Still, it was the first time ever that they'd dared to retaliate. In a way I think it marked the beginning of an end for her. What touched me most was when I followed Ouma out to the burnt-out ruin the next morning and stood beside her as she stared straight at the black rubble. Without turning her head, almost as if talking to herself, not the slightest hint of sorrow in her voice, very quietly, she said: 'Poor Casper. This is where he used to come for his port every day. Now his place won't know him any more.'

In the front right-hand corner of the top drawer in her dressing table she shows him what will from now on be 'his' place: she's bought him a comb and a toothbrush to be kept there.

Somewhere in his writings Sartre tells the anecdote of two manuscripts he'd received from different writers at roughly the same time. One dealt with Hiroshima; the other, if I remember correctly, was set in a mental institution. But in the course of his reading, says Sartre, a remarkable interchange took place. He gained the impression that the Hiroshima story ultimately projected a vision of a world gone mad, whereas the one about the lunatics was an exploration of the kind of world made possible by Hiroshima. Something to that effect. Which should not surprise anyone. It can be no coincidence that Ovid's *Metamorphoses* is one of the seminal writings of the West.

(Cf. Harry Mulisch in *The Assault*: 'It was as if he were saying that life is a metaphor for another story, and that it is our business to discover that other story.')

How to articulate, within the desperate exclusiveness of their love, the weight and madness of the violence surrounding them? Yes: that is what continues to intimidate me while at the same time making it more urgent for me to keep grappling with this emergent story. How else can I hope to understand? The mindless devastation of the month of August was more than an escalation of what had gone before: as the State of Emergency began to take effect a wholly new phase in the violent history of the previous year was set into motion. In Natal the immediate cause was the murder, by four 'unknown men', of Mrs Nonyamezelo Mxenge whose husband, a leading lawyer in political cases, had been killed a few years earlier in equally sinister circumstances. Demonstrations in Durban, violently broken up by police, soon spread to Umlazi, to Kwamashu and other areas, to the Witwatersrand; even the Western Cape, traditionally much more easy-going, erupted in the worst violence of the year. Mrs Mxenge's funeral on 11 August (in the Ciskei, where her husband had been buried earlier) set fire to the whole of the Eastern Cape, notably to Duncan Village near East London where police repression became so blatant (to the point of interfering with the Red Cross when they tried to evacuate victims) that the Supreme Court in Grahamstown had to intervene.

It came as no surprise that Mrs Winnie Mandela was singled out for 'special attention': the small house in Brandfort to which she had been banished a number of years ago was raided by the Special Branch, and in the raid her two-year-old grandson disappeared. Soon afterwards the house was 'inexplicably' burnt down. (Milton Thaya, who happened to be in the township with a group of teachers at the time, told me about his visit to the charred house, and of the way in which the whole community rallied round that remarkable woman, and of a staunch Afrikaner café owner who commented, when Milton went to buy a cold drink from him after the fire: 'Now that's a really bad thing, *jong*. This Winnie Mandela has done nothing but good since she came to live in our town.') Throughout the month – throughout the year – Nelson Mandela's name had been a blazing beacon in the struggle; in every black township in the country his words of more than twenty years ago still flamed on:

'During my lifetime I have dedicated myself to this struggle of the African people. I have fought against white domination and I have fought against black domination. I have cherished the ideal of a democratic and free society . . . It is an ideal which I hope to live for and to achieve. But if need be it is an ideal for which I am prepared to die.'

(*Amandla! Ngawethu!*)

Early in the year the state president had tried to get some political mileage out of the situation by offering Mandela his freedom in exchange for an undertaking to renounce violence. There were thousands of his supporters present in Soweto when his daughter Zinzi read out his reply (which could not be reported in the South African press, of course):

'What freedom am I being offered while the organization of the people remains banned? What freedom am I being offered when I may be arrested on a pass offence? What freedom am I being offered to live my life as a family with my dear wife who remains in banishment in Brandfort? What freedom am I being offered when I need a stamp in my pass to seek work? What freedom am I being offered when my very South African citizenship is at stake? . . .

'I cannot and will not give any undertaking at a time when I and you, the people, are not free. Your freedom and mine cannot be separated. I *will* return.'

(*Mayibuye!*)

As the month smouldered on the official death toll in what had euphemistically become known as the 'unrest' rose to over 160; thousands of people, many of them children, were arrested. (Among them was the trade unionist Oscar Mpetha, apparently regarded as such a danger to the state that he was detained in spite of being seventy-five years old, and diabetic, and having had one leg amputated.)

Even leading businessmen became so concerned about the winds of change fanning the flames that a deputation was sent to Lusaka for discussions with the ANC.

Beleaguered on all sides, the government nevertheless persisted in believing that the unrest amounted to no more than ephemeral and local disturbances – the work of 'groupuscules' – which could be quelled by a show of force. In the midst of all this upheaval great expectations were raised for a speech by the state president on August the fifteenth, which however turned out to be a pathetic anticlimax. In about sixty minutes this gentleman brought the country's economy to its knees, caused the collapse of the currency and destroyed most of what remained of South Africa's credibility in the Western world: an act of political, economic and moral devastation which, if committed by anyone else, might well have resulted in a charge of high treason.

There is a break in the text of Jane Ferguson's diary after her brief account of the crisis caused by Chris de Villiers' discovery that two of the waiters had been taken away by the police for 'questioning' in connection with the burning of the shed. Did she need a rest at this point? Did she first go out on one of her long walks to clear her head, calm down her emotions? Whatever the reason, the rest of the page is left blank and one has to turn it over for the resumption of her laconic notes:

*Was sure I'd never see him again. How could the police fail to recognize him? But he did come back. In a black depression. Couldn't find any lawyer in that small town willing to 'interfere'. Once the waiters were charged with an offence, OK. But there was nothing one could do in the mean time. So C. went straight to the police station himself. Received very cordially, but their attitude changed when they heard what he'd come for. Quite an argument. To make things worse, Uncle Jock also drove to the station. Total chaos, as far as I could make out. In the end the guinea-fowl didn't even feature any more and C. was actually threatened with arrest for 'trying to defeat the ends of justice'. There was nothing he could do but come back to the farm.*

*One important shift though. Was it some time that night he told me, or during the next day (yesterday)? Can't remember. There was so much we talked about. But this I do know: that trip to the police station had changed all his plans for the future. Ours.*

She supplies very little detail on this point. Charles Ferguson filled in something when he brought me the diary; but because, obviously, I hadn't yet read it I couldn't put any pertinent questions. The gist of his information was that Chris had given up his plans to leave the country. How could he sit it out in Swaziland or Mozambique while others like Jackson and Freddie or whatever their names were had to bear the brunt? Et cetera. No, he had no option but to go back to Johannesburg. 'I'm not a criminal, Jane,' one can imagine him arguing. 'Why should I act like one? I don't know how much I can still get done before they come for me, but at least I'll be of more use inside the country than outside.'

How she would dread having to put the question – but sooner or later, surely, she would have had to: 'And if they do take you in? What then?'

'I don't know, Jane. But it's no use speculating. That's too sterile, too paralysing. Perhaps they'll come up with a charge of treason. It's such an easy way for them nowadays to keep one out of circulation for a while. Otherwise, quite simply, detention. Don't break your head over it.' With, undoubtedly, a touch of bitterness: 'Whatever happens, however obscene it may be, I still have the protection of my white skin. They won't dare to – '

A pause.

She: 'To do what, Chris?'

'Well, to do whatever they might do to me if I were black. You see, that's the reason why I must go back. I cannot allow anyone to make an exception of me just because I happen to be white.'

'And when will that be?'

'Soon.'

I suppose an imagined conversation like the above might have led up to the few lines of dialogue she does quote:

*I was quaking. 'If it's really the end for us,' I said, 'please, my love, promise me you won't tell me when it's the last time.'*

*His eyes in mine. 'No, Jane. I can't. You've got to know. No matter how terrible it is. We must know, both of us.'*

*'You mean – ?'*

*The merest nod of his head above mine. His shadow thrown up high against the wall by the bedside lamp.*

*'Yes, this is our last night. I must leave first thing in the morning.'*

*And at daybreak this morning he left. Uncle Jock: 'Not a bloody moment too soon. I don't know how I can ever look your father in the face again.'*

*'I'll face him myself.'*

*To escape from their sneering eyes (Sylvia positively gloats) I withdrew here into my room. To write it down. Even though it can hardly make a difference. I feel my guts, my womb, contract. C., C., C. I dare not even write out your name any more. And outside, in the wood, somewhere, there's a rainbird throbbing out the sad sweet sounds Dad interpreted for me as a child:*

*'Wafababa, wafamame, ngafa iszunqu-nqu-nqu – '*

*'My father is dead, my mother is dead, I am dying of loneliness.'*


Milton Thaya again. He's just come back to me, as I expected he would, which would make it possible to follow up, in my story, the previous episode in which I made him intrude into Philip's life.* Another deeply upsetting visit. He seemed as cheerful as ever, talking about all kinds of things as they bubbled up in his mind; but I could see, from the fidgeting of his hands, the pulling of his knuckles, the crossing and recrossing of his stout legs, that he was tense. And at last he came out with it:

'So they picked up Vuyani. Thought you'd like to know.'

'After everything we did to prevent it?'

'Well, it's the Emergency, you know. Everything goes.'

'Did they track him down in Cradock?'

'No, he left there long ago. Got too hot for him, especially after Goniwe and the others got killed. So he kept on the move. Queenstown first, a spell in Bisho, then back to Grahamstown and on to P.E. That's where they caught up with him. New Brighton.'

No need to go into all the details. Together with the hundreds of others rounded up in the Eastern Cape in terms of the

---

* Pages 117–20.

Emergency regulations Vuyani was taken to St Alban's in Port Elizabeth to be 'processed'. The family only learnt about his detention when another youngster, barely fourteen, was released after a fortnight and brought news about Vuyani. What he related about general conditions in that prison was sickening enough (up to forty or fifty detainees crammed into cells meant for six or eight; among them children of eleven or twelve picked up at random in the streets or in pinball arcades because the mere fact that they hadn't been at school had shown them up as agitators and criminals in the eye of the police; the wretched food; lack of washing facilities; the systematic assaults: every morning six names would be called at the door of the cell and it would be late afternoon before the six were dragged back, in a sorry state, some of them unconscious), but what concerns me here is the specific information the youngster supplied about Vuyani. How from the first day he'd been singled out for 'special treatment' on account of his reputation. How on two occasions when Vuyani was brought back in the afternoon they thought he was dead. (On one of these occasions the two SB men who'd dragged him in kicked the limp body to see whether he would twitch or groan; then they poured water over him and drew open his eyelids; whereupon one of them said: 'Jesus, he's dead'; and then both scurried away and only came back the next morning.)

The youth honestly didn't think Vuyani would survive his detention.

Milton and I talked for hours about what could be done. The only effective remedy seemed to be an application to the Supreme Court, but Milton was adamant that the youth would be too scared to testify; he'd already tried everything he could to persuade the boy. 'No ways, man. That kid is scared out of his wits. You expect him to come forward with his story and be picked up by the *boere* again? This time they'll kill him.'

Using this incident in my story would make it acceptable for me to send Philip back to the Security Police offices. Another interview with the colonel. Painfully polite.

'Really, professor, you should know better than to go overboard over wild rumours. The State of Emergency makes it easy for people to spread the most horrifying stories about the police. I wish I could take you with us on one of our trips into the townships. Do you know what the body of a community councillor looks like who's been stoned and kicked to death by a mob? Or a girl of three raped and necklaced just because her father happens to be a black policeman? These people are savages, professor. We're working under impossible conditions. Look, I'll be frank with you: nobody's perfect, it is possible that we also occasionally make mistakes. But can you imagine what will become of this country if we don't try to maintain law and order?'

'I'm not doubting your good intentions, colonel. All I'm trying to do is to discuss one specific case which has come to my notice. I've told you the facts.'

'Professor.' An indulgent smile. 'What you call the facts – where do they come from?'

'I told you I cannot divulge my source. He's afraid of being arrested.'

'How convenient. Why should he be afraid if he's telling the truth? If we arrest someone it means we have good reasons for it. And if it turns out that he's innocent we let him go.'

'I know that Vuyani is innocent. I also believe that he's in danger of being killed by the police.'

'That is an extremely serious allegation, professor.'

'All I was hoping to do was to get some kind of assurance from you.'

'You have my assurance that the truth will come out.' Behind the taut smile there flickers, if only for a moment, a hint of how differently this courteous, formal man might behave if this room with its barred windows were locked; if one were not his visitor but his prisoner.

Philip rises. 'Well, then I suppose there's nothing else I can do.'

'Good day, Professor Malan.'

As Philip reaches the door to the passage the officer says in a casual, almost friendly tone of voice: 'Cute little blonde, that Melissa whatshername, Lotman, in your department, isn't it?'

He swings round. The face of the man behind the desk remains expressionless as he meticulously rearranges the files on his desk.

*

In a copy of *Le Monde* which reached me belatedly I have just come across an interview conducted a few days before his death with the philosopher Michel de Certeau: 'What do you think of Lévinas' idea', asks the interviewer, 'that "the other" is not just an *alter ego* but also everything I am not?'

To which Certeau replies: 'Because they are what I am not, others bring to me the tidings of my own frontiers, my inadequacies, in the final analysis of my death.'


A small, intensely visual impression to be worked in somewhere: Melissa standing under the shower eating a mango, the sweet sticky juice running down on her breasts.

Perhaps it might be linked, in one way or another, to a recollection from her youth. 'Remember I told you about my friend Irene? When we were in high school – fourteen or fifteen or thereabouts – we would sometimes sneak out on their roof in the rain and take off all our clothes and sit there, naked, until we were so cold and our teeth chattered so much that we *had* to crawl back. There was a strange feeling of elation in it. I can't explain. It wasn't a dare, we weren't trying to be provocative or defiant or anything. It was just a sensation of freedom. Can you imagine what would have happened if someone had seen us? What with her father being a dominee and all.'


And this for Philip. (To be incorporated in an earlier episode?) 'Those weeks in Paris in '68. I think it was the most complete experience I've ever had of what you once called "being there" (remember?). It wasn't just because of Claire. It was everything happening around us and to us: the most private moments were caught up in the whole sweep of events that carried us along. Or so it felt at the time. Today, when I think back, it is almost frightening. How momentous it all seemed at the time; but what has, really, remained of it all? A mere ripple on the surface of history. And yet, and yet – *I was there!* Not that it was exuberance all the time. There were deeply disturbing experiences too. At one stage, I remember, the student leader Cohn-Bendit was refused permission to re-enter France after a trip abroad. Because he wasn't a French citizen, you see, but a German Jew. But he arranged to be smuggled back and one evening in the Sorbonne – there he was. I remember Claire jumping up and down with excitement, beside herself. And then there was a big protest march through the city. Students, workers, housewives, children, ordinary little bourgeois people, the whole of Paris was in the streets that afternoon. A million people, some newspapers said. I'd never seen anything like that in my life before. Not that I wanted to get involved, but Claire dragged me along, insisted that I had to "show solidarity". So there we were, a million of us, like a vast torrent through the boulevards, the two of us among them, and everybody chanting: *"Nous sommes tous des juifs allemands!"* A demonstration of collective rage, hysteria, passion, madness almost. "We are all German Jews! We are all German Jews!" I was there with them, in the middle of that great roar of sound, yet I couldn't bring myself to shout with them. I was sweating, a sweat of fear, of rage, of rebellion, I don't know what, but I couldn't utter a sound. I knew they were passionately convinced of what they were shouting. There's something moving in any show of solidarity. But something terrifying too. To be marching down those streets, proclaiming ourselves to be German Jews, twenty years after the war, in Paris, so remote, so safe, made me feel sick. I'd visited Dachau; I knew what being a German Jew really meant. And from that day I've been terrified of marches, the voice of the masses. Ortega y Gasset. I know I'm being unfair to many who are truly persuaded of the nobility of their causes. But I cannot join in. I can support something I believe in, there's much I can truly express solidarity with. But don't expect me to march in a crowd. It's obscene. It's too easy, too gross. It makes me puke.'

'Yet there are times when nothing else will do, prof! Those marches in Durban, in Cape Town, in Joh'burg – even if they were broken up. What happens if no one dares to protest at all?'

'I know. That's what makes it so bewildering. I agree with you as I agreed with Claire. And yet it seems such a waste if a cause can only be promoted by overstating and oversimplifying it. It's an insult to the intellect.'

'Isn't it a matter of living lucidly and choosing the means to match the circumstances?'

'I'm not a pragmatist.'

'No. You're a literary theoretician.' She smiles. 'And I love you for it. But that can also be taken too far, you know.'

'At the moment I want to forget about the streets and just be with you. We have little enough time together as it is.'

'How would Claire have reacted if you wanted to drag her away from the streets?'

'Why do you ask that?'

'I want to know more about her. More about you. Tell me about Claire.'


There will be less and less of this as the story progresses: memories, recollections, flashbacks. In the beginning, obviously, it will be their only natural frame of reference, and their most important means of verbal access to each other. The future is, provisionally at least, excluded; the present world surrounding them a menace. So the past is where they can be most safely themselves. But as it progresses it must inevitably change. I can foresee a moment when he will acknowledge with a sense of real discovery that she hardly ever refers to her previous lovers any more; she no longer needs to reassure herself, define herself, in terms of them. She's catching up with herself, with us. We are here now. But that means that there are decisions to be made.


' – and then she told me – you know Lizzie, don't you, that voluptuous creature in Sociology – anyway, *she* told me, you could knock me down with a feather, she'd heard from Lucas Wilson (I think there's something between her and Lucas, they're always doing things together) about this juicy affair between prof Malan and that blonde in his department, you know, Melissa Lotman, now I know Lizzie can be quite a bitch and she's got a fertile imagination, but coming from Lucas I'm sure it's true, even if it's hard to believe of a man like Malan, I mean, he and his wife are such a nice couple, but then I suppose men will be boys, won't they, and faced with a sexy little bobtail like that, but don't you think it's blarry disgusting – ?'


Received a rather neutral letter from Charles Ferguson today (I realize of course that he cannot afford to be personal) in reply to my query about the story of Ntombinde, daughter of king Usikulumi.*

*For three years she pleaded with her father for permission to go to the forbidden waters of Ilulange, but he refused. Whoever goes there never comes back, he said. But after three years he gave in and allowed her to leave. She selected a hundred bridesmaids, the most beautiful virgins of the tribe, which surprised everybody as there had been no talk about an imminent marriage. Whenever Usikulumi had mentioned the subject in the past Ntombinde had shaken her head, saying she hadn't even given it a thought yet.*

*The whole tribe stood watching as the procession of girls left, led by Ntombinde. High above them in the clear sky soared a whole flock of mountain eagles, gliding smoothly on the currents of air, which stirred up fear in the heart of Usikulumi, for the Zulu people know that this sign means war; but nothing could deter Ntombinde.*

*Through the mountains of Zululand the long procession trekked, and from afar one could hear the tinkling of their bracelets and their ankle rings, and their tiny aprons swayed as they walked. Up they went, to the tallest mountain of all, where they found the waters of Ilulange. There Ntombinde took off her rings and bracelets and the apron that hid the entrance to her womb, and all the bridesmaids did likewise. She stepped into the water, followed by her maidens.*

*While they were bathing the mountain monster, the Isikqukquma-devu, the one no human being had ever set eyes on, stole their aprons and their rings. This caused a great commotion when it was discovered. All the girls fell on their knees and pleaded with the monster to return their clothes, which he did. Only Ntombinde refused to plead. I'm the*

* See page 147.

*daughter of a king, she said, I don't plead with anybody. Then, all of a sudden, the waters of Ilulange rose up and grabbed her and dragged her away, deep, deep, deep below the earth and under the mountains.*

*The girls hurried back home to spread the news. And Usikulumi sent out men to search for his daughter, but the water had swallowed her.*

*In the meantime Ntombinde had been cast up by the water far, far, far away, beyond the mountains, in the land the Sun retires to at night after it has disappeared behind the mountains. Never in her life had Ntombinde seen someone so beautiful, and when he asked her to marry him she consented and became his bride.*

*Back home Usikulumi was still doing all he could to find his beloved daughter, but in vain. He sent many flocks of cattle to Ilulange as sacrifices to the Isikqukqumadevu, but they were all swallowed by the water. Then he sent out his prize impis but they, too, were swallowed by the water. Until at last Usikulumi summoned the greatest witch doctor in the world to his place, and with his muti he drew Ntombinde back from where she was, passing under the mountains and through the waters of Ilulange.*

*Usikulumi was overjoyed to see his daughter again, but she was inconsolable. She couldn't live without her husband, the Sun. She grew thinner and thinner until she was only skin and bone. No one could find out what the matter was with her. She refused to say a word. Only to the Moon did she confide, when one night it visited her, that she was pining for her husband, the Sun. The Moon conveyed the message to him in the land far, far, far away, beyond the mountains. And the following night she brought back a reply, saying that the Sun would come to visit her in her hut every night to sleep with her after the people had gone to bed. Only, the hut had to remain closed at all times and not a soul was allowed to know about it, otherwise the Sun would never come again.*

*Ntombinde told the Moon to tell the Sun that she would do as he wished. Then she went down to the river to wash, and rubbed new fat into her body, and the next morning she accepted food. From that time on the Sun came to visit her every night to sleep with her in her hut. And Ntombinde grew beautiful again and in all the world there was no other woman to compare with her.*

*But now that her beauty was restored there were many men, coming from near and far, who wanted to marry her. She refused even to look at them. This made her father very sad. But whenever he asked her about it she would only say: 'I don't need a man. I am happy the way I am.'*

*Nothing Usikulumi did or said could persuade Ntombinde to divulge her secret. So her father decided to keep a watch on her. Late one afternoon, when Ntombinde had gone down to the river to cleanse herself for the night, Usikulumi slipped into her hut and hid under a pile of skins. He waited for so long that he fell asleep. But when the Sun arrived in the middle of the night, Usikulumi was awakened by the blazing light. Amazed, he watched as the dazzling stranger knelt in front of his daughter and undid the small apron that hid the entrance to her womb and laid down beside her on her mat of reeds. But before the Sun could enter her, Usikulumi moved under the skins. And immediately the Sun jumped up.*

*'I've been betrayed!' he shouted.*

*And in the violence of his rage he set fire to the mat and to the skins and to the hut, and throughout the village the fire raged. Ntombinde fled into the night and watched from afar how everything was consumed by the fire: every man and woman and child of her tribe, and every single hut; and from there the flames sped up the mountain, burning down everything in their way until the whole mountain was ablaze.*

*'Don't go away! Don't go away!' shouted Ntombinde, but the flames of the Sun raced further and further into the mountains. In despair she ran after the fire, with her bare feet on the scorched black earth, scaling the tallest cliffs, until she reached the top. From there she saw the whole mountain burst open from the heat. And deep inside she saw the fire raging on like a lake of flames. With one great leap Ntombinde hurled herself into that furious whirlpool to be reunited with her lover. And that was the end of Ntombinde and that is the end of the story.*


To work into one of the previous episodes:

Melissa: 'The other day after you left I lay on the bed wondering whether people differ significantly in their experience or perception of orgasm. Remember, I told you about the first time I came, that unnerving episode on the bicycle. And then there was that cousin of my father's, the one who used to "play" with me when he was supposed to baby-sit. In this case, I presume, it was something that gave him a hold on me, some kind of power over me. It was something I knew I should try to avoid, yet I didn't entirely want to either. I always had to control myself not to cry out, not to make a sound; I was scared to death that if someone came in I wouldn't be able to lie still. (And he never stopped when it began to hurt.) That fear, drowning out everything else. Is that why, no matter how fully I abandon myself, I continue to associate orgasm with a feeling of helplessness, with revolt, with pain, even with panic? I wonder sometimes if, at the time, I might actually have enjoyed it if I'd known what was happening, if I'd been able to put a name to it. Would that have changed the fear into pleasure? (And was that why, in spite of everything, I allowed him to go on?) God knows what was going on in *his* head – '


In September,* as the number of detainees in terms of the Emergency regulations approached the 3,000 mark, more and more violence characterized police and army repression of peaceful demonstrations, notably in the black townships and on the university campuses. Even on the conservative Afrikaans campus of the University of Stellenbosch there was, to the 'deep chagrin' of the rector, a small demonstration. After nearly 500 so-called 'Coloured' schools and colleges in the Western Cape were closed down by the Minister, and the largely moderate black students' organization COSAS was banned, a new wave of stayaways and protests was provoked throughout the country.

In Port Elizabeth the young district surgeon, Dr Wendy Orr, supported by several other people, applied to the Supreme Court for an interdict against the 'daily abuse' of detainees under her supervision. Early in October this resulted in her being unofficially denied further access to prisoners.

Some of the worst clashes of the Emergency period took place in Cape Town when a massive police force broke up a small peaceful demonstration led by a group of singing women in the centre of the city. With water cannons, batons, sjamboks, tear-

---

* It is now exactly a year later, and the most recent estimate of the number of people detained during the three months since the declaration of the latest State of Emergency amounts to about 20,000, several thousand of whom are children.

gas and other means the police set on the lunchtime crowds and even arrested TV crews. At roughly the same time the hanging of the alleged 'terrorist' Benjamin Moloise (after the State President in his wisdom had decided to turn down representations which indicated the existence of possible judicial grounds for a reprieve) provoked running battles between the police and the public in Johannesburg as well.

The most shocking event of this period, known as the Trojan Horse episode, occurred on 15 October when security forces in Athlone, Cape Town, used railway trucks loaded with crates to provoke children at the corner of Thornton and St Simon's Road into throwing stones, whereupon armed men jumping from the crates started shooting blindly at everybody in sight, killing and wounding several children.

In Grahamstown in the Eastern Cape a young black schoolgirl was killed when a policeman fired a rubber bullet into her face at point-blank range in what was said to be a prank.

When a group of students from Stellenbosch University announced their intention to travel to Lusaka for discussions with the youth wing of the ANC the State President (who is also the chancellor of that university) denied them passports. Why should there be discussions, the Government obviously reasoned, for as long as the regime can rely on violence to remain in power?


For the story to succeed, a sense of emergency will have to work through to all levels. So sooner or later the university itself must also be drawn into the conflict. To effect this, a confrontation between Philip and Lucas Wilson seems to me inevitable. I see it as the prelude to a whole cluster of episodes. But the prelude as such may assume different forms. For example, it may be triggered off by the visit of a right-wing academic or preacher from the US (a species regularly welcomed in this country and given almost unlimited television coverage, to prove to the world that 'distinguished' visitors think highly enough of South Africa and its policies to defy international bans and boycotts). It isn't difficult to imagine such a lecture disrupted by a group of radical students, possibly the BSM,* which would trigger off feverish academic debate afterwards. In such a situation one can see Lucas taking a leading role in organizing a petition to demand assurances from the administration that in future – at least for the duration of the Emergency – such lecturers be banned from the campus.

From this would flow the confrontation in Philip's office, which the reader will recognize as one of the settings suggested for the first encounter between the professor and Melissa.† Philip seated behind the big sapele desk, Lucas on a straight-backed chair opposite him. On the walls, a number of prints (Van Gogh, Marini, a *Don Quixote* by Picasso). Books, journals, senate agendas, fat files, wads of notes, all arranged with meticulous precision on the desk and the two spare tables, on shelves, in cabinets and cupboards. A single splash of colour: a bunch of nasturtiums in a tumbler on the desk. (Will his visitor guess their origin?)

'I'm sorry, Lucas, but I cannot possibly sign such a petition. You may think I have an old-fashioned view of a university, but I can only feel safe as an academic if the institution I belong to has sufficient faith in the enquiries of the human mind to permit total freedom of speech. Or as close to total freedom as one can aspire to in any given situation.'

'Allowing men like this American to address our university has nothing to do with free speech, prof. It is simply a way of taking advantage of the situation to strengthen the stranglehold the system already has on us. Don't you see? Twenty per cent of our students are black: they represent the great voiceless majority of our society who are being suppressed in the most violent way imaginable. This man didn't come here to extend the range of our enquiry, but simply to represent the voice of the oppressor.'

'Must I remind you of Voltaire?'

Lucas finds it difficult to hide his irritation. 'The eighteenth century was a far cry from our time, prof. Circumstances have changed a hell of a lot.'

'Are any circumstances sufficient pretext for liberals to become illiberal?'

---

* Black Students' Movement.
†See pages 18–19.

A derisive little grin. 'You're not trying to tell me that you're still clinging to the outmoded ideals of European liberalism, prof? Come on! Our time needs more radical approaches.'

'You mean you want to match intolerance with intolerance? And if circumstances change even further: would you want to match violence with violence?'

'There are circumstances which can only be changed through violence. Or do you really expect the people in the townships to turn the other cheek?'

'Whatever the responses the townships may come up with – *we* are academics. Members of a university. We should respond in terms of the system of values we attach to a university.'

'But can't you see that the entire function of a university has changed? How can we remain aloof and uncommitted when the country all around us is burning?'

'I can in no way compromise the need to enquire, to search for truth.'

'Even if it means that by the time you come up with the answers there no longer exists a society to which they may be relevant? Learning for the sake of learning very easily becomes a *reductio ad absurdum*.'

'Are we here to find answers? Or to search for the pertinent questions?'

'Fiddling while the city burns?'

'No. But if I have a choice I prefer Archimedes' death to Byron's.'

'The point about Archimedes is that he could have saved his life – and advanced the course of science – by not trying to opt out of the realities of his world.'

'You mean he should have kissed the feet of the Roman conqueror?'

'Don't be ridiculous, prof. It is precisely to *stop* the kissing of feet – and arses – that I want people like last night's speaker silenced.'

'You'll make a good inquisitor, Lucas,' says Philip, more bitingly than one might expect of him. 'Or a security policeman for that matter.'

The pale face flushes in anger. 'I was hoping you'd be more understanding. I didn't think you would be quite so out of touch.'

'And I was expecting more academic responsibility from *you*.'

And behind this moment of naked anger flares, in both their minds, a single name. Melissa.*

The angle of approach might also be different, involving, say, the government's ban on COSAS. Which would provoke a protest movement among students at the university, spreading rapidly to radical younger members of staff. The deep structure of the scene, however, will remain unchanged.

'Call me what you wish, Lucas,' one can imagine Philip saying. (The setting would be the same: his study in the Arts Block where on that distant autumn night he took out the bottle of sweet sherry – a din of protesting students in the distant background – to offer Melissa a drink.) 'To me the university is a centre of learning. No strings attached. I know we live in a secular and cynical age, but we're still in pursuit of truth, aren't we? And that is possible only if we can isolate ourselves from the turmoil surrounding us.'

'With all due respect, prof: your vision of a splendid nineteenth-century isolation is wholly out of touch with what is going on right now. How can you close your eyes?'

'I don't think it's closing one's eyes. It's a matter of distinguishing between functions. As a man, as a citizen, I respond to what is happening around me. As an academic, I have different priorities.† It's a matter of defining the true function of a university.'

---

* It is difficult to render simultaneity in literature. If this were a film I would have used the dialogue as off-screen voices speaking over a collage of Melissa images as recalled by both men. They are not discussing university matters at all: the thrusts and parries of their dialectic are no more than the signs of an altogether different discourse. Both of them love her. This is the crux. Their tussle is the derailment of love.

† It is tempting to make Philip react in a completely different way here, reflecting the profound and inevitable change the scene in the forest (page 120 etc) must have wrought in him. How can he persist in thinking in terms of such tidy structures? But I find this the clearest way to illustrate the most insidious aspect of Lucas's influence on him: this perversity which forces

'Then it's on the nature of that function that we differ.' Is there a momentary narrowing of the colourless eyes?

'You want to organize a protest march against the COSAS ban. I agree the ban is upsetting, revolting. I even agree that students should protest, because the ban affects them all. But the university as an institution should stay out of it.'

'Then we cannot count on your support?'

'Not if it means marching through the streets with a poster round my neck. Proclaiming I'm a German Jew.'

Lucas stares at him in mild bewilderment.

Philip looks back, unrelenting, almost fascinated. It is the first time he really sees Lucas, not as a colleague or an opponent, but as a physical being: *this man*. The angular body, strangely pliant, soft, boneless, the ginger hair, the freckled face and hands. The man looks like a used condom, he thinks with uncharacteristic viciousness.

From this point the different possible approaches may converge in a more personal clash.

Lucas: 'I think we need another discussion soon. As you know, a decision about the new dean will come before faculty at our next meeting.'

'I have no wish to influence the election.'

'Of course not. But it may be important for those who support your candidacy to know exactly where they stand with you.'

'Don't they know already?'

'That's what I'd like to establish. Beyond all doubt.'

'Meaning?'

A long pause. The sheer weight of time.

'I'll be frank with you, prof. Look, as I see it, a deanship

---

him to revert to a structuralist world the forest scene has revealed to be inadequate.

Perhaps the undercurrents of the scene can be underscored by adding a sly touch (but only if it can be done very deftly, subtly): either in this episode or in a follow-up scene Lucas may bring the professor a sprig of mistletoe, which he impishly, ceremoniously, lays on the immaculate desk. ('I noticed you always have flowers on your desk. But this was all I could find – although it *is* a bit early for Christmas.')

requires more than academic or administrative competence. If that was all there was to it, I think the choice would be straightforward.'

He says nothing, asks nothing, just stares silently into the pale eyes. The young man has stood up, is now leaning slightly forward, his hands on the straight back of the chair. White knuckles.

'I'm speaking of moral integrity. One should like to be sure that the dean of a faculty is worthy in all respects.'

'And you don't think I meet the requirements?'

'That's not what I said. Perhaps I meant it as a question more than anything else.'

'I have nothing to be ashamed of.'

'That may be too strong a word. But you will appreciate that in a small community like ours, which tends to be somewhat conservative – '

'We do have our share of radicals,' he says pertinently.

'What I'm trying to say is that even if no one thinks that marriage is as sacrosanct as it used to be, there is still a premium on the kinds of relationships permissible between academics and their students.'

He gets up. 'Why beat about the bush, Lucas? Are you afraid of coming out with it?'

'It's not in my nature to poke my nose into other people's affairs, prof. I just wanted to leave a thought with you.'

'Good luck with your demo.'

When Lucas has left he sits down again. He can feel his heart beating. After a while he goes to his secretary's office to cadge a cigarette. He doesn't react to the look of incredulity in her eyes.

At table that night he has an unnerving experience: a sudden spell of dizziness followed by a trembling in his sight, as if he's staring at the world through running water. And even that vision is restricted: he can see straight ahead, but Greta and the children, seated on either side of the table, are invisible to him.

'What's the matter, Philip?'

'Nothing,' he says quickly. 'It's nothing at all.'

He is aware of her narrowed eyes watching him intently, but makes an effort to keep calm.

After a few minutes his sight returns to normal.

'I don't think it is anything to worry about,' says the doctor the following day. 'But it would be wise to make a few tests. At your age one shouldn't take risks.'

A brief entry, dated 28 January, in Jane Ferguson's diary: *Sensational reports in all the papers. C. arrested by the SB in J'burg today. Article 29 of the Internal Security Act. That can mean anything. Anything.*

On the morning of the boycott only two students turn up at Philip's 9.35 lecture and he sends them home. This leaves him with a few free hours to spend in the library on research for an article he's been planning for some time. When he returns to his department just before lunch he finds the building practically deserted. Only his secretary is in her office, drinking tea, standing in front of the window which overlooks the quad, spilling in her saucer; no sign of her usual matronly calm.

'Anything wrong, Mrs Shaw?' he asks from the door.

She almost drops her cup as she swings round to face him. 'Professor! You gave me such a fright. Where've you been all morning?'

'But I told you I was going to the library, didn't I?'

'You mean you didn't see what happened?'

'Please tell me what is going on.'

She's seen it all. A secretary from another department came to call her and with a crowd of other staff members they watched from the windows of the senior common room where one had a full view of the front lawns.

Lucas's demonstration started off rather unimpressively, it transpires. Perhaps a hundred students and about a dozen staff members, lined up with posters on the front lawn well inside the campus boundary. Then a convoy of police vehicles arrived in the street below and a phalanx of constables armed with green, orange and yellow quirts spilled out to take up position opposite the demonstrators. More and more vehicles arrived. Behind them the customary bustle of the town centre seemed to draw back, ebbing away, leaving only an anxious silence that pressed heavily on the spring morning. Some of the students shouted wisecracks and taunts at the police; two or three of them gave the Africa salute. More police drew up from behind, armed with rifles. Dogs tugging at their leashes. Suddenly, without any warning, they charged. A few of the staff members stood their ground, looking like mealie stalks on a land devastated by hail. The others were either trampled down in the charge or forced to turn and join the stampede. Four or five constables came straight at Lucas and started dragging him off towards the nearest van. A stout officer, trotting up from behind, breathing heavily, shouted: 'Right, boys. Give him hell!' The first blow broke his glasses. A kick in the stomach as he stumbled forward. Then he went down in the milling, running, tumbling mass of bodies. Flamboyant sjamboks swishing, arms flailing: all of it in a kind of unreal slow motion, as if one were watching it on film.

'It was downright disgusting,' says Mrs Shaw, 'the way those police went for the girls. You know' – a brief hesitation before she sweeps aside her usual prudence – 'hitting them across the breasts, kicking them between the legs. Quite deliberately.' A gulp of tea from her shaking cup restores her hold on herself. 'Not that it lasted very long. A few minutes, I should think, no more. Then the lawns were deserted. Only shoes and bits and pieces of clothing left behind. And the vans drove off. They must have taken away twenty or thirty students, men and women. And Lucas Wilson, of course. Professor, I still can't believe what I saw. One moment everything was peaceful, like a harmless student prank on a sunny morning. Then all this violence. Just because of a few posters. I never thought words could be so dangerous.'

What else can he say except, from force of habit: 'Didn't you know a word is the most dangerous weapon of all, Mrs Shaw?'

But later that afternoon, on his way back from the mass meeting which formed almost spontaneously in front of the Students' Union (how on earth did *he* get there? But practically everybody was there, in the wave of indignation and anger that swept through the university like a tide), he cannot suppress his confused rage as he says to Melissa: 'What's the use of just talking? Of all those slogans? One has got to *do* something, Melissa!'

(Like a small island in the tide of students eddying past them, they stand holding hands, staring excitedly at each other, not caring a damn about who sees them.)

'We can join tomorrow's march.'

(At the meeting: 'So they want to stop us marching tomorrow? Right. Then we'll march. Not twenty or a hundred or two hundred of us, but everybody on this campus.')

Startled, he looks at her. 'You really mean it?'

'They need us. They need *everybody*.'

'What was the use of half a million so-called German Jews in the streets of Paris twenty years ago?'

'There are times when one's just got to *be there*.'

'Will you be there?'

She nods.

And suddenly, shedding an ancient weight, he knows: Of course. She's right. There are times like that. This isn't Paris, 1968: these aren't a crowd of strangers in a distant city in Europe: this is here, now, today. This concerns *me*.

'I'll come to pick you up,' he says. Thinking: I'll come to you openly, not surreptitiously like before. This time, this once, we'll march together for all the world to see. Even the prospect of possible violence seems to hold a new and compelling fascination for him.

From the university he drives to the police station where a whole crowd of students and hangers-on, black and white, are thronging and jostling. It takes fifteen minutes or more for him to battle his way through to the charge office. The detainees, as it turns out, have not yet been 'processed'.

'I'd like to pay bail for Lucas Wilson,' he tells one of the busy young attorneys who are scuttling to and fro between cells and charge office.

'No need to,' says the lawyer, wiping perspiration from his pale, tense face with the back of his hand. 'The university has already offered to pay bail for everybody.'

'I'd like to pay for Dr Wilson anyway.'

He has to wait for hours on a corner of the dusty grey steps of the charge office before the detained students, and Lucas among them, are released; the sun has set long ago, the street lights are burning. Under the hooded lamps armoured vehicles are parked, surrounded by clusters of police in combat gear.

He gets up when he sees Lucas approaching, walking with difficulty.

'Can I take you home?'

'One of the students has already offered me a lift.'

'I've been waiting for you to come out.'

'Why the hell did you pay my bail?'

They reach Philip's car.

'You're a colleague.'

'You trying to buy me?'

'Don't flatter yourself. I would have done the same for any colleague.'

'It would have been better for you to be at the demo. Instead of trying to salve your conscience afterwards.'

'I'll be there tomorrow.'

'It's always easier the second time.' A snort of anger. 'Look, prof, if you think – '

'I hope you'll continue to lobby against me for the deanship, Lucas. You don't owe me anything.' Adding, as he moves into the driver's seat: 'Nor I you.'

And the next morning they march with all the others in the innocent sun of spring. Philip and Melissa hand in hand; Lucas, still hobbling slightly, a few yards in front of them, carrying a banner. Once he glances over his shoulder – his face is swollen and bruised – but his eyes remain without expression, as if he hasn't recognized them.

Yesterday morning at the demonstration there were a hundred. At the meeting in the afternoon, five hundred. This morning over a thousand. The logic of violence, thinks Philip. What else did the police expect? Hit a man over the head with a truncheon, bruise the breasts of a girl with a sjambok, break up a peaceful demonstration: and twenty-four hours later even people like me join the march.

It is a silent procession. No one speaks. Language is reduced to slogans on banners and posters. A year ago, he thinks, no one would have dared to show the colours of the ANC in public, or to display its slogans (except for graffiti hastily sprayed on some wall or fly-over at night): today it happens openly, throughout the country. It can no longer be stopped; the tide cannot be turned back. We're all becoming German Jews. And there is a strange exhilaration in a march like this: because of the silence, perhaps, the dignity of the black and scarlet gowns, row upon row upon row, all the way from the library, in a large question mark around the campus, through the main building, across the wide lawns where sunbirds and butterflies are fluttering among the flowers.

Below them, opposite the main entrance, the town has come to a standstill. Cars are damming up. The crowds have stopped in their tracks as if a movie has suddenly been frozen in a still. A sense of mute expectation. Not even the sun makes a sound.

As they spread out across the wide sweep of the lawns where yesterday's little band was overrun, there is a low drone in the background; and soon the police vans, the armoured trucks, the Buffels and Casspirs and Hippos approach in an endless slow procession. Drawing a cordon of mute violence between town and campus, spectators and demonstrators. The only movement (apart from the sunbirds and the butterflies) is that of the banners, fluttering from time to time in a breath of wind; an arm raised here or there; hair stroked back. (Blonde and loose and unruly hers tumbles about her shoulders.) And the police taking up position across the street with their quirts and batons, backed up by a second row with rifles and tear-gas canisters and dogs. All the formality and precision of an old-fashioned gentleman's war. Crusaders against Saracens. The terrible simplifications of lines of battle.

Someone addresses them. His gown flaps gently in the breeze, an indolent provocation to the security forces on whom he has turned his back to face the massed protesters. Then they break into song. *Nkosi sikelel' iAfrika*. The saddest and most beautiful anthem in the world, Philip thinks.

Hand in hand he stands with her. He doesn't sing with them, only recites the words in his mind. She is standing with her eyes closed. He can feel her trembling slightly, but it is not in fear. A kind of ecstasy, almost a trance, more than bravado: an excess of passion and conviction which spreads through her, through him. Obscure thoughts he couldn't grasp many years ago suddenly become clear. There is no 'I' or 'you' left; they are no longer a thousand individuals standing there: in the simplicity of this singing all separateness is transcended. No sentiment or thought or conviction is located 'inside' anyone any more: they have been transformed into pure energy, a single, vast electric field.

Waiting for the order to be barked, the violence to be let loose, the sudden movement to be unleashed: prepared for it, defiant, ready. Today there will be no stampede to run away. Today they will stand their ground. They will all have to be killed or dragged away with force.

Is that the reason why nothing happens? Have the police, for once, been intimidated by a dignity, a silence beyond the range of their simplistic calculations? Or have they decided (been ordered) beforehand not to 'act'? For ten minutes, a quarter of an hour, the two groups stand staring at each other. Even the light breeze has died down. Only among the flowers the trembling sunbirds, the flickering butterflies persist, unimpressed. In exactly the same instant the opposing parties begin to move: the police back to their trucks, the protesters to their university. Nothing has 'happened', nothing has been solved. And yet, thinks Philip, deep inside the darkness of their collective consciousness something has been decided. An ant cannot do combat against an elephant: it will be flattened instantly by a foot. Yet the ant can persevere, and each one killed is replaced by five or ten others. Yesterday there were a hundred, today a thousand. And one day, one day the ant will penetrate to the vital organs and the brain of the elephant. Then that whole mighty carcass will come tumbling down.

Through the dispersing crowd he walks with her, across the lawns, along the streets, back to her room in the scrappy yard. Hand in hand, swinging their arms, like two teenagers in love for the first time. Only, this isn't innocence: it is provocation. Look, look at us: we love each other, we *want* the world to see.

As they come through the rickety gate in the hedge overgrown with nasturtiums and creepers and weeds, her landlord waves at them from the back porch.

'Hi, Jack!' she calls back. 'Why aren't you working today?'

'What's the use? I got no customers left with the black boycott. So I thought I'd rather catch up on the jobs at home.'

She unlocks the door; Philip lets her enter first, then closes it behind them. She leans back against him, her hair covering his face; his hands on her breasts. The world is peeled from them like the shedding of clothes, skins. After the harsh clarity of winter the luxuriant wisteria in front of her window has invaded her room with an unworldly purple luminosity which makes them feel deliriously new.

It is as if the events of the morning have torn open new depths inside them which must be plummeted immediately, urgently, passionately, triumphantly. Her orgasm is so violent that in a sudden rush of fear he wonders whether she's lost consciousness; he has to check that her heart has not stopped beating. Her eyes flutter. She stares at him from afar, in a daze, as if she doesn't know where she is. At last she recognizes him and moves the tip of her finger along the lines of his face as if it were the map of a newly discovered territory with whose contours she is not yet familiar.

This is what it was like in Paris, he thinks. Love and violence meeting, intersecting, reinforcing one another: each discovering, obscurely, something of the other in the self, unsettling synonyms.

When at last she gets up it is to kneel beside the record player on the floor where she puts on a record, skipping a few cuts to find the groove she wants. Nana Mouskouri.

'Listen to the words,' she says, then flits away to the small kitchen down the narrow passage.

> *Ce qui arrivera demain*
> *Ne changera plus jamais rien*
> *A nous*
> *Je veux te dire quand même*
> *Comme l'on dit je t'aime*
> *Je n'ai pas peur de mourir*
> *Avec toi.*

She returns with the tray and puts it on the bed, seating herself at his feet, humming the last phrases of the music: *'Je n'ai pas peur de mourir avec toi.'* Looking up, through the wildness of her hair. 'That is what I kept on thinking this morning. You know, when the police took up position opposite us, I suddenly realized that I was no longer afraid. All my life I've been scared of violence. But this morning it just slipped away from me. Not for a moment did I doubt that they would charge at us and beat us down, but I didn't mind. I was with you. I knew I wouldn't run away but just stay there with you. And if they dragged us off to jail, that too would be all right. Perhaps they'd be merciful and lock us up together. I almost *wanted* to get killed with you. I knew that in a strange way it would mean victory for us. And for the first time I think I really understood what the black people in the townships are feeling.'

She leans over the tray to kiss him on the forehead, a small chaste gesture, with a serenity, a matter-of-factness, which moves him.

'I want to tell you something,' he says. 'And I don't mean it in a sentimental kind of way, but as a simple fact. I know now what it means to be in heaven. So if I have to go to hell after this, I'll accept it.'

After a long time, with a little sigh, she helps him dress; surprised, he discovers that they have been in such a hurry that he hasn't even taken off his watch.

The landlord is still hammering away on the back porch.

As Philip reaches the gate, ready to step out on the sidewalk, a car hoots on the opposite side of the street.

Annoyed, he looks up.

It is Greta in her small white Mazda.

'Come here,' she says, leaning over to open the passenger door for him. 'Get in.'

Essential to the love story: the substance of bodies.* It would suit the structuralist approach, as it suited Plato, to conceive of the human being as a collection of parts, one of which is the

---

* 'Body and body: I love you.' Cf. page 134. From the Donne quotation on page 17 one may proceed to the Woman as the Book (Barthes). Writing, narration, as an act of love.

body, another of which is the soul (usually with the assumption that, somehow, the soul is more 'essential', the 'real' person, which 'inhabits' the body as if the latter were a mere place of abode). But that is untenable. The alternative, as a love story demonstrates, need not imply that I am 'only' my body. As F. Sommers argues in 'Dualism in Descartes: the logical grounds',* a university can be described in terms of many different code systems – the topography of its campus, the constitution of its courses, its politics, the nature of its finances, etc. But these do not exist as separate compartments, islands, entities: 'To have been shown its grounds is to have been shown the university. Sometimes we are piously told that a university is not a set of buildings and grounds, but this is a mistake. A university is not *just* a physical plant; it is that and more.' The lover is more than body, his or hers: but that 'more' is not 'something else'. It is at most a different aspect which can be foregrounded or illuminated by looking at the lover from a different angle or another ideology. The body 'is' the love it makes. The book 'is' the story it tells. The story 'is' the world. The world 'is' the word.

'Thinking back now,' said Charles Ferguson, that day he brought me the book, 'I find it inexplicable that they didn't arrest Jane as well. Unless they thought that by leaving her free she might be of more use to them, perhaps by unwittingly leading them to whatever it was they were looking for. They certainly put her under tremendous pressure. But frail as she seemed she had resources nobody but I knew about.

'Within a day or two of Chris's arrest they came to see her. A whole contingent from Durban. By that time she'd come back to me in Empangeni and she'd already told me about her and Chris. In fact, she'd even given me her diary to hide. I don't know whether she was actually expecting something to happen, but it was just as well I had it. I hid it in one of our ranger's huts.

---

* In Michael Hooker (ed.), *Descartes: critical and interpretative essays*, Baltimore, 1978.

No matter how discreet her references to Chris were, the diary might have complicated things for her. And it was bad enough as it was.

'You see, the day she'd left the holiday farm she'd torn the page with his name on it from the hotel register. The pseudonym, I mean, Clive de Vos. And this they found in her room when they came for her and turned the whole house upside down. Like a bloody hurricane passing through the place.

'They questioned her for hours, then left. But the next day they came back. And no matter where she went during the next week or so, she was always tailed by strangers. So I insisted on going with her all the time. One never knows with those bastards. I mean, we know what happened to Goniwe and his friends in Cradock, don't we?

'It was tough on the nerves, I can tell you. But Jane didn't crack up. I was proud of her. I don't know what Jock and the others on the farm told the SB – for they went there too, of course, and as it turned out that really was the last straw for poor old Jock: a month later he just packed up and left, didn't even bother to find a buyer, just boarded up the windows and locked the doors and cleared out. Now where was I? Oh yes, the SB pestered them too, and every time after they'd been there they came back to Jane. Pressed her about that torn-out page. (Why hadn't she burned the damn thing? She'd meant to, she told me when I asked her. But she didn't have the heart to. It was all she had of him, that false name in his handwriting. Imagine.)

'No matter how they prodded and pried and pressed her, she insisted that she knew nothing about Chris's political activities. She didn't mind admitting that they'd been lovers. Almost proud of it, it seemed. You should have heard the questions they asked. Made it sound like an autopsy. But all she was prepared to say was that they'd spent a few nights together, and that she'd shown him around. Sweet blow-all about politics. I swear, if this were the fifteenth century and they'd burnt her on the stake she still wouldn't have told them anything.

'Then why had she torn out the page? As a souvenir of the man she'd loved, she said. But why had she waited until the news of his arrest had become known? Precisely because it had become known, because she'd realized then that he wouldn't come back. Same reason why she'd kept all the newspaper cuttings. You should have seen those reports, especially in the Afrikaans press: predicting "shocking disclosures" in the near future about "plans to overthrow the state". And in the English press the equally predictable eulogies about "a man of courageous principles", demands to "charge or release". Somewhere among all those simplifications the man himself had disappeared. Chris de Villiers. Or Clive de Vos, or whatever you want to call him. If it's true that history is only that which is recorded, then I suppose in the long run a person also exists only in terms of what has been verbalized about him. I find it a distressing thought. Anyway, Jane had kept everything. Including the newspaper photographs. You know, the protest march by the black trade unionists after they'd been locked out by the factory bosses who refused to negotiate. Chris among them. The police charging in with batons and sjamboks and dogs. Chris grabbed by four or five policemen. One of the papers reported that a bystander had seen a stout officer rushing up to them and ordering his men to "give him hell". The others were released the next day. But Chris was detained. The rest you know.'


Greta stares straight ahead of her as she drives on with Philip beside her; past the university, out of town, up the winding mountain road, a cloud of dust behind them.

'Where are we going?' he asks.

She doesn't answer. He notices the whiteness of her knuckles on the steering wheel.

'Couldn't you have waited?' he asks. (Why?)

Greta still gives no answer. He is used to her formidable self-control, but this time it is even more unnerving than usual.

When they reach the wood she turns off into a side track. My God, he thinks, does she know that this is where I found Melissa that late afternoon – ?

Without bothering to pull off the road – apart from the occasional donkey cart loaded with firewood there is never any traffic along this deserted track – she stops and switches off the ignition. Turns down her window. He opens his door to let in the breeze, but remains sitting beside her. A light rustling of leaves. The smell of eucalyptus. The whispering of pines. Gradually the sounds of birds are insinuated into the conscious mind, an abundance of invisible life among the trees. Space defined by sound. Sound surrounded by silence. Spheres within spheres. There is no end. There was no beginning.

'Well?' she asks, both hands still on the wheel, as if, though motionless, she continues to drive through immeasurable space.

'What do you want me to say?' he asks wretchedly.

'It's up to you.'

'Listen, Greta – '

'Whatever you do, don't try to apologize. Don't try to explain. Just tell me the truth.'

'I didn't intend to apologize. I cannot feel guilty about what's happened. All I want you to believe is that I never meant to hurt you.'

'But now you have.' Slowly her voice becomes suffused with anger. 'You're threatening to destroy what it took us fifteen years to build up.'

'Let's try to remain reasonable,' he says, also beginning to lose control. 'Drama will bring us nowhere.'

'You're the one who got involved in a cheap little sitcom.' Her voice stalls. She snaps open her handbag, takes out her cigarettes, lights one. Fascinated, as if he's never seen anyone smoke before, he stares at her. After inhaling she holds her breath for a while before slowly blowing out the smoke through her mouth. 'It isn't pleasant to hear from a friend – not even a friend, just a woman you meet at parties or in the supermarket from time to time – that your husband is spending most of his time with a girl young enough to be his daughter.'

'Who told you that?'

'Does it make any difference? It would seem that everybody's known about it for months. Except me.'

Very far away a rainbird is calling.

(Nothing can happen to birds that has not happened before.)

He gets out of the car. She remains behind the wheel. Aimlessly he wanders across the narrow dusty track, in among the first trees. The cool–warm smell of resin. A thick pelt of pine needles on the ground. (Somewhere here, close by, invisible, must be the rock, the circle of trees caught in that day's fire. She was lying down, as if in a sleep of a hundred years. Then she sat up, knees drawn up to her chest, hands clasping her feet. The perfect small round nails of her toes. Dark red drops of dragon blood.) Momentarily he is overcome by the same dizziness which assailed him the other night. It is different this time: a kind of double vision. As if he is staring at two altogether different scenes at the same time, superimposed on one another, the lines incongruous. But it goes away again. He draws in his breath, aware of the coolness of the light mountain wind on the perspiration on his forehead; then returns to the small white car and stops outside her window.

'Would you understand, would you accept,' he says, 'if I told you that it is possible to love two people at the same time?'

'No.'

'Then there's nothing more I can say.'

'What I mean, Philip, is that even if I could understand it with my head I refuse to accept it.'

'I haven't stopped loving you. But I cannot lie to you and pretend I don't love Melissa too.'

'I don't buy it. It's too easy. We're *married*, aren't we? There were certain things we promised each other. You expect me to keep my side of the bargain while you keep on exploring other possibilities.'

'Try to understand, Greta. Something happens to one's love in the course of fifteen years. It grows broader, deeper, more secure, more dependable, more predictable. But it cannot make one immune from another kind of love which is irresistible because it is so new and adventurous and fresh.'

'And with no strings attached, no responsibilities, no humdrum realities?' A brief, bitter laugh. 'What you're really saying is that in the course of fifteen years you've got used to me. You've learned to take me for granted. It was easy because I was always there. Now, suddenly, there's someone who's young and beautiful and full of life, and now your old love seems so tawdry and threadbare by comparison that you think it's expendable.'

'I never felt the need to replace one love with another.'

'Of course not. Not while you could have your cake and eat it. But that's what *you* wanted. You didn't stop to consider what *I* might wish. Or even she. It's pure selfishness, don't you see?'

For God's sake, he wants to say, that isn't true. It may seem like that to *you*. But how can you see what it looks like from where I am? I've kept these worlds so meticulously apart; it was possible to survive in each of them. I *have* survived, haven't I? Tell me I have. Don't let this happen. Don't let everything crumble to pieces.

'It's not just you and me,' she presses on. 'What about the children? We're a family.'

'I didn't *want* it to happen, Greta. And certainly not this way.'

'Do you live your life or does it live you? It's as simple as that.' She leans through the window. 'You're forgetting something very important, Philip. When we got married you were a man of experience. Also in terms of women. You'd even been married before. I was terribly young. I was about Melissa's age then: perhaps that should make you think. I was head over heels in love with you, right, but at the same time I was scared. How could I really be sure of you? How could I take the place of your wife who'd died? And then it was you who said: *because* of your experience, *because* you were older, *because* you'd spent such a long time thinking about getting married again, you could guarantee that you really knew what you were letting yourself in for. You not only wanted me, you wanted to marry me and stay married to me. Till death us do part. That's what you said. Have you forgotten?'

'I know I said that. And I meant it. Very deeply. But how can one foresee what may happen fifteen years later?'

'What is marriage if not a voluntary exclusion of other alternatives? For better or for worse? Even if other possibilities do arise later – more beautiful ones, younger ones, easier ones, more adventurous ones – they don't *exist* as alternatives, they're irrelevant. Because you've made your choice. Unless that choice is exclusive there can never be trust. And trust, it seems to me, is what it's all about.'

'How can one be tied to a choice forever, no matter how sincerely it was made? It's a matter of context. People change, Greta.'

'Well, if things have really become so unbearable I think it's time you make up your mind: either you accept the situation you first chose so freely and responsibly, or you make a clean break. You don't just muddle on.' Suddenly, directly: 'Do you want to marry Melissa?'

'We've never even thought of such a possibility yet.'

'How easy for you.' Now she is really getting angry. 'And in the mean time you expect me to sit waiting quietly until my lord and master has decided what to do with my life?'

'As long as no one knew about it no one could get hurt.'

'How naïve can you be?' In a rage she opens her door and gets out to face him more directly. 'It's the indignity of it, Philip! At least, if something like this had to happen, couldn't you have been more discreet, a bit more intelligent, a bit more sensible in your choice?'

'What do you mean? How can you judge so easily?'

'You're the laughing stock of the town,' she storms. 'It's sickening. Such a cheap little affair. Middle-aged man in his menopause, or whatever you men call it – and a little tart who knows a good fling when she sees one. Surely you don't think you're the only man in her life? Haven't you heard what people say about her – ?'

'You won't strengthen your case by insulting Melissa,' he hits back.

She begins to cry. And suddenly he finds himself curiously detached from her, from the whole situation: as if he is watching two other characters in a badly rehearsed play. Incredulous, he listens to the world she is conjuring up for him: a sordid affair in dark rooms, underground, dishonest, insignificant, perverse. Nothing of what she says is relevant to him. It cannot be Melissa and him she is talking about. (So detached does he feel that he finds time for a literary reflection. Lacan: 'It is the world of words which creates the world of things.') She is fabricating an existence wholly strange to him, a world that has no right or reason to exist. And his initial detachment gives way to anguish, almost to despair, as he wonders: What is true? Does that small cool room exist in which he was with Melissa but an hour ago, with its roughly plastered uneven walls, the crevices in the ceiling, the white curtains with their yellow ribbons, the light filtering through the foliage? Does that bed exist, with its grey-and-yellow duvet? The table with its piles of books, its scattered papers? The untidy little kitchen, the shower cubicle, the drawer with his comb and toothbrush in it? Does the deserted garden exist, and this wood, and the night they first met? – What happened that night? Did she come to him in his study? Did he drive her from the airport to a cottage in the dunes and tangled milkwood where they could hear the sea? Did he pick her up, soiled and abused, in some deserted street? Did they spend the night in a hotel where a bomb might go off at any moment? He isn't sure: he can no longer tell. He doesn't know *anything* any more.

As I find myself writing about Philip's distress amid his splintering separate worlds, I must confess a bemusement in myself. There he stands, wondering whether Melissa's room, or the past, or memory exists. Whereas he himself doesn't exist! He owes the possibility of his own being to me as I sit here writing him into literary existence. (Does that make me exist?)

In dejected, uncomprehending silence I let them drive back from the hostile wood.

Across the distant valleys beyond the densely wooded slopes the rainbird is still shaking out the clear droplets of its call.

There is a quote from Robinson Jeffers which continues to haunt me:

> A great love is a fire
> That burns the beams of the roof
> The doorposts are flaming and the house falls.

*3 March. Last night, the radio announced this morning, the notorious ANC activist Dr Chris de Villiers committed suicide in his cell at John Vorster Square. According to a police spokesman he hanged himself on strips torn from his blanket.*

*4 March. Drove back to the holiday farm in the mountains. The first time since C. was arrested. What kept me away so long? Not the constant surveillance by the SB. Not any dread to reopen wounds. But rather – even though I know it sounds strange – a kind of awe. Even disbelief. The fear of discovering that the memory was illusion, that nothing had really happened. Perhaps that farm was an island of the mind, an air bubble in the blood, a pressure on the brain, not a real place. Now C. is dead. (What certainty do I have even about that? I have only their word to go by, and I know that even if he had died it could never have happened the way they said: a man like C. doesn't commit suicide.)*

*When I got there everything was deserted. Except, when I went round to the kitchen (all the doors in front were locked, the windows boarded up) I saw the back door gaping and the shutters of one window broken. On the unkempt back lawn sat a group of Zulu people. Probably came up from the village below. They didn't seem to be waiting for something, just sat there as if they belonged to the place. I stopped. A few scrambled to their feet. Expecting trouble? From the back door came a man and two or three women, followed by a number of children, carrying things. Tins, boxes, bundles of newspapers, bits and pieces of furniture. The people on the lawn called out to them in warning. The looters stopped dead, dropping some of their loot.*

*Swallowing my panic I waved, shouted 'Sanibonani nina!' There was an uneasy pause. Then smiles broke out as a few voices called back: 'Sawubona ntombi!' They picked up the stuff they'd dropped and I walked on, round the burnt-down shed – could hear the guinea-fowl clicking inside, they'd taken over completely – and across the tatty lawns and terraces, past the pool, now all green and slimy, with fat frogs on the surface, some of them already dead and bloated, others copulating. I threw a stone at them but that didn't disturb them.*

*Stopped at the little cemetery, wondering whether I shouldn't come back sometime to do some weeding and tidying up, to make the dead more comfortable. But what's the use? No one even knows who they were any more. If one starts tending the graves in this country there won't be time for anything else. Almost with a feeling of guilt I remembered that dream I'd had. And that brought everything back. C., and the waterfall, and the story of Ntombinde, and the child who got burnt in the fire, and our nights together, and his going away.*

*What I was most keenly aware of was the feeling of revolt in me. Not against the fact of his death (though even now I can hardly bring myself to put it in words) but against everything denied us as a result of it. Not*

*success or victory in the struggle or anything heroic like that. But the*
*most mundane, ordinary things we'll never be allowed to share. To go*
*out for a meal, or prepare our own in the kitchen and sit down at our*
*dining table, to lock up the garage at night and take out the dog to pee, to*
*hang my panties over his towel in the bathroom, to use his razor for*
*shaving my legs, to go for a walk, to quarrel and make up, to wake up*
*beside each other in the morning.*

*No. I had to control myself. Not break apart. For his sake. I didn't*
*know (still don't) how to cope with the fact. Even if he is dead something*
*remains. Sooner or later I'll have to come to terms with it. I owe it to*
*him. Like those flames carried by runners, those torches, over mountains*
*and plains, through winters and summers, handing it on, one to the*
*other, the kind of flame that never goes out.*

*I walked back. A detour round the shed so as not to disturb the guinea-*
*fowl. I was glad they'd settled in again. Glad those people had begun to*
*take possession of the house, at the same time beginning slowly to break*
*it down. Perhaps it is a necessary process, I thought. Everything we*
*whites have built here over the years. The signs of our obtrusion. All*
*superfluity must first be levelled with the earth again before, one day,*
*someone can start anew.*

*'Hamba kahle,' the people called to me: 'Go well.'*
*'Salani kahle': 'Stay well.'*

*When I arrived at the front of the main building I saw the pale green*
*Toyota lower down the slope, among the trees of the driveway. Men*
*inside. They didn't get out. I didn't stop. In a way I suppose I'd been*
*expecting them. When I got into my old Volkswagen the Toyota started*
*up and drove off towards the main road. I didn't look back at the*
*farmhouse again. I knew it was the end of something. What I don't know*
*is whether something else has already begun.*


To keep things apart, distinct, separate (man and woman; life
and death; beginning and end; the inside and the outside of a
text; life and story), to define them in terms of their exclusivity
rather than in terms of what they have in common, must end in
schizophrenia, in the collapse of the mind which tries to keep the
distinctions going. In this lies the failure of apartheid, and the
failure, as I see it, of structuralism. What is suppressed, Jung

said somewhere, comes back to take its bloody revenge. And surely the most terrible revenge must come from the denial of the fluid oneness of things in favour of the principle of isolation.

The flash of insight in Kristeva's devastating remark: 'It is the critic's task, and there is hardly a more comical one, to coagulate an island of meaning upon a sea of negativity.'

Walking from the campus to her room, Philip would be aware of the shift that has taken place. That encounter with Greta in the wood was a watershed both of consciousness and of conscience. He is aware of walking along a perilous route, not the earlier dangers of police and trucks and guns, which were precise and definable, but something dark and ubiquitous: a route leading through danger to love; love surrounded by danger; love, who knows, *because of* danger. Provided one knows where to tread, he thinks, there is no need to fear the abyss: yet once you're conscious of the abyss, how can you be sure of your step?

She's expecting him. He came round the day before and left a note to tell her about Greta (she wasn't home then; the landlord said that she'd borrowed his van 'to take that black chap somewhere, you know, the one who always comes here, Milton something, just up to mischief again if you ask me, but you know how stroppy that girl can be'). She's wearing a faded T-shirt and her old jeans, her hair tied into a pony tail, her expression hidden behind a mask of make-up. But the paleness shows, her eyes are tired.

'Shall we drive out to our hotel for tea?'

'Yes. It's so stuffy in the room today.'

But there is more in returning to the hotel in the mountains than a wish to escape: perhaps it also contains (certainly this is what I'd like to convey if I fill out the scene) the need of affirmation. That the place exists, that it is there, not just an island of the mind, an air bubble in the blood, a pressure on the brain.

'Was it Milton you saw yesterday?' he asks as they drive out of town.

'Yes. Who told you?'

'Jack.'

'Poor man, I think he's jealous. Even of Milton. He's been eyeing me for so long himself. And always trying to persuade me you're too old for me. But he's a good sort. Quite harmless.'

'You don't discuss us with him, do you?'

'Of course not. But his eyes are peeled.'

'We're becoming public property.'

Up there on the mountain, to their left, only yesterday, that conversation with Greta in the wood; now so remote. Yet the nerve-ends are still too frayed for words to touch.

'Milton in trouble again?' he asks, not really interested; but it is a way out.

She shrugs. 'It's difficult to tell: you know how casual he can be. Sees everything as a joke. But I got the idea he's beginning to feel the pressure. The SB's been keeping watch on his house. So he thought it might be better to clear out and lie low for a while.'

'Where's he gone to?'

'I took him to a farm at Seven Fountains. No one will ever think of looking for him there, it's right out in the *bundu*.'

He says nothing. This is not what they have come out to discuss. But how to broach what both know has become unavoidable? They drive along in silence to their outlandish garden, that other territory where they have always managed to elude the world.

A place, as always, of opposites, extremes.

On the one hand there are signs of work in progress: terraces and flower beds weeded and raked, the lawns partly cut, the broken chairs and tables piled up under the new green foliage of the trees. Someone has even begun – but without either conviction or skill – to repair the roof of the outbuilding; but the wind has plundered it and strewn the thatch all over the place. On the other hand, alarmingly, the decay has gone further than before. The last rusty wires around the cemetery have been torn from their rickety posts, the bougainvillaea looks tattered, there are broken panes in the front windows of the main building.

But the reception inside is as effusive as before. (Can they really be the only people who ever come here?)

'Another week,' says the elderly woman in the turban which fails to hide the desperate grey wisps of her hair, 'then our menu will be ready.'

'We're planning a gala opening,' says the old man in the baggy khaki shorts, his face purple and blunt like the head of a penis. 'You must give us your address, we'll be sending out invitations soon.'

'We're getting an interior decorator from P.E.,' confides the overripe blonde, shoving her right hand down the front of her dress to scratch her left armpit; an overripe breast swings briefly into view. If it isn't plucked soon it will fall.

'So what'll it be today?' asks the old man, suddenly business-like. 'Champers on ice? You look as if you're celebrating something.'

'Just the usual tea, please. Outside.'

'Of course.' Raising his hands in apology: 'Sorry about those chairs, hey, but the bloody factory is keeping us waiting. It won't be long now, though.'

The swimming pool, they discover, has deteriorated again. (Perhaps, perversely, it is tended only in the winter months?) There must be a leak somewhere, for most of the water has seeped out, leaving a slimy green liquid with large frogs on the surface, some already dead and bloated, others copulating. Philip throws a stone among them, but that doesn't disturb their amorous concentration.

She turns away from him and heads for a shady spot at the far end of the lawn. (He thinks: 'Light clothes you in its deadly flame'. Neruda.) She sits down and pulls off her sandals. He comes to her. She lies back, her head on his lap.

'What's going to happen?' she asks. He can feel the tautness of her body. Her eyes are closed. He cannot think of anything to say. Under her closed lashes is a suggestion of tears.

'It is the end for us, isn't it?' she asks.

'I can't go on without you.'

She shakes her head, her eyes still closed; through the leaves above them flickerings of dazzling light move across her face.

'It'll get worse all the time,' she says. 'It's no longer just the two of us. Others are involved now. We can't go on hurting them, and getting hurt ourselves.'

'There must be a way out.'

'Like what?' For a moment she opens her eyes. 'There's nothing we can do, Philip. It was different while she didn't know. To hurt her consciously can only tear us apart. It's like – like making love on a grave. You remember my dream?'

'It was the first time we came here.'

'We were still innocent then. We didn't know yet.'

The waiter approaches with the tray, walking slowly, formally, as if in an invisible solemn procession. Like moving in a dream. Perhaps it *is* a dream.

Philip leans over to pour the tea; she watches him, turned on her stomach, chewing a blade of grass.

'We can get married,' he says quietly, pouring the tea, spilling some in her saucer.

'Is it really so easy?'

'Nothing is easy. But it can be done.'

Heat is shimmering among the trees. A few cicadas are shrilling.

She takes her cup, puts it down again to light a cigarette first. The little flame is blown out. He takes the matches from her, but the second attempt also fails. Only when they shield it with all four of their hands does he succeed.

'You have a career to think of,' she says. 'You have children. You have Greta. You can't just shrug them off.'

'Is it my problems you're worried about, or do you have misgivings of your own?'

'I suppose it's just that I've never possessed anyone or thought in terms of possession before. No, that's not quite true. Perhaps there were a few times when I possessed someone, but not because I wanted to, only because they allowed themselves to be reduced to it.' She smokes in silence for a minute. 'There were men who wanted to possess *me*, of course. But that invariably made me so scared that I backed off.'

'Don't you think it's different this time?'

'Of course. I know. But getting married is something else. I think it would frighten me.'

'There's no hurry.'

'True. But if it comes to a choice, if you give up what you have now, that'll inevitably put pressure on us. It'll be so different. There's so much we'll have to learn to live with.'

'I'm willing to risk it. What about you?'

'Not if it's at the expense of others.'

Yes, the innocence has gone, he thinks. Already it is different. The silence inside their bubble has been disturbed. Now they are exposed to the full glare of the light.

Wordless, they gaze at the deserted garden surrounding them. Nature taking over. Yet the signs of human presence cannot be effaced so easily. How few places there are left, he thinks, not yet contaminated by us. There is only one space which can be relied on ultimately: this imagined space between you and me.

When they arrive back at his car in front of the main building they both notice the pale green Toyota lower down among the trees of the driveway. There are men inside. Philip and Melissa do not stop. In a way, perhaps, they have been expecting the visitors. When they get into his car the Toyota starts up and drives off towards the distant main road.

'Promise me one thing,' she says when they get back to her room. 'If it's really the end for us, please, Philip, promise me you won't tell me when it's the last time.'

There is only one entry in Jane Ferguson's diary during the three months following her description of her last return to the resort in the mountains. Dated 2 June, it is very short. *Visitor from J'burg this morning. Could have been a man from another planet. No: from the dead. No traveller returns? This one did. No need for a name – what difference does it make? An inmate from John Vorster Square, released a week ago. Brought me this:*

A strip of toilet paper is sellotaped to the page, folded a few times and densely inscribed with what must have been a very blunt pencil, so that it is almost illegible. The date appears to be twenty-something February, i.e. a week or ten days before the death of 'the notorious ANC activist Dr Chris de Villiers' was reported. Part of the top, as well as the bottom of the paper is missing; it is difficult to make out how much has been lost:

ever get this? No matter. What is important is to write. Remember Winston Smith: 'The act of marking the paper was the decisive one.' I won't bore you with the details of my routine, so many prisoners have left their grey records. The Gulag, Buenos Aires, Santiago, Pretoria, it's all the same. The grey walls, the graffiti, the barred windows (illegible) hands wide, the small walled-in quad into which, once a day, a ray of sun filters through the steel mesh above, the mattress on the wooden bench, the shit bucket, the samp and greasy gravy, the mug of what looks like weak coffee, vaguely tastes like tea, and may be dishwater, the (illegible). Only the singing, I'm sure, must be unique. Those deep full voices, heartrendingly beautiful, utterly human yet unlike any sound I've heard man or woman utter before, a sound of entrails and blood, as if the deepest darkness of the earth itself has (illegible). The saddest, the most terrible thing of all is to wake up in the middle of the night and hear a man crying somewhere. For a moment not to have any idea of where one is, and then to remember. And to want to be with you, and to know there's no way in the world I can make anything easier for you. But I don't want you (illegible) about me. Oh they're doing their damnedest, but one reaches a stillness within oneself where they cannot (illegible). The worst, I suppose, isn't (illegible) but boredom. My main diversion in the long hours between interrogation – that is, when I am able to concentrate, when I am fully conscious – is a long line of black ants running diagonally up one wall carrying grains of sand, mortar, food, something. (Illegible) knows where they come from or head for. But there is something admirable, something truly astounding about their (illegible). And I am fascinated by the thought that they may in fact be busy breaking down and carrying away this entire building grain by grain. They have time on their side, the patience of history. What will happen will (illegible). Nothing, in the long run, can withstand this painstaking erosion by amicable ants who no doubt know what they have undertaken. I try to imagine how one day (illegible) nothing left of all their jails, admin buildings, mausoleums, granite monuments, the (illegible) some people insist to equate with 'white christian civilization'. The ants will remain, though. And all of those – us – who have the patience of ants. There's an almost perverse satisfaction in knowing that whatever they do they can never (illegible). The only way to survive is never to allow oneself to be dragged down to their level. Moral superiority. Which is (illegible). They've tried to persuade(!) me to testify against some of my best friends. Do they really think they can (illegible)? *Don't worry. I'll survive. One day I will be free again and we'll resume the struggle, which is the only thing that's* (illegible). *You know I've never believed in wasting my time with futile and* (illegible) *feelings of guilt. Yet in a very profound sense I feel I'm purging my own whiteness. There's a kind of* (illegible) *in knowing I'm no longer allowed to be exceptional, I'm not spared anything because I'm white. Their trust has not been misplaced. And what trust it was, and is. There's very little* (illegible), *but from time to time I spend moments together with some of the black* (illegible) *in the quad, in a passage, in an interrogation room, in* (illegible). *More often than not we're not allowed to speak. But a manacled hand brushing one's shoulder, a nod of the head, an expression in the eyes* (illegible). *We're in it together. The colour of our skins no longer separates us. Actually, this has been the best of it all along, since I first got involved in the unions. There was a time when they avoided whites, had to do it on their own. Not in the unions. They had enough trust to want us to* (illegible). *Together. And that is the beginning of something more important than* (illegible). *Well,* (illegible) *outlast the individual. What counts is the struggle itself. We are no more than the skins it sheds along the way. One day I'll* (illegible), *we shall all of us get out of this place. You see, it's not a matter of 'Abandon ye all hope – ' In a curious way this is a place of hope. Amandla! Ngawethu!* (Illegible) *seen so much hope for the future. We whites so often tend to think of the 'catastrophe' ahead, the great 'explosion', the 'apocalypse'. But it's really only a blind wall caving in to reveal a landscape which is* (illegible) *no, not 'beautiful' in any utopian sense, but worth while. Yes, that's it.* Worth while. *Worth everything. I don't know whether this makes sense to you, but* (illegible). *There is no time to grope for coherence, to formulate neatly or even correctly, and I'm not even sure you will* (illegible) *but I want you to be sustained by it as I am. Whatever you do, don't ever despair, don't even* (illegible). *I'm all right, I promise you, I shall be all right.* (Illegible) *time when I was a great follower of Camus, you know, truth, justice, freedom. But I'm much more modest now, perhaps more practical, more* (illegible). *To keep the revolution going, each new day to* (illegible), *the way ants work.* (Illegible) *of seeking martyrdom, the struggle has had enough martyrs already and it's more important to live for a cause than to die for it.* (Illegible) *do, they can never win, not in the long run, there are too many of us, black and white* (illegible) *consolation. For three centuries their meticulous colonialism has kept blacks 'in their place'. Good old christian work ethic. 'Arbeit macht frei'. It's changing now and we're all in (illegible). I have no doubt there will be all kinds of (illegible) about us, about me (illegible). Don't be disheartened or deluded. Don't think you're impotent. Report me and my (illegible). That should keep you busy! So whatever you do, however great the temptation to (illegible), I'm (illegible), I assure you I shall*

In the heart of every story lurks what Frank Kermode called 'the sense of an ending'*: to him it is, in fact, the distinguishing generic feature of a novel. Especially when it comes to a love story I presume the reader has a certain expectation of a climax. Isn't that what love is conventionally supposed to be directed at?

My own answer would be, emphatically, *no*.

Maybe this is the most profound discovery feminism has brought to the novel? – the awareness that sexual love is not primarily, exclusively, directed towards orgasm as its result and conclusion. Sophie Chauveau draws the crude but significant parallel between sex and eating, orgasm and the breaking of wind after the meal. If you've eaten well, she says, the burp comes naturally: you do not eat 'for the sake of' the burp. Which is why she can go on to say: 'Of course love creates fear, but what else is there to grapple with? What other kind of adventure is still left to us? *It is the only adventure of which we do not know the end.*' (My italics.) Which involves more than Eliot's distinction between the bang and the whimper. Perhaps one should rather think in terms of Flaubert's dictum: *'La bêtise consiste à vouloir conclure.'*

Which is why Madame Chauveau can launch into such a passionate tirade: 'Stop using your erect sexes like the batons of policemen, as if they are meant only to establish law and order in the disorder of my senses, to offer a target for my emotions, justification for our embrace, aimed at a conclusion, always the same, which you know by heart, and which never ceases to disappoint you and subvert your contortions.'

---

* And although for us the end has perhaps lost its naïve *imminence*, its shadow still lies on the crises of our fictions; we 'may speak of it as *immanent*' (*The Sense of an Ending*, Oxford University Press, 1977, p. 6).

It was on the white beach of Mauritius* that I first read Sophie Chauveau's *Débandade* (Jean-Jacques Pauvert, 1982), at the edge of an expanse of turquoise water in which the uncertain white line of the coral reef tried, tentatively, to draw a line, to indicate a frontier, a circumscription, a conclusion, before giving it up again as across the full length of the reef the ocean came gently flowing in, spilling its excesses on the beach.

One afternoon while she is dozing in his arms, I can see him gazing at her as he thinks with exquisite self-pity: 'My love, my love, will you remember, thirty years from now, when I am dead and you about as old as I am now, your lover of this deranged year? Will you still remember how desperately I loved you, and how beautiful it was, and how sad, and how full of pain?'

Apropos: asked what had struck him during his most recent rereading of *Don Quixote*, Carlos Fuentes says in an interview:
  'I discovered for the first time that Don Quixote knows he has invented Dulcinea. I realized that he knows very well that she is an invention of his, and that *Don Quixote* is perhaps one of the most beautiful love stories ever written, because Don Quixote knows that Dulcinea is a lowly woman, that she smells of garlic, that she has a voice like a bellows, yet for him she is a princess because he loves her, and therefore she's incomparable.' As a result, says Fuentes, the knight succeeds in postponing his own death. 'I think that this is the role of Dulcinea always, she postpones our death, whoever Dulcinea may be.'
  'But if that postponement comes from the creating of character,' asks the interviewer, 'how much are you, Carlos

---

* Perhaps the concept of the island, like the concept of the novel as a rounded whole, the perfect circle, the magical ring, is not just a manifestation of the urge to escape, to deny the world, to seek refuge from what you cannot handle, but the result of the need for self-preservation and survival. In which case the supreme irony is that on the island we recreate the conditions of the world we try to escape. *Robinson Crusoe. Lord of the Flies.*

Fuentes the novelist, postponing your own death by writing novels?'

To which Fuentes replies: 'That is what novels are about – a postponement of death.'*

A piece of dialogue for Greta: 'Forget what I said the other day, Philip. I was unreasonable. I don't want to force any choices on you. I know it isn't just a summer cold. I love you. For God's sake, I'm prepared to give you time. I know you'll come back to me in the end. If I go away now and leave you to her you can only get hurt, and I don't want you to be alone when that happens.'

Only days after receiving Chris de Villiers' letter from the dead Jane Ferguson began to work on her novella, making brief side notes in her diary. For example:

*7 June. Now I can start writing. Want to. Must. I must find the words for it. Words of fire, like a blazing stick forming patterns in the dark. About the gulls (nine of them sweeping over the sea in front of my window this morning). About the restoration of dreams and how (impossible) it is to live innocently and anew; how it is to (have to) prepare constantly to start again, to (want to) continue believing in the values I believe I believe in. About the fear that these things and this trembling may depart from me; that the intimate knowledge I have acquired may be irrelevant; that I may be left without passion again. Previously I knew the tides, but without feeling the water growing in myself. I knew autumn, but without experiencing the way it happens in the leaves.*

---

* Quoted in *The Listener*, 14 August 1986. All these quotes! J. Feral remarks, apropos of Kristeva, that 'a given text always constitutes a kind of mosaic of quotations, [and] that it is an abstraction and a transformation of others'. What assumes the form, at the moment, of an agglomeration of citations will eventually – if I proceed to transform notes into story – be absorbed by that text to exist only, as Barthes termed it, as 'mirages'. Cf. the footnote on pages 18–19.

The intimation of the end is also a preparation for entering into the dark night of the soul. And although physical night need not be part of it, I should like to introduce the following sequence with a scene set pertinently in the dark – that dark Donington refers to, in his discussion of *Götterdämmerung*, as akin to the alchemists' *nigrado* (blackening) and *putrefactio* (dissolution) which precede the dawn of insight.

Philip will experience it as a night not so much hot as oppressive, close, stifling, with a stillness which is not the absence of sound but the muffling of obscure and threatening things lurking, invisible, in the dark. The night is holding its breath for fear that at the first sound or movement some unseen evil power may discover the presence of life and pounce on it. He has woken up in the middle of it, knowing that he has been dreaming but unable to recall the dream, remembering only that it has been frightening. Beside him Greta will be sleeping peacefully; the whole house is asleep. So is the town. (But what is happening in those dark townships on the periphery of white consciousness?)

He lies with his legs drawn up, in a foetal position, caught in a vortex of ancient guilt and memories, surrounded by the whorl of all that has happened. That first unreal night: when he picked up a half-conscious mumbling waif in the streets and brought her home and cared for her and abused her – no: when he brought her from the airport and impulsively turned off to the secluded cottage by the sea where he spent an irresponsible weekend with her in chaste and idyllic isolation – no: when they fled from a boring reception to his hotel where the possibility of a bomb drove them into the precarious sanctuary of lovemaking (God, the shock of the telephone, her hands pressing against his head, the fumbling with her cigarette, the silhouette of her breasts against the window) – no: when she came up to his study after the political meeting and he offered her cloying sweet sherry in a mug, which they shared, and their hands touched, and she looked at him, and they kissed, and knew they had no choice but to become lovers –

Their fugues and evasions; the compulsive returns to the submarine interior of her little room with its light changing according to the seasons – an icy white in winter, purple in spring, an intensifying green in summer. The never-ending threats to the integrity of their love: saved from the everyday, but by that very circumstance marked for destruction. That one special day accorded them to spend together, when Greta was away: and then Milton Thaya came and by the time he left the day was nearly over; and when at last he found her – that far-off rock, fire-encircled – the sun was already setting. Their brief apotheosis on the day of the demonstration, and its consecration afterwards in her room: and Greta waiting for him in the small white car outside. Every time, every time.

Why is he haunted by it all tonight? So many thoughts caving in on him like collapsing walls, a medieval castle crumbling: and what grail, what mystic rose or ring is to be salvaged from the ruins?

Something must be wrong. Why else should these memories oppress him so? Something must have happened to her. She is in danger. She needs him. That is the only explanation.

Impossible to stay in bed any longer. He must get up. No matter whether it's two or three or four o'clock. He must go to her without delay.

But he also knows that if he does, something will have been decided once and for all. Return will be impossible.

Can a decision so momentous, of so much weight, really be taken so easily? But perhaps it has been decided long ago, somewhere within him, below the grasp of his tormented consciousness; leaving to him only the execution of actions which must result from a choice already made.

Cautiously, so as not to wake up Greta, he slides out of the bed, stopping for a moment to make sure she is still asleep, before he begins to put on his clothes in the dark. His movements are leisurely, calculated. Now that he knows what is to be done there is no room for hesitation or further thought.

He goes downstairs to his study. Without turning on the light he assembles what he needs. Cheque book and credit cards, a few books, a file with personal documents. Puts them into his briefcase, then returns upstairs to pack some clothes.

Outside the night still weighs, heavy, secret, silent, on the town. For a moment he stops in front of the small window on the staircase. There is no light at all outside, not even in the streets.

Must be a power failure. Medieval darkness. It makes him nervous again.

As he tiptoes along the passage past the other bedrooms, carrying his suitcase, a small sound makes him stop. A light moan from his daughter's room. She must be dreaming. He can hear her mumbling and complaining in her sleep, but cannot make out the words.

When she was small she often had nightmares. Invariably he was the one who, at the very first sound, hurried to her bed to take her in his arms and comfort her and coax her into drinking some water or milk: 'It's all right, my darling, Daddy's here with you, don't worry, there's nothing to be afraid of.'

Standing at her open door, waiting for her breathing to become regular and peaceful again, he abandons himself to memories. One day when she was very small, about two or three, they went to the sea. She lay sleeping on the back seat and when they crossed the last hill Greta woke her up so that she could look at the sea. To their surprise she burst into tears. 'Where's my cup?' she cried. 'I want my cup.'

'What cup?' they asked.

'My little red cup. The cup I buried in the sand.'

'But we've never been here before, my darling. Daddy's just bought us the cottage. And you've never had a red cup in your life.'

The child was inconsolable. It was getting on their nerves. In the cottage they unpacked – the girl refused to get out of the car and stayed there on the back seat, moaning and fretting – and prepared lunch and tidied up; and in the course of the afternoon they went down to the beach. Immediately the child brightened up. On the beach she broke away from them and ran straight to a tall white dune, her sturdy little baby legs wobbling in the sand. Near the top she flopped down heavily and started burrowing. They watched, bemused. Only a few inches into the sand she brought to light a little red plastic mug – surprisingly well preserved, as if it had been buried only a few hours before – which she triumphantly waved at them.

'My cup!' she shouted, chortling with glee.

Ever since that day his feelings for this child have been more than just paternal love. There is a kind of awe mixed with it, and amazement; as if he senses in her something still in touch with a beyond neither he nor any other grown-up could hope to understand.

And now, tonight.

Another light moan in her sleep. He goes into the room and sits on the edge of the bed, starts talking to her in gentle, comforting tones; leans over to kiss the slight dampness of her head, and stays with her until at last her sleep is deep and untroubled again.

With a sigh he goes back to his bedroom and unpacks his clothes in the cupboard, undresses, and gets into the bed again.

'What's the matter?' Greta asks in a dazed voice. 'Can't you sleep?'

'Just been to the bathroom.'

She drifts off into sleep again. He lies on his back, staring up at the dark ceiling. The night is as oppressive as before. But inside him something has changed.

All he can do now is to wait for the day to break.

But when he arrives at Melissa's room at nine, bleary-eyed and dull after his sleepness night, her door is closed and there is no response to his knocking. With a heaviness in the pit of his stomach he goes away, only to return an hour later, and again at eleven, but there is still so sign of either her or her landlord.

It is a blazing hot day, as if the sun is shining through a giant burning-glass, all the white beams refracted towards a single spot; the world can go up in flames at any moment.

He even cancels a late-morning lecture to return to her messy backyard, but she is still not home.

At lunch Greta enquires anxiously about his health; he snaps at her, irritable and morose.

It is three o'clock in the afternoon before he finally finds Melissa in her backyard on a rock in the overgrown nasturtium bed. She is barefoot, her feet pressed into the soft earth as if in search of something reassuringly solid or cool.

'Melissa!'

She glances up, her eyes defensive. Her shoulders are drooping.

'What's the matter? I've been so desperately worried about you. Couldn't sleep at all last night. And this morning – '

'Can we go for a drive? I must get out.'

The town is purple with jacaranda blossoms.

Gradually, as they drive along the mountain road towards the forest – intuition sends him there; she seems to take it for granted that they must come here – she unburdens to him. It's Ntombazana, the child of her landlord's char. (Philip – and hopefully the reader – will remember the impudent, bright-eyed little girl who wanted to know whether he was Melissa's 'boyfriend'.*) Yesterday, on her way home from her lessons in Melissa's room, she crossed the Market Square with four or five of her friends to catch a bus. Near the bus shelter a few *Casspirs* were lined up, and a group of bored young policemen stood leaning against the vehicles. No one paid much attention to them, they'd become part of the daily scene. As Ntombazana came skipping past – the bus was preparing to leave – one of the constables called out to her: 'Hey, you!'

They all stopped at once, cowering, suspicious.

'Come here.'

They didn't budge.

The constable took a few sweets from his pocket and held it out to them.

One or two of the kids hesitated for a moment, then darted off like frightened hares to the far side of the square. Ntombazana didn't know what to do. She looked round to see what had become of her friends.

'Stay where you are!' Was it a game? Was he serious? (Afterwards, some of the bystanders said, he burst into tears and swore he'd meant it as a joke.)

She drew up her arms and prepared to make a dash for it. He raised his pistol. He pulled the trigger. At point-blank range he shot her in the head. She was killed instantly.

Rosie, her mother, only heard about it that evening. It was impossible to do anything about it at that stage. The police, expecting trouble, had formed a cordon round the townships (from the opposite hill searchlights were trained on the area throughout the night so that nothing would be secret) and no one could get through to the town or the hospital.

---

* Cf. page 108.

Early in the morning Rosie arrived on Jack's doorstep with the news. But he was on his way out – there were rumours of a march into town to attack white businesses and he had to go and defend his shop – so Melissa had to take charge. To the police office, where she was curtly turned away ('Why are you asking about the case? Do you have any personal interest in the matter? What's your name and address?'). Then to the hospital. The morgue. After they'd identified the body, Melissa took Rosie to a lawyer. Then back to the police.

'What happened to the constable?' Philip asks.

'Didn't turn up for work today, as far as I could make out. Apparently he's in quite a state. Eighteen years old, I believe. Guns have never been meant as toys for children.'

'How's her mother taking it?'

'You know Rosie. The most placid, motherly person in the world. Never cared for politics. But you should have heard her this morning. In between the bouts of crying she spoke about her two little boys. She's always been so proud of them: wanted them to become teachers or doctors one day. But all that has changed. There's only one thing she's going to bring them up for now, she says. To kill policemen.' She bursts into desperate tears. 'How are we ever going to get out of this mess again, Philip? What's happening to us? How does a society deserve to survive if children are being killed as a joke?'

High up on the slope, where the wood begins, they turn from the dusty road into a narrow side track. He stops the car in a small opening among the trees. From there they follow a narrow footpath – she leads him by the hand; she knows the way – over a knuckle in the mountain into a deep valley beyond, towards the rock where he found her on that distant, unbelievable day.

Liquid bird-sounds. The bush-dove uttering its forlorn call: 'It is my little girl – it is my little girl – it is my little girl!'

A Piet-my-vrou calling its mate.

A rainbird in the distance: 'My father is dead – my mother is dead – '

As their ears get tuned in to the silence the myriad of other calls become intelligible to them, like before. Sudden blinding flashes of light stabbing at them through the branches overhead.

He stretches himself out on his back. She sits beside him in her ancient posture, knees drawn up, sandals kicked off, narrow feet together. After a while she also lies back, their bodies touching. Without speaking, they lie there, delivered to silence. As if the mountains, and the trees, and the hard earth beneath them, and their very bodies, have no relevance in themselves, but serve only as obstacles, objects to make space possible, discernible.

From time to time she still contracts in a sob.

'Philip,' she says at last, 'for God's sake, don't ever leave me. I won't be able to bear it. I'll go mad, I think. You know what happens to a woman who goes mad? Internal combustion. She burns. That's what happens. She burns.'

He presses her against him until at last the tenseness leaves her.

The first time we were here, he thinks, I had to come through flames to reach you; now the fire is inside me, in my blood. Desire stirs in him; he feels the urge to make love to her, here, now. He senses his penis erect like a weapon, a sword, between them. But this very image disturbs and disarms him. In her experience sex has so often been associated with violence. How can he take advantage of her? (That first night – but that was different!) Also, it is too open, too exposed here. He needs the reassurance of more defined surroundings and shapes: floors and walls and ceilings, bed. They are both too vulnerable here.

Far overhead two crows fly past.

She sits up again to light a cigarette.

'I'd like one too,' he says.

'I've never seen you smoke before.' She wipes away her tears before she puts a cigarette in his mouth and leans over so that he can light it from hers.

'How strange,' she says after some time. 'Remember, the other day I told you that something inside me seizes up with fear when I think of getting married, of being possessed.' She pauses. He sits looking at her in silence, as if he already knows what she is going to say. 'Something has changed now. I can think of nothing else I want more than to be married to you. Not for the excitement or the adventure of it, but for the most ordinary little things you can imagine. To go out for a meal, or to make our own food and have it at our dining table. To lock up the garage at night and take out the dog to pee. To hang my panties over your towel in the bathroom, or use your razor to shave my legs. To go for a walk, without being disturbed by combi-loads of drunken students terrorizing us as if we were criminals. To quarrel, and make up again.' She blows out smoke. 'Do you realize that we've never even quarrelled yet? It's abnormal. It's because we can only share an hour or two at a time. I want you for ever.'

He stubs out his half-smoked cigarette and presses it into the ground. 'I never want to be without you again either,' he says.

With almost ceremonial precision she stubs out her cigarette too and lies back again, propped up on her elbows, her head thrown back. High above them, through the trees, she can see clouds sailing past without a sound.

'The clouds don't even know what's happening to them,' she says. 'They just keep on drifting. They're never the same, yet they're always there. Vapour. Water.' A brief laugh. 'Not that that explains anything.'

'Eighty per cent of us is water too.'

'If only it could have been a hundred per cent.'

'I'm not sure of what you're trying to say,' he says against her cheek. 'But I agree. Totally.'

'We must go back.' She is composed again. 'Please forget what I said. I didn't mean it. I know it's impossible.'

Why don't you start burrowing in the ground? he thinks. I'm sure you'll find the decayed rim of a little red plastic mug. This is the end of the rainbow. Didn't you know?

Back in the town, he stops in front of the gate to her backyard and opens the door for her. Wistful for a moment, he turns to look back towards the hills where they have been. And starts. For high up in the mountains, in the dark patch of the wood, a thin spiral of smoke is visible. In front of their eyes it becomes more dense, more black. She grabs him by the arm, unable to speak. From the yard her landlord comes towards them; his frayed blue overalls are stained with grease.

'Fireworks again,' he says nonchalantly. 'Always happens on the first hot day of summer, have you noticed? It's the bloody berg wind.'

He stands looking at the distant fire with them, then shakes his head and returns to whatever odd job he's been doing.

'We've set fire to the wood,' she whispers. 'My God, Philip – '

'Impossible. We stubbed those cigarettes out so thoroughly.'

'How can one be *sure*?'

He points: there – there – in at least three other places – no, four – plumes of smoke are spiralling up from the wood. Within ten minutes entire trees are exploding in spectacular eruptions of fire, sending a heavy black cloud of smoke drifting over the town.

'There'll be nothing left of the wood,' he says.

'There'll be nothing left of *anything*.'

By now, sirens of the fire brigade are howling through the streets, like a stampede of obsolete animals trying to escape the burning of their familiar world.

Right through the night, and the following day, and the second night, the mountain continues to burn. The whole town is pervaded by the smell of soot and charcoal. Arson, rumour has it: it's the blacks taking revenge for the killing of the child. The next to be set alight will be the white suburbs. More armoured vehicles are brought from Port Elizabeth to quell any possible outbreaks of violence. Troop reinforcements are sent from as far away as Oudtshoorn. The Eastern Cape, this ancient battlefield of white and black, is set to explode again. Will anything ever be the same again? It is as if an entire familiar order is passing away. The town is surrounded by a wasteland of black soot, grey ash.

But it isn't only the trees. There is something in himself, in them, he thinks, that has been destroyed in this fire. A sanctuary, an island has been taken from them. He shakes his head. No. It has always been penetrable, vulnerable, even if they haven't realized it. Even in their most intimate moments they have been at the mercy of memories, other loves, other people. The clouds go on drifting by, changing, passing overhead. Nothing can happen to clouds and birds. They do not know. But we do. We know *now*. From the very beginning we have been invaded – not only by the past, but by the future. Since the first dawn this day has been dormant in the wood. From the first germination of a seed the fire smoulders within it.

With apocalyptic violence the months of November and December broke upon the country, their excesses like a sensational backcloth, painted in fire and blood, to an overstated opera. Donington speaks of 'the voluntary sacrifice of outworn values': only, this was not voluntary, and in the spasms and contortions of the year's end violence seemed only to beget more violence. On 2 November the Government, unable to control the forces its policies had unleashed, tried to black out the symptoms by banning all TV coverage of events in emergency areas. From that day, the daily average of people killed in the unrest increased alarmingly. In the township of Mlungisi outside Queenstown a desperate mob, armed with stones, attacked police who responded with shotgun fire, killing at least fourteen people (the unofficial death toll was much higher). Conditions in the township were so appalling that arrangements had to be made for food supplies to be brought in; but white ratepayers appealed to the Government to withhold emergency aid until the black boycotters were brought to their knees. In Mamelodi, near Pretoria, a clash at the Development Board offices between blacks and police resulted in an official death toll of thirteen. In the mean time, peaceful black leaders like Mkhuseli Jack and Henry Fazzi who tried to negotiate an end to the consumer boycotts in Port Elizabeth were rearrested. Clearly, a peaceful settlement would act against the by now well-established policy of the security forces to use as much force as possible in quelling violence they themselves had, at least in part, provoked. Soon afterwards, when boycotts in the Eastern Cape did get called off – to allow the Government six months in which to prove its serious intentions with reform – a new wave of boycotts, violence and tension broke out in the Transvaal. In an unprecedented move members of the Defence Force were given extraordinary powers of detention and 'unrest control'.

A significant development in this period was the formation of a new umbrella organization of militant black trade unions, COSATU, designed to organize and direct political agitation of the oppressed black majority within the context of labour.

During December a land-mine explosion in the border area of the Northern Transvaal killed two women and four children; just before Christmas a bomb in a shopping centre in Amanzimtoti wreaked havoc (five dead, sixty-one injured). In Natal a charge of high treason against sixteen UDF leaders was finally withdrawn after the case had dragged on for God knows how long. In the Cape a gathering to sing carols by candlelight was banned as being subversive. Soon afterwards, a sandcastle competition on the beach in aid of ECC was banned on the same grounds.

Zinzi Mandela reported that her father was effectively being held in solitary confinement in Pollsmoor Prison, where he spent 'his worst Christmas since 1964'.

The value of the South African currency continued to decline as pressure from abroad increased. It became clearer by the day that the country's problems could no longer be isolated from the body of humanity. Only the State President in his end-of-the-year messages on TV professed faith in peace and prosperity under the guidance of his violent regime. Behind his blunt arrogant eyes slumbered the incomprehension of someone left behind by history. *Südafrika, Südafrika über alles.*


It is even worse now, as I am writing this in the blazing heat of a new summer. Much worse. Unable to control the situation its own actions had provoked, exposed by an uninterrupted flow of news about the excesses of the security forces and challenged by several court decisions, the Government imposed a new set of emergency regulations at the beginning of December. Media coverage of 'unrest' is now restricted to official statements by the State Bureau of Information, and consequently it is now illegal – at the risk of a ten-year prison sentence – to make any statement about security force action, boycotts, the treatment of detainees, 'people's courts' or street committees, or to advocate the release of detainees, or to discredit or undermine the system of compulsory military service.*

This did not prevent Milton Thaya from visiting me – even though for reasons of personal safety these visits are now

---

* In its edition of 12–18 December 1986, the Johannesburg *Weekly Mail* warns that 'This means you could be in trouble if you make such a statement at the dinner table, in casual conversation, or even in private notebooks.'

restricted to a minimum – to keep me up to date with events in his life. (He has just returned to Fingo Village after spending almost three weeks on the farm at Seven Fountains where he lay low to get the SB off his neck.) Conscious as I may be of the risk I run by divulging what he told me this afternoon, as a writer I have no choice but to proceed. How else can one retain one's self-respect? He left in the early evening, as soon as it was dark enough to get away unnoticed; if I close my eyes I can still see him in the big beige chair opposite me, his whole body enthusiastically involved in the act of telling.

It happened two nights ago, while many of the township people were outside to escape the oven heat of their shacks. Milton himself was standing at the wire fence in front of his home, chatting to friends while keeping one eye on a police van crammed with *amangundwane*, which came cruising down the street very, very slowly.

A stranger – a gaunt fellow in a tattered check shirt and faded khaki pants – came walking quite briskly down 'Durban', the street that runs down from the Chinaman's shop on the main road. (Officially, the streets are only named, A, B, C, etc., but the people have rechristened them 'Durban', or 'Angola', or 'Libya', and so on.) As he reached the corner of B Street where Milton lives, the police van, coming from the left, drew up right next to him and two of the *amangundwane* jumped out. Not a word was said. In front of all the township people out to enjoy a bit of fresh air, the two policemen opened fire and the stranger collapsed in the gutter.* Pandemonium, as one can well imagine. A couple of drunken youngsters, staggering home from the beer hall, started shouting abuse at the police, apparently under the impression that the man shot down was one of their friends. All the other *amangundwane* came tumbling out of the van, guns in hand. The drunken youngsters tried to get away, but one was caught by some of the policemen. 'Come on,' they shouted, setting to work on him with professional efficiency. 'Say "*Kubo!*" Say "*Kubo!*" ' Even in his inebriated state he must have known what would happen then: it is the battle cry of the young comrades in the township.

---

* In a manner of speaking. The township streets have no gutters.

217

In the mean time, the other *amangundwane* were spreading out in all directions, ordering the bystanders back into their homes. No one stopped to argue. In fact, there was something of a stampede to get out of reach as fast as possible.

On the corner of B Street and Durban the two cops were still trying to provoke the drunken youngster. 'Say *"Kubo!"* Come on, damn you!'

Then a Buffel arrived and suddenly there were white soldiers swarming all over the place. The *amangundwane* retreated into their van to watch. The drunken youth was still standing in the middle of the intersection, swaying on his feet, shouting at them. One of the soldiers, taking his rifle by the barrel, bludgeoned him to the ground. Screams of protest from all the windows in the neighbourhood caused the soldier to hesitate and stand back. The youth scrambled to his feet and dashed into the nearest backyard, which happened to be Milton's. The blinding searchlight on the Buffel was turned on as the massive vehicle thundered into the yard, knocking down one of the flimsy corrugated-iron shanties closest to the gate. But they never found their quarry.

The body of the stranger still lay, deserted, in the gutter on the corner.

An official statement by the Bureau of Information subsequently informed the public that a suspected terrorist had opened fire on the police in Fingo Village and that, forced to retaliate in self-defence, they had shot and killed him.

'Is there really nothing one can do about it, Milton?' I asked.

'Of course not.' He shrugged. 'It happens every day, doesn't it?'

'People must be *told*.'

'You want to burn me?'

I couldn't grasp what he was trying to say. Without warning he got up from the easy chair and made for the door as if, suddenly, he couldn't stand being there any longer. But after a moment he came back. 'You don't understand?' He was breathing deeply. 'I *knew* that man.'

'How do you mean you knew him? Who was he?'

'It was the man I stayed with when I went into hiding at Seven

Fountains. Just got his name from somebody and tried my luck, you see. An ordinary farm labourer. Everybody called him Fivebob. His name was Khayalethu, but that was what they called him. Fivebob. He and his family took me in, just like that. No questions, nothing. He earned twenty rand a month, but he took me in, shared everything with me.'

'I don't understand, Milton. What was he doing in town then?'

'Thrown off the farm after I left. I found out about it only this morning. Seems the farmer came to his hut and told him he and his family had twenty-four hours to clear out. Somebody had split on him: told his boss he'd been sheltering strangers in his hut. Terrorists, most likely. So he was on his way to my place to see if I could help him find somewhere to stay for his family.'

'We must be one of the most violent nations on earth,' said Charles Ferguson, picking at his pipe. 'We're surrounded by it. We articulate through it. It has become our language. And the problem is that, in order to make sure people keep on listening, we are forced to speak more and more loudly, through more and more excesses of brutality, just to make ourselves understood. What scares me is the thought that one day we'll have to resort to violence, more and more of it, in order simply to say: I love you.'

The death of the dog. Not an indispensable episode, perhaps, yet I feel compelled to try it.

For months now they would have been discussing the fate of the dog. The smelly, clumsy, long-haired, wolf-like creature that has been part of the family since before the first child was born. For the last year it is almost too arthritic to move, its sight has deteriorated, it is incontinent, it sheds its hairs all over the place. But whenever the question of euthanasia is raised at least one child volubly rebels.

Now the dog has been drawn into the other tensions in the family. What Greta cannot, or does not want to, discuss with Philip is taken out on the dog; when the children burst into the bedroom, without knocking, in search of Sellotape or erasers or scissors, and find Greta in tears on the bed, they flee in consternation to vent their fears and frustrations on the wretched old animal. When Philip comes home, guilty and tired (he's always tired these days, a weariness to the bone; at night he cannot sleep), then once again it is the shaggy hunk that must bear the brunt of it.

'It can't go on like this, I'll go mad, I tell you!' Greta explodes one evening.

'Don't blame me. Every time I want to do something about it, you or the children insist on prolonging his suffering.'

And the next morning, with the children off to school and Greta gone to town, he heaves the stubborn animal into his car and drives him to the vet. What he hasn't bargained for is that the officious white-coated man should order him to lift the dog on the table and hold him there. (A puddle of urine on the floor, a squirt over his sleeve.)

'All right, all right, don't panic,' he tries to reassure the animal, combing his fingers through the matted hair. The dog lies shivering under his hands while the vet prepares his syringe.

It is a very small, very banal operation. The rubber band round the upper leg; a spot shaved clean; a dab of methylated spirits. The needle. A few seconds – ten? – even less. Then a sigh, and the ungainly shaggy dog relaxes under his hands.

'It's all over,' says the vet.

All of a sudden everything that was, no longer is. Complete peace. Unable to grasp it, he remains behind for a moment. His glasses are foggy. Blindly he stumbles down the passage which smells of disinfectant and, yes, of death. Back to the sun. But the receptionist calls him back. He still has to pay, and get his receipt.

Just a sigh, he thinks. The only frontier between life and death. A sigh. (His father too, these many years ago.) Less than the movement of a cloud through the sky.

What shall one call it? – denial, betrayal, murder? The names do not matter. There is only this emptiness.

'What on earth has happened to the dog?' Greta asks at lunch. (The children are not yet home from school.) 'I've looked for him all over.' A sudden pause. Her wide, shocked eyes staring at him. 'Philip, don't tell me – ?'

'You said last night it couldn't go on like this.'

'I never thought you really would.' Her mouth contorts. 'Have you killed our dog?'

'What else was there to do?'

'But dead!' She begins to cry. 'No matter how old and miserable he was, he looked after the house. Who'll protect us now?'

'Don't make it sound like the bloody end of the world!' he snarls at her.

'How could you do it? You're totally heartless, you have no feelings.'

He pushes his chair back in anger. Gets up.

'Where are you going?' she calls after him.

'I'll come back when you can talk sense again.' His voice is shallow, harsh, trembling.

She makes an effort to control herself. 'You know it's not the dog.'

'Then don't use it as a pretext.'

'How easy to have a dog put down.' Her voice is empty. 'If only one could get rid of everything else so easily.' She bends her head. A long silence. 'I know it's hard for you too. I'm sorry. Why should we all have to suffer like this?'

'It's all we've got left,' he says, almost inaudibly. 'Suffering is all we can still be sure about.'


A note from Melissa, with a sprig of jasmine on the envelope:

'I don't know how to say it, I love you so much, I have such a need in me to see you every day, all day, all night, but at the same time I can't bear the hide-and-seek and the lies and the discoveries and the tears and the gossip and the knowing looks and the dishonesties and the drama. Every day there is some new story or speculation about us which makes it seem like just another cheap little affair, and I don't want that. We can't go on doing this to ourselves and to Greta. Lucas used to tell me I had no conscience, but I find it unbearable to live with what little I have left. What is going to happen? What is going to become of us? We seem to be going down the drain together with the rest of this goddamned country.'


Another sign of the approaching end. On their way to the hotel in the mountains (the heat of the past few weeks has been interrupted by this mild misty day) she says unexpectedly:

'I'll have to find another place to live. Jack told me yesterday. He's had to close down his shop, the black boycott has ruined him. So he's going to sell his house and move in with his brother in Joh'burg.'

'When?'

Flickering images, as from an old-time movie, race through his mind: the mornings, afternoons in that secluded and serene little room – the familiar chaos of her books and clothes, towels, records, dirty dishes, cups, ashtrays – the green light filtering through the window – the undoing of the yellow ribbons and the sensual grace of the white calico curtains as they fall into position – the red glow of the heater on cold days – the trembling of her breasts as she moves – his watch on the bedside table – her smothered moan when he enters her – Melissa, Melissa, I love you.

'As soon as possible,' she says. 'I've already begun to ask around. This afternoon I'm going to look at a couple of places.' A touch of despair: 'But they're all modern flats. I don't want to live up in the air, Philip. I need a place where I can feel the ground under my feet.' A sudden choking sound. 'And the dog – '

He doesn't know what to say. She needs reassurance from him now; he cannot afford to let her discover the panic in himself. (How is it going to affect them if she has to move out of that little room which has become like a subconscious dimension to their love, something indispensable, as much a definition of their togetherness as a place of abode? Space. Silence. That innocence towards which she continues so urgently to grope.)

'Is there no other way out for Jack?'

'No, he's thought about everything. He has no choice.'

'I'll help you. Perhaps we can even find a better place than the old one.'

'Perhaps.' She doesn't believe him. He doesn't either. 'Poor Jack is quite shattered,' she says, more composed now. 'He spent almost the whole of last night talking to me and drinking himself out of his wits. Just couldn't face his empty house.'

He cannot suppress a hint of irritation: 'He certainly knows where to find sympathy.'

A weary little laugh. 'You know, it was the first time he asked me to go out with him. Sometime next weekend perhaps. He's always kept so much to himself. Never tried to take advantage of me, not even when I was depressed or sad or angry or lonely.'

'Did that happen so often?'

'Of course.'

He is unnerved by the directness of her answer. Not knowing what to say he changes the subject: 'You're not going to accept his invitation, are you?'

'Why not?' She seems genuinely surprised. 'He's feeling so miserable, he can do with a bit of comforting.'

'But suppose he just wants to take advantage of your sympathy? Suppose he tries to get you into bed?'

(Ashamed, he thinks: This has never happened between us before, neither of us has ever felt jealous, it has never even entered the picture: our love has always been wholly free. To what indignities can one be reduced?)

'What if he does?'

'But Melissa!'

'It it really so important?' There is an edge to her voice.

'What's the use of trying to comfort him for a night? I'm sure there can't be more in it for either of you. So *why*?'

'Why not? You're just upset because it concerns someone else. If it had been you I'm sure you wouldn't have minded. Be honest, Philip. The poor man is down and out, he's lost everything he's had. And if I can offer him a bit of comfort, why shouldn't I? The world is such an inhospitable place.'

'Think of how it may affect us.'

'What are you talking about?' She shakes her head. 'It's not as if we're on the point of getting married or something, is it? What have we got? We're living in a world that's falling to pieces.'

'Nothing has been finalized yet. Anything may still happen.'

'Really? Anything?'

He stares straight ahead. His hands are sweating on the steering wheel. They turn out of the main road and charge uphill, followed by a churning cloud of dust.

They find the hotel completely deserted. Doors locked, windows boarded up. But going round to the back they discover that the kitchen door is gaping open and some of the shutters have been torn from the windows. On the unkempt back lawn a group of black people sit huddled together, mostly women and children. They do not seem to be waiting for something; it is as if they simply belong there.

Philip stops; Melissa beside him. Some of the people jump to their feet as if expecting trouble. At the same time a man and two or three women emerge from the back door, followed by a troop of children, all of them carrying stuff in their arms. Tins, boxes, piles of newspapers, bits and pieces of furniture. From the lawn voices call out to them in Xhosa. The looters stop in their tracks, some of the smaller ones dropping their booty.

Then Melissa breaks the tension, waving at them and moving on; after a moment her greeting is answered by relieved calls of 'Molo!'

Apart from the group on the lawn there is no other sign of life. They consider going round to the side lawn where they usually had their tea; but it is too cool today to tarry there. Restless, at a loss, they wander about for a while, reluctant to face the finality of a decision.

In the little cemetery Melissa squats down beside one of the graves and starts picking aimlessly at tufts of grass and weeds. A futile action, but it helps to concentrate her mind. In an open spot she begins to scoop out gravel and sand, not really knowing why. She becomes aware of Philip standing behind her, watching her, and his presence makes her persevere, as if her pointless activity is now of tremendous importance.

'What are you looking for?' he asks lightly. 'The Grail?'

Embarrassed, she glances up and begins to flatten the ground again. Looks up again, with a little grimace. 'It's too late for that, isn't it? Why are you staring at me like that?'

'I don't know,' he says slowly. 'I have a strange feeling that I saw you doing this in exactly the same way, long ago. Digging into a grave like that. I must have dreamt it.'

'You must have.'

She gets up. He wants to take her hand but she pulls away. Reluctantly, almost sadly, they stroll back across the patchy lawn, stopping from time to time as if in search of something, a sign perhaps, which may persuade them to stay. But there is nothing. The place has lost its familiarity and turned against them. There is nothing more they can do but leave.

The last entry in Jane Ferguson's diary:

*29 June. Writing like someone possessed. Day and night. The only grasp I have on the one experience which seems to have made my life worth while. Yet it scares me too. What is realized on paper becomes a betrayal of what one has aimed at, what one has hoped for, what one has believed in. Words, words.*

*I have no wish merely to report or record what has happened. It is the hereness of it, on the paper, which is important. The most one can do, it seems to me, is to prophesy the past.*

*C., C., I need you, I love you. I'm trying to write you. I can never possess you.*

Narratively speaking, it would be improper to leave Lucas Wilson where I last abandoned him. At the same time I am reluctant to yield to the old-fashioned impulse towards the 'well-made story' which involves a too tidy pulling together of threads.

Still, the circumstances within which I continue to compile my notes and undertake my trial flights suggest possibilities which it would be a pity not to explore.

One of these involves the call-up for army duty in the townships of a number of younger academics from the university. 'Standard procedure,' the Government would assure anxious opposition politicians enquiring about the move; yet it would seem a curious coincidence that so many of the most vociferous radical young members of staff should find themselves in the ranks of those called up with only twenty-four hours' warning. Among them, inevitably, would be Lucas Wilson.

Melissa knows nothing about it: the call-up coincides with her move into her new digs (helped by Milton who transports her furniture in his rickety truck). A small two-bedroomed flat on the second storey of a face-brick building near the university. Knowing in advance that she won't be able to sleep that night – the move has upset her too much; the last late afternoon walk with Rex in the woods was depressing rather than comforting; the strange, bare surroundings, still impregnated with the lives of the strangers who inhabited the place before her, upset her – she takes a sleeping pill when, close to midnight, she cannot avoid going to bed any longer. Impossible to tell for how long the front doorbell has been ringing before it penetrates to her consciousness. Startled out of her wits she jumps up, looking round in the room she doesn't recognize, trying to contain her dazed, scattered thoughts. Ten past two, say the luminous hands on the alarm clock beside her bed. She can't believe it. Perhaps it was a bad dream. But then the door bell goes again, shrill, insistent, aggressive.

Without bothering to put on a gown, wearing only her well-worn pyjama top, she stumbles to the door, not yet able to think coherently.

Lucas on the doorstep.

She stares at him, her head throbbing.

'For God's sake let me in before somebody sees me!' He pushes past her. She stands petrified, not even thinking of closing the door until, agitated, he pulls her inside by the arm and shoves it shut behind her.

'What are you doing here?' Slowly her thoughts become more manageable. 'Do you know what time it is?'

'They're looking for me.'

'Who? Why?'

'I need a drink.' Uninvited, he goes into the kitchen and rummages in the fridge. 'Got any beer?' he calls from there.

'No.'

He reappears in the door. 'Well, what else can you offer me?'
'Sherry?'
'You know I can't stand the stuff.'
She shrugs, unable to hide a touch of perverse satisfaction.
'Brandy?'
'I'm not sure.' She points vaguely at the piles of boxes still standing haphazardly on the floor. Then becomes aware of the look in his eyes as he glares at her; a look she knows only too well. Without a word she scurries back to the bedroom, stumbling over things in her way; finds her pyjama trousers, and her dark red dressing gown, puts them on (the trousers back to front). When she returns he has already poured himself what must be at least a triple tot of brandy.

'I don't want you here, Lucas. You must know by this time – ' (Tonight Jack isn't near in case of need; and she hasn't even met her neighbours yet.)

'I'm in trouble.' He takes a big gulp. His matted red hair appears to be on fire.

Backed up against the frame of the middle door she looks at him, unrelenting, on the defence.

'I got called up by the army, day before yesterday. Had to report by noon yesterday. I refused, of course. One's got to make a stand. There are two or three of the others in it with me. Now we're in hiding. The SB are looking for us.'

'What's the SB got to do with it? Surely it's a matter for the military?'

'Because the call-up was just a pretext. They've been after my blood ever since that demo. Don't you know – ?'

'I'm not interested. What do you want from me?'

'I want to stay here until I can make other plans.' A pause. 'Please.' It sounds more like an order.

'We've been through this before.'

'Can't you see it's different? It's for an important cause. And my life is in danger. If they catch me – ' Suddenly his voice breaks. He is close to tears. 'Would you rather turn me over to them? Don't you know what can happen to me in their hands?'

'Haven't you – Lucas, why didn't you think about it before you did what you've done?'

'There was no time.' He has lost most of his aggressive self-assurance, looking like a wretched little orphan. 'Melissa, please! I promise you – I'm just looking for a place to stay. Nothing else. I won't come near you if that's the way you want it.'

'It is.'

'So I can stay?'

'I don't know.' She feels miserable, resentful, cornered, guilty, angry. 'Why didn't you go to someone else?'

'It's safe here.' He comes towards her; instinctively her body tautens in revulsion. He must have noticed, for he stops. 'Look, if you insist, I'll leave in the morning. God, Melissa, you can't throw me to the dogs like this.'

She turns away, clutching the door frame. How in God's name is it possible that she should relent, feel sorry for him? But what will happen if she turns him out? How can she ever live with it if they arrest him while she could have prevented it? Perhaps, if the circumstances had been different – but the *army*! Inexplicably, illogically, Louis enters into it. A way of atoning for his death perhaps? Reaching out beyond the grave – that charred stump, those black sticks of arms – to the brother she'd known before the change began.

'Lucas, if you swear you'll behave yourself and leave first thing in the morning – '

'I give you my word for it.'

She sighs, her head throbbing. 'I'll make you a bed on the floor in the spare room. If you don't mind the mess.'

He sits down on the old sofa she's picked up at a second-hand furniture dealer's that afternoon; sipping his brandy, watching her unpack several boxes to find sheets, blankets, a pillow, a towel, with which she goes to the small spare room opposite hers. (Thank God this flat has more space; what would she have done in her old room?) Five minutes later she reappears in the middle door.

'If you don't mind, I'm going back to bed, I feel terrible.'

'Thanks, love.' He gets up and comes towards her. 'You're a brick.'

She goes to her bed, but in spite of the sleeping pill she took earlier she finds it impossible to relax. With every muscle in her body tensed, she listens to him still fidgeting about in the front room. (Why doesn't he go to his bedroom?) Papers rustling. Is

228

he going through her books, her boxes, all the half-unpacked things strewn about on the floor? When, much later, she hears his footsteps in the short passage outside her open door, she raises her head and sees him passing, naked, to the bathroom where he urinates voluminously. Her stomach contracts. She has to lie back to overcome the nausea rising in her. Waiting. Knowing what is coming.

Still naked, he comes into the bedroom and sits down at the foot of her bed.

'You asleep?'

'Lucas, please – '

'Jesus, Melissa, this whole thing's been such a shock. I don't think I'll sleep a wink tonight.'

'I can give you a sleeping pill.'

He ignores her offer. 'You realize they may be taking me in tomorrow.'

'You knew that when you made your decision, didn't you?'

'Yes. But when it comes it still takes one by surprise.' He leans over her. 'Promise me you won't tell a soul I've been here tonight. Don't breathe a word to Philip Malan. OK?'

'I won't. Now just go to bed, please.'

But he doesn't. She is so exhausted that at one stage she sinks into a daze; when she comes to, he is in bed with her, fondling her, pressing himself against her. The aggressive baton of his sex. His breathing in her ear. She pushes him away, tries to ward him off, but he persists.

'Lucas, you promised!' She sits up, her head reeling. 'If you don't stop, I *will* tell Philip about it.'

This makes him mad. He forces her back against the pillows and manoeuvres himself on top of her. But she manages to squirm away, out of reach, huddled up against the wall. And so it goes on for what must be hours. Only this time she refuses to give in, keeps on fighting, no matter how furious or violent it makes him.

At the first light of dawn she jumps out of bed and flees to the front room, putting on her dressing gown as she goes. He follows her to the door, his sex at half-mast.

'Melissa – '

She swings round like a cornered *meerkat*. 'So this is your great cause,' she sneers. 'Fighting for justice, for the things you believe in. Resisting your call-up. Cocking a snook at the Security Police. Carrying on the great fight underground. Who do you think you are? A hero like Chris de Villiers or Neil Aggett or someone? Do you realize that during this night hundreds of people may have been in danger of their lives, fighting, getting arrested, beaten up, tortured: while to you it's been nothing more than a chance for a quick fuck!'

'How dare you!' He comes at her, white with anger, but ridiculous in his nakedness, his sad appendages dangling, his eyes myopic without their customary thick lenses, like mouse-pussies in rut. She begins to laugh, harshly, cruelly, helplessly; and that, at last, disarms him.

'Fuck you anyway!' he hisses, as he turns away, back to the bedroom where, she suspects from past experience, he may now proceed to relieve his tension and vent his rage by masturbating. When she goes past his open door to the bathroom half an hour later he is fast asleep in her bed. She spends the next few hours dozing fitfully in a chair in the front room, waking up at last with a blinding headache to hear him splashing in the bathroom. (He has left the door open.) She slips into the bedroom to get dressed.

'Well!' he says when at last he reappears, looking at her with a sneer. 'Thanks for the hospitality.' He moves through to the front room, and glances back. 'See you later.'

'No!' she shouts after him.

Surprised, he stops to look at her. 'What do you mean?'

'Don't say "See you later". Because I won't ever see you again. You understand? Once you're out of that door you're never coming back. And don't give me that spiel about the SB again. I don't care a damn if they catch you. In fact, if you ever set foot here again I'll personally go and tell them where to find you.' She bursts into hysterical sobs, only half aware of his stunned colourless eyes staring at her. When at last she manages to control her sobbing, he is gone.

Later in the day, on her way out of the face-brick building, she notices a pale green Toyota parked opposite the entrance, a man behind the wheel. When she comes back a few hours later, the car is parked in a different spot, but still in view of the front door. And when she tiptoes out in the evening to have another peep, she sees the car again, and the light of a cigarette behind the steering wheel. Waiting.

Is there a way out? Is it true, as Annie Leclerc says,* that the only significant love stories are those dealing with a love either impossible or frustrated, or ending at the point of entrance into love? ('After that, separation is all that can be told. Or death. The most beautiful love stories end unhappily.') Eros, she maintains, exposes one to an experience radically different from that of order, regularity, equilibrium, common sense. Love propels one towards the transgression of frontiers: it exists only in terms of the quality of that transgression.

So what can be in store for Philip and Melissa?

I must approach it from a different angle; his.

This time there is no hesitation in him. Everything has been decided beforehand; all the arrangements have been made, meticulously, responsibly, gladly.

During the morning, while Greta is out shopping, he packs a suitcase. Only enough clothes for a week or two, to start with. He locks the suitcase away in the boot of his car and drives to the university. There are still examination scripts to be marked, administrative duties to perform, a committee meeting in the afternoon. All he feels guilty about is having to telephone Greta to ask her to go to the Wassenaars on her own for the drinks they've been invited to: he's still tied up at the office, he tells her; he'll drive straight to the party afterwards to join her there. This makes it possible for him to go home after she has left, to leave in the post box the letter he's already written in the morning, with a cheque to cover expenses during his absence. The letter is short and to the point – he is embarrassed by the triteness of the gesture, but there is no other way – not wanting to demean it with sentimentality. (Except for one paragraph: 'I know I've

---

* *Hommes et femmes*, Editions de poche, Paris, 1985.

failed you in what you were entitled to expect of me. I'm sorry. Forgive me if you can. And if you won't find it cynical of me – for I promise you it isn't meant like that – I want to tell you that, in my own way, I still love you.')

In the early dusk he rings the bell at the door of the flat Melissa has moved into a few days ago; he hasn't been able to come round yet; she has been curiously reticent the last few days. (All he feels relieved about is that Jack had to go to Port Elizabeth the previous weekend to make arrangements for his trek to the north; so nothing could come of his intended date with Melissa.) He feels ill at ease on this exposed landing running along the face-brick wall, the row of identical doors.

'Philip!' She clearly hasn't expected him. She looks tired, dirty, sweaty, her hair in a mess; wearing a crumpled yellow shirt and white shorts. 'What are you doing here?'

'Can I come in?'

'Do you have time?'

'Oodles.'

Incredulous, she stands aside to let him in. He takes her in his arms, but she detaches herself. 'No, I'm filthy, look at me.'

'You're lovely.'

'I've been cleaning up all day but nothing seems to get done. I hate this bloody place.'

He looks round, curious. The familiar bits of furniture look oddly out of place in the strange surroundings. A redefinition of what has been taken for granted; unnerving shifts.

'Philip, what are you *doing* here?'

'I've come to pick you up.' He closes the door behind him. 'Go and have a bath and get ready. We're going away.'

'Where?'

'To the moon.'

'No use. At the stroke of midnight we'll have to be back.'

'No. This time the coach won't be changing into a pumpkin again.'

'Don't make jokes, Philip. I'm flaked.'

'I'm deadly serious. Where's the bathroom?'

She points at the middle door. Ignoring her protests he goes down the short passage to the bathroom, puts in the plug, opens the taps.

'Philip, are you out of your mind?'

'Absolutely. Aren't you glad? Think of how many people go through life without ever going mad.'

'I'm not in a mood for games,' she says, a tired edge of warning in her voice.

'This isn't a game. Come here.' He begins to unbutton her shirt. Instinctively she puts her hands on his to restrain him, then gives in with a brief sigh. Holding on to his arm she kicks off her shorts.

He checks the water. 'Right. You can get in.' Afterwards he helps to dry her. 'Now pack a few things. Mostly casual, but add something for special occasions. Make sure you're prepared for both rain and sunshine. And the evenings may be cool.'

'Philip, honestly – '

'Don't forget your passport.'

They are half-way to Port Elizabeth before she slowly, almost reluctantly, begins to relax. 'Now tell me where you're abducting me to.'

'I'm not abducting you. We're eloping. Tonight we're starting from scratch. A new life. Just the two of us.'

'You really think it's possible?'

'Wait and see.'

They spend the night in a hotel on the beachfront. (This time there is no bomb scare.) Early the next morning he takes her to the airport, where he leaves his car in the lock-up garage.

In Durban they have to wait for a few hours, longer than he's anticipated, as the plane to Mauritius, scheduled for 14.15, is almost three hours late. So it is already deep in the tropical night before they emerge from the airport at the other end and get into the dirty, dilapidated taxi which drives them, for an hour and a half, at hair-raising speed, through plantations of dark sugar cane, and sprawling towns, and clusters of palms, to their hotel in the far north-west of the island.

At an incredibly early hour the sun breaks out over the sea, where a white line of foam traces the embrace of a coral reef a few hundred yards from the beach; pale green translucent wavelets break placidly on the sand where large umbrellas are already sprouting like huge exotic flowers.

'I can't believe it,' she says, breathless.

They're standing in front of the window in their bungalow, naked, staring out.

'This is happily ever after,' he says. 'Why shouldn't a modern love story end on a positive note for once?'

'How long does "ever after" last?' she asks.

(A momentary thought: Eighty matches – ?)

'Let's not think about the future right now,' he says, holding her. 'For the moment it's enough just to be here. Let the sea wash everything from us. Pain, memory, history, everything. All that matters now is being together. And knowing that nothing will part us again.'

'But – '

He puts a finger on her lips. She smiles, and takes him by the hand and leads him back to the bed. The vagaries and inventions of love. (Soon he hears her breath coming in deeper gasps and she begins to utter the moans of her imminent orgasm, her hands pressed against the sides of his head as she tries to force him more urgently into the ozone of her overwhelming femininity; while far outside the sea turns and sighs like some vast luminous animal, its wet waves breaking on the sand.)

I cannot resist the temptation (for the last time?) to interrupt with these lines from Borges, quoted in an article on the death of the great Argentinian, during my own recent week on Mauritius:

> He who embraces a woman is Adam. The woman is Eve.
> Everything happens for the first time.
> He who lights a match in the dark is inventing fire.
> He who reads my words is inventing them.

The liquid days flow into each other, merge; there are no demarcations between them, no frontiers. Late in the morning they stumble out to the sea where they laze and loll. In the afternoon, after lunch and the siesta, they stroll to the entrance of the hotel and hail a taxi to explore the island. Only a hundred yards or so from the hotel the shanties and shacks of the inhabitants begin to line the narrow roads: shops with let-down flaps to exhibit the wares – coconuts, tomatoes, turnips, cabbages – surrounded by clouds of flies; clusters of people thronging in doorways or the streets, talking and laughing and gesticulating, flashing white teeth as one comes past. Fern trees among rubbish dumps. Lean dogs – the bitches weighed down by swollen, swinging teats – in narrow lanes between black walls and hedges overgrown with green foliage and purple waves of bougainvillaea; untamed fertile nature taking over the moment man relaxes his grasp. Patches of wheat, the ubiquitous cane fields, interspersed with piles of black volcanic rocks gathered by peasants (some of the mounds covered with dazzling orange flowers). Women and children planting or cutting cane. Men on bicycles with bundles on the back carriers. Chickens scratching beside the road – angry suspicious amber eyes – shaking their bedraggled white or black-and-red feathers. A goat tied with a thong to a peg driven into the ground. Occasionally, a groaning wooden cart drawn by an ox with a tall hump and menacing wide horns.

Strange to think that the whole island arose from the fire of primordial volcanoes. Now life flourishes among the remains of lava.

Every now and then cars approach, usually taxis with no sign of suspension, racing wildly through groups of people and animals, hooting away, to be greeted by huge outbursts of laughter and waving arms.

Here and there they come past sugar refineries spreading a nauseating bitter-sweet smell across the landscape, belching black smoke from tall chimneys. Everywhere one finds half-built houses abandoned without apparent reason, piles of unused concrete blocks still stacked beside them. Clusters of red flags fluttering from tall thin poles in front of Hindu homes; mosques with outrageous domes and minarets; ugly little Catholic chapels.

Big-eyed children bunch beside the roads, or stare through the dusty panes of dark hovels. In spite of the unmistakable signs of dire poverty everybody seems to be smiling, even jubilant. Deep below that exterior, one suspects, must lurk the ageless patience which goes with surviving flies, cockroaches, changing weather, disease, an unpredictable meagre income. Wherever one goes the greeting resounds: 'How are you, my friend?' And no matter what you ask of anyone or how grave your distress or inconvenience, the reply is invariably: 'No problem.'

Then it's back to the hotel with its white-warm beach: pedalos, waterskis, canoes, glass-bottom boats to take you gliding across unimagined worlds below the surface. In the shallow water: small soft tufts of green seaweed, like the pubic hair of mermaids. Smooth long-haired girls with bronze breasts. Exotic cocktails made of rum and fruit juices, served in hollowed-out pineapples or segments of bamboo. Cool coconuts in the blazing sun. Palm fronds frayed by the wind. In the evenings the beautiful people abandon themselves to dancing, to the accompaniment of electric guitars and drums. Women in transparent chiffon. Men in white shirts unbuttoned to the navel, exposing black coir mats on their chests. The rhythms of the *sega*. At night, the geckos on the walls of their bedroom, uttering smacking sounds in the dark, like passionate kisses. Before dawn, the boats coming in from the reef or distant beaches, loaded with coral and shells gaping like the shameless shiny pink vulvas of giant women. Sometimes, when the tide comes in, there is the deeper boom of waves on the coral reef. Far beyond it, on the horizon, as unreal as dreams, men-of-war glide past from time to time. The detached realization: if a world war should break out now, we won't even know about it on this remote island.

Yet close by: the hovels and the teeming bodies of the poor, the tatty fields, the big-eyed children, the mounds of volcanic rock from prehistoric eruptions. How are you, my friend?


No. An end like this is out of the question. It will convince no one. Romantic evasion. Narrative naïvety. A facile betrayal of everything which has made the story possible. Such a conclusion is simply unthinkable.

Yet in the case of Jane Ferguson a conclusion appeared plausible: that terrible yet purifying act of self-immolation which rounds off an entire existence and perhaps makes a new beginning possible. Or was that illusion too? I wonder: can it be that I invented Jane Ferguson (and her father, and Chris de Villiers) simply to obtain a grasp on Melissa's elusive codes? Or was Melissa a strategy to develop Jane's story?

An alternative (more in keeping with the latest twist provided by Lucas Wilson's function in the plot): after having made all the elaborate preparations described on page 231, Philip drives to Melissa's new flat in the early dusk, parking under a grevillaea which sheds yellow flowers on the bonnet of his car. He checks the row of post boxes in the lobby for her name, but it is not yet there. He goes upstairs, perturbed by not having found even that meagre written proof of her existence, and rings the bell on what he expects to be her door.

No answer.

He rings again. And again. Becoming more agitated. How can she not be here after everything he has done to prepare the surprise for her?

He keeps his thumb pressed down on the button. He'll ring all night if he has to.

The door of the neighbouring flat opens and an angry head in curlers is poked through it.

'What's this blarry racket?'

'Sorry,' he says, 'but I have to find Miss Lotman very urgently.'

'Well, she's not here.' An inquisitive (or accusing?) stare. 'You from the police too?'

'No, of course not.' Stabbed by sudden fear he asks: 'What makes you think that?'

'Well, the cops have been coming and going all day. Since they took them away this morning.'

'Who did they take away?'

'The girl who lives here. Who else? Miss Lotman, whatever you said her name was. And that redhead, suppose he's her boyfriend. Just as well they caught them, I tell you. We're law-abiding citizens in this place, they're not the types one wants to have next door. Before you know where you are you get murdered in your sleep. Blarry bunch of terrorists.'

'Madam, please – ' He feels sick. 'Won't you just tell me what happened?' Adding clumsily: 'Miss Lotman is one of my staff members. I've got to know.'

'Oh well, then.' The woman comes out on the landing, clutching the flaps of her magenta candlewick gown to her scrawny chest. 'As far's I could make out this chap was hiding away here 'cause the army was looking for him, but he AWOLed. You know? They been watching him all along. Won't be surprised if he brought explosives and stuff in here, right under our noses. One never knows with these lefties, is what I always say. So anyway, early this morning the police swooped and found him here, and took both of them away, because it's clear as daylight she's just as guilty as he is, not so? Can you imagine sleeping with a terrorist in your own bed? She must be a very kinky lady, is all I can say. So off they went and I hope they lock them up for good. By rights, people like that should swing by their necks. Look at the state the country's in, and all because of communists like them. And *whites* too. I mean, you kind of expect it from the blacks. But what's civilization coming to if whites start betraying their own kind? It's enough to make God turn in his grave, if you know what I mean – '

As he drives back home he notices in his rear-view mirror a pale green car following him.


How the hell can I go on? I haven't slept a wink all night. How could I? Milton Ṭhaya is dead. My friend – that ebullient, irrepressible man – is dead. And I'm supposed to go on writing about love.

His wife came to me late yesterday afternoon. Thokozile. She's stayed the night. Sleeping now, at last, I think. I've given her a sedative.

No tears. ('The fight,' she said, 'goes on.' The rage of clichés.) But she couldn't stop talking. All night long. Milton, Milton. Her husband. Her children's father. My friend.

Day before yesterday. Shortly after the curfew. A voice in the street, B-street, in the township. Calling out: 'Hey, Milton! Milton Thaya! Milton!'

Something was wrong. She knew it immediately; just knew it. 'Milton, don't go out. You stay right here.'

But he went. Had he ever turned away a man who came for help, or advice, or a chat, or a drink? He was Milton Thaya, for God's sake.

He went outside. A low murmur of voices. Someone grabbed

the door from outside and slammed it in her face. Shouts.
Sounds of a struggle. Then a brief burst of gunfire.

She heard her own voice screaming as she ran to the door.
Two, three, four shots splintering the wood, inches from her
face.

'You open that door and it's good-bye with you!'

The children huddling round her. Not another sound from
outside. But one couldn't risk anything: they might be waiting.

Who *were* they? Comrades? Security Branch? The army? The
*amangundwane*? Ordinary young hooligans, the Khmer Rouge of
the townships, armed with scorpion guns they'd made themselves?

The body was lying in the street when the sun came up and
they went out. Just outside the gate.

An incident so trifling, so ordinary, the State Bureau for
Information may not even mention it in its daily report.

Thokozile is sleeping now. She's left her children with friends
in Tantyi. The two girls, the young boy. (When will he, too,
learn to handle a scorpion and avenge the death of his father?
This burning generation, this land in flames.)

And all I have is a word. I am weary to the bone. But I have no
choice. In the beginning was the word; it is still with us. The only
remaining sign, perhaps, of our dignity. We must tell stories
because it is the stuff we're made on. And our little life, dear
God, is rounded with Thokozile's sleep.


To resume: another possibility:

Philip drives through the town weighed down by a sense of
doom, the way one might drive through a bombed city, staring,
uncomprehending, at the rubble in the streets. (Those curious
bourgeois sightseers from the suburbs of Paris who drove to the
Latin Quarter on the Sunday afternoon, after the devastating
night of 10 May.) Outside the broken gate of the backyard where
Melissa used to live he stops, waiting for several minutes before
he finds the courage to get out and pick his way through the
weeds and rubble in the yard. Her door is closed. Not even Rex
is there to bark and welcome him. Behind the green creepers

covering her window he can see that the curtains are gone. Forcing his way through the branches he presses his face against a pane, his hands shielding his eyes, to peer inside; but, as he has suspected, it is empty. There is not even nostalgia in his attempt to look inside, to look back. It's more a numb feeling of sordid guilt as if he's peered through someone's bathroom window.

He drives on again, without any specific aim, yet knowing subliminally where he will end up. In a long slow curve the road winds up the mountain slope, through the black waste land. Here and there whole charred skeletons of trees still stand gawkily upright, but most have been burnt out, leaving only stumps and mounds of ash stirring blackly, greyly, in the warm wind. One can see very far now, there are no obstacles left. He can even discern, in the distance, the large flat rock where they were together on that magic late afternoon. How young and innocent they were then, how uncomplicated their love. There is no sign of birds today, nothing to lend significance to space or relief to silence.

Then on again, to the deserted garden. The hotel is still empty, lifeless, boarded up, like the previous time. Only more derelict. Even the back lawn is deserted now. All he is conscious of is the clicking of guinea-fowl in the outbuilding, but he doesn't go there.

If he closes his eyes, perhaps, everything will return: they will be lying here on the grass again, and a waiter in ill-fitting formal clothes will approach with a tray from the main building, and she will tell him about her erotic dreams or the lovers from her past, she will laugh or cry on his shoulder. But he keeps his eyes open. The December light is without compromise, does not permit of illusion.

He drives back, slowly, to the town. At last his mind is made up, the final decision taken. This journey has confirmed what was already unavoidable. Resigned, philosophical, detached, as if he has come a very long way through distant regions and spanning ages, he stops in the garage, gets out, follows the paved garden path to the back door.

'Hello!' he calls.

'I'm in the spare room,' comes Greta's voice from upstairs.

'What are you doing here?' he asks from the door.

'Making the bed.'

'Do we have a guest then?'

She stands up. Her face is pale, but calm. 'No. I'll be sleeping here tonight.'

He feels something pressing down on his heart. Once again he experiences that strange, unsettling dizziness which affects his sight. (It may become serious, the doctor warned. You should see a specialist. At your age – )

'I've now taken my time to think about the whole business, Philip. I saw a lawyer this afternoon.'

He shakes his head in disbelief, thinking: This is like one of those cheap, sensational movies which begin with the doctor saying 'You have six months (or three, or one) to live – '

'Are you serious?' he asks, leaning against the frame of the door to contain his dizziness.

'Of course.'

'I've also had time to think,' he says. 'I've decided I want to come back to you.'

'I'm no longer interested, Philip,' she says quietly. 'All our married life I've been thinking first of all of you. Your welfare. Your happiness. Your wishes. Your needs. It's taken me a long time to discover that I'm a person in my own right too. I don't think it's selfishness. It's simply a matter of survival. Whatever it is, I'm no longer prepared to tie my life to yours.'

'You want me to go?'

'I won't be unreasonable,' she says. 'I don't expect you to pack your bags and leave, just like that. You may still sleep here tonight, which is why I've made my bed here in the spare room. But I want you to start making arrangements tomorrow. I've already spoken to the children.'

He is shaken by unreasonable rage. 'You needn't be charitable to me!' he says, trembling. 'If this is how you feel, I'll go straight away. I *have* a place to sleep.'

In a frenzy he hurls pieces of clothing into a suitcase. Pertinently ignoring her, he goes down the passage past her, and down the stairs, buoyed up by an excessive, almost childish feeling of malicious joy.

Not caring much about stop signs or even traffic lights on the way he drives recklessly to the large block of flats where Melissa moved in a few days ago. Only once on his way is he forced to stop, yielding – impatient and rebellious – to a convoy of military vehicles rolling towards the black townships. At last, at the end of his tether, he drives on again. Leaving the suitcase in the car, he runs upstairs ('at your age') and presses the bell on her door.

Inside there is at first no sound, but the lights are on and he is aware – unless it is his imagination? – of inaudible scurrying movements. She must be home.

He rings again, feeling his heart beating uncontrollably.

Another pause. Then, so unexpectedly that it startles him, the door is opened. She is wearing a yellow shirt – most of the buttons undone – which barely covers her panties. She is, of course, barefoot, her hair in disarray.

'Philip! What are you doing here?'

Over her shoulder, he notices a large pillow on the carpet; two glasses of red wine, half filled. There is a record on the turntable. Pop music.

'I need you,' he says simply.

From the bedroom a strange man's voice calls out: 'Melissa, who's at the door?'


Yet another possibility: that image of the two lovers walking in the night. After the day of wandering and soul-searching described in the previous episode Philip is driven back to Melissa. There is a whole future to discuss, to resolve. Hand in hand they proceed through the night: a windy evening, the street lamps inhaling light rather than emitting it. As they pass a large blank wall covered in graffiti – *Life is a sexually transmitted disease* – a combi filled with students returning from a binge comes charging round a corner, heading straight towards them. Exposed in the glare of the headlights, in a din of drunken jeering, cat-calls, wolf-whistles, Philip grabs Melissa by the arm to escape along a dark alley. But when they emerge at the far end the combi comes veering round the corner, hooting with aggressive glee. The hunt is on. No matter how many garden walls they scale, through how many backyards they stumble, whenever they return to the streets as from time to time they must, the combi is there again.

Only after a final erratic detour along dark vacant lots filled with mounds of rubble or patches of weeds and brambles, do they manage to elude their pursuers and return, breathless, to the unfamiliar flat in which she now resides. Once inside, not yet daring to put on the light, he tries to secure the safety chain but finds the socket broken and dangling from a single screw. Huddled together, gasping for breath, still unable to speak, they stand listening, waiting. And soon they can hear it approaching from street to street: the screeching of tyres, the hooting, the chorus of maniacal voices like the cackling of a flight of furies or birds of prey invading the room in which they have momentarily believed themselves to be safe. The lights from outside streak and flicker along their walls.

And another conclusion – but it can't go on like this.* There can be no end to what has had no beginning. I find myself back where I started. ('The end of all our explorations – '?) The primal couple caught in a circle of fire. The ring of artifice, wrought in words; the verbal image of that basic sign: Woman: the Vulva. Novels have ends, stories run on in everlasting spirals, circles, rings. No, I don't think I shall be writing my book after all.

If ever we wander through that deserted garden again, in a dream perhaps – the cries of ghost peacocks, of hadidas, of Valkyries, of mountain eagles soaring over the cliffs – and an autumn leaf drifts down to settle on your head and you grant me the wish that should by rights be yours, what shall I ask? I don't

---

* 'In Latin *concludere* means "to shut up". Peace and quiet. Constriction. Confinement. Guarded silence. *Ludere* means "to play". Inside this final sign, then, lies a game, a finishing lure, another possibility, a further clue, a lasting con.' (Vincent B. Leitch, *Deconstructive criticism*, New York, 1983.)

know. I honestly don't know. Perhaps only the freedom, the openness, the open-endedness, the endlessness – the silence, as you called it – of a country for which the future is still possible, a love not yet circumscribed, a story not yet written.

1985–1987

# Glossary

*ag* (Afrikaans):   oh well
*amandla ngawethu* (Xhosa):   Power to the people (ANC slogan)
*bakkie* (Afrikaans):   small truck
*biltong* (Afrikaans):   strips of dried salted meat
*boere* (Afrikaans):   white policemen and/or soldiers
*Buffel:*   military vehicle
*bundu* (probably Shona):   wilderness
*buti* (Xhosa):   brother
*Capab*:   Performing Arts Board of the Cape Province
*Casspir*:   military vehicle used by South African police for riot control
*COSAS*:   Congress of South African Students
*dagga* (Afrikaans):   cannabis
*dominee* (Afrikaans):   preacher of the Dutch Reformed Church
*ECC*:   End Conscription Campaign
*hamba kahle* (Zulu):   Go well
*hamba suka!* (Xhosa):   Go away quickly! Scram!
*hippo*:   military vehicle
*impi* (Zulu):   organized group of black warriors
*impimpi* (Xhosa):   informer
*jong* (Afrikaans):   familiar form of address, like 'old chap', but can be used for both masculine and feminine
*kierie* (Afrikaans):   stick, cane
*kubo!* (Xhosa):   Attack! (Literally: At them!)
*kwedini* (Xhosa):   young boys
*mayibuye iAfrika* (Zulu):   Come back, Africa
*mealie meal*:   maize flour
*meerkat* (Afrikaans):   mongoose
*mkulu* (Xhosa):   old man
*mlungu* (Xhosa):   white man
*molo* (Xhosa):   Good day
*mos* (Afrikaans):   (roughly) anyway, in any case
*muti* (Zulu):   medicine, magic potion
*nkosi sikelel' iAfrika* (Xhosa):   God bless Africa (Black national anthem)
*ouma* (Afrikaans):   grandmother

*oupa* (Afrikaans): grandfather
*piet-my-vrou* (Afrikaans): onomatopoeic bird name
*sala kakuhle* (Xhosa): Stay well (singular)
*salani kahle* (Zulu): Go well (plural)
*sawubona ntombi* (Zulu): Good day, young woman
*sanibonani nina* (Zulu): Good day, people
*SB*: Special Branch (Security Police)
*sega*: Creole dance on the isle of Mauritius
*vlei* (Afrikaans): marsh